THROUGH FIRE AND SHADOW

THE FORGED AND THE FALLEN - BOOK 2

R.M. SCHULTZ

SKY SEA AND SWORD PUBLISHING

CONTENTS

Dedication	vii
BY R.M. SCHULTZ	ix
Prologue	1
1. Cyran Orendain	9
2. Cyran Orendain	15
3. Sirra Brackenglave	27
4. Cyran Orendain	37
5. Pravon the Dragon Thief	43
6. Cyran Orendain	56
7. Jaslin Orendain	68
8. Cyran Orendain	77
9. Sirra Brackenglave	88
10. Cyran Orendain	100
11. Cyran Orendain	108
12. Jaslin Orendain	115
13. Cyran Orendain	127
14. Cyran Orendain	137
15. Pravon the Dragon Thief	145
16. Cyran Orendain	157
17. Jaslin Orendain	168
18. Cyran Orendain	183
19. Sirra Brackenglave	195
20. Cyran Orendain	204
21. Pravon the Dragon Thief	217
22. Cyran Orendain	231
23. Jaslin Orendain	242
24. Sirra Brackenglave	251
25. Cyran Orendain	260
26. Pravon the Dragon Thief	269
27. Cyran Orendain	281
28. Jaslin Orendain	288

29. Cyran Orendain	299
30. Cyran Orendain	310
31. Sirra Brackenglave	321
32. Cyran Orendain	330
33. Jaslin Orendain	342
34. Pravon the Dragon Thief	353
35. Cyran Orendain	360
36. Sirra Brackenglave	367
37. Jaslin Orendain	373
38. Cyran Orendain	383
39. Pravon the Dragon Thief	390
40. Jaslin Orendain	398
41. Cyran Orendain	406
42. Sirra Brackenglave	415
43. Jaslin Orendain	423
44. Cyran Orendain	432
45. Pravon the Dragon Thief	439
46. Jaslin Orendain	443
47. Cyran Orendain	453
48. Sirra Brackenglave	461
49. Jaslin Orendain	466
50. Cyran Orendain	472
51. Jaslin Orendain	480
52. Cyran Orendain	485
53. Jaslin Orendain	491
54. Sirra Brackenglave	496
55. Cyran Orendain	500
56. Jaslin Orendain	506
57. Cyran Orendain	514
58. Cyran Orendain	526
59. Pravon the Dragon Thief	530
60. Jaslin Orendain	538
61. Cyran Orendain	544

Receive a free The Forged and The Fallen prequel!	559
Book 3 coming in 2024!	563
Glossary	565
Acknowledgments	569
About the Author	571

To all those who still dare to read and tread the worlds of imagination.

BY R.M. SCHULTZ

The Forged and The Fallen

Novels
Through Blood and Dragons
Through Fire and Shadow

Novella
The Taming and The Betrayal

North Cimeren

PROLOGUE

Orinia

A STRANGE ANIMAL RESEMBLING A CAT BUT WHOSE FUR LOOKED more like moss rustled in the grasses. Orinia hunched down in the brush behind the crook of a beech tree, watching through the dark curls dangling over her eyes.

"Here, kitty," she whispered under her breath.

The beast scampered farther away from the village, only its dark green topline and the violet tufts on its ears appearing and disappearing within the heads of wheat. The animal looked to be two to three times bigger than a typical cat, but not large enough that it should pose any serious danger. Not unless she cornered it.

The creature had to be an angoia cat, if the myths she heard about such beasts were true. The general descriptions matched. Such cats were never supposed to leave the forest, never venture beyond the angoias, much less the boundaries of the Evenmeres. Something must have driven it from its home.

Orinia crept between the divided trunk, stalking the animal. At the very least, she needed to see its entire head, or no one in the village would believe her when she told them she had seen an angoia cat. No one would probably believe her anyway, but if she saw its face, she would know for certain.

"It has to be an angoia cat." Her eyes burned as she fought off the urge to blink, hoping not to miss any potential glimpse.

The violet tufts on the beast's ears flicked back when Orinia's foot crunched in the wheat. She paused. So did the creature. It was supposed to be a dark omen to spot an angoia cat, but that was probably because no one should venture into the old woods —the angoias. That was the only place where the cats lived, and those regions had turned deadly. If Orinia was fortunate enough to be the first person to ever spot one in a field, the portent should mean something much different.

She bit her lip and reassured herself with her logical thinking as she carefully took another step closer. The cat's ears flicked again as it tensed and then bolted off through the field, creating waves within the wheat. Orinia cried out and sprinted after it.

The creature's bounding green shoulders and backend moved much faster than Orinia could run, but its head quickly swiveled around in her direction. Copper eyes glinted as it regarded her, one clear emotion seeping from them—fear.

Orinia froze as her foot slapped against the ground. She stared. It *was* an angoia cat.

The creature looked at her for a full minute, as if beseeching her to stop her pursuit. The terror it exuded was much too drastic to be brought about by a young girl chasing it, a girl who could not nearly keep pace with such an animal.

The cat jolted and darted away, bursting up a hill and vanishing over its rise.

"Stop!" A tingle of excitement arced through Orinia as her

fingers clutched at her small tunic. She had actually done it—seen an angoia cat. No one currently living in the village had ever laid eyes on such a creature, but stories claimed that some of the great elders had, back when they didn't know better and ventured into the old woods.

A scream pierced the late afternoon sky like a crack of thunder.

Orinia whipped around in surprise, and a lance of fear stabbed at her insides. *Someone in the village...*

The forest just beyond the village appeared out of place—something was strange, unfamiliar. The maple she would often climb on and then sit and rest her back against was not the nearest tree. The boundary of the woods was closer than it should be, and two conifers partially obscured the maple she knew so well. Those conifers should not have been there.

The pines and oaks near the margins of the forest then shifted and moved, but the trees didn't advance by walking with their trunks or by swinging their limbs about any more than a typical tree stirred by the wind. These trees glided across the ground, and a rising mound formed beneath them, rushing for the village.

Men, women, and children darted away from the forest, frantically shouting and pointing. Orinia shrieked and hurtled toward her house.

A howl erupted from the woods and bounded over the village and fields before rolling away and echoing in the distance. The gliding pines and oaks stopped, along with their rising mounds.

Orinia slammed to a halt and crouched in the wheat. The ensuing silence lingered like the deep inhale before a dragon released its fiery breath.

A few heartbeats later, more howls answered, and hunched forms burst from the tree line, dashing into the dead grasses between the forest and village. None of the figures were tall enough to be seen clearly. Nothing more than their spiked armor and black weapons poked above the foliage. These things tunneled through the grasses, sending waves rolling in their wake.

Orinia remained frozen in her hiding spot.

One of the creatures' blades jabbed out from the brush and impaled a man who was yelling at someone in the distance. The victim screamed and doubled over. On opposite sides of the man, dark arms and hands reached from the vegetation and yanked him down. He disappeared into a rustling of blades of grass.

Orinia gasped and covered her mouth.

Howling erupted around the woods, and many of the moving lines in the foliage altered course and converged on the area where the villager had been brought down. A man's dying cry sounded, followed by the gnashing of teeth.

"By the Assassin's own hand." Orinia took a step back in retreat, her arms shaking, her mouth unable to respond to any command to yell for help.

Something rustled in the wheat to her left, and she turned just in time to watch a jagged blade sink into her thigh. She shrieked and flailed her arms as she stumbled back, the blade still buried in her flesh. The same diverging beech trunk she had hidden behind earlier pressed into her side. She wheeled about and, with her good leg, leapt upward, grabbing for branches and hauling herself up.

Something strong encircled her ankle and jerked her downward. She wailed and kicked with her other leg, connecting with the helm of a hunched and gray-skinned monster. Its leering face snapped sideways, and Orinia scrambled higher. Once she was beyond the beast's reach, she glanced down again.

The single creature seemed to be the only one in her area. It snarled, and a sting of drool strung from its lower lip, its sharpened teeth and tusks yellow and stained. Orinia kept an eye on the monster as she climbed higher, but the stunted tree she scaled started to bow and sag.

The monster's snarl vanished as it gripped the trunk with both hands and shook it. The beech swayed, but its roots did not give. The creature growled and then glanced around at the scene of screeching and fleeing villagers, monsters roaming about, and floating lights that emerged from the forest and danced around the periphery of the area. Then the beast's jaws gaped, and a sinister look of gloating sank into its dark and piggish eyes.

It's going to howl. Then others will come to kill me. "Please, don't make any noise!" Orinia reached for the blade still stuck in her leg. Her fingers quivered as she wrapped them around the weapon's hilt and ripped the blade from her thigh, which caused a fleshy sound upon its release.

The monster inhaled a massive breath and tilted its head back, the lump on its throat descending and then jolting upward.

Orinia closed her eyes and whimpered as she clutched the monster's blade in both hands. She kicked herself away from the trunk and fell, leading with the weapon. The blade drove downward under her weight and sank through the open mouth of the beast, its howl dying out with only a bubbly gurgle.

The monster coughed up dark blood that ran over Orinia's hands. She lurched, releasing the weapon, and the creature collapsed beneath her. She found her feet and reached out to steady herself, bracing against the trunk, her palm slipping and leaving behind a smear of both red and black blood. The chaos of weaving balls of light and berserk monsters that heaved for breath continued to assault the village.

Orinia's heart rammed against her breastbone again and again as she glanced about. Across the way, the village's horses galloped around inside their stables, their eyes rolling, their ears flicking as their neighs rang out like screams.

Orinia stumbled toward the stables, holding a hand over the wound on her thigh while cursing the Assassin under her breath. Her leggings were soaked through with blood, and there was nothing she could do to help the village now. Her only hope was to ride to the nearby outpost and ask the soldiers there for aid.

She limped along, stooping over so she could flee like the angoia cat and use the wheat for cover. She glanced over her shoulder. No rustling waves rushed after her, but she left a swath of crushed wheat in her path and a stream of blood marked her trail.

She swallowed and pushed herself to move faster.

1

CYRAN ORENDAIN

The breath of the Evenmeres gusted and tore across the battlements, flinging Cyran's hair about his cheeks and neck. He strode along, watching the woods, his dragonsteel armor of green and gray for Nevergrace clanking as he moved.

"Anything at all to raise concerns?" Cyran asked a soldier with a spear, who stood rigid near a merlon and gazed into the distance.

"No, Sir Cyran." The soldier hardly blinked as he watched.

Cyran nodded and paced on. A myriad of converging events and horrors could descend on the outpost at any moment, and everyone knew it. He looked into the shadows of the oaks, pines, and maples and then beyond to the towering pale trunks of the angoias, which created a wall to the north. He was one of the guard now, something he had dreamed of for most of his life, and not only that—he was also a dragonknight.

The Dragon Queen had gone down somewhere in those woods, and her body had not been recovered. A chill slithered up Cyran's spine with the thought of her sneaking away through the angoias and returning to Murgare. He feared she might not be dead and that she could be nursed back to health. Then she would return, unleash her vengeance, and rain destruction down upon what was left of the decimated Never.

Cyran followed the scarred and pocked walkway of the battlements, passing a few more soldiers who watched the Evenmeres with untiring eyes. The sensation of a growing anger festered beneath those boughs. Cyran had encountered many strange creatures after being caught out in the woods. Hopefully those monsters would now serve a purpose and kill the Dragon Queen, if she was not already dead.

Twilight settled over the sky sea and the horizon, casting purples and oranges across a bank of clouds as mid to late autumn's chill hovered in the air. Neither Cyran nor the rest of the guard could continue searching for the Dragon Queen's body this day.

"They will find her tomorrow." Laren, a dragonsquire and friend of Cyran's, stepped up a staircase and onto the walk of the outer curtain. Brelle trailed him, her thick hips swinging as she moved.

Cyran nodded with feigned optimism. "Any day now."

"But once the king and his legions leave the outpost, we're as dead as rats trapped in a barrel of mead," Brelle said and sucked at her lower lip. "Except we won't have the nice drunken feeling first."

"Then we won't have to wait long." Dage, the hulking dragonsquire, followed them up. "King Igare and all of his men will depart at daybreak."

"Oh, is that why they've been preparing all their dragons?" Brelle snapped, her tone riddled with facetious nervousness. "Finding the Dragon Queen's body will hardly matter if Murgare's legions swoop down on us and Cyran and Eidelmere are our last remaining guard and dragon."

"Igare will leave others to protect the outpost." Laren flashed his boyish grin, which lifted a dark cloud from Cyran's thoughts. "He is a just and kind king."

"In her current condition, Nevergrace could hardly defend herself from a pack of forest hares." Brelle spat over a merlon as she motioned to the crushed portions of the inner and outer curtains and to the keep, its upper half toppled over. "If we're not left with more guard and dragons, and Murgare exploits our weaknesses, the outpost will fall without a fight. Unless you decide to call what will be Cyran's and Eidelmere's brief attempts at defense 'fighting'. Then Murgare's legions and onyx guard will spill across all of Belvenguard."

"Damn Garmeen for all of this." Dage's chin jutted out as he glared off into the distance. "Traitor. Bloody bastard. Who knows how much destruction, if any, the Never would have felt if he hadn't betrayed us all."

"I still don't know what to think about all that." Disbelief lightened Laren's voice. "I've known Garmeen my entire life. I cannot even imagine him assisting Murgare or doing anything those rumors claim."

"Maybe he was tricked into giving them information... somehow." Brelle folded her arms across her chest.

"But the king and his council didn't have any doubts about Garmeen's involvement and guilt." Cyran tore his attention away from the shifting shadows beneath the canopy of the Evenmeres and glanced to the western horizon, the southern fields, and the Scyne Road stretching away to the east. A stab of pain sank into his heart, and anger radiated out of the well it created. Garmeen, the former leader of the dragonsquires of Nevergrace, had been well respected, not to mention completely trusted by the guard, especially by Sir Kayom, who died during the recent events. Garmeen had probably even saved Cyran's life once—when a flaming figure in a cloak appeared outside the Evenmeres.

How could Garmeen betray his fellow squires and all of

Nevergrace, all his people, for the enemy? To sway such a man, the reward or threat or promise Murgare offered him must have been mighty indeed.

Cyran paused and squinted. Something staggered in the distance to the east. A long shadow stretched across the fields and roadway behind whatever this something was, making it appear like a hunched giant. Cyran gripped the hilt of the Flame in the Forest.

"What is it?" Dage stepped closer, towering over Cyran, the dragonsquire's long blond hair stirring in the wind.

"Something approaches the Never," Cyran whispered.

The guard closest to them tensed and crouched, eyeing the woods before glancing back at Cyran and noticing his attention was not directed to the north.

"It may only take one man to overthrow the outpost now." Brelle held a hand to her forehead as she strained to see into the distance.

A lone person out there rode horseback along the Scyne Road, and if Cyran ignored the tremendous and distorted shadow following them, they might have only been a child or other small human. The horse limped along toward the outpost, and the rider swayed in their seat.

Cyran rushed along the northern wall to the northeastern corner of the castle, studying the figure as best he could. This was no farmer riding through their fields, and with everyone on edge from the recent occupation and battle at the outpost, it did not take much to kindle anyone's nerves.

Cyran paused at a merlon near the corner and leaned over the crenelation.

The horse stumbled, and its rider toppled over and crashed onto the ground, where they lay in a heap.

"Watch the woods for anything." Cyran gestured at the

soldiers along the northern wall. "This could be a distraction. If a tree so much as looks strange, blow the horns."

"Of course, Sir Cyran." A soldier nodded.

"I must find out who approaches the Never." Cyran dashed down the nearest stairway and into the outer bailey before making for the gates of the outpost.

"What if you—our guard—are being drawn into their diversion?" Laren jogged along behind him.

"Eidelmere is already saddled and prepared for any attack." Cyran did not look back. "And Murgare would be foolish to strike while the king and all his legions are still here."

"But you do not suspect that this person is a distraction." Brelle's voice carried from behind Laren. "You hope it is the Dragon Queen, mortally wounded and crawling back to the outpost in search of aid."

Cyran bit his lip. If this was the Dragon Queen, and she was alone and weak enough to fall off a horse, she should not pose too much of a challenge to all the legions currently at the Never.

Cyran grabbed a saddled gelding from the stables, swung onto its back, and galloped past the soldiers watching the gates. His steed's hoofs thundered on the dry ground of the Scyne Road. Hundreds of dragons of more varieties than he had ever seen before the king's visit to Nevergrace slumbered out in the fields to the south.

Three dark shapes tore through the rising moonlight and shadows stealing across the fields. Cyran tensed but quickly recognized the smaller Smoke and the outpost's two other wolves. They must have overheard his hasty departure and chased him.

Cyran rode on before Smoke's familiar howl erupted to his left in the thickening night.

"You may accompany me in case I need aid," Cyran said in

the direction of the howl, although Smoke would do so with or without his permission.

The silhouette of a horse stood in the road ahead, and Cyran reined his mount to a swift halt, the gelding's shoes and hoofs sliding across the ground. The horse in question did not move, and neither did the heaped form lying beside it.

Cyran drew the Flame in the Forest, and its green glow lit up its blade and the night around him. He swung off the gelding, his armored boots landing with a thud as he faced the prone figure.

The sound of galloping hoofbeats came from the direction of the outpost and drew closer.

Cyran crept toward the downed figure, holding his blade aloft and quickly glancing at the motionless horse beside this person. The animal appeared like a typical steed, not a monster conjured from some dark realm. He used the tip of his blade to lift a cloak covering the figure, and he steeled himself and prepared to look upon the face of the Dragon Queen.

The cloak slid aside. Beneath lay a small girl, and blood had soaked through her leggings and splattered her tunic.

2

CYRAN ORENDAIN

The little girl mumbled and rolled over beneath a pile of furs. Ezul, the Never's nyren, dribbled water onto her forehead as torchlight danced about the walls of the chamber inside the lower keep. Tiros, King Igare's nyren and councilmember, assisted with dressing a wound on the girl's thigh. The chain around Tiros's waist clinked as he worked. It appeared similar to Ezul's, but the king's nyren's belt was composed of more links of different kinds of metals than the Never's nyren's belt.

Cyran stood against a wall, waiting. When he had picked up the girl, she was nearly unconscious and delirious, muttering gibberish, and she was pale from blood loss.

Emellefer held a pot of water and assisted the nyrens. She glanced Cyran's way and cast him a quick look of acknowledgment before turning back, tucking her dark hair behind an ear, and regaining a solemn air. Cyran tried to return the greeting, but he was not quick enough. Emellefer had been busy serving the king and his entourage since Igare's arrival, and Cyran had been on watch for most of that time. He hadn't found many opportunities to speak with this beautiful young woman of the

Never since the outpost had been reclaimed, nothing more than a greeting and farewell.

The little girl mumbled again and tossed about, her movements growing stronger. She screamed and sat up, scrambling back on the bed, her eyes wild with terror.

Cyran leapt forward and grabbed her wrists before she fell off the bed and crashed into a nyren, but she wailed and jerked against Cyran's grip. A messenger waiting by the door of the chamber darted outside and disappeared.

"You are safe." Cyran attempted to hold on to the girl's wrists but not squeeze too tightly as she struggled against him. "We are inside the keep of Nevergrace."

The girl's gaping eyes relaxed a touch, and she stopped pulling against Cyran as she heaved for breath.

"You are weak," Ezul said to her, "and you tire easily because your blood is thin. You have lost much of it. Rest, my child." He reached out a gnarled hand and smoothed her hair as she spun around to regard him.

"We found you out on the Scyne Road." Cyran released her. "You rode almost all the way to the outpost, but you fell from your mount."

The girl studied him without blinking, her matted hair pressed against her scalp.

"What is your name?" Cyran asked.

The girl swallowed, and her jaw worked a few times before she spoke. "Orinia."

"Where are you from, Orinia?" Cyran knelt at her bedside.

"From Gernlet." She glanced at the bearded nyrens and trembled. "Out east toward Bransheer."

Cyran had heard of the village, or hamlet rather, but had never known anyone from there. "And what brings you to Nevergrace as a lone and wounded rider?"

"My village was attacked."

Cyran stiffened. *The Dragon Queen.* "Can you describe your attacker?"

Footsteps rang out in the hall, and a half-dozen people entered the chamber.

"It was the forest itself," Orinia said. "The forest attacked us."

A gasp and murmuring sounded from near the doorway.

"The forest?" Cyran asked with an eyebrow raised. Images of everything he had encountered in those woods stampeded through his mind—elves, forest feeders, dragon fae, the flaming Harrowed. Trees had also moved and spontaneously combusted in violet flames, but none of them had attacked him.

Orinia nodded. "I don't know how else to tell it. The trees came first. Then... things I cannot describe. Fiends is what I'd call them. One of them stabbed me, and they killed all the others."

"All of your people?"

She nodded again. "As far as I could tell. The fiends were slaughtering them when I ran."

There could still be survivors.

"It must be an attack from Murgare." The king's orator, Riscott, stepped forward, his gray robes shifting as he moved. "At this castle, their legion was crushed, and now the Dragon Queen sends out her wicked servants to spread fear and destruction in retaliation."

Orinia pulled her knees up closer to her chin and scooted away as Riscott approached while rubbing at his goatee.

"I told you prior that I'd encountered similar things in the woods," Cyran said.

Riscott regarded Cyran with large dark eyes. "Indeed, but you never showed me any evidence that they are not servants of the north. Murgare is responsible for cursing the Evenmeres and any creatures lurking in its depths."

Cyran bit his lip but did not have further knowledge or

reason to argue with the orator and challenge his opinion. "I will take Eidelmere and fly to Gernlet."

"There is a report of a similar incident in the north." Cartaya, the king's conjuror, sidled along the wall to find a better view of Orinia while speaking. "Or so my informants tell me. One of these people mentioned a Murgare village located just outside the Evenmeres that was razed to the ground."

"Such an attack could have been staged, or even carried out for one purpose—to cause uncertainty." King Igare Dragonblade stepped up beside Cyran and smiled and nodded at Orinia, his kind face revealing warmth and understanding. He brushed his unruly blond locks away from his cheek. "There have been several large-scale heists in our kingdom recently, heists involving dragons. A sun dragon was even taken from its den in Somerlian. Many are attributing the events to a particularly powerful and enigmatic—if not mythical—guild of thieves that has members ranging across all of Cimeren."

"The rumor of an attack in the north being caused by something in the Evenmeres is probably nothing more than a Murgare ploy," Riscott said. "To make us believe there is something in the forest not under their influence. They seek to have us waste time hunting for these fiends and ignore the true evil right before our eyes, although I would not doubt that Murgare may have even unleashed their wicked creatures on some of their own as a sacrifice—in hopes of further deceiving us. They will strike with their full legions when we are distracted and weakened."

"We must separate fact from fiction." Tiros wadded up a bloodied bandage and placed it into a pot near the bed.

A quiet voice sounded near the doorway as the king's clergyman, Lisain, prayed to one or more of the nine gods. The young man's head was bowed, and blond hair covered his face. His fingers were interlaced at his chest. "The Paladin speaks of a great evil stirring in the north. My prayer to the Shield Maiden summons images of war and of the Assassin and Thief. And the Siren of the Sea suggests that treachery and deception lie heavy in the present and will persist until the day the sky sea rains blood."

A few heartbeats of silence lingered.

Until the day the sky sea rains blood... Cyran's thoughts turned over that ominous portent.

"Another informant of mine has spoken of trees at the edge of the Evenmeres shifting into the marshlands and moving and sinking into the Lake on Fire." Cartaya pushed back her hood, and her stark white hair spilled out, framing her strangely young-appearing face. "Initially, I thought it was nothing more than rumors created by a drunken crowd celebrating outside Galvenstone after we reclaimed Nevergrace. But now?" She spread her hands to emphasize her question. "Given the current discussion, I believe these rumors should be considered."

"Then I further encourage us to decipher hearsay from truths." Tiros glanced around at the members of the king's small council. "We must investigate these matters. It will be quick and easy to send a dragon to Gernlet, and only slightly more difficult and time-consuming to have another inspect the area where the lake becomes marsh. But to request that anyone explore the northern margins of the Evenmeres is another matter entirely."

"We cannot send anyone through that forest and to Murgare simply to verify that a village has been razed." Igare paced, rubbing at his chin, his head lowered in thought.

"We could dispatch a few moon dragons and ensure that they arrive at the kingdom at night." Riscott ran two fingers down his goatee. "They could have a look around the village in question and retreat as soon as they have done so."

The king shook his head. "It cannot be done. None but a storm dragon can cross the Lake on Fire in less than several days, and a defenseless storm would not survive any Murgare attack. And perhaps only a shadow dragon can pass over the Evenmeres's angoias. A legion of ours will never be able to achieve their aim during a single night, and thus even moon dragons will be spotted and attacked."

Silence fell over the chamber and swirled about them as Orinia paled further, and she clutched her shins and pulled her knees up against her face.

"We must know if Murgare is also being attacked by whatever creatures reside in the Evenmeres," Tiros said. "If those of the north are also victims, we have another issue to consider. If the creatures in the woods are indeed the minions of Murgare, then we can concentrate on our known enemy."

King Igare nodded as he paced. "We will have to send someone, but I fear this someone or small legion would never return to enlighten us about these issues."

"I will travel to the northern village." Cyran faced the king, and the chamber turned quiet again. "I have traveled along the outskirts of the angoias. Nevergrace's forest dragons came from those woods. Eidelmere can navigate the canopy, and with a little luck, he will hopefully be able to cross through the old growths. Then I could find this village that lies along the border of the Evenmeres, inspect it, and return with any information."

Igare studied him, his expression grave. "I will not send my newest dragonknight. You cannot be lost. Your place is here at your outpost. The Never no longer has other guard to defend her walls."

"The Never is already in need of assistance." Cyran stood straighter and placed his arms behind his back. "All of us here hope you are willing to leave a few from your legions behind. But, if I may, I would disagree with the remainder of your assessment. A dragonknight would be the perfect soldier to send to Murgare, even one as inexperienced as me. Any of the rest of the guard would need numbers for protection against Murgare's ranks, but with the bond my dragon and I share, I should be able to fly in and scout about, outmaneuver any attackers, defend myself if needed, and still return."

Igare exhaled slowly and loudly.

"The dragonknight's suggestion is the most reasonable option we have to slip into Murgare and fly away unseen." Cartaya strode forward and stood before Cyran. She ran a supple hand along his cheek as she stared into his eyes. "And it is our best chance to not lose any guard or initiate war. Most of the forest dragons have forgotten their old ways, but Cyran rides the oldest of them all. Eidelmere could still remember the old woods."

"It will still be far too dangerous." Igare clenched his jaw and frowned.

"It is likely that any one guard—even a dragonknight—will not return to Belvenguard alive." Tiros sidestepped Ezul and approached his king. "The loss of one of our few dragonknights, even if this boy is young and inexperienced, could weaken our legions. Should Murgare send all their dragon hordes upon us, we would be more likely to fall."

"Cyran cannot fly into Murgare alone." Igare's kind face hardened.

"I will not be alone," Cyran said. "I will bring my two archers and my dragon with me."

"We could send a few more forest dragons to accompany him." Riscott glanced about, looking for support.

"All the other forest dragons of Nevergrace have been killed." Cyran's heart twinged as he acknowledged this out loud. "And forest dragons that have been reared in the hatcheries at Galvenstone could not understand the Evenmeres like Eidelmere does. Such dragons would also be guided by a mage who is directed by a guard, which does not allow for quick reactions. They will likely slow Eidelmere down and make it easier for Murgare to catch us."

The king grimaced before slowly closing his eyes in capitulation.

"Then who shall we send to Gernlet and the marshes?" Riscott asked. "Both attacks, as well as this rumor, should be investigated as soon as possible if we're to prove that the forces behind them are one and the same."

"I shall fly to Gernlet." A man armored in red and gold stepped through the doorway—Sir Paltere, the dragonknight of Galvenstone. His svelte body and armor would stand out amongst all the broad and hulking dragonguard anywhere. "A swift storm dragon bearing a guard known for his abilities of deduction can fly to the marshes." Paltere smiled at Cyran and spoke to him. "We shall work as one, fellow dragonknight, although we will be separated by many leagues."

Cyran nodded as Paltere crossed his forearms and bumped fists with Cyran.

Riscott stepped closer to Igare. "If we find that whatever is hiding in the angoias is also attacking Murgare, we will have another matter to deal with. But if these events are all the workings of the north—as I expect them to be—then we shall begin clearing the Evenmeres's paths of their brigands and widening the trails near Nevergrace. That way, we will be able to use the paths like a funnel blockade with a mass of our soldiers and knights clashing against much fewer of theirs at any given time. When Murgare decides to march an army through the woods to initiate their war and flank Galvenstone, we best be ready."

The king's tone carried an edge of worry. "We shall send these dragon riders this night, in case any storm dragon of Murgare hides in the clouds and watches us."

"I humbly request a few guard for the Never, Your Grace." The former young lady of the outpost—now the only lady of

Nevergrace—slipped through the doorway and approached the king. Menoria's blond hair streamed behind her, her face radiant.

Cyran's gaze was drawn behind her to where his sister, Jaslin, followed at the lady's heels. Jaslin and Menoria had grown close during the Dragon Queen's occupation of the keep, when they were both hostages. Jaslin's eyes met Cyran's, her expression focused and determined, although she still played with a shard of that ancient pottery Cyran had smashed, the one that seemed to influence her and make her want to venture out into the Evenmeres.

Igare rubbed at his temple, where a vein throbbed lightly. "Of course, lady of the Never. I cannot replace all of the fallen of your castle, but I shall replace whatever Galvenstone can spare. I will appoint three of my best forest dragons, all with their mages and guard and archers. These men and dragons will make Nevergrace their residence. Permanently."

Menoria bowed her head in gratitude.

"Then be off, my dragonknights," Igare said. "And return quickly and safely. Cyran, use the forest as cover and search only around its northern boundary. The rest of us shall prepare Belvenguard for the time when the sky sea rains blood."

Cyran gave his king a brief bow of his head and made for the doorway. Jaslin took Cyran's arm as he passed, playing the part of ushering him outside.

"I've already lost one brother," Jaslin said when they stepped through the doorway and scooted out of the way of the others exiting the chamber. Jaslin's auburn hair with its lighter ends reflected torchlight and appeared to burn. She met Cyran's gaze, standing nearly as tall as him, her blue eyes tinged with the redness of tears she was attempting to hold back. She toyed nervously with her shard. Smoke bounded up and sat on his haunches beside her, his tongue lolling out in a pant. "And now your duty will likely get you killed."

Cyran took her hand without the shard in it and squeezed. "I cannot avoid everything that is happening around us, and I wish to make Belvenguard safe for everyone. If someone had done so sooner, maybe Tamar would still be alive."

A single tear trickled down her cheek. "Will it have been worth it when you are dead? If I die as well?"

"I go so you will not die."

She spun the crystal shard between her fingers as she stared at the ground. "I haven't forgiven this world of the nine gods for what happened to Tamar." She reached out, hugged him, and kissed his cheek before resting her face on his chest. "I beg you to do one thing before you leave."

"And what is that?"

"Follow me." Jaslin turned, and she and Smoke led Cyran through the keep to the outer curtain where the walls had been decimated by dragon fire. She stopped at the edge of the destruction, where the last intact stone of the walk was shattered and blackened, nothing but empty air extending beyond. She pulled a small box from a pouch at her waist and removed its lid. "I've been waiting to do this for far too long." She reached into the box, scooped out a handful of ash, and blew it into the wind. The dark dust flowed like a river in the air before slowly dispersing over the grounds and remnants of the wall below. She then took a handful of blue petals—those of a glacial rose, which were said to have grown and become the angoias and the Evenmeres—from the box and scattered them in the wind. "Tamar would have worked harder than any to restore his outpost to its former glory."

Cyran's eyes burned. *Tamar.* "He would have."

Smoke howled a long and woeful sound as Jaslin held the box out to Cyran. He scooped out as much ash as he could in one fistful before slowly uncurling his fingers and allowing the wind streaming off the Evenmeres to take what was left of his brother and strew it around the Never. He plucked a single petal from the box and watched as a gust carried it away.

There had been enough blood spilt around the outpost to water all the surrounding earth that had been scorched by dragon fire. More glacial blue roses would then grow from the grounds and the cracks in the stones, and their color would embrace the walls of the outpost, bathing them in haunting beauty.

Tears cascaded down Cyran's cheeks as he spoke the ancient words a dying forest dragon had once taught him to help souls enter the other realm—the *neblír*. "*Mörenth toi boménth bi droth su llith.* Till the end of days we soar. *Mörenth toi boménth bi nomth su praëm.* Till the end of nights we reign. *Röith moirten íli. Ílith ëmdrien tiu gládthe.* You honor me. My soul sees yours."

"Tamar will never be replaced." Jaslin sobbed and emptied the remainder of the ashes into the wind. "The hole he leaves in my heart can never be filled." She clung to Cyran's arm. "I cannot lose my last brother, but I know I cannot stop you or overrule the orders of a king. Please, travel safe."

Cyran kissed the top of her head and tousled her hair as he wiped at his eyes and choked back far too much emotion for what should be a brief farewell. If he displayed too much of his feelings, he feared it would only make Jaslin sadder and cause her to worry more. "I will have Eidelmere and two fine dragonarchers with me. Just stay out of the forest, *please*."

"We'll help watch over the outpost while your brother is away." Brelle approached from the walkway behind them, striding before Laren, Dage, and Emellefer. Brelle's curls bounced against her forehead as she folded her arms across her chest and shot Cyran a rueful grin. "And we'll probably all be a little safer if Cyran is not in charge of our new guard."

Cyran grinned in reply. "Then I shall take my leave. Jaslin, you'll remain in good hands with this lot. Not clean hands, but good ones."

When Jaslin looked up, a deluge of tears struggled against the brim of her lower eyelids, fighting to be released. There was no hint of casual mockery in her expression or reply as she sniffed and fought off more emotion. "Find the village and then return straight to Nevergrace, Brother. Before the sky sea rains blood."

Cyran bowed to her, patted Smoke's chest, kissed his muzzle, and wheeled about, marching down the walk past Brelle and his other friends, headed for the dragon's den.

3

SIRRA BRACKENGLAVE

Sunlight sifted down in faint wisps, slipping through the angoias towering around Sirra. She limped as she paced north through the Evenmeres, the forest's one safe path—the trail—not in sight, not in this region. But she had been here before. Not long ago, the Harrowed leader had taken the Sky Sea Pearl from where it had been lost inside an angoia, thus placing Cimeren's way of life at stake.

The copse of angoias thinned around her, allowing sunlight to reach the forest floor, which she had not witnessed since she'd descended from the canopy after traveling by that route. Her black dragonsteel armor was as silent as leather when she moved, at least when she needed to remain undetected. At other times, she welcomed the clatter of its steel to instill fear.

Memories of when she had worn white armor and wielded white weapons upon a snow dragon flooded her thoughts. She was not too much different then than she was today. She only appeared vastly different, and white had never suited her demeanor. The feeling of home calling to her nestled into her bones, as it often did when she remembered her early days so long ago.

"Be gone," she said over her shoulder and motioned.

A forest dragon clinging to the trunk of an angoia moaned and scampered along after her before leaping to the next closest tree. "Will you ever return to our woods?"

"You should wish to be free of me and to *never* have to see me again."

The dragon's tongue flicked out. "But you are not like the others, not like the men who have passed through these woods. And you are also not akin to the Harrowed."

"I appreciate the assistance you've offered me in traversing the Evenmeres, but the time has come when we must separate." She marched over to the creature, tromping across bracken.

The dragon fell silent, a sense of longing and sadness seeping from it and flooding the other realm.

"Do not fear," Sirra said. "You will not become a lost one—one of the *siosaires*. Our bond will not be broken, as neither of us will die this day. But I must return to another. For I have been bonded to her for over five centuries."

"So be it, Dragon Queen." The forest dragon scrambled up a trunk, headed for the canopy. "But if for any reason, your shadow dragon is no longer a good fit for you, find me."

Sirra waved to dismiss the dragon's request. *Shadowmar is wounded but still far stronger than you or any other.*

Sirra trudged on through the undergrowth, and the forest dragon disappeared behind a trunk.

Dramlavola. Sirra grasped a thread from the *neblír* and tugged on its fibers, as its power had faded. Strength flowed anew through her muscles and bones. Her recently broken arm and shattered femur continued realigning and stitching themselves together, sewing bone across their fracture gaps. If not for the power of the dragon realm, she might not have survived the recent tilt in the sky. Not that her fall, which ended the confrontation with the boy of a dragonknight who had broken her arm, was all that far—barely above the canopy of the typical pines and oaks—but if she had not been able to call upon the increased strength, speed, agility, and healing properties of *dramlavola,* she might have been immobile for too long. Then the vile creatures roving the forest floor would have hunted her down and killed her.

The forest dragon she just dismissed had brought her far to the north in half a fortnight, and she no longer required the creature's abilities. She stepped past an angoia and into southern Murgare as she wondered what fates had befallen Sir Vladden and his mage, Quarren, in their errands of attempted diplomacy with the southern cities and kingdoms. The pines and oaks and maples around her grew sparser as fields stretched northward. Dark crags of peaks loomed against the vast horizon.

The beating of massive wings thundered overhead, and a dark shape blotted out the sunlight piercing the sky sea. Shadowmar wheeled overhead and shrieked, releasing a cry of rage and angst that Sirra had rarely heard her make.

The winged shadow of the creature dragged across the field ahead, circling and growing larger as the dragon descended. Shadowmar landed, burying her talons into the earth while flinging dirt and rock in her wake, punishing anything around her with her wrath. Her left eye was closed, and the shaft of a dragonbolt protruded from her scaled lid. Dried blood and fluid caked the area. Shadowmar shrieked again.

"You're *alive*, my Dragon Queen." Yenthor, the hulking archer on the quarterdeck, tore his black horned helm from his head and studied her. His red beard and hair tumbled past his shoulders.

"And she has passed through the entire length of the Evenmeres without aid." Zaldica stepped out of the lower turret, which was dangerously close to being crushed between the shadow dragon's lowered chest and the ground. Zaldica cradled her helm against her side, her thin face and closely cropped hair exposed.

"I did find aid in the woods." Sirra strode closer, barely feeling any pain in her leg. "From a forest dragon." She reached for the end of the bolt still embedded in Shadowmar's eye. "Allow me to remove this."

Shadowmar lowered her head and growled as Sirra grasped the shaft of the bolt just beyond its fletching. The projectile was solidly planted, lodged deep in the bone beneath.

"I... we"—Yenthor motioned to the two other archers on the quarterdeck and then to the turret—"wanted to remove it, but she would not let us get anywhere near it."

"We also thought she may throw us from her back after you were unseated—" Zaldica caught herself and stopped abruptly, probably worried that the Dragon Queen's temper would flare with the reminder of a boy of a dragonknight besting her in a tilt. "But Shadowmar flew through her exhaustion and returned us to Murgare."

"She took us out to the sea, where she found rocks to rest on some nights, and back around the angoias." Yenthor wiped his brow. "It took us many days, but she brought us home. Then, over this past day, I began thinking we were her prisoners. Till now."

Zaldica stepped closer to the embedded bolt and studied it. "We discussed how we wanted to head back to Northsheeren, but Shadowmar would not leave the margins of the Evenmeres." The archer studied Sirra, and the look of a confirmed suspicion narrowed Zaldica's features. "She knew you were still alive. Otherwise, she *would* have thrown us and been rid of us for good."

"This will hurt." Sirra placed a palm on Shadowmar's cheek and paused. She called upon her enhanced strength and, with a sudden burst of movement, yanked on the bolt. It broke free with a crunch and a tearing of flesh as the broadhead ripped through the dragon's scaled eyelid.

Shadowmar roared and flung her head back, screaming into the heavens and cursing all the gods but the Dragon. Sirra tossed the dragonbolt aside as easily as if it were a typical crossbow bolt and not one fashioned of heavy dragonsteel, then covered her ears until the thunderous ringing died out around her. The archers had fallen and lay prone either on the quarterdeck or on the ground.

Fury deluged the other realm. Blood seeped across and sealed over Shadowmar's scarred eyelid before thickening. This lid would never again open.

"We will revisit how to deal with the young dragonknight and his archers before the time comes." Sirra gestured, and Shadowmar lowered her head again. Sirra climbed into her saddle just behind the spikes running along the back of the dragon's head. "And next time, we will not be so bold as to believe we can easily take them or one of Belvenguard's outposts with only a small legion. But do not worry, my beast. We will face them again when war unfolds its mighty hand across all of Cimeren."

Shadowmar snorted, and her breath hurled clouds of steam into the air.

Sirra adjusted her horned black helm as Zaldica and Yenthor scrambled to retake their positions, and Sirra said, "We should learn if anything has significantly changed in Murgare after we were driven from Nevergrace, but we also must stop any uprisings triggered by the death of King Restebarge. It is paramount that we maintain Murgare's unity before the lands fracture apart, and we will show any who doubt the power of the north that we have not been weakened and we will not tolerate insolence."

Shadowmar's wings unfurled, each leathery segment

between bony shafts filling with wind and billowing like all the sails on the mainmast of a galley.

"During our travels here, we spoke with a few people from Murgare," Zaldica said. "Primarily, we heard about the same revolt we caught wind of while we were at Nevergrace."

"Then we fly to the eastern reach and the shores of the Ilmoor Sea." Sirra glanced in the direction of the rising sun. "We will start by quashing the unrest there."

∿

Days later, sunlight glittered off the vast expanse of the sea ahead, throwing blinding light back up at Sirra as she banked Shadowmar to the north. Somewhere along this coastline, a band of would-be pirates was accosting any ship sailing for or departing these shores.

Wreckage burned to the northeast, out over the water, and clouds of seabirds circled above the area, screeching in droves. Sirra veered her mount in that direction and circled lower, causing the gulls to scatter and fly away. Below, the mast of a ship resembled a smoking torch. Clouds of smoke erupted from the decks beyond. Anyone still aboard was probably dead, and by the look of what remained, the fires could have been days old.

Shadowmar swooped past, and Sirra slowed her mount until they hovered above the area, the black smoke not affecting either Sirra or her dragon. Smoke did not affect most dragons or someone who had been raised with the Smoke Breathers of the north. However, the archers hacked and covered their lower helms with wetted cloths.

Around the periphery of the wreckage, planks of wood bobbed on the water, but their distinct appearances made it clear that these were not random debris. Each was fashioned into a 'V' shape, and something lay atop them, something besides gulls. Sirra angled Shadowmar lower until her mount flapped and skimmed along just over the water. Seabirds launched from the flotsam and screeched as they soared away. Dozens of the V-shaped structures floated around the burning ship, and as the objects sitting atop them came closer, they became more apparent—men.

"Someone in the Reach has left us a dire warning." Sirra slowed Shadowmar until they hovered above one floating person and their planks.

The man's body was pale, his oily hair dangling into the water. His hands and feet were tied to planks that had been lashed together at only one end, which kept him from slipping off his frame and into the sea. He did not move. A few barnacles had gathered on the boards in addition to portions of the man's flesh and clothes. Many small punctures reminiscent of the work of gull beaks dotted his exposed flesh.

"Bring me closer." Sirra pointed at the man.

Shadowmar extended her neck, and Sirra stepped onto her stirrup ladder.

"What madness is this?" Yenthor glanced around at the carnage.

"Is there any life still left in you?" Sirra asked the victim as her ladder's bottom dipped into the Ilmoor Sea.

The man did not respond, his head lolling back with each bob of the waves, his hair plunging into and rising out of the water.

"He is surely dead," Zaldica said from behind Sirra.

Sirra crouched, anchoring herself on her ladder with her uninjured arm and leg while reaching out with her other foot and tapping the victim's hand.

The man jerked, his head snapping up as he glanced around. One of his eyes was missing, his socket deep and sunken. His other eye was wide and unfocused. "What is it?"

"What happened here?" Sirra asked. "To your ship and crew?"

A small crab scuttled out of the man's empty eye socket and sidled down his cheek before dropping into the water with a plunk. Sirra ignored it. An archer behind her retched. The others hacked and gagged.

"Are you the Finned Corsair's blood letter?" The man's voice was dry and raspy, like the inside of a windy tunnel.

"Who I am is of no consequence to anyone here but those involved in a reported uprising."

"I beg you, let me bleed, blood letter. I cannot endure such suffering any longer."

"First, can you tell me anything about what has happened?"

"The Finned Corsair has come."

"And this Finned Corsair is responsible for all of this destruction?"

"He demands tariffs and kills those who resist. He takes everything on board."

Sirra nodded. "I will ease your passing." She drew her blade, and black flames erupted along its length.

"Please do so quickly. Do not allow my blood to drip, or *they* will finish me. I beg of you, blood letter." The man's one eye turned wild and darted about beneath the cloudy haze on its exterior.

"I will do as you request." Sirra brought her blade down and cleanly beheaded the man without straining. His head dropped into the sea with a splash. Her sword's black fire charred the margins of the body's wounds and cauterized most vessels, but a trickle of blood seeped from the stump of its neck. It dripped into the sea.

A sense of urgency and anticipation, emitted by Shadowmar, bloomed in the other realm. Then Sirra felt it too—the approach of many souls primarily occupying that realm.

"Lift us away." Sirra grasped her saddle as best she could manage as Shadowmar flapped her wings, and they rose. Sirra glanced about at the relatively calm waters. "They have been lurking around the area the entire time, waiting for blood."

Shadowmar released a low and throaty growl.

Sirra climbed into her saddle, the discomfort in her healing arm and leg barely noticeable. Billowing black smoke swarmed around them, but the sea remained silent, as if waiting for its predator to strike.

A bubble of steam gurgled beneath the headless body and its makeshift raft. The sea erupted in a turbulent storm—creatures thrashing beneath its surface and blowing their scalding hot breaths through the water.

"Sea dragons." Sirra looked over the wreckage again and then toward the shoreline of the Reach.

A scaled head snapped out of the sea and seized the body with its teeth, yanking it and the raft down into the deeps and leaving only a frothy wake and bubbles to mark its passing.

"By the blood of the Great Smith," Yenthor cursed.

An unsatisfied sensation seeped out from the other realm, originating from the creatures below. Shadowmar's anger answered and overpowered their emotions.

"We will ignore these sea creatures," Sirra said as she laid a hand on Shadowmar's scaled neck, "but we will face the young dragonknight who has plagued you more than once, my beast. Soon, we will soar over Belvenguard again. One last time before the kingdom is given a new name. However, there is something in the Reach that we must address first, because it bends and strains the unity of Murgare." Sirra's gaze settled far away on the distant shore, on the city of Eastwatch. "The people of the port city will better understand what is transpiring in their waters."

Shadowmar flew west toward land, passing through curtains of dense smoke and over bodies floating on precarious rafts.

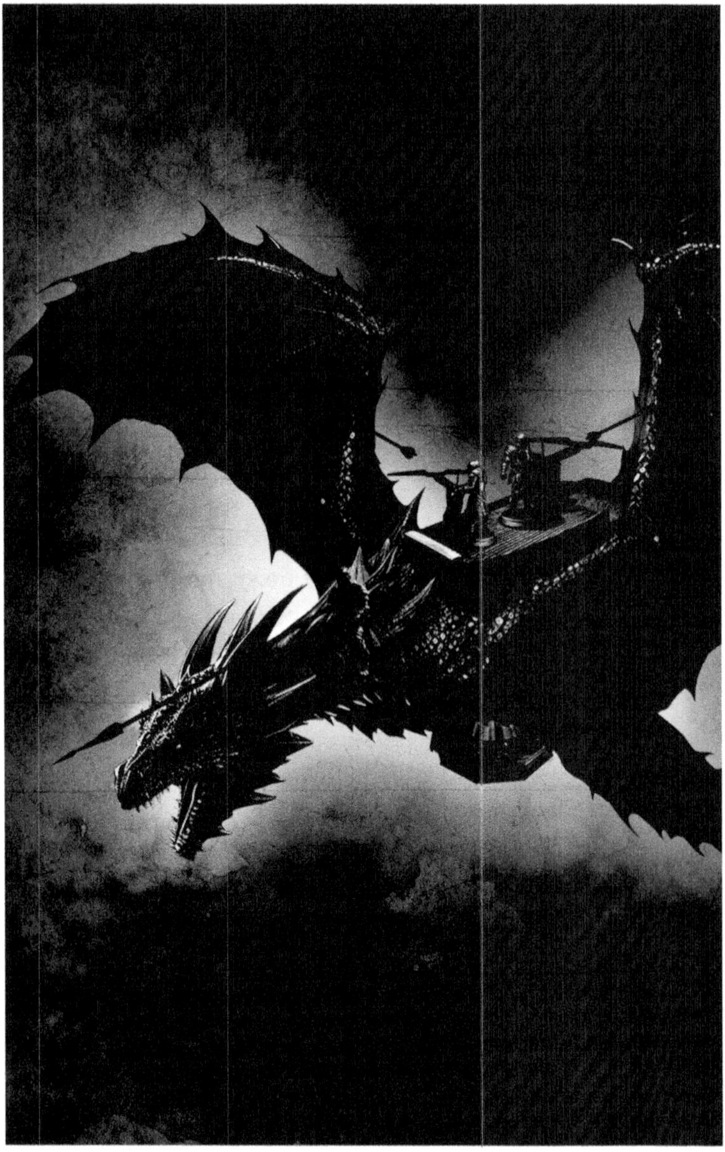

4

CYRAN ORENDAIN

Eidelmere soared over the smaller woods of the Evenmeres, the pines and oaks and maples appearing like a green and brown sea waving far, far below. The dragon braced with his wings as the limbs of the first angoia drew near.

Cyran allowed Eidelmere to maneuver and guide them as the old dragon thought best. Cyran had ventured here before, but he had not gone far beyond the margins of the old copses. Eidelmere's experience and knowledge would probably only be hindered if Cyran tried to direct him.

The dragon landed on the outer branches of a bough and scampered along its length, heading toward the trunk.

"When these conflicts with Murgare are all over, I'd be more than happy if I earned enough coin to settle down on the shores of the lake," Vyk rumbled from the quarterdeck on Eidelmere's back, his loud voice carrying on a conversation with Ineri, who was stationed in the turret below the dragon.

Cyran could only imagine Ineri huddled in the lower position, terrified of being smashed as the forest dragon ran up the limb. But turrets only hung to a level around a dragon's knees, although in front of their knees, and there was no fear in Ineri's tone.

"The Lake on Fire?" Ineri asked before falling into a bout of hacking and coughing.

"Of course. Not some little lake like the Lake of the Arrow or smaller."

"But you've got a large family. It will take a lot of coin for all of you to live along the shores."

Vyk huffed. "Might need an entire hamlet for my lot." He chuckled. "But there, we could live off the water and what it provides. We'd sail about in a skiff all day and catch lake trout and clams and snails and scrapper bottoms. We'd live like kings."

"If kings lived in a hamlet." Cyran glanced over his shoulder.

Vyk grinned and shrugged. "We wouldn't work harder than any king. How about that? We'd just lounge as our skiffs bobbed about until we eventually returned and cooked up our catch. We'd relax and drink ale and mead to the end of our days."

Ineri did not answer.

"You are less... agitated than before," Cyran said to Vyk, although Cyran returned his attention to Eidelmere's path as the dragon clambered around the angoia's trunk and out onto a bough on its far side.

"You mean less agitated than before we visited your outpost when that whore of a Dragon Queen occupied it?" the archer asked.

Cyran nodded.

"Don't concern yourself." Vyk's bearded cheeks lifted in a smirk, and the long braid of his hair trailed behind him. "You'll see that side of me again. When the time comes."

Cyran laughed and shook his head.

"If I end up living along the shores of the lake, I'll make a hammock specifically for you, Ineri," Vyk said. "One you can lounge in anytime. And maybe I'll even fashion one for our dragonknight friend here, if he isn't dining with the king every night afterward. But for all that to happen, Cyran has to make sure we survive this little adventure he's volunteered us for." A twinge of animosity cut into the archer's words.

Cyran's heart clenched. He had wanted to volunteer and help Belvenguard in any way he could, but prior to convincing Igare to send him, he hadn't considered that he would also be volunteering Vyk, Ineri, and Eidelmere. Nothing of great importance could be accomplished by any one man. He should have realized the implications sooner and asked his dragon and archers about it before swaying the king.

Ineri cleared her throat so loudly that the sound carried over the patter of Eidelmere's feet. She said, "I only wish to live long enough to see Murgare fall into ruin and despair. To watch the north have to live with the repercussions of their wicked ways. Is that too much to ask? Is it too vindictive?"

"No, it is not, my lady friend." Vyk's words had softened and taken on a hint of remorse. "I hope that day comes soon. May all of Belvenguard rejoice in such times."

The companions fell silent, and Eidelmere leapt from the end of a branch, his wings filling with wind as they glided through the open air to a bough on the nearest angoia.

"And what will you do, my friend?" Cyran rested his palm on Eidelmere's neck.

"Me?" Eidelmere landed, and the limb bowed several horse lengths before rising and wobbling and then maintaining its position. The dragon's head whipped around to study Cyran, the cracked old scales around the dragon's eyes compressing as he squinted. "A boy such as you would not understand the desires of an ancient dragon."

"I realize and remember that you are one of the *sïosaires*, and that I am not Morden," Cyran said. The sensation of Eidelmere's sadness in the other realm—due to his severed bond with his former dragonmage—had ebbed only slightly since the event. "Our bond may never be as deep as yours and his was, but I am still asking. As a friend."

Eidelmere huffed and faced forward again while dashing along as fast as his old limbs could manage. The dragon leapt onto a trunk and paused. He sucked in a deep breath, his nostrils buried against the bark of the angoia, and his eyes closed as he savored its scent. He gingerly gnawed at the bark and flicked his tongue across its surface. "I waste my breath on you, boy, but if you ask, I will tell you. I would like to return to this forest again. Not as we are now, but alone. Without any mage or knight. To find the last of my kin and live out the rest of my days with them. If I—a dragon who has done the bidding of men for nearly all the long centuries of my life—have not become too foreign to my kind."

Thoughts spun in Cyran's mind. Eidelmere was ancient, even for a forest dragon. How long he had left in this world, Cyran could only guess. The dragon treasured these woods, even though he had been taken from them when he was not much older than a hatchling. His life had been dedicated to a much higher purpose, but a life in the forest would have been far more peaceful.

The angoias rose in their ominous beauty all around them. Had Murgare truly planted these trees in the past age and also cursed the woods to divide the lands of Cimeren? All the tales claimed that the north had done so in order to work their vile magic without scrutiny. Eidelmere had told Cyran much about the past—about the Dragon Wars and the shining city of Cimerenden, a place of the elves, who were now believed to be extinct, their city decimated. Cyran had encountered a few elves in the woods after crashing on a wounded dragon, but those elves had all died after trying to attack him and the dragon, who hadn't been quite dead yet.

Cyran reached behind his head and gripped the hilt of his silver blade rather than the Flame in the Forest's, imagining silver runes and their bluish glow. Even though he carried the Flame in the Forest, the properties of the silver blade had saved his life as well—against the dragon fae of these woods.

"How far are we from the marshlands?" Cyran asked.

Vyk grumbled something incomprehensible.

"Not far," Eidelmere said only inside Cyran's mind. *"We work our way north through the thinnest region of the angoias, which is along the outskirts of the marshes."*

"Why do you ask about the marshes?" Ineri coughed.

"The king's conjuror mentioned something about people insisting that trees moved from the Evenmeres and out into the marshes and then the lake," Cyran said. "Another strange event."

Vyk laughed. "That notion is absurd."

Cyran turned around in his saddle. "Others are supposed to look into it, but we're so close. I'd like to see if there is any truth to the rumor." He paused and looked back at Vyk. "You would not want to set eyes upon what I've seen lurking down below in these woods. I do not discount any kind of magic here."

Vyk's jovial smile dropped flat.

"I do not wish to delay finding this village in the north," Cyran said, "but if we are so close, perhaps we should have a look at the marshlands during our travels."

Eidelmere grumbled, "I would not have told you if I'd have known what you would ask of me."

"The dragon didn't tell you anything," Vyk said. "Did he?"

Cyran nodded and gestured at his own skull, as if that would explain their communication, but Vyk's brow wrinkled in confusion and protruded just below the lip of his helm.

"It will add time to our journey." Eidelmere lunged from a branch and glided along with open wings.

"We were meant to gather information about any attacks related to this forest." Cyran's hand found the hilt of his mounted lance, and he ran his fingers over it. "Confirming if the forest is somehow moving into the marsh could end up being of importance."

"If the time comes when we intend to occupy the marshes?" Vyk chortled. "No army has been able to pass through those lands since... ever."

"We should find out if Murgare is rearranging trees and potentially creating another, wider path through the Evenmeres," Ineri said.

Cyran nodded his agreement. "And we may end up being the only ones with firsthand accounts who can determine if the change resembles anything that occurred around the Murgare village in question." He addressed Eidelmere. "Turn to the west."

Eidelmere angled westward and soared along through the shadows of the copse before landing on the next angoia. "You will get us all killed one day, boy."

5

PRAVON THE DRAGON THIEF

The looming walls of Castle Scyne waited on the hilltop ahead, beneath a drizzle of autumn rain.

"The Weltermores." Pravon turned his lanky body around in his horse's saddle and glanced behind their trio. In the distance, the River Scyne rushed south, separating the kingdom of Belvenguard from these lands. A stone bridge spanning the river stood like a small fortification with a tower guarding each border. "This is the first time I've been allowed to enter this kingdom."

Aneen's palfrey stepped lightly, but Aneen watched their surroundings with a consuming wariness. Something caught her eye, and her red hair whipped across the one shaved side of her head as she turned. After a few heartbeats, she settled a little. "I am not supposed to ever return here." She cast Pravon a smirk, and he studied her with interest.

"You two can reminisce about all the details of your sad little lives after we have finished our work." Kridmore's black steed pushed between Aneen's and Pravon's, the dragon assassin's dark cloak snapping behind him and emphasizing his impatience. "There is still much to accomplish before the end."

Before the war begins—what all those of Cimeren are referring to as the time when the sky sea will rain blood. Pravon watched the assassin ride away, his growing contempt for Kridmore leaving a burning pit in his stomach.

"Imagining getting my hands on coin from the Weltermores gives me a little tingle." Aneen's fingers repeatedly gripped and released the hilt of her sword as her horse slogged on.

"We won't be taking much coin on this errand." Kridmore's ever-hooded head pivoted in their direction, only his shovel chin and ivory teeth visible along with his smirk. "But you can take anything that readily offers itself to you during our travels."

Aneen slowed and allowed Kridmore to increase the gap between them.

"What makes him believe he is now the uncontested leader of our trio?" she asked. "That mad assassin? He'll likely get us all killed."

Pravon rubbed at his hooked nose and whispered, "He has no interest in discretion or restraint when he has the opportunity to kill anyone or anything." Recollections of their most recent encounter with their contact for their current blood contract surfaced in Pravon's mind—a man in a dark cloak with a pointed and dimpled chin protruding from his hood. Their contact often wiped at his lips with two fingers and exposed crooked yellow teeth. He had also shared a secretive final discussion with only Kridmore. It would likely be a decent amount of time before they met with their contact again. That meant Kridmore would be leading them for some time to come.

Kridmore slowed his steed's steps, as if he had heard them speaking, but he was too far away to have caught their words and he didn't turn to address them again.

The sight unleashed buried memories that assaulted Pravon. Such memories harkened back to when he was a child in the city and his wealthy father made all of the decisions for Pravon and the rest of his large family. During his childhood, Pravon had access to more food and clothing than he could ever need, but the discipline his father demanded Pravon follow just to live in their noble family and maintain his lowest rank of its eight sons rankled him. Whenever he had visited a lord's or noble's house with his father, Pravon often found himself stealing things—jewelry, coin, art—simply for the thrill and because he realized he could and no one noticed, at least until one day when he was an adolescent and his father caught him sneaking out with a platinum chalice. His father shrieked at him and said he was worth nothing and would never become anyone, then banished him from the houses and told him to go find his way as a beggar. Pravon was forced to grow up and forever live on the streets.

"If it comes to it, swear to me that you will take my side and we will join against Kridmore," Aneen said, interrupting Pravon's reverie as her head drooped and she studied her saddle in an atypically meek manner before Kridmore rode farther away.

"There is no honor among thieves," Pravon said, still mulling over his memories. One day, he would grow more powerful and wealthier than his father and confront the man again. Working for blood contracts and stealing dragons was probably the riskiest and rarest trade in all of Cimeren—there were very few indeed who could execute such feats—but it allowed him the opportunity to procure vast amounts of coin. He had yet to discover how to attain true power through such means, but he imagined once he had enough coin, power would follow. After their current unimaginably deceptive but richly paying blood contract was fulfilled, he would be far more wary of the men behind their contracts, but following a long respite, he would likely take another. Or should he give it all up and live a comfortable but humble life?

"That old saying is a lie, and you know it." Aneen's head shot up, and she studied him.

"But what can I ever swear to that will make you believe me?"

"Do not try to pretend that you are something more than a thief. Swear to the Assassin and the Thief. One of them should hold you to your word, the same as with any accepted contract."

"Unless those two gods find entertainment or a bit of mirth in me betraying you." Pravon brooded on it. "But I will. I have no love for our companion. I swear now to the Assassin and the Thief to take your side if anything should arise between you and Kridmore. But I have doubts that even both of us will be able to stand against the magics we've seen that conjuror-assassin bend to his will."

Aneen sighed and rode on. She and Pravon spoke no more until, after a couple hours, they began to follow a twisting road that led up to where the castle resided.

"Outside of the Weltermores, and behind his back, people call the ruler of these lands the Burro King," Aneen said as she studied the countryside, breaking Pravon's contemplation of how he had wound up in this situation with a dragon assassin and another dragon thief.

Pravon's eyebrow climbed his forehead with a confused interest as he faced her. "I'm sure there is a story behind that one. Is he stubborn?"

Aneen snickered. "No more so than any other king. But he has a fondness for small burros."

Pravon's eyes gaped.

"Nothing heinous like you are thinking. As far as I've heard, it is more of a fascination with a type of animal or pet. He has the creatures roaming everywhere around his kingdom." She pointed to a cluster of distant spots that in any other kingdom would have been livestock on the hillsides. "He chuckles every time he sees them."

Burros? Pravon continued riding up the winding road toward the hilltop, imagining the animals and what could possibly be so amusing about them and their orneriness.

"I want to know what our primary objective is now," Pravon said, "if we're no longer focusing on killing dragonmages to weaken legions. I believe our contact has accepted that Kridmore is our leader and will only be informing the assassin from now on."

"It's not so different from most of the contracts I've taken," Aneen replied.

Kridmore had slowed his pace and was not far ahead of them again. A few travelers meandered along the road, one ox pulling a cart at their rear. The travelers stared at the trio as they passed by, but no one uttered a word. On the hilltop ahead, two storm dragons stretched their wings outside the castle. One shook its scaled head like a dog.

Any storm dragons from the castle would be kept inside and in a den of some sort. Pravon leaned closer to Aneen and said, "There are distant travelers already here."

"It's probably our targets," she replied.

"But if they are already inside the castle, we will have a difficult time locating and then..." Pravon studied Kridmore's back before whispering, "I do not want the assassin to do something rash and get us all trapped and killed in there."

"The emissaries who are already here are not our primary target." Kridmore didn't turn around, but he must have heard Pravon's mere whisper at twenty or more horse lengths away.

Pravon swallowed. *Damn this man.* "Then who is our primary target? Surely not the Burro King."

"Burro?" Kridmore's shovel chin arced around in Pravon's

direction. An expression Pravon had never seen before on Kridmore revealed itself—confusion.

"It is an old tale." Aneen rode past the assassin.

Kridmore followed her, and Pravon took up the rear. When they neared the storm dragons, one of the beasts let out a low caw like a bird and studied them.

If only you knew who we are. Pravon pushed his hood back and smiled at the dragon, his brown hair settling around his shoulders. These beasts were not sleeping and would not allow him to get close enough to stick them with a poisoned spike, not without creating a commotion.

Kridmore dismounted and slowly and calmly approached the closest dragon. It blinked as it reared up and regarded him. Storms were much smaller than most dragons, at their full height not even reaching a quarter or half as tall as average pines and maples. The beast's deep blue scales caught the late afternoon sunlight and shimmered. Kridmore reached out his hand. The dragon opened its maw and hissed.

"What are you doing?" Pravon asked in a strained whisper.

Aneen's hand strayed to something beneath her cloak.

"What we came here for." Kridmore advanced on the dragon, clicking to it like a stable hand would to a horse. He unfurled his fingers, and purple flames danced on his palm.

The dragon's eyes widened, and it sniffed.

Kridmore made a kissing sound. "It is all right, my beast. Breathe in the flame."

The dragon lowered its long neck and sniffed at the fire. Kridmore flicked his hand upward and slammed his palm into the dragon's snout. The beast huffed in surprise and jerked back, but Kridmore grasped one of the spines on the side of its head. The dragon pulled Kridmore with it, and the assassin heaved himself up in a whirling arc, pressing himself against the side of the creature's head. He reached out with his hand that had been burning, but he now clutched something golden in his grip. He buried a portion of the object into the base of the dragon's skull.

The golden hilt of a dagger protruded from the storm's scales, and a golden band showed on the assassin's arm as he settled into the saddle on the dragon's neck. The beast shrieked and spit lightning that arced into the air and crackled. Soldiers along the walls shouted. In the distance, a horn blasted.

"Shit on the Thief's cloak." Pravon reached for one of his spikes, wondering if Kridmore expected him and Aneen to try to claim the other dragon.

Aneen rushed forward, wielding a spike tipped with black liquid.

The second storm dragon unfurled its wings and flapped them, blasting Aneen and Pravon with a gust. Pravon cursed again as one of the creature's feet lifted off the ground. He would never reach its neck in time. Damn that assassin. He could have at least warned them.

Another horn blared along the castle's walls, and thoughts of being thrown into a foreign kingdom's dungeons, where Pravon's skills would be wasted, flashed through his mind. He reached back and hurled his dragonsteel spike at the storm's neck, aiming for the groove where its jugular vein would lie.

The thin spear sailed through the air and sank into a scale under the beast's neck as easily as a needle would pass through fabric.

Not a direct hit, though.

This was the time when a dragon would kill a dragon thief—if the creature had not been properly stuck. The beast inhaled a massive breath and directed its gaping jaws at Pravon. Pravon could only cringe and lower his head.

As the dragon's other foot left the ground, Aneen leapt upon one of its talons and stabbed her spike into its leg, but she did not bury her needle deep. She drove it in so that it entered at a flat angle.

The dragon screeched as it turned its maw toward Aneen. Pravon dived aside, and a blast of lightning arced from the dragon's jaws and slammed into the ground in a blinding flash of blue that bounced up and struck the castle walls with a crack.

Pravon rolled to his feet, remaining in a crouch.

The storm dragon wobbled as it attempted to beat its wings, but its wings moved out of synchronization. Aneen still clung to its ankle and toe, retracting her spike along its flat angle—one intended to match the path of the underlying vasculature. This technique would have the best chance of hitting a vessel's lumen, which Pravon always attempted to do as well, although he did not have an adequate opportunity in this instance.

The storm dragon settled onto the ground, and Aneen scaled its spikes as she said, "There are more veins on a dragon than just its jugular." She cast Pravon a wry wink. "It can be fun to change it up once in a while." The storm dragon no longer resisted her as she climbed onto its saddle and spoke to it.

"I didn't have much of a choice." Pravon glared at Kridmore, who sat quietly on the neck of his dragon, the assassin's hand gripping his golden dagger. The black jewel at the hilt's base swirled with clouds of teal and jade. The creature's eyes had rolled back in its head and misted over.

Pravon stepped forward and removed his spike from the other dragon's neck. A spurt of dark blood shot out with its release and splattered his arm.

"This *is* interesting." Aneen motioned for Pravon to take a seat in the mage's saddle behind her. "It seems your poison must have also coursed through the dragon's veins, although the beast did not receive a large enough dose to immediately sever her bond with her mage. She is responsive to me, but at the same time, she could also listen to you."

Pravon's mind spun as he studied his comrade. He had never heard of such a thing, but then again, a dragon thief did not destroy a bond and then form a new one in the other realm. Their power over a dragon resided in promises. A thief would only give a dragon the antidote for their poison before the beast suffered and died if the dragon obeyed them fully.

"You're welcome." Aneen gestured again for him to join her. "Now you owe me and must definitely take my side."

Pravon quickly glanced at Kridmore before climbing up behind Aneen. He ran a hand along the storm's scales. "I am here too, my beast. I also carry the antidote, one you will never find among my stash of vials if I am dead."

The tromping of hundreds of booted feet carried from near the castle's gates, and someone shouted from the outer walls, "Desist at once!" A soldier on the battlements pointed at the storm dragons with his spear. "You will dismount from the emissaries' dragons."

Kridmore flashed the soldier the sign of a closed fist pressed against his chin, something crass and insulting.

Other soldiers poured out of the castle and encircled them.

"Would you please at least warn us of what you intend to do next time?" Pravon glared at Kridmore, rage and frustration leaking from his pores. "You nearly got us both killed."

Kridmore ignored him and addressed the regiment of soldiers. "You are all wearing steel, and my dragon breathes lightning. I would not venture any closer."

Most of the soldiers took a few steps back.

"Now, we would like to share a few words with your Burro King." Kridmore pointed to the soldiers on the battlements.

The soldiers there shared a tense look before one answered. "The king will not speak with you."

"Then tell him—"

"I am here." A man wearing a platinum crown over his

graying hair strode boldly up to a crenellation and glared down at Kridmore. He stood in a hunched posture, his voice raspy, although he was probably only middle-aged. "I am Weerin, king of the Weltermores. The Burro King, as you have called me." His voice only carried pride. "What have you to say about this disruption of my lands before my legions of dragonguard swarm down on you and destroy you?"

Pravon glanced around. There was no sign of any dragons filling the skies or rising from within the castle, although a tumult carried out from within the baileys.

Kridmore's smirk remained as arrogant as ever. "I have only this to say—whatever offer the Dragon Queen's emissary promised you in coin or marriage pacts, even if it is to the lady of the Never, those offers are no longer on the table. The Dragon Queen does not rule Murgare. Neither does King Restebarge or Queen Elra. Both are dead. Oomaren is now the rightful king in the northlands."

Weerin's face paled before a flush of red lit up his cheeks. "And you are who? And from where?"

"We are emissaries from Belvenguard," Kridmore said with a haughty and sarcastic tone as he tapped his chin, his ivory teeth flashing. He rubbed at the jewel on his dagger's hilt.

"I find that nearly impossible to believe." The king folded his arms across his chest. "Even though we were waiting for such emissaries, those from Galvenstone arrived just before you did. And they flew in on those two dragons."

"Those are our dragons!" A man in red and gold robes emerged between merlons and pointed at Kridmore.

"They are no longer." Kridmore smiled up at him.

"You cannot simply claim a dragon." The emissary searched about. "What did you do with my mage?"

"Your mage is not dead and was not involved in your dragon's severed bond and new ownership," Pravon said.

"Then how did you manage this?" The man's jaw fell open. "Who are you?"

Kridmore's smirk broadened. "If the Burro King does not believe me, then we will both have to wonder and not trust each other."

The emissary beside the king shifted about. "*We* have come from Galvenstone to parlay with the Burro—the king of the Weltermores, rather. Per King Igare Dragonblade's direct orders."

Kridmore addressed the Burro King. "Leave the offer of the young lady of the Never alone, and you will be free of us. For now. Then Cimeren may still find peace. You all desire peace, no?"

Weerin slowly nodded. "A war between Murgare and Belvenguard will destroy all of Cimeren with its reach and its aftermath."

"And how would you attempt to keep the peace?" Kridmore cocked his hooded head.

"By helping settle any disputes between the two kingdoms."

The beating of dragon wings rose from within the castle's walls.

"Then do what you can, for the time when you will be able to do nothing is nearly upon us." Kridmore tapped his dragon's head, and the beast's wings stretched. "Do not listen to anything these emissaries whisper in your ear."

The king's lips parted, but he did not speak.

Kridmore's dragon lifted into the sky, and Pravon prodded Aneen, who urged their mount to follow. An ember dragon of deep gray with flecks of orange and fiery eyes emerged above the walls and shrieked in their direction. Its breath would unleash smoldering particles that would explode with fire upon striking something.

Kridmore's storm dragon sailed away in a burst of speed, and

Pravon and Aneen trailed behind. The ember dragon, an ash dragon, and an emerald dragon all pursued them but quickly became small dots between them and the castle.

"We should make for the clouds." Pravon pointed upward. "None can match a storm dragon's speed, but better yet to fly higher than they can as well."

Kridmore veered sharply off to the left and nearly crashed his scaled steed into a hillside.

"What do you mean to do now?" Pravon barked at the assassin.

"I want to keep an eye on him." Aneen banked their dragon into a sharp turn, pursuing Kridmore. "We should be safe enough, as long as we're on storm dragons."

Pravon gritted his teeth and attempted to suppress his outrage.

Kridmore's dragon dived low and snapped up a burro from the hillside, crunching on its torso with her jaws. The animal fell limp in her teeth. Kridmore wheeled back around, heading for the castle, soaring even faster than when fleeing. He maneuvered to approach the castle from its eastern walls, keeping his distance from the dragons pursuing them.

Aneen commanded their storm dragon to climb higher into the sky. She kept a decent distance between them but chased after the assassin and tracked his course while watching the approaching ember dragon and its company.

When Kridmore swooped over the castle's walls, his mount buzzed through a legion of rising dragons and caused all the soldiers on the battlements to dive for cover. Bolts flew around his dragon as he dodged and weaved. The assassin's beast flicked its neck and flung the burro from its mouth. The carcass of the animal crashed onto the walk, striking one of the emissaries in the process. The emissary was thrown backward, and they smacked their head on the stones and lay still.

Kridmore's storm dragon screamed past the castle and veered away, blasting past Pravon, the wind from her passing nearly throwing the thief from his seat. A dozen bolts whistled as they flew after Kridmore and his mount.

"I guess we should follow him." Aneen spun their dragon in a tight arc and chased after the assassin again while watching for and avoiding more flying bolts.

A few storm dragons from the Weltermores shrieked in the distance and streaked closer.

Pravon turned and watched the beasts. *The only chance they have of catching us is with those dragons.* But storm dragons were not strong enough to carry dragonarchers or even a fully armed and armored dragonguard.

Kridmore ascended toward the clouds, and Aneen followed.

Once they gained on their untrustworthy comrade, Pravon donned thick furs and hunkered down against their dragon's hot body. He yelled at the assassin over the howling wind. "What was the point of all that madness? Simply to draw out the king and kill a single emissary?"

"Our true targets were not the emissaries." Kridmore patted his dragon's neck. The assassin wore only his cloak and didn't act as if the biting chill of the sky affected him. "This time we were only supposed to take the dragons. They offer us the swiftest passage to where we need to be, per our contact, and all without having to travel across land or by sea. The simple Weltermores hardly require us to spend much of our time here. We now make for a much larger kingdom."

The dragon assassin soared south and disappeared into a bank of clouds.

To the Rorenlands, then?

6

CYRAN ORENDAIN

A TENSE SILENCE FELL LIKE A DOME OVER EIDELMERE AND CYRAN'S companions, only the rustle of the enormous leaves around them and the dragon's feet thumping on bark disrupting the quiet. Far below in the Evenmeres, a crack and crash rang out and radiated upward, sounding like the toppling of a massive tree. A series of crunches followed, terminating in a thunderous boom. A flash of violet light lit up the canopy and snuffed out.

Cyran's breath caught in his throat as he glanced back at his companions, each of them probably too afraid to mention the terrors lurking down below in these woods. Eidelmere ventured onward even faster.

"Let us use some of this additional time for training." Vyk patted the steel arms of his mounted crossbow, pretending to act unconcerned.

"That's a grand idea." Cyran altered the angle of his shield. "Make sure you have your crossbows ready and finely tuned, in case we find ourselves in sudden need. I'll work with the new lance." When he gripped the weapon's hilt, the lance's length glowed the dull green of the Never's dragonsteel—iron amalgamated with the scales of a forest dragon.

Vyk chuckled again, a deep throaty sound. "We all know you've taken the oaths and are now a dragonknight of Belvenguard. Trust me, we do. But even so, put a few swift ice or fire dragons on our tail and even with all your abilities, this old forest dragon and we riders are as good as dead."

A surge of defensive anger bubbled over in the *neblír* as Eidelmere sneered at the insult.

"All the more reason to keep your prowess with the crossbow at its peak," Cyran replied.

Vyk guffawed. "All the more reason for *you* to learn how to hit the broadside of a keep with a dragonbolt while you're flying."

"I am the acting guard." Cyran's eyebrows pinched together with confusion.

Vyk shook his head in a condescending manner.

"The guard of whom?" Eidelmere answered aloud. "This Smoke Breather look-alike on my quarterdeck is more likely to die from intoxication than live through any war."

Vyk fell into a stunned silence.

Cyran glanced at the quarterdeck and his saddle and then leaned over to try to see the turret beneath Eidelmere's chest and belly, but he only caught sight of the lower portion of one pole and the turret's base. "I am the guard for all of us."

"If you haven't noticed, there isn't a mage riding behind you." The claw at Eidelmere's wingtip indicated the empty area on his neck behind Cyran.

Vyk recovered from Eidelmere's insult, and the archer's booming voice rang out. "If you, dragonknight, haven't noticed that we've been without a mage since the first time we climbed aboard with you, I really don't know how we managed to survive an encounter with the Dragon Queen." He bellowed and shook his head.

"Unlike Sir Kayom, *you* have no mage to protect," Eidelmere said to Cyran.

"We will only lose control of this dragon if you fail to protect yourself." Ineri's voice carried up from below.

"But I wield the dragonlance against our enemies," Cyran said.

"How often does any guard have a chance to use their lance against an attacking dragon compared to how often dragonarchers loose their bolts?" Ineri's question was clearly rhetorical. "You should still be able to control this dragon no matter where you sit or stand on it, right?"

Cyran hesitated. If he was in Eidelmere's immediate vicinity, he could command the dragon, but he had never tested how far away he could go and still maintain control over the creature.

"So why not at least try learning how to man a mounted crossbow on the quarterdeck or inside the turret?" Ineri added.

"Sir Paltere does not—"

"So if you haven't seen Sir Paltere, your fellow dragonknight, act as an archer, then neither can you?" Eidelmere snapped.

Cyran instinctively leaned back, as if that would defend him against the attacks of all three of his comrades. The idea of him acting as an archer seemed foreign, but he didn't know exactly why. Maybe because he'd only pictured himself as a guard who could control a dragon and hadn't looked or thought beyond that, not with everything that had happened since he'd discovered his abilities.

"I may not always be here," Ineri said in a quieter tone before coughing several times.

"Neither Ineri nor I have been at Nevergrace long," Vyk said, "but we've both heard at least a half-dozen times about how a certain young dragonknight was once the best ground archer in the entire outpost. He used to make the other squires look like fools."

Through Fire and Shadow

Eidelmere flapped a few times to carry them toward a branch in the distance as Cyran's thoughts ran rampant.

"It's time to learn how to adapt those skills of yours and use them while flying on the back of a dragon." Ineri's smile revealed itself in her words.

Cyran sat in silence for a minute, feeling a bit foolish before releasing his lance and shield and scaling down Eidelmere's neck to the quarterdeck. "Just so you all know, if you haven't heard or have forgotten, I manned both the turret and quarterdeck crossbows during our attempts to defend and reclaim Nevergrace. I was not spectacular with either of them."

"I'm not surprised to hear that." Vyk unlaced the quarterdeck's bootstraps from his feet. "You aren't better than most men in all aspects of battle, and no man is born deft with the mounted crossbow while soaring atop a dragon. That's not something passed down through bloodlines. And when you're up here, it doesn't matter how good you were when taking careful aim from a safe and steady spot on the ground, or even on horseback."

A howl and hollow scream carried up from the darkness below, and then all fell silent.

Cyran hesitated before swallowing a lump in his throat and climbing onto the quarterdeck. He grasped the barred handholds embedded in its planks.

Vyk reached to release his harness. "You're still able to control this dragon and make sure he doesn't do anything out of sorts, right?"

Cyran nodded. "If I must."

Vyk unclasped his harness from the frame of the crossbow. His hands shook as he stepped from the swiveling base to the rear of the quarterdeck and hooked himself onto a hold there. Cyran pulled himself up using the crossbow and its frame for assistance and strapped himself in. A dragonsteel bolt was already loaded, the crossbow's rope cocked, its fibers so taut they felt like steel.

"Consider Ineri's story and her skill for a moment," Vyk said. "Rumors claim she is the best damn dragonarcher in all the kingdom. She could shoot the wings off a sparrow while in a squall, if a dragonbolt wouldn't just pop the sparrow into a few feathers."

"I could have taken the wings from a bird." Ineri hacked and sputtered. "At one time. When using training bolts."

As long as Cyran had known Ineri, she'd been weak and tired, and she often reacted more slowly than expected. Vyk had also been intoxicated during their last battle, and his ensuing rage almost consumed him entirely. When the archer was not in the midst of his battle fury, he usually lounged around and drank, similar to how he claimed he wanted to live out the rest of his days. Bonds and friendships between dragonguard, mages, and archers were not treated lightly. At least not in Belvenguard. These two had been appointed to aid Cyran before he'd even been dubbed and named as a guard, mage, and knight. Cyran had grown to trust them, and they formed a friendship during the battle to reclaim the Never, but it was likely that these two were available for a reason. Perhaps they were great archers at one time. Now they might not be a guard's first choice.

Cyran examined the long dragonsteel bolt with its flared broadhead and massive fletching extending before him. Maybe he should try to become adept with the ballista or, at the minimum, more familiar with the mounted crossbow on the quarterdeck. He slowly eased the tension from the rope of the crossbow, removed the bolt, and slid it into a pile of others that were strapped to the quarterdeck. He pulled out a training bolt—a shaft of wood with fletching—and cranked the windlass to cock the rope into its locked position.

"Aim for one of the branches." Vyk pointed at the limb of an adjacent tree.

"That's a lot smaller than a dragon." Cyran sighted down the shaft of the bolt.

"But dragons weave and dodge. That poor limb cannot move or defend itself."

Cyran squeezed the trigger handle toward the tiller just as Eidelmere dipped during a long glide. The rope snapped forward, and the metal arms of the crossbow thumped and thrummed as the bolt screamed away.

The projectile sailed through a gap between leaves, disappearing and imparting only an image of failure.

"If a guard and mage allowed a dragon to do what the dragon wanted at times," Eidelmere said, "such as being able to visit its home instead of keeping it locked inside a den, maybe that dragon would not attempt little tricks to make things more difficult for its archer. Dragons receiving such treatment would also do more for their guard and mages in return—be better fliers and engines of war. In addition, we could offer less resistance to our riders."

Cyran sighed, immediately recalling the dip Eidelmere had taken as soon as he loosed the projectile. He loaded another training bolt and cranked the windlass.

Eidelmere gestured with his wing at a cluster of buds and newly unfurling leaves. "Full angoia leaves are too big. Anyone could hit them." The young leaves he indicated were almost the size of a man's torso. "The two archers I carry may have at one time been worth their dirty hair and pale skin, but I've seen scores of dragonarchers come and go. I would consider these two mediocre at best."

Vyk glowered at the dragon and folded his large arms across his chest.

Eidelmere continued, "Those who were the most adroit with

the bow were unmatched at being able to anticipate where their dragon, their bolt, and their target would all be when everything aligned and collided in that instant. They did not aim for where their target currently was. They compensated and adjusted for their and their target's future position."

"I—" Cyran began.

"I know—you question everything unless it is Sir Paltere who teaches or speaks to you." Eidelmere exhaled a breath of frustration. "But in this one instance, listen to me."

The dragon's advice did ring of something Sir Paltere had taught Cyran about dragonknights jousting. Those of the guard could not account for their dragon's coming movements, and instead they had to adjust after their mage maneuvered their mount. It was much different for a dragonknight. But if what Eidelmere was suggesting would be more advantageous, as the crossbow could be used much more often in battle compared to the lance, then why had the dragonknight of Galvenstone not taken to the ballistae?

"Aim at the smallest target you can visualize, and then when you miss, you could get lucky enough to hit what is around it." Eidelmere flapped his wings as a gust lifted them. "If the time indeed comes, target an enemy dragon's heart and you could hit his tail, or even his hind leg."

Cyran scoffed. He swiveled the crossbow around and tilted it toward one of the small leaves, sighted, and gripped the trigger. Eidelmere nearly veered aside, but Cyran sensed the motion coming. Through their bond in the other realm, he held the forest dragon steady.

It is the same as during a joust. Like with the tilt against the Dragon Queen.

A dragonknight held a vast advantage not only over other guard but also over dragonarchers. If Cyran learned to handle a mounted crossbow while flying, he could account for all of his dragon's movements, and then he could...

Cyran continued to hold Eidelmere's path steady, and he loosed.

The bolt whizzed away, missing the young leaves, but it punched a hole through a large leaf behind the others. Cyran basked in the beam of sunlight that streamed through the metaphorical wound, and he shrugged. "Not too bad."

"It would not be bad if you hit a dragon's wing." Eidelmere soared westward and landed on a bough. "But the dragon would have to be sitting still on a branch, waiting to be killed. Unfortunately, the massive wings of my kind are the easiest targets, and if you hit them, you inflict relatively little, if any, damage."

Cyran groaned and loaded another bolt. He trained for a few hours amidst eerie calls and shrieks or shuffling trees far below, but he only achieved similar results before the angoias thinned. A vast expanse of marshland opened before them. Cyran held his breath as he gazed west past the sparsely treed marshes to the Lake on Fire and its mirror-like surface.

"We should not venture any farther west," Cyran said. "We do not want to be spotted by the watchtowers of Galvenstone, who will likely believe us to be an enemy. Even if they thought we could be from Nevergrace, they would send a legion after us to make sure, and any of Murgare's watching storm dragons would then be clued in to our passing."

Eidelmere angled northward.

"Wait! Stop." Cyran twisted his torso around in his saddle, and the forest dragon landed on a limb and halted. In the far south, the black spires of watchtowers rimmed the shores near Galvenstone, which was no more than a mass of unidentifiable gray—resembling rolling hills—on the horizon. "If anyone from Galvenstone saw trees moving into the marshlands and then the lake, the event would have to have taken place somewhere in this region or farther south."

"There!" Vyk pointed.

A few leagues or so closer to Galvenstone, what resembled the tops of scores of pines and oaks peeked out from the placid waters of the lake. These treetops were visible just beyond the borders of the marshlands.

Trees do not belong in an area where they are almost fully submerged.

"The lake could not have expanded over that area in recent months," Ineri said. "The waters would overtake the marshlands before covering any new areas."

"Well, if we eventually return, we can certainly tell the king that those trees would never have grown there," Vyk added.

"But even if it is possible, why would trees move *into* the lake?" Cyran asked, more to himself than the others.

"The ways of the cursed forest are as obscure to me as they are to you." Eidelmere cocked his head, as if trying to get a better look.

"At least we now know that some of the rumors Cartaya mentioned are true." Cyran glanced northward. "We should make haste and find the village in question. It will likely take nearly a fortnight to cross the Evenmeres, even with a forest dragon doing the traveling."

The others did not respond, and Eidelmere leapt into the air and wheeled about, diving back into the thick of the angoias. More questions than answers swirled in Cyran's mind.

"If Sir Kayom ever allowed you to visit the woods by yourself, would you have heeded his call and returned to the outpost when you were needed?" Cyran asked Eidelmere through their mental connection. The dragon could not lie to him, not to a bonded mage. The other realm did not allow for it. *"Or would you have*

roamed so far away that his dragonmage could never touch and control you again? So you could ignore their summons?"

Eidelmere did not respond for several minutes as they navigated the canopy world of the Evenmeres—leaves and shadow and sunlight all stringing past in bursts.

"It would likely depend on how long the guard allowed me to visit my home," the dragon finally replied. *"Too little and I would do anything to not have to return. I would also appreciate being asked if I was in agreement with whatever incursion or event they planned for me to assist them with."*

"But would a forest dragon ever want to help support the wars of men?"

"If such a war threatened to reshape the world of Cimeren or our realm, then yes. But most dragons would probably like to be offered the choice."

Was a guard's and mage's relationship with their dragon any different from that of a knight and warhorse? Surely no horse would willingly assist men with charging into battle when there was a high possibility of death and another option for freedom and an open field. Where would such a line between man and his steeds and weapons be drawn? If one kingdom did not utilize dragons or horses or soldiers and knights, they would be crushed by another who did not follow the same rules. Supposedly, this was exactly what had happened to the ancient elves.

Cyran reached into the other realm, searching for Eidelmere's true name and the threads of his soul. This dragon definitely had his own personality and beliefs, like any other man or beast, but weighing the ability to defend oneself against evil kingdoms versus allowing dragons to do as they wished and granting them complete freedom would be a tricky scale to balance. Humans would always have to weigh advantages against disadvantages, and many choices mortals were forced to make in this world were not easy. Surely, many men had made the wrong decisions in the past, and those decisions might have shaped Cimeren more so than any just and honorable choices.

Cyran closed his eyes. *"Eidelmerendren, if you assist me with Murgare's coming war, and if the blood raining from the sky sea stops and we survive, I will free you, my friend. I swear that you will be able to live out the rest of your years in the forest with whatever remains of your kin. May you find your lost relatives and rejoice amongst the angoias."*

A flash of surprise and disbelief wafted through the other realm followed by a twinge of anger and bitterness. The dragon believed Cyran's promise was a lie, nothing more than a ruse to entice him into becoming more compliant. Humans could lie to dragons, but most dragons honored their oaths from the other realm.

A half hour passed in silence as a tumult of emotion stormed through the dragon realm.

"I was not attempting to deceive you with that promise," Cyran said. *"I swear it."*

An overwhelming tide of sadness and relief—both sensations slipping past any barriers Eidelmere had—clashed against Cyran's heart and twisted his beating organ. Eidelmere feared he would be lied to, or he worried that the day of freedom would never come.

"I've heard similar false statements from your kind," Eidelmere snapped in Cyran's mind, resentment saturating his response. *"Do not aim to bring me hope only to tear it away when your oaths become inconvenient. Also, do not make such vows if you believe we will never survive to see the day when you must fulfill them."*

Cyran winced but tried to embrace his empathy and shove it into the other realm.

"You cannot force emotions into my world," Eidelmere said. *"The threads only accept true feelings."*

Cyran sighed. *"I cannot promise that we will live through any war with Murgare, but I will do everything I can to make it so. And if our enemy is decimated and no longer an immediate threat, I shall take you into the heart of the Evenmeres myself and kiss you before wishing you Godspeed."*

If the sensation of tears clawing their way past a shield of bitter resentment could be felt through the other realm, their salty drips seemed to hit Cyran in sheets.

7

JASLIN ORENDAIN

Menoria glided into her bedchamber, her head downcast, her cheeks pale.

Jaslin stood from the chair in her lady's room, closing her book and setting it aside. "What is it?"

"King Igare is departing the outpost." Menoria slumped onto the bed and covered her eyes, her fine blond hair cascading over her hands and face.

Jaslin was taken aback. There had to be more affecting her mood than just the king leaving. Everyone knew Igare and his legions would return to Galvenstone soon. He was supposed to have left days ago, but then that girl from the attacked village showed up and altered his plans.

"He promised to leave us three fully manned forest dragons." Jaslin shuffled over and settled a hand on the lady's shoulder. "Nevergrace will have the same size legion as it did before the Dragon Queen came to the outpost. More once Cyran returns."

Menoria sobbed.

"Surely that is a good thing." Jaslin rubbed her back.

"I do not wish to leave the outpost. I never have."

Jaslin's forehead wrinkled in confusion. "Why would you be leaving?"

"Riscott asked me to accompany the king to Galvenstone." Menoria staggered to her feet and rushed out of the room, covering her face.

Questions tumbled over each other in Jaslin's mind. Her hand crept down for the crystal shard she kept in a pouch at her waist. She drew the object out and hurried after Menoria, turning the shard over in her fingers. A familiar melody spun through her head, and she hummed as she trailed her friend.

Menoria disappeared through an archway down the hall, where stairs led to the first floor of the keep. Jaslin pursued her, not knowing what to expect. Menoria's reactions were usually calm and controlled. She would make a fine lady of the Never. Surely accompanying the king and his legion was an honor, and she could return soon. Maybe a few repairs on the Never's walls and keep would even have been completed by then.

Jaslin descended the stairs and followed Menoria out across the courtyard and then up another set of stairs leading to the walk along the battlements of the inner curtain. Once Jaslin reached the walkway, Menoria stood calmly and gazed out over the castle and lands below.

In the baileys and in the fields beyond the Never's walls, guard and mages and archers hustled around, preparing their dragons. These dragons varied in size from small storm dragons of deep blue to enormous gray stone dragons that carried many archers as well as a trebuchet. There were so many other dragons in between those sizes, and their colors varied from rose red, to emerald, to sapphire, to silver, and to as golden as the sun. There were even several black moon dragons that were blind in the daylight and should not be flown when the sun was up. These creatures had probably been brought in case an attack came during the dark hours, and they would probably not be leaving until nightfall.

Menoria slowly pivoted about, taking in the outpost—its decimated walls and half keep that had been toppled over by crashing dragons. Huge stones still lay strewn about the baileys and beyond. Scores of farmhands, woodsmen, and builders worked on dragging off some of the rubble.

"This may be the last time I ever see her." Menoria's eyes remained wide and unblinking.

"What are you talking about?" Jaslin stayed a pace away from the lady and toyed with her shard. "You are now the lady of Nevergrace. You could decline the invitation if you are overly worried about your outpost's safety."

Menoria scoffed and shook her head. "If the orator has spoken, then the king has essentially asked me to travel to Galvenstone. I cannot ignore the request, no matter how kindly it was made."

The pounding din of builders hammering on the upper stones of the keep rang and swept over the castle.

"Surely with everything that has happened here, they would understand," Jaslin said.

"I am the new lady of the Never." Menoria frowned. "Perhaps if I were a woodsman or a servant, it would be different."

"Then accompany the king and his legions." Jaslin shrugged. "See them safe to Galvenstone and return straightaway."

The look in Menoria's eyes turned distant. "All I've ever wanted was to remain at Nevergrace and help the castle and its people. A people who come from long lines of defenders and guardians of the kingdom. We are proud. Even now amidst this ruin." She waved a hand over their surroundings.

Jaslin nodded and kept her voice near a whisper. "I have wanted a similar life. To remain at the Never with my brothers while Tamar worked and took care of the outpost and Cyran stood watch as a knight or with the guard. My dreams have been crushed as well. Tamar was killed by a falling tree… if it was not something more sinister lurking in the forest, and now Cyran has departed and may never return."

"I fear what this summons could mean." A tear trickled down Menoria's sculpted nose and cheeks. She stepped dangerously close to the edge of the wall where a few stones had been torn from the merlons, creating a vacant opening.

"Did you do something wrong?"

"I was born a woman. Since I came of age, I've been waiting to see where my father would send me in order to strengthen ties with other lords. But these past years before my father died, he was not well, and he did not seem as keen on the idea as he had prior."

Jaslin stepped up to the gap in the battlement and looked down. Someone could potentially survive a fall from this height, but it was unlikely.

"The Dragon Queen asked me questions when she occupied the Never." Menoria shuffled closer to the lip of the wall, and Jaslin grabbed her hand. "About if I would be happier if she brought a suitor to live here with me."

Jaslin squeezed her hand.

"I had never felt so relieved in all my life." More tears streamed down Menoria's cheeks. "I hate the Dragon Queen with every fiber of my being, and yet I desired what she offered. I fear I will not find a similar proposition in Galvenstone."

"All will be well," Jaslin said in a consoling voice. "If they have an idea for a suitor for you, maybe this person will return to Nevergrace with you."

Menoria slowly shook her head. "The orator will never leave Galvenstone, and it was he who asked me to accompany their entourage to Castle Dashtok."

Jaslin stifled a gasp. "You believe Riscott wishes to wed you?"

Menoria's eyes closed, and her chin dipped.

"It may not be so," Jaslin said, tugging Menoria a half step away from the lip of the wall. "Just because Riscott asked you, and he is not married, does not mean he seeks your hand. He has a son. I've heard it mentioned several times. If you are meant for his son, you could both yet return to the Never. No young man would willingly want to remain in the orator's company or vicinity for too many years, especially if their other choice is to rule a castle of their own far away from such a father."

"I've heard that Riscott is pressuring his son, Jaken, to wed the king's only daughter—Princess Nistene."

So Jaken can one day become king of Belvenguard.

"Even though the young man only has eyes for the conjuror's beguiling daughter," Menoria continued. "I also received this." She was barely able to raise her arm. In her hand, she clutched a parchment. A seal of red wax had been broken.

Jaslin grabbed the parchment and skimmed its contents. The note was brief, addressed to Menoria but signed by no one. It simply read: *If this message has been delivered to you, then the queen of Belvenguard is already dead.*

Jaslin inhaled, and her hand started shaking. "Queen Hyceth?"

Menoria shrugged.

"That would mean the queen has left Igare without a son." Jaslin pondered the possibilities. "Nistene is his only heir. Such a situation could be what Riscott wants for Jaken."

"There is another possibility."

There were many other possibilities. "And which one do you believe you are headed toward?"

"That Igare still desires a son, and he is looking for a new queen."

∼

"Your letter is similar to one Cyran said he and the squires received when they were at a tavern in Galvenstone." Jaslin hurried along, glancing back to make sure Menoria was still following her through the crowds working on the keep, groups of king's men, and all those helping them make preparations for their departure. "Laren and Brelle should know more about it."

Smoke and the two other wolves stood just within the front gates of the Never and whined while staring outside. Jaslin crouched beside Cyran's wolf and pet his head. Smoke's tongue lolled from his mouth, but his eyes remained wild.

A forest dragon lumbered through the open gates and roared. Jaslin froze. The two other wolves turned and fled into the bailey. Smoke whimpered but sat on his haunches and panted erratically. A dragonmage rode on the dragon's neck behind the guard's saddle. Two other forest dragons followed the first, and they glanced about, taking in the wreckage around them. Three dragonguard on foot then entered with their archers.

Brelle, Laren, Dage, and a score of other dragonsquires trailed the procession. Jaslin stepped out of their way and waited as the dragons passed, their footfalls rumbling the ground as they made for the rear of the castle, likely for the den.

"We've been given what could be three of the Merchant's offspring as our new guard rather than children of the Paladin or the Shield Maiden." The sarcastic timbre in Brelle's words was thicker than normal, and she spat as she marched along behind the guard and dragons and brushed her curly hair behind an ear. To Laren, she said, "You'd make a finer guard and could defend Nevergrace better than any of them."

"You cannot tell that just by looking at them." Laren's boyish grin vanished as he studied the guard in their red and gold armor of Galvenstone as they trailed the forest dragons. "They have probably trained as much as any and have earned the right to bear the lance."

"They were probably born with certain important fathers and were given—"

"Do not disrespect any of the guard." Dage's long blond hair dangled across his broad shoulders. "They are much more skilled than you."

Brelle spun about to face Dage.

"Brelle." Jaslin hurried over to them, and Brelle, Laren, and Dage turned to her as the other dragonsquires followed the forest dragons. Jaslin held out the parchment in question as Menoria waited behind Jaslin. "Menoria found this slipped under her bedchamber door the other morning."

Brelle took the letter and scanned the writing before flipping it over and studying the seal. "Is our queen really dead?"

Laren shook his head. "Not that I've heard."

Dage agreed with Laren.

"This message is just like the one we received in the Tavern of the Shield Maiden," Brelle said.

"Same writing." Laren pursed his lips. "At least I think so."

Jaslin faced Dage and asked, "Did the anonymous letter you received also look the same as this?"

Dage's forehead furrowed. "You all keep asking me questions about that damn message. I cannot remember what the writing on it looked like."

"Cyran said yours suggested not to join the dragonguard even if you were asked to." Jaslin scrutinized the hulking dragonsquire.

"The message said it would be in my best interest not to answer such a summons." Dage's cheeks reddened. "But when I am finally offered the chance, I will become a guard. I am not afraid of anyone who hides behind parchments and words."

"And your message said to beware of someone in the king's council?" Jaslin faced Laren and Brelle.

Brelle nodded. "It was addressed to us 'dragonsquires.' Sir Kayom received a letter as well."

"Then they mean nothing." Dage turned to follow the procession of the Never's new dragons. "The queen is not dead, Sir Kayom is, and Brelle and Laren have spoken to many others about their message, which they said it specifically told them not to do."

"I don't know what to make of the letters." Brelle folded up the parchment and handed it back to Jaslin.

Laren shrugged.

Emellefer stood in the distance but called to the squires, her shimmery dark hair a bit disheveled. "See to putting away your new dragons and making them comfortable, and by then, I'll have your suppers ready."

Renily, the little redheaded girl, skipped about beside Emellefer, and Ezul, the Never's nyren, stood silently behind them as he ran a hand down his white beard. Whenever Jaslin saw the nyren now, she immediately got an image of long white hair dangling from his eyebrows, face, and beneath his tunic around his nipples—wizard nipples, Brelle had called them.

"I cannot promise it will be as good as Ulba's stews," Emellefer added, "but I'm trying my best."

"Ulba's stews tasted like she dropped an apple or two of horseshit in them." Brelle paced after Dage. "Especially whenever she and I discussed something before dinner."

"You mean when you argued with her and then insulted her," Laren said, striding beside Brelle.

Their conversation faded into a murmur.

Renily kept skipping about, staring at the ground. "I wish Cyran was here to play the lute during the king's departure."

"Me, too." Emellefer sighed, a look of longing crossing her

face. "He had to leave far too soon, and just before everything should be getting back to normal."

I wish he were here as well. Jaslin took a deep breath as she handed the parchment back to Menoria, who brushed aside a few tears.

"We should prepare to depart as well." Jaslin ruffled Smoke's fur and headed for the keep.

"We?" Menoria asked.

Jaslin stopped and faced her. "Of course. I am your handmaid now, remember? If you're going to Castle Dashtok, you will need your caretakers to accompany you."

A hint of a grin tugged at the corner of Menoria's lips.

"I should pack your clothes." Jaslin stepped away.

"My real maids have already packed my belongings and loaded them onto a dragon. You are simply... my friend. Why else would I let you lounge around and read stories all day?"

Jaslin smiled. "Should we go see where the king lives?"

"You should pack. Quickly."

Jaslin absently clutched at the shard in her pouch. "I don't own anything I need to take with me, and both of my brothers are already gone."

"Not even your books?"

"I've read all the books in Nevergrace a dozen times, and the Summerswept Keep should have more stories than I could ever hope to get through in one lifetime. I will be fine."

Menoria turned and walked out the front gates. Jaslin paced after her.

In the fields beyond, a hundred dragons growled and shrieked as the legion prepared to escort the king of Belvenguard home.

8

CYRAN ORENDAIN

Cyran loosed another training bolt. The crossbow's arms whipped forward and launched the projectile with blurring speed. The bolt sailed over the leaf of an angoia and disappeared into a cluster of shadows.

Eidelmere's disappointment broadened, lying heavy in the other realm. The dragon had not spoken more than a word or two in response to anything Cyran asked in the days since they'd left the marshlands and once again headed north toward Murgare.

"Do you have any words of wisdom for me, Ineri?" Cyran asked. If she was once the most accurate dragonarcher in the kingdom, surely training with her would be superior to listening to a dragon.

"No." Her turret's crossbow creaked as it swiveled about. "I've tried teaching others, but I am not adept at instructing anyone. I aim and I hit my targets. There is nothing more I can explain."

Cyran scoffed and glanced back at Vyk, who rubbed his arms to keep himself from getting too cold, simply shrugged, and said, "I've told you everything I can. Just keep practicing. If you were once as good with the hand crossbow as we've heard, you should eventually learn how to handle the mounted crossbow... while on a dragon."

Sunlight cascaded around them and hit Cyran like a slap to the eyes. He squinted and glanced eastward. Eidelmere sailed past the last line of angoias and soared over the pines far below. They were now in the unknown lands, over the forest between the walls of angoias separating Murgare and Belvenguard. Forest dragons might still travel these lands, but it had probably been centuries since any dragon riders had done so.

The verdant green of the woods stretched to the horizons in the east and west. Far to the north, another massive wall of even older and more gnarled angoias rose into the clouds, which skimmed along beneath the belly of the sky sea.

A sense of awe replaced Eidelmere's darker emotions, and the dragon's wings billowed as he flapped and carried them on in silence. Only the wind gusted around them, and no other dragons swirled in the sky, making Cyran feel as if he were on a ship out in the middle of the sea, sailing for an unknown island.

After many hours of uninterrupted and quiet traveling passed, the sunlight faded into the west, and Cyran returned to his guard's saddle. Darkness stole across the forest.

"Where will we find rest between the angoias?" Vyk asked.

Cyran glanced down into the woods, and he shuddered. He hoped he wouldn't have to see the things he had encountered on the south side of the angoias—even closer to Nevergrace—ever again. It was likely there would be eviler creatures secluded in the areas between the kingdoms. Over the past days of travel, Eidelmere had taken rest among the angoia branches high above the cursed forest, but tonight they would not have that luxury.

"I will fly on through the night and following day until we reach the next wall of angoias," Eidelmere stated indifferently.

Cyran nodded and allowed the dragon to guide them

onward. Night engulfed them, and the light of the thousand moons silvered the woods below and the walls of trees to the north and south.

Hours crawled by, and Cyran nodded and jerked, awakening himself in his saddle. Eidelmere still flapped along with the steady beating of his leathery wings. The breath of the Evenmeres gusted and tugged on Cyran's hair with invisible hands. Eidelmere's weariness showed in his sagging eyelids.

"You make all the sacrifices now, my friend." Cyran laid a palm against the dragon's neck. "My sacrifices will come later."

The dragon made no indication of responding.

"If you grow too tired, we can try to find a spot to rest," Cyran said.

"Not down there." A shiver ran down Eidelmere's spine, jostling Cyran's saddle. "Your memory is poor if you have already forgotten what lurks in the woods."

"I haven't, but you *need* rest."

"I will rest when it is safe to do so."

Eidelmere flew on through the night and next day. Then, after night fell again, they finally neared a wall of angoias, and Eidelmere drifted onto a branch. The dragon's exhaustion seeped from his scales.

"Please, take your well-deserved rest," Cyran said and patted Eidelmere's neck.

The dragon shook himself like a dog before Ineri stepped from the turret and uncinched it, allowing its frame to rest on a fork in the boughs. Vyk yawned, stretched, and climbed down the rope ladder from the quarterdeck. Eidelmere slumped over and closed his eyes.

"Might as well catch a bit of rest myself." Vyk walked along the limb, and although it was much wider than most castle walkways, he glanced around nervously as if he could tumble off at any moment.

"You've done nothing but sleep these past couple days." Ineri coughed so hard she doubled over. Once she recovered, she dug into her saddlebags and retrieved an apple and bread.

Cyran climbed down from his saddle, chewing on jerked venison. He wandered along the bough, trying to peek through the leaves and into the night sky. Vyk slumped down with his back against the angoia's trunk and closed his eyes. His head tilted forward, and his chin rested on his chest. Within a few minutes, he began snoring.

Hours crawled by while worries accosted Cyran. Thoughts of Nevergrace, the attacked hamlet and village, Murgare and Belvenguard in general, and most of all Jaslin, tormented him. The crystal shard his sister still carried even after he had shattered the decanter made him uneasy. Eventually, his eyelids drooped.

Faint music carried up from somewhere below.

Cyran jolted, cocking his head to listen, making sure it wasn't only his mind playing tricks on him, given his recent thoughts of Jaslin and that shard. She had been humming the tune far too often, the same tune Tamar had been whistling before he died.

The melody rang of something light and joyous, and yet foreboding undertones haunted its background. It was familiar, reminiscent of something Cyran couldn't quite grasp or recall. It had to be an old song, a very old song. The hair on the back of his neck spiked as he tried to rest, and the tune wormed its way into his psyche.

It is in the key of the Dragon, but in minor. Notes of the Siren's, the flat note of the Great Smith's, and one of the Assassin's rang in a strange harmony with each other, along with a chord of notes Cyran could not place.

Far in the distance below, over the canopy of the forest proper, spots of light drifted and swirled about in a fiendish dance. Cyran's blood chilled.

"They call to us." Eidelmere's lips twitched as he mumbled, but his eyes did not open.

Cyran reached for the hilt of his silver sword—the only weapon he had found to be effective against the dragon fae. Thankfully, the creatures still had a long way to fly in order to reach them. But far below, something shifted in the silvered trees of the forest. Whatever it was, it was large, and it might have been the trees themselves, as some branches appeared to wind through the others.

"Their song lightens my heart." Ineri hummed before hacking a few times.

"I never should have been so foolish as to stop along the outskirts of the angoia wall." A low growl sounded in Eidelmere's throat. "When we were flying over the open forest, they probably spotted us. We should travel deeper into the woods and lose ourselves from them before we rest. Otherwise" —he glanced at Ineri—"we risk being drawn to them or them to us." The dragon groaned and used his winged limbs to push his torso up. "Damn the curse placed on this forest *and* these creatures that have taken up residence in my old home and have made it their own."

"They are a long way from us." Ineri closed her eyes, her head bobbing slightly to the tune. "And it is such a pleasant sound."

"Only because you haven't encountered them before." Cyran stood. "If those creatures eventually fly up here and find us, they will kill us. Trust Eidelmere. He is tired and has more reason than any to find sleep."

Eidelmere quickly regarded Cyran but then ignored the comment.

Ineri's eyes slid open. She studied Cyran for a moment and nodded. "I will reattach the turret."

Eidelmere unfurled his wings, each of his joints appearing

gnarled and lumpy with age, his movements stiff. He stood on his hind legs but stooped over as Ineri and Cyran looped the turret's cinch straps through the belts binding the quarterdeck to the dragon's torso. Once the turret was reattached, Ineri climbed inside its poled frame, and Eidelmere stood taller.

"Vyk." Cyran shoved against the archer's shoulder.

"Mount up, archer, or we will leave you behind." Eidelmere's voice blasted over Vyk, and the archer's beard and braid lifted in the gust created by the dragon's breath.

Vyk's eyes popped open. "I was dreaming of luscious mead, and the songs in the tavern were pure and sentimental."

Eidelmere leaned in closer to Vyk's face, his lip lifting in a snarl. "That is the melody of the dragon fae. Mount up or we will leave you to them."

Vyk scrambled to his feet, glancing around at the branches before looking down at the lights swirling in a swarm over the forest. He hurried for the quarterdeck's ladder and hoisted himself up.

Eidelmere cursed under his breath as Cyran took his seat in the guard's saddle, and the dragon lumbered along the limb toward the trunk. Memories of the dragon fae's vicious bite and the venom they carried—which Eidelmere said would corrupt a man's conscience—hit Cyran like a punch to the temple.

"Have you heard the tale of the dragon fae?" Eidelmere's voice rang in Cyran's head.

A sense of foreboding clawed at Cyran's chest. There was a tale about them? "No. I am curious, but I am also not sure I want to hear it."

"I heard the song of the fae at some stage in my life, although I cannot remember when or where." Eidelmere reached the angoia's trunk, leapt up, latched onto its bark with the claws at his wingtips and those on his hind limbs, and scaled upward. "Perhaps it was when I was a mere dragonet in these angoias. It is said that the fae are those who crept out from the *neblír* during the times of the Great Dragon, when only She walked the young world."

Cyran had trouble imagining a great dragon as anything other than a behemoth of a beast or perhaps the Dragon, one of the nine gods.

Eidelmere stopped scaling and wound around the trunk before climbing out on a branch on the far side of the tree. There, he lunged along the length of the bough, leapt into the pale moonlight, and glided onward.

"The dragon fae believed their time to flee the *neblír* and overpower the Great Dragon had come." Eidelmere's voice turned distant as they traveled through the copse of angoias. "They were prideful little beings who wanted to extend their reach beyond the dragon realm and conquer the realm of the mortals. They were no match for the Great Dragon and her children, but they did not see themselves as small. Their vision was one of grandeur and victory. They made a pact with the Assassin, who granted them the venom in their bite. But the Great Smith and the Dragon found them during their meeting with the Assassin and told them of a third realm—one with more creatures and beings to rule than that in the realm of men. The greedy fae flocked to the new realm, and the Great Smith and Dragon locked all of them inside this realm of mystery, where place and passing of time is nothing like the others. It is said that while in the third realm, the fae ceaselessly used their new gift of venom to entrance and control all creatures birthed since the dawn of Cimeren."

A slosh of bile rumbled about in Cyran's stomach.

"You will continue to hone your skills while I spin any tales." Eidelmere's tone was thick with spite. "If I must push through my exhaustion, the least you can do is keep up your end of your vow and try your best to ensure that we survive the time of the raining blood. You can train while you listen."

A sensation of sheepish guilt settled in Cyran's chest, and he grabbed his lance's hilt and swiveled it around, targeting small areas on leaves as they sailed along. He felt Eidelmere's movements somewhere deep inside him, and the tip of his lance split the stem of a leaf on a nearby limb.

Cyran grinned with pride. He watched the leaf drop and spiral about as it drifted slowly downward.

"Your skills with the lance are sufficient." Eidelmere did not sound any less rankled with Cyran. "You should train with the crossbow. Your skills with it are far less than adequate."

"But it is night, and I can hardly see."

"Dragons attack outposts at night, remember?"

Cyran fell silent as memories of the Dragon Queen's arrival at Nevergrace bombarded him. "But I won't even be able to see if I hit my target."

"You won't hit it. Perhaps it is best for you to practice with the lance for now, but when it is daylight, you will take up the crossbow again."

An ember of irritation sparked inside Cyran. He controlled this cantankerous old dragon, not the other way around. He should follow the path that he thought would be most beneficial.

"Your comrades were right—the mounted crossbows on the backs of dragons have taken and saved far more lives than all the lances in Cimeren ever will." Eidelmere dipped a wing and whipped around a few leaves, attempting to disorient Cyran and make him miss his target.

Cyran sensed the dragon's movements coming, and after that initial dip, he held Eidelmere still.

"You should try not controlling my every movement,"

Eidelmere snapped. "You would become a much greater dragonknight if you did so."

Cyran's lance split an angoia leaf in half. "And allow you to make me miss my targets?"

"Feel where I go instead. That way, you can concentrate on what you need to do, and I can concentrate on what I am doing and take the most beneficial route as each situation unfolds."

"I cannot let you take a safer path when I see a more advantageous one for a coming tilt."

Eidelmere scoffed. "You must learn how to trust a *dragon* completely. How to trust me with your own life. That is what scares you, the sense of not being in control of a terrible beast that could kill you or get you killed."

Cyran swallowed. In his heart, he knew most of what Eidelmere said was true. "What if you choose the wrong path?"

The dragon scowled. "What if *you* choose the wrong path? I've seen many more battles than you ever will in the short years of your lifespan. You could direct my movements and actions while jousting, as we are both looking ahead at the same things, but if you ever want to become a master of the crossbow, and I mean a real master, you will have to let go of your fear and trust a scaled monster to do the best it can not only for itself but also for you."

Cyran imagined what could have happened after Sir Kayom and Morden were unseated and Cyran had to quickly learn to command Eidelmere. If he had not been able to do so, Eidelmere would have torn the quarterdeck and turret loose, along with Cyran and the other archer, and they would have plummeted to their deaths.

Cyran's mouth felt as dry as one of Jaslin's old book pages. "Sir Paltere never—"

"Sir Paltere, Sir Paltere," Eidelmere barked. "*Sir Paltere* is not an accomplished archer, and neither will you be if you cannot see the possibilities I lay out before you. If you allow me to fly the best course, you could swivel about behind those metal arms and watch what approaches us from all sides. You could feel where I'm headed and what I'm about to do and know where your bolt would be when you loosed. If needed, you could even hold me still for a moment just as you squeeze the trigger, so in that instant your bolt would not fly astray. But hold me for too long, and I could fly straight into death's open maw—something you may not see coming when you are distracted."

A sickening pull tugged at Cyran with the thought of allowing a dragon to direct and control his flight, a dragon that could benefit from his death and then find its freedom. It might not matter if the shattering of their bond was initially painful.

Cyran sighted his next target—a knot on an approaching branch, one as small as a man's heart. After grasping at the thread of Eidelmere's soul in the other realm, he squeezed. He controlled Eidelmere's movements, making the dragon bob and weave through a gauntlet of incoming foliage. The capped tip of his lance smacked against the knot with a hollow thump, and Cyran released the weapon and dragon and allowed Eidelmere to settle onto the branch.

"I may never be the greatest dragonknight who ever lived, but no guard can match something like that." Cyran said it evenly, trying not to reveal any pride or emotion that could further irritate the dragon. "They just can't. Not without being able to direct their dragon and create the movements needed for everything to align."

Eidelmere's anger sheeted through the *neblír*. "You are not ready. You cannot be made into one of the greatest dragonarchers Cimeren has ever seen. Not with such lack of vision and an inability to aim a bolt while upon one of my kind."

Cyran's smile fell flat. Eidelmere ran along the branch in silence as Cyran felt a pit of regret forming. Perhaps he should have just allowed the dragon to do as he wished, lightening his bitterness for the time being. The beast was utterly exhausted. Cyran clenched his jaw and cursed himself.

They veered toward one massive leaf, almost as if Eidelmere wanted it to smack Cyran in the face, but Cyran ducked as it whipped past. The leaf dragged over Eidelmere's neck and hit Vyk with a slap.

"Ah!" Vyk thrashed about, punching and kicking at the leaf to get it off him.

"Is there any more to that tale about the dragon fae?" Ineri asked from below.

Eidelmere's anger settled a bit. "This boy on my neck would never use any knowledge passed down to him to behoove us, but I would not mind telling the final outcome for you, archer."

Vyk fished a strip of an angoia leaf from his beard and cast it aside.

Cyran remained silent, hoping to further avoid the forest dragon's ire.

Eidelmere continued, "The legend concludes by alleging that during the Dragon Wars, when all were distracted, someone —perhaps the Assassin—released the fae from the third realm and allowed them to return to ours. Now these creatures have taken up residence and have grown strong in the shadows of the Evenmeres."

9

SIRRA BRACKENGLAVE

The shipyard waited just ahead. Sirra marched along, Yenthor and Zaldica flanking her under a mist of cold rain. Shadowmar loomed over the docks beyond the shoreline. Anyone who had not fled when the shadow dragon landed now hid behind crates as Sirra's boots clomped on the boards of the walkway.

Sirra paused and turned her helmed head. A boy hunched beside a stack of rope.

"Where is the master of this yard?" Sirra asked the boy.

The boy stuttered but didn't speak. He pointed to a building down the way.

Sirra paced on and stepped inside the open doorway of the building. A man sat behind a desk and stacks of parchment. He glanced up when Sirra entered.

"Are you the master of the shipyard?" Sirra strode up to the desk.

The man ran a hand through wisps of gray hair and nodded. "You are from Northsheeren?"

"You'd know her if you saw her dragon." Zaldica halted just beyond Sirra's left side.

The man gulped. "You are the Dragon Queen?"

"What is occurring out in the bay?" Sirra folded her armored arms across her chest. "Master..."

"Raltan." He forced a welcoming smile. "There is a man out there who refers to himself as the Finned Corsair."

"He is named this because he comes from the Bay of Fins?"

The master rubbed his eyes. "No. Because he and his blood letters feed the finned dragons of the deep. He stops every ship coming to and leaving Northwatch and Eastwatch."

"What have you done about this?"

"Me?" Raltan touched his chest. "I've sent word to Northsheeren, but I do not command dragons or any naval ships that can retaliate against him. My messengers had to travel the long way around to reach the castle—far south to the Reach Road. However, there is also talk of strange happenings down there, and some say my messengers probably did not survive."

"How long have you allowed this Finned Corsair to control the bay?"

"I-I did not *allow* him, but he and his blood letters showed up soon after the rumors of King Restebarge's death spread."

"And where do he and his men reside? I will burn him."

The master shrugged. "*If* you can find him. Some say he dwells on Dawn Breaker Isle. Others say he and his men sleep in the waves or crawl out of floating rocks."

Sirra paused in thought. It might not be as easy to crush this pirate and his uprising as she initially believed. The stitches holding Murgare's lands together were stretching. She had to pull them tight again before her kingdom began to fray.

"The Finned Corsair binds the crew from the ships he takes to wreckage and makes them float out on the water?" Sirra asked.

"Until they beg to be bled so their suffering will cease."

Raltan glanced away. "But still their lives end in a surge of terror."

"We will simply draw him out." Sirra turned to the open window and stared over the bay and the isles to the north.

"If you came in on your dragon, the Finned Corsair likely already knows you're here." The master tapped two fingers against his desk. "And the Finned Corsair is no longer the only pirate in the area. Another man, who the people call the Hammer, and his crew have plundered many incoming ships as well."

Sirra clenched her fist, her annoyance flooding the *neblír*. Somewhere outside, Shadowmar shrieked. Raltan jolted, his eyes wide as he glanced about.

"She will not harm you, as long as you are not part of this uprising." Sirra studied the man and muttered a word from the other realm—*desirité*. If he spoke an untruth, she would feel its presence.

The master slowly nodded. "Most certainly I am not."

The threads of the dragon realm burned with Raltan's lie. Sirra focused on him. What would a master of Eastwatch's shipyard have to gain by employing a corsair? Wheels upon wheels of deceptions, ones she had seen or heard about in her centuries of life, scrolled through her thoughts. If this man controlled the corsairs, he could claim that all his goods were taken and thus avoid tariffs and taxes from Northsheeren. He could also plunder all the ships meant for Northwatch. With the death of Murgare's king, this master probably believed he could run the ploy for some time before pointing a finger at the Finned Corsair.

"The only good news about the rise of the Hammer," Raltan continued, "is that the two corsairs do not seem to like each other, and they have gotten into a few skirmishes of their own."

"We will borrow as many ships as you have on hand and

make it appear as if they are loaded with goods and mean to sail as fast as they can for distant lands. This will force these pirates to send all of their ships out to intercept them. We will also gather up the floating crewmembers and ease the passing of any who cannot be saved."

"With your recent arrival, the corsairs will suspect a trap."

"It will not entirely be a trap. You will have your workers load up all the goods you were too afraid to ship across the sea these past fortnights, and make sure all the typical people see this. Then send the vessels east and north. If neither of these corsairs show, you should make a profit."

"I will send word at once." Raltan stood and bowed his head, his hands shaking as he passed around Sirra.

She turned to follow him.

The master cast her a nervous grin before calling out for a deckhand. To Sirra, he said, "I work faster alone."

"I will not slow you down too much."

∽

The following morning, seven ships disembarked from the harbor of Eastwatch. Their sails rippled as the gusting wind caught and snapped them, which spread their deep violet and sea-green fabrics wide.

Sirra sat astride Shadowmar, overlooking the bay. No other vessels sailed the waters. She waited as the ships bobbed eastward across the bay, and then some turned north to sail the gap between the shoreline and Dawn Breaker Isle.

The master of the shipyard exited his building to watch. Zaldica followed him. She had been observing him and everyone he dealt with since Sirra first spoke with him.

Best to know everyone who is involved and if the master is truly at the head of this gambit.

Raltan paced nervously, rubbing at his temples as he watched his ships. He turned to Sirra. "I fear what is about to happen. I do not know if even your dragon can stop all the pirates in these waters."

"We only have to apprehend their leaders," she replied in as light a tone as she could muster.

Raltan paled.

Within half an hour, a smattering of sails filled the sea between the isles and the departing ships.

"They are coming." Raltan pointed. "All my wares will be taken. My crews killed."

"How many are there?" Sirra asked as Shadowmar stretched her neck and flexed her wings.

Yenthor grabbed a spyglass from the master and extended it. His forehead wrinkled as he peered into the device. He moved the spyglass about to view the waters for a minute or so. "A dozen ships."

"That is a lot of ships for only a couple pirates." Sirra studied Raltan. "How did they get ahold of so many?"

"They started with only one," the master said. "The others they raided and took for their own."

Sirra waited until the corsair ships increased their distance from the isles, sailing closer and closer. "We fly." Sirra gestured for Yenthor and Zaldica to mount up.

Zaldica grabbed Raltan by the arm and guided him toward Shadowmar.

"What are you doing?" the master shouted as they neared the dragon's head. "I cannot fly on a dragon."

"We insist that you ride with us." Zaldica shoved him against the quarterdeck's rope ladder while Yenthor and another archer grabbed his wrists and hauled him up, his feet kicking wildly when they left the ground. Once on the quarterdeck, Yenthor wrapped a harness around Raltan's waist and strapped him to a holding bar.

"My old heart cannot handle this." The master pulled at his wisps of hair. "I will not survive."

"We need you to make sure the negotiations go smoothly." Sirra grinned beneath her helm, and Shadowmar leapt into the air and beat her enormous wings.

Sirra's steed of scales swooped out over the water and careened toward the merchant vessels. Within a few minutes, Shadowmar overtook the ships and whizzed past them. The corsair ships did not retreat or even turn about when the dragon's vast shadow fell across the sea before them.

"They do not show fear." Yenthor cranked his crossbow, and its metal arms creaked with tension.

They must fully trust their leader or believe they somehow hold the upper hand.

"They must be taught fear and respect," Zaldica said. "Shadowmar will burn their ships to ashes."

Wheels within wheels. Sirra glanced back at the master of the shipyard. His eyes were clamped shut as he knelt on the quarterdeck, grasping at every hold he could find. "They must have a trap of their own and want us to spring it."

"What could they hope to do to us?" Yenthor's tone was arrogant—too arrogant—and that was what the corsairs would be hoping for. "Shadowmar could crush one of their ships simply by landing on it."

"Maybe they have heavy crossbows mounted behind the bulwarks." Zaldica's turret whirred with her movements.

"Perhaps." Sirra considered the implications of putting her mount in danger, and she had Shadowmar swoop low over the water to avoid becoming an easy target. "But there has been no need for these ships to carry such weapons prior. They would have to have fortified them after Restebarge's death. Not impossible, but..." She strummed a thread in the other realm that she seldom called upon. "Ëagothor." What felt like a beacon of light flared in the *neblír* in the area of the largest ship. "They have a dragonmage with them. A powerful one." *But these corsairs are too young to understand the power of the Dragon Queen.*

Shadowmar shrieked as they sailed closer to the line of approaching ships.

"They would have trouble hiding much more than a few storm dragons on those ships." Yenthor's arrogance did not wane. "I don't believe they could even have a mist or fire dragon with them."

Such dragons would not explain why they are unafraid. Sirra studied the sea flashing below them. She jerked Shadowmar up against her will. The shadow dragon roared as Sirra bent her wings and neck and forced her to swoop upward.

The sea erupted, and a massive form burst from its surface, jaws as long as carracks lunging upward and snapping.

Sirra rolled Shadowmar upside down and to the side as the sea beast's bulk—probably three times that of Shadowmar's—emerged. Its relatively small wings flapped and propelled the creature higher. Sirra weaved to the side, drawing her sword and slashing at her attacker's maw in one movement. Her blade nicked its flesh just before the beast plunged back into the sea, sending waves bigger than the cargo ships rolling outward.

Shouts of fear radiated from the corsairs. Raltan cried out and wept.

Sirra remained focused on the sea. That creature was larger than any sea dragon she had ever encountered or heard of. Much larger. It might have even been bigger than the ancient cave dragons the dwarves had freed from the depths of their mines, creatures that had been trapped in ages past but had not stopped growing as they formed their own caverns to live in.

The arms of a crossbow thrummed, drawing Sirra's attention. Two bolts screamed away from the corsair ships, flying toward Shadowmar, who was now a much easier target in the sky.

"*Fall,*" Sirra said in her mind, and Shadowmar's wings folded inward. The dragon dropped from the sky like a mountain, narrowly avoiding the projectiles that would have punched holes in her hide or the leathery flaps of her appendages. The dragon snapped her limbs out again, and the sea wind broke their fall as it billowed the segments of her wings.

A massive monster lurked below, unseen, a beast that Sirra imagined as a whale dragon.

Shadowmar flapped and soared onward, releasing a blast of black fire as the first wave created by the whale dragon's breach reached the corsair ships. The lead ship ignited in dark flames, and a few screams rang out but quickly died under the roar of an ensuing inferno. The wave then smashed into the vessel, tilting it onto its side, tearing the masts from the decks, and throwing the crew into the sea.

The other vessels turned and faced the wave head on, rolling over it, and when it passed, they spun around and scattered as they fled for the isles. In the other realm, Sirra sensed the presence of the mage, as well as the mage's bond with the whale dragon. That thread was more akin to a chain, strong indeed. Typically, a bond could only be severed if a mage or dragon died, but such laws did not hold true for the Dragon Queen, not if she had made a deeper connection by possessing some physical aspect of the creature.

She swiped her hand across the edge of her flaming blade and pressed her fingers together, crushing a droplet of dragon blood that would not burn away. In the *neblír*, she grasped the chain of the beast's bond and squeezed.

"Utheliambrendorean," she muttered. "I know your name, sea beast."

A hollow wail sounded from the deeps and echoed through the air around them.

"You will travel east and stop those seeking to flee around Dawn Breaker Isle," Sirra said through her new bond. *"We go north."*

Shadowmar quickly overtook the fleeing ships, and as they veered to avoid her, she herded them back toward the isle. In the distance, the gigantic whale dragon surfaced and shrieked, beating its tail at the incoming vessels. The corsairs swung about, hoping to avoid certain death.

Within a few minutes, Sirra trapped the remaining eleven ships between Shadowmar and the whale dragon. She skimmed over the corsair vessels, and her dragon's wings snapped the tops off two masts before Shadowmar landed on the whale dragon's back. Shadowmar folded her wings in against her sides and perched on the gargantuan beast like a bird on a rock. Zaldica or the other archer in the lower turret released a gasp. Those two would be so close to the sea beast that they would be able to make out its individual scales.

Utter silence engulfed the corsair ships. Raltan sobbed uncontrollably.

"Bring out the Finned Corsair and the Hammer," Sirra called out.

Several minutes of silence passed.

"Or you will all be burned by the black fire that consumes souls." Sirra added the final embellishment to strike fear into their hearts, but it was not true.

A moment later, two men shuffled onto the foredecks of two different ships and faced her. On one of the ships, the outline of a red fin on the mainsail contrasted with the sail's black background.

"You have attacked Murgare vessels and have taken your spoils as well as lives." Sirra spoke in an emotionless tone. "Tell me why you have done so." Shadowmar's neck extended, and

Sirra stood and strode along the top of her mount's skull, down between her eyes, and to the dragon's snout before stepping off onto the foredeck of the ship with the fin sail. A man whose face was covered in so many blue tattoos that only a few fins could be distinguished amongst the myriad of designs stood before her, his nose dripping with water.

"Be careful, Dragon Queen," Yenthor called. "He may not look like much, but he is a murderer and you've cornered him."

Sirra did not heed the archer's words as she faced the tattooed man. "You are the Finned Corsair?"

The man nodded. "The Murgare king is dead, and the lands have grown wild."

"You are all still residing in Murgare waters and are thus beholden to the laws of the kingdom." Sirra drew her sword, and its black flames snapped and crackled. "While Castle Northsheeren still stands, you will not defy her."

The Finned Corsair bowed his head. A crippled young man with a staff hobbled up onto the foredeck, half of his face pale with scar tissue, the other half darkened by the sun.

The dragonmage of the whale dragon. Sirra ignored the mage and addressed the Finned Corsair. "*Desirité*. Was it per your orders that your men carried out the carnage in the bay? The torture?"

The Finned Corsair's chest expanded, the slats of his ribs shoving outward as he sucked in a deep breath. "I undertook some of the efforts, but not the lashing of men to planks and setting them adrift in the sea. That was the Hammer's doing."

Truth.

The Finned Corsair looked beyond Sirra to Shadowmar's quarterdeck and said, "The entire affair was arranged by the master of the shipyards at Eastwatch. Master Raltan. He specifically requested some form of torment that would strike fear into the hearts of many."

Truth.

Raltan screamed, "You lie! The Finned Corsair is lying to you, Dragon Queen."

"The dragon realm does not readily accept lies." Sirra faced the other man who had come to the foredeck on the adjacent ship, the Hammer—a stout man with a wooly beard. "You are responsible for the persecution of the sailors?"

The man sneered.

"Why?" Sirra asked.

"Because I enjoy it. Same as you."

"The Siren of the Sea take you." Sirra motioned, and Shadowmar's tail lashed out. The barb at its tip impaled the Hammer's chest.

The Hammer lurched back. His face drained of color, and his underlying veins blackened so deeply that they stood out under his skin as they branched and climbed up his neck and cheeks. His mouth gaped as he gasped for breath. White froth bubbled from his lips, and he collapsed in a heap.

Sirra ascended Shadowmar's snout and head and followed the dragon's topline to the quarterdeck, where she faced Raltan with her sword poised. "You were behind all of this. Your lies are as potent as your fear."

The master dropped to his knees and trembled. "I... I didn't think it would go this far. Please!"

Truth. Sirra brought her blade down and cleanly severed the man's head from his neck. It dropped onto the quarterdeck and rolled over the edge and into the sea.

"We will answer the call for our banners and uphold Murgare's rule." The Finned Corsair genuflected in Sirra's direction, and the mage hobbled up beside him. "As the other regions of the kingdom are now doing. And we will help gather all of the able across the Reach and journey west to the shores of the Lake on Fire."

A wave of bewilderment hit Sirra. "The banners have been called to the lake?"

The Finned Corsair glanced up, studying her, intrigued with her surprise. The mage beside him grinned.

"Who has called all the banners of Murgare?" Sirra asked.

"Northsheeren."

10

CYRAN ORENDAIN

Cyran loosed a training bolt at a leaf as Eidelmere soared past. The bolt clipped the edge of its target but flew well wide of its mark—the center. Cyran cursed in frustration as he squeezed the tiller, as if hoping to crush it.

"You didn't miss by as large a margin as you often do." Vyk leaned against his harness, which was clipped to the rear of the quarterdeck. His attempt at optimism only spurred on Cyran's annoyance with himself.

Cyran unstrapped his harness from the quarterdeck and ascended Eidelmere's neck, knowing the dragon's every movement and not having to struggle to reach the guard's saddle. He gripped his lance, and its green sheen lit up the settling twilight.

Eidelmere dipped below a cluster of leaves, and the angoias opened up before them. Below, an expanse of more typical forest sprawled outward to either side and to the north. Beyond a league or so of the trees directly ahead, the forest ended.

The lands of Murgare. Cyran held his breath as a shudder of anticipation jolted through his bones. The gleam of his lance seemed a hundred shades brighter without cover around them. He angled the weapon in its mount, pointing its capped tip downward and into its resting position as he released its hilt. Its radiance faded. At least the glow from the lance was not as bright as that from the Flame in the Forest. "We should fly low now. So we are not seen."

Eidelmere's disdain for the command leaked through the other realm, but the dragon folded his wings. They plunged downward toward the canopy of pines. Cyran worried that the flash of green light from his lance could have looked like a burst of magic to anyone or anything in the vicinity. Whatever outpost Murgare had watching over these woods might have noticed and then caught sight of them exiting the angoia cluster.

A tingle of dread ran across the nape of Cyran's neck.

Eidelmere plummeted but spread his wings just in time to stop himself from colliding with the treetops. The sudden change jerked them, flinging Cyran against the pommel of his saddle. Only his bond with the dragon saved him from sailing over Eidelmere's head. Vyk grunted behind him.

Eidelmere swooped out over the canopy, the treetops brushing against Ineri's turret as they traveled more slowly, headed north. The color of their forest dragon's scales would blend in with the greenery beneath them.

"We should only leave the angoia cluster at night." Cyran glanced around the edges of the forest as the last of a deep blue dusk shone through the sky sea in the west. "It will be much more difficult to find the village in question, but it will also be much less likely that we'll be spotted by any watchtowers."

"Sounds like a fine plan for the hopes of saving our skins here," Vyk said. "But unless this destroyed village still has torches burning, we may never spot it."

Cyran considered that. Perhaps they should fly out during the daylight. Maybe early morning would offer them some cover —because watchers would have a more difficult time determining the type of their dragon in the early lighting—and also allow them to see more than they could at the present. He cursed to himself and wished they had a moon dragon accompanying them.

"Whatever watchtowers Murgare has, I fear they do not function the same as those in Nevergrace." Cyran gritted his teeth as they flew along. "We may not understand their methods here. The north probably either utilizes deception and does not light any beacons or torches in their towers, so none will see their locations, *or* the entire woods are the result of their dark magic and so Murgare would not consider it possible for any dragon of Belvenguard to make the crossing. Then the north should only have a few scouts, if they have anyone, lurking at different locations near the forest's boundaries."

"But if the forest is theirs, then their soldiers and monsters could also be watching from within the woods." Ineri's words cast a spell of foreboding around them.

"I can barely see my own beard hairs out here," Vyk said. "I don't know how well you two can see, but if your eyes are anything like mine, we're never going to find a destroyed village beyond the tree line."

After they soared around for twenty minutes, Cyran spotted a few specks of firelight burning in the distant darkness. Eidelmere glided closer to them but kept his distance and remained low over the forest.

"It is nothing more than a hamlet," Ineri said, "and each abode has a torch burning inside."

"Then it's not the village we're searching for." Cyran guided Eidelmere away.

They flew about for several hours, but nothing else stood out in the veiled light of the thousand moons. Murgare must have far fewer villages along the forest's border than Belvenguard did. Maybe the north knew something Cyran didn't, or perhaps they had known about the darkness in the Evenmeres long ago and their people did not wish to live so close to it. The reason should not be that Murgare had a much smaller population. The north was supposed to have more people than the southern kingdoms.

A flash of light caught Cyran's eye, and he swung his head about. In the distance, a shimmer of movement followed. Wings extended.

Cyran pointed. "There's something over there!"

An armored person on the ground clambered onto a reflective beast, and the creature's wings flapped. The shimmering form rose into the air and swung toward them.

"They're coming at us," Vyk said. "It's a crystal dragon. Hopefully it doesn't know we're outsiders and thinks Eidelmere has emerald and not forest green scales."

Eidelmere grumbled something incomprehensible.

"Sight them," Cyran said. "And loose as soon as we know it either has identified us as unfriendly or when you can hit it in a vital area. I will draw it toward us."

Cyran swung Eidelmere away but did not speed up his flight, hoping to keep their pursuer from growing nervous. The crystal dragon followed, flapping easily and gaining on them. Cyran wheeled his mount around in a wide arc. He raised a hand against the moonlight, hoping to make the gesture appear as a friendly greeting.

Their adversary swooped closer until it was within ten or so dragon lengths from them. Then it paused and hovered. A few heartbeats passed like minutes as they stared at each other across the darkness. Eidelmere flapped slowly and blinked, his breathing shallow.

The crystal dragon shrieked, and crossbow ropes snapped. Screaming projectiles tore across the gap from both sides as their opponent whipped about.

Cyran folded one of Eidelmere's wings in and had his dragon fall. This caused them to plunge downward as well as diagonally and to their right and allowed them to narrowly avoid two incoming bolts. Metal scraped against crystal and skittered away as Vyk's and Ineri's projectiles were deflected by the scales of the beast.

"Sharp-edged weapons are of little use against a crystal dragon," Eidelmere said in a resentful rumble.

Cyran gripped his lance. *"Eidelmere, prepare for a tilt, and fly me as fast as you can."*

The forest dragon beat his wings and raced at the Murgare beast as the crystal banked and fled directly away, shrieking into the night.

Cyran swallowed as he glanced around. "It's going for reinforcements. Bring it down. In any way you can."

"We've got blunted bolts with heads like steel clubs," Ineri said.

"Let's see if those will smash this beast apart!" Vyk roared.

Windlasses cranked behind Cyran as Eidelmere climbed and chased their adversary. Cyran cursed under his breath and squeezed the hilt of his lance, feeling useless. He glanced back at his quarterdeck. Vyk flew into a rant as he swung his mounted crossbow about, aiming and tightening the rope of his ballista at the same time.

Eidelmere gained on their prey as its glass-like wings glinted under moonlight. They swooped past a clump of pines, and another deafening cry sounded, causing Cyran to lurch and cover one ear as he turned. A massive beast nearly twice the size of Eidelmere rose from behind the trees in ambush, its scales deep red with a speckling of dark gray. Bloody tears dripped from its eyes.

Cyran shuddered in horror. Eidelmere flared his wings, jerking them to a halt and throwing Cyran forward. Cyran quickly regained his composure and angled his lance as he urged Eidelmere to fly them onward. The blood dragon advanced, blocking their path.

"Careful!" Ineri said. "The blood and tears of those beasts can ignite nearly anything and create a conflagration, and tears cannot always be shielded by the wings of your mount."

The idea that Murgare beasts without discipline or honor might use such tactics on one of their own kind and not reserve their breaths and abilities for fighting non-dragons—per their oaths in the other realm—did not surprise Cyran. He looked beyond the monstrous dragon as they rushed closer. The crystal dragon tore away, streaking northward.

Fuck. Cyran tilted his lance, driving Eidelmere upward and at an angle. "Aim for the crystal," he shouted back at Vyk and Ineri. "I will try to deal with this fiend."

The blood dragon shrieked and hurtled closer, its guard adjusting his lance and obstructing the Murgare archers' line of attack. Cyran kept Eidelmere angled straight ahead, knowing he was also inhibiting his archers' shots at this beast but not at their fleeing target.

Ineri's and Vyk's crossbows thumped, and projectiles screamed away. A second later, metal clanked against scale, creating a sound like glass shattering and tinkling as it fell. The crystal dragon roared in pain as it shook its neck and breathed a blizzard of flying shards skyward.

Cyran swung Eidelmere to the right and then left, forcing the guard who faced him to bob back and forth to try to follow his movements. Cyran flicked his weapon's tiny tiller handle—which was often damaged during a tilt—to remove the blunt cap on the end of his lance as he made several quick movements during the last few flaps. The blood's jaws gaped, and red saliva pooled on its tongue and dripped from its teeth. The moment before they clashed, Cyran held his breath as he angled his lance downward and had his dragon drop on the monster. His lance impaled the creature, releasing a crunch and crack as the weapon sank deep into its skull. The guard's lance whistled as it passed just over Cyran's head, where he had been a split-second prior.

The guard shouted in anger, and the light in the creature's eyes blinked and darkened as Eidelmere collided with it. Cyran's lance exploded with red fire, the flames erupting from his target's skull and the puncture wound there. Cyran released his lance, shielding himself from the flames as he ripped his sword from its sheath, the weapon's blade radiant with green light. He swiped just above the guard's shield and cleaved through the top of the man's head before swiftly bringing his blade down on the mage behind him and hewing apart that man's torso.

The blood dragon fell like a stone. Its skull slipped off the remaining stump of Cyran's lance, and the beast hit the earth with a clatter and a spray of blood. Its saddles, guard's lance, and then quarterdeck and riders ignited with flame. Cyran released the mount attachment holding the lance to his saddle and let the blazing weapon fall, leaving a smoking trail in its wake.

Ahead, the crystal dragon raced on, but its wings beat erratically. One bolt was lodged into its shoulder. Eidelmere soared closer, quickly overtaking the beast as its archers loosed more projectiles and Cyran attempted to weave his mount around them, although one punched a hole in a leathery flap of Eidelmere's wing. Eidelmere cursed, and a shot of pain flooded the other realm.

Cyran gritted his teeth. He would no longer have a weapon to defend Eidelmere and his companions for as long as they were in Murgare. Once Eidelmere climbed above their adversary, Cyran had the forest dragon dive while he unfastened the attachments for his shield. They whipped past the crystal's quarterdeck, angling for the creature's neck, and just as its mage glanced back, Cyran used both hands to hurl his shield into the mage's back. When the shield struck the man, he was flung forward. He smacked into his dragon's scales with a crack, bounced off, and was launched out into the night.

Eidelmere gripped the Murgare beast with his talons, catching one wing and its neck as he swung around and flung the creature away. The crystal arced downward and to their left, smashing into a pile of boulders. Its scales exploded and rained over the rocks as its guard thwacked into the face of a boulder, issuing a crunching of metal.

Cyran glanced about. No other beasts or men appeared to be in the vicinity. He sighed with relief, but the bodies of dragons and men littered the area below.

"We need to clean this up," Vyk said, the madness in his voice ebbing.

Eidelmere cursed in a tongue Cyran did not understand as Eidelmere resisted his control and landed beside the remnants of crystal blocks and shards. Their adversary's lance was too short for the length of Eidelmere's head, curtailing any hope that Cyran could replace his lost weapon. The forest dragon sucked in a deep breath and spewed a deluge of water over the rocks several times, creating a stream that rushed over everything, picking up most of the remains and carrying them down to the cluster of pines. Once the area was clean of scraps of bodies and the wreckage from the quarterdeck and turret, Eidelmere flew back to where the blood dragon's remains were heaped and smoldering, and he repeated his cleanup, washing most everything into the trees.

"I took a bolt because of your actions," Eidelmere said in Cyran's head, his tone even more bitter than usual. *"But, once again, you did not."*

11

CYRAN ORENDAIN

"We should find a place to rest for the night." Cyran steered Eidelmere in a circle, the dragon's pain due to the injury in his wing minimal. Cyran had already apologized profusely, but the dragon had ignored him. "Back to the angoias. We will venture out again around daybreak and then at dusk."

Eidelmere climbed through the air currents as they veered toward the closest copse of old woods. The kingdom of Murgare grew more distant, but the companions' view of it broadened as they ascended. Cyran watched over his shoulder to make sure no one had spotted them and was in pursuit. In the distance, silver moonlight fell in swaths across the northern lands. A thread of a road ran to the west and east beyond the Evenmeres —the Reach Road. Ezul had spoken of it, and Cyran had seen it on maps, although no one knew if Belvenguard's old maps of Murgare were still accurate.

Within a sheet of moonlight less than a league from the Reach Road lay a blackened circle. Cyran twisted himself around in his saddle. The area was too precise to be a natural copse, and given that the light of the moons came from so many different directions, it probably wasn't a shadow cast by some massive structure.

"What is it?" Vyk swiveled his mounted crossbow around so he could look over Eidelmere's hind end and tail.

"There's something beyond the Reach Road." Cyran pointed to the darker area.

Vyk shrugged.

Ineri's turret rattled and rumbled as she adjusted position. "I see it as well."

Vyk scratched his beard.

Was the archer night blind? Cyran wheeled Eidelmere away from the angoias and toward the area in question, sending the dragon low again as they flew north as silently as they could, this time without a guard's lance or shield to help protect them. Eidelmere skimmed over the treetops. Once they neared the edge of the woods, Cyran eased Eidelmere to a slow glide. They carried out over an open expanse, and Cyran's nerves thrummed. He glanced all around, feeling as if eyes watched them from every angle.

"Is there any kind of clearing in this part of the forest where you can hide?" Cyran asked his steed.

"No." Eidelmere tilted his head to each side, discontent ripe in his words. "Not in woods as thick as these."

"Then stay low, but bring us back over the forest." Cyran hunched down in his saddle, as if that might help them remain unseen. "Hopefully in this light no one will be able to tell the color of your scales. Please take us down right along the tree line, and try to hide yourself against the trunks and boughs."

Eidelmere adjusted his wings, and he swooped lower. His talons dug into the earth with a scraping sound before his feet thumped down. Cyran held his breath, fearing that horns from watchers in the forest would blast around them.

After a minute of persisting silence, Cyran swung out of his saddle and scaled down its stirrup ladder. Once he did not have Eidelmere's body heat wrapped around him, the nightly chill sank its teeth through his armor and leathers. During their travels, he believed that the growing frigidness was due to the higher altitudes they had been passing through, but winter must arrive much sooner in Murgare. Either that or the bitter cold in these lands never abated. "We walk from here." He weighed keeping his dragonsteel armor on for protection versus taking it off and moving quicker and stealthier.

Vyk and Ineri released themselves from their restraints and joined him as he decided the armor was more beneficial for war and when mounted. If Vyk and Ineri didn't have as much protection, then neither should he, and it would greatly slow them down if they needed to run. He unstrapped his breastplate and eased it into the grass, then quickly removed the larger pieces of plate, keeping only those on his arms and lower legs. In case they needed to leave in a hurry, he strapped the armor he had removed to his saddle.

Before them, an open expanse of fields not unlike those of Belvenguard extended to the Reach Road. Beyond the road lay grassy fields and hills backdropped by looming peaks that filled the northern sky. Thankfully, the mountains were many leagues away, and they would not have to travel over them for this errand in Murgare.

Ineri hacked and doubled over. Cyran waited until her fit passed.

"It will not be a short jaunt," Cyran said. "Ineri, perhaps you should wait here with Eidelmere and help defend our dragon if any of north's legions come along."

Ineri eyed Cyran, and she stood straighter. "I can make it."

"We both know you can." Vyk smacked her on the back, and she stumbled forward. "But we need you here."

She studied both of them before eventually nodding, folding

her arms across her chest, and planting herself in her current position. Cyran led Vyk away from the trees, hunching over as he dashed toward the road and a lone maple. The thought that the north did not keep prisoners and soon killed anyone they took kept running through his mind... although the Dragon Queen had not done that with all of the Never's people. Hopefully the recent death of the Murgare king allowed for a more open interpretation of their laws.

When Cyran reached the trunk of the maple, he stopped beneath its boughs and looked around. Nothing in the fields or along the road moved. He rushed from his cover and sprinted through the last of the fields before the emptiness of the Reach Road surrounded him. He swallowed and hurtled along, darting from one cover to the next while heading in the general direction of the black circular region he had seen. Vyk's large form lumbered along behind him, the archer attempting to take mincing steps but failing miserably. Cyran stifled a sigh of chagrin and carried on.

Soon, they found a spur of a trail that veered north, away from the Reach Road, and they followed it. In less than half an hour, they approached the area in question—a blackened swath of land. Cyran strained to listen as he scrutinized everything around them. Several times he tensed with fear when he thought he saw movement, but he ultimately convinced himself it was only the blowing of grasses and the exposure of their lighter underbellies in the moonlight. The brush around the spur road appeared to be dying, but none had been burned.

Cyran halted just before a distinct line where the ground turned black. A few burned and cracked remnants of logs lay scattered about the area along with heaps of debris, but most of whatever had been standing here had been incinerated.

Dragon fire? Surely no dragons of Belvenguard had journeyed to this area in recent years. But wild dragons did not attack villages, unless the native beasts of Murgare were as heinous and barbaric as its people. Given that predilection for the people of the north, it was more than possible that they had destroyed and murdered some of their own. The notion didn't seem shocking, not with everything else Cyran had heard about the ways of Murgare and their late king, Restebarge.

This village had once had a circular wall, which seemed different from what Cyran had seen with most villages, even those he had heard about in the north. A single maple outside its walls was also burned, but not from the trunk up—from the top to around its middle. It resembled other trees Cyran had seen that had been struck by lightning, or perhaps dragon fire from above had seared this one. A single lance had also been embedded into the earth outside the charred area, as if a marker.

Cyran tentatively lifted his foot and stepped across the threshold of the blackened site. His dragonsteel boot crunched through a layer of ashes. Somewhere in the distance, a night owl screeched, and insects trilled.

"What are you doing?" Vyk's whisper cracked with tension. "The village has been decimated. We came here to confirm that. That was all."

"We came here to confirm if the village had been destroyed in the same method as Gernlet. These remains suggest something different from what Orinia described occurring to her hamlet." Cyran crept along toward the closest mound. Scorched and broken beams were heaped on top of each other as if a structure had collapsed on itself. He checked his surroundings to make sure nothing was watching him or flying overhead before leaning down and slowly moving some of the logs. Soot rubbed off on his gloves, and it coated his tunic and the pieces of his armor whenever he brushed up against some of the remains.

Vyk eventually arrived at his side and aided him. "What are you hoping to find?"

"I don't know. But if we find nothing else, I will be satisfied."

After nearly an hour of digging about and sifting through rubble, Vyk heaved and lifted a beam. It snapped in half, and the debris resting on top of it fell with a clatter and rolled off the mound.

Cyran winced and grabbed his sword's hilt as he crouched and studied their surroundings. Nothing moved. After several minutes, Cyran relaxed and returned his attention to what was left of the Murgare building Vyk had been inspecting. Vyk stood frozen, staring at something within the cinders. A shaft of blackened material was exposed below where the beam had been, and where other debris had rolled away lay a patch of white.

Vyk leaned over and grabbed the object. It slipped free from the surrounding scraps, and he held it up into the moonlight, studying its pale region. The ends of the shaft were knobby and bent.

"A femur," Cyran said.

Vyk dropped it and leapt back. "Human?"

Cyran retrieved the bone and held it up beside Vyk's upper leg. "It's about your size."

Vyk glared at him. "Don't do that."

Cyran pulled it away.

"Now can we return to Belvenguard?" Vyk asked.

Cyran held the femur before him as he looked about the area and its cinder mounds. "It would take many nights to search all of this—what was not long ago an outpost or village. We've found enough. It appears that people were burned alive inside their walls here."

Vyk exhaled and studied the skies, an inkling of horror that would arise in full if he spotted any dragon silhouettes prevalent in his eyes. "Thank the Great Smith's right arm. And the Siren's left breast."

"But we cannot yet return to Belvenguard."

"Shit." Vyk cursed several more times. "And why would you say such a thing?"

"We were sent to determine if a village in Murgare was decimated in the same manner as Gernlet."

"We've seen that it wasn't."

Cyran shook his head as he glanced eastward and then to the west. "We should cover all the lands along the borders of the Evenmeres. We may have gotten lucky and simply stumbled upon this scene, but there could be another. Or many more. And those could be different."

"The Paladin riding a gelded rouncey." Vyk kicked at a piece of scrap.

"We ventured all the way through the Evenmeres." Cyran headed back toward the Reach Road, eyeing the dark walls of angoias in the distance. "As far as we know, besides for groups of travelers following the trail through the woods and storm dragon messengers flying over, the only others to have ever accomplished such a thing are the Dragon Queen and a small legion of hers. We've already made the sacrifice and overcome the biggest obstacle. I must know if there is or is not a Murgare village that met the same fate as Gernlet."

12

JASLIN ORENDAIN

Jaslin sat along the edge of a huge bath and rinsed out Menoria's golden hair. Steam rose in wisps around the lady of the Never. A few other noblewomen leaned back in the sunken bath at Castle Dashtok while others conversed in whispers. Jaslin arrived at the castle several days ago, and a somber mood had hung around the place the entire time.

Jaslin's robe clung to her damp skin as she worked. The humidity in this lower chamber drew beads of sweat out on her forehead. She tucked away the book she had been reading, sliding it under a robe to keep it from getting too damp. Its story delved into the relationships of a king and a much younger queen.

Menoria soaked in silence while other women waded through the water and steam and exited the bath. Servants wrapped the departing women in robes and accompanied them up the stairs leading out of the chamber.

"You are in no hurry to attend the king's feast?" Only one woman remained behind, an older woman with gray locks.

Menoria shook her head, and sorrow and regret tugged at her words. "I will not be late."

"But you seem... to be in low spirits." The woman leaned back and closed her eyes.

"I feel the melancholy hovering around us." Menoria splashed water on her face. "And I am homesick."

"She just needs for me to read her a few good stories." Jaslin forced a smile. "That always cheers her up."

"Not many books are kept here." The lady pursed her lips in thought. "There are probably some in the archives, but most of all the scrolls stored in there are court records."

Jaslin nodded, hiding her surprise and disappointment about this place while Menoria remained silent.

"Tonight they will celebrate and mourn the queen, and then all will be well again." The woman sighed. "Or as well as can be with the threat of Murgare looming."

"Mourn *who*?" Jaslin asked as Menoria was lost in thought.

"The queen."

"Queen Hyceth?" Jaslin's fingers curled like hooks in Menoria's hair. *The letter was right?*

"Of course." The woman released a dry chuckle. "Everyone is saddened when the king is heartbroken. The poor man. He lost his lovely wife while he was away on duty. Didn't even get to say farewell to her."

Menoria tensed but still did not speak, so Jaslin asked, "What happened to her?"

The woman dismissed the question with a wave. "There are many rumors carrying around the court. Igare and the kingsknights have been investigating the matter since his return. I heard they found her stabbed in the back, but the king will address all the rumors tonight—within the hour, rather."

Menoria waded forward, dragging her hair from Jaslin's fingers, although a few strands were pulled from her scalp. The lady moved to the exiting steps and climbed from the scalding water as Jaslin hurried around the side of the bath, grabbed a robe, and draped it over Menoria's naked flesh.

Jaslin met Menoria's eyes. A dark anticipation and fear lingered beneath the lady's exterior.

"Come." Jaslin ushered her along. "I will help you dress for the feast."

∼

Jaslin entered the feast hall, pacing directly behind Menoria. Joined tables in the middle of the chamber formed three sides of a square. Most seats were already filled, and people at the tables stopped talking and stared when Menoria passed.

"Your seat is over here." An attendant in an elegant tunic of red and gold stood rigid and gestured for Menoria to follow him.

Menoria held her head high as she was shown around the periphery of the tables and past a man who had to be Sir Paltere the dragonknight, per Cyran's incessant mentioning of the man. Others of the guard were seated amongst what must have been a hundred attendees. When the servant led them beyond the side table and turned for the king's end table, Jaslin's senses sharpened.

Several of the seats ahead were still empty. Princess Nistene sat quietly with her head bowed, and beside her was her friend, Vysoria, the conjuror's daughter. On Vysoria's other side sat Jaken, the orator's son. Everyone stared at Menoria now as she walked along. The wooden throne chair at the center of the end table waited ahead. Beside it was a similar empty chair—the queen's seat.

"Here you are, lady of the Never." The attendant motioned to a seat two away from the king's.

Menoria exhaled with relief and sat as the man helped her slide her chair in behind her.

The servant faced Jaslin. "You are welcome to attend the feast and dine, but your seat is at the end of the other side table." He pointed to the last chair on the far side of the chamber.

Jaslin smiled and nodded. "Of course." She hurried over and took a seat beside the older woman they had spoken with in the baths.

"I did not expect to be seated beside the handmaid of the lady of the Never." The woman held out two fingers. "But I am pleased to have even been invited. I am Fileena, mother of the king's orator."

A sinking feeling fell through Jaslin, but she took the woman's fingers in her hand and kissed the backs of them. That meant this woman was Jaken's grandmother. "I hope my presence does not offend you, milady."

Fileena shook her head. "Don't be foolish. I merely attend these events to hear the latest facts and rumors. I do not care two sweaty halfpennies whom I sit with."

Two doors at the rear of the chamber parted, and several kingsknights in glistening golden armor strode forth, holding open the doors. A procession of people entered—Tiros, Lisain, Cartaya, Riscott, and Igare.

They are coming directly from a meeting of the small council.

The councilmembers took their seats, and the chamber fell silent. Igare stood behind his queen's chair and bowed his head. He wept, his shoulders shaking, and he wiped his eyes before looking up again.

"Tonight we feast in honor of our late queen." Igare pulled out his chair and sat, and everyone in the chamber stood.

Jaslin quickly followed suit. The king motioned for a servant to fill the chalice before the queen's chair, and the servant poured a dark wine into it and then filled the king's goblet.

Igare raised his drink. "To Queen Hyceth and everything she

stood for—beauty, faithfulness, kindness, honor. A wife who cannot be compared to or replaced." The king drank deeply.

Goblets clanked around the chamber. Jaslin waited for Fileena to offer and then tapped her goblet to the lady's, and they drank. The mulled wine hit Jaslin's tongue with a bitter bite, and she tried not to wince.

"I realize you all wish to hear of the events concerning your queen's sudden and untimely death." Igare held up a hand. "But first we will dine in her honor and remember the woman she was. When we are finished and we have paid our respects, then we will discuss all we know of the matter."

The king motioned, and servants waiting along the walls of the chamber stepped forward bearing platters overflowing with roasted duck, dark fruits, and orange tubers. Two attendants hauled in a boar that had been spitted and fired, a single apple jammed into its mouth. They set the boar on a table between the three others and carved off hunks of pale meat.

A plate with a roasted game bird dripping in plum sauce and a side of fired carrots was placed before Jaslin. Her mouth watered as she waited. When Igare's plate was placed before him —the king was the last of all to be served—he nodded to the queen's chair and her meal.

"We eat." Igare stabbed a hunk of pork and bit into it. The attendees ate in silence, although the chamber was filled with the clinking of goblets and goldware, the scraping of plates, and the scuffing of chairs.

After most people finished, many having taken second helpings of duck or boar from the servants, they leaned back and sipped from consistently refilled goblets. Igare slowly stood. He forced a deep breath and then paused and drank.

"It is with a broken and leaden heart that I must discuss any of this so soon after the death of my greatest love." The king's voice wavered with emotion.

Princess Nistene burst out in a sob, but she quickly covered her mouth and bowed her head to hide her tears. Vysoria placed a comforting hand on her back, and Jaken leaned against Vysoria and whispered something in the conjuror's daughter's ear.

"Only those who I completely trust are gathered in the feast hall this night." Igare wiped at his eyes, his graying blond locks dangling over his face. "You all know that Queen Hyceth was murdered while I was away dealing with the events at Nevergrace, which her assassin could have been waiting for. It seems there are many assassins in the employment of our ancient enemies, and this is the second time they have slipped past my soldiers and knights." He pointed at each doorway where a pair of gilded kingsknights stood on guard. "No more! I have set additional men on a tireless watch."

Jaslin wondered about the assassin Cyran had spoken of after he visited Galvenstone. He had seen the assassin hanged. If her brother were here now, she would ask him more about the prior situation. She never thought to do so at the time, although she had asked questions that were spurred by morbid interest.

Cyran. Her heart ached. Both of her brothers were gone, and at least one would never return.

"They first came for the Murgare queen when she was our prisoner, in hopes of inciting the war they have desired for decades." Igare clenched his fists. "They came for Nevergrace, in hopes of dividing our legions and to flank Galvenstone. Then they came for Hyceth, our queen."

Nistene's sobbing sounded through the hand she held over her mouth.

"I do not understand why these assassins seek out queens and not myself," the king continued, "but I have long tried to grasp the ways of the heinous north. Even after all these years, their methods still elude me. They may wish to torment me, to make me suffer, because I am your king, the king of the free people of Belvenguard. A large part of me wants to say that I no longer care to try to see the world through their eyes and that I welcome war with them with open arms, but I fear that could be their intent—to loose the bloody rain of the sky sea that will wash over all of Cimeren. They wish to plunge our kingdom into the same darkness that covers the north. To have dragons swirl in the skies not for defense but to instill fear and compliance. No kingdom and no man, woman, or child will be safe if such war begins. Because of this, I"—he clutched at his midsection in anguish and took a deep breath—"must bottle up my feelings and desires and not immediately unleash my rage and avenge Hyceth. I risk making myself appear weak before the souls of my wife and my forebearers for Belvenguard's safety. What I do is not without cost. My heart grows old and withers within my chest, and I fear I will never find the antidote for such poison."

The king paced behind the table, and the attendees watched him, a myriad of expressions upon their faces. No one uttered a word.

Sir Paltere stood and glanced around at those gathered in the chamber. "Part of me wishes for the north to come, although I know it is wrong. We could stamp out their evil forever and then live in peace. We would no longer have to fear that assassins could take our loved ones from us in the night."

Several guard who were seated with the other guests banged their fists against the tables. Riscott turned to address Menoria, and the orator placed a hand on her shoulder as he whispered in her ear. Jaslin cringed. The orator's mother, who was still sitting beside Jaslin, seemed nice enough, but Jaslin would not be able to ask her about Riscott's intentions. The orator was probably thirty years Menoria's elder. From everything Cyran said of the council, Riscott was the one who seemed the most untrustworthy.

"But we will not engage in war." Riscott stood and folded his hands at his waist. "Not unless it is brought to us. The small council has spent the past days weighing our options. This is the king's decision. For the betterment of Belvenguard." He sat and whispered something else to Menoria, who paled but nodded politely.

"There is one other issue." Cartaya brushed her white hair behind her ears, revealing more of her face. She appeared so young, maybe twenty and five by the look of her skin, but something about her seemed much older. "The king has no son."

"He has the princess." Riscott smiled in an affable manner and motioned to Nistene. "Whichever man weds the princess shall become Igare's rightful heir."

Jaken straightened in his seat, leaning away from Vysoria as he looked at his father and then to the princess. The princess's bulbous nose, protruding teeth, and absent chin contrasted with Vysoria's haunting beauty and dark features.

Jaken does not fancy the princess.

"The princess has many potential suitors from every city in Belvenguard, the Rorenlands, and the Weltermores." Riscott beamed.

"But their gifts have meant nothing." Cartaya's tone turned confrontational. "Not when she has already been promised to your son. And now our banners do not heed our calls. The cities of Belvenguard should have all arrived with dragon legions, soldiers, and knights to help defend Galvenstone against an attack from the north. They should have been here long before we returned from Nevergrace."

Menoria shifted uneasily in her seat as she snuck a quick glance at Riscott. Her upper lip quivered as if she were disgusted.

"Your ploys may weaken our kingdom, orator." Cartaya opened her palm, and a white flame sprang to life.

People shuffled with awkward tension and muttered to one another.

Fileena scowled and said, "The conjuror wishes for the king to remarry and to take her daughter as his wife. She despises my son and grandson."

Jaslin glanced at Vysoria. The conjuror's daughter was even younger than Menoria, not quite a fully grown woman. The king was probably a few years younger than Riscott, but that hardly mattered.

"The king should have a son." Tiros remained relaxed in his chair. "The passing of the throne has always been more secure with a son."

Lisain folded his hands against his white robes as he bowed his head. "The Paladin and the Shield Maiden have spoken plainly, and they have showed me that the future of Belvenguard is less obscure and more stable if Igare fathers a male heir."

A cloud passed over Riscott's expression, but he remained silent.

"It would be wise if the king announced who will be his betrothed before the war begins." Tiros did not look up or challenge the king, his tone even and neutral.

"That is enough," Igare said without anger, although his tone carried enough sternness that no one spoke. He studied everyone seated in the chamber. "This is a tense time for all. Forgive my council for their bickering. It is their duty to question every action and decision I make and to fight for their opinions to be heard. That is why I chose these people in particular and the reason I keep them by my side. I wish to hear all of their ideas and never only those in agreement with mine. But they make for poor mourning companions." He swallowed, and a few soft chuckles filled the chamber. "Tonight, I will not dishonor Hyceth by announcing whether or not I'll take a new wife, but in the coming days, I will make some decisions and you'll all hear from me again. I must face this question for the good of Belvenguard."

"For Belvenguard," many attendees answered in unison, and the echo of their voices carried around the chamber.

"Now drink and celebrate as Hyceth would have wanted us to do." Igare raised his goblet and gulped its contents. He motioned to the servants.

Several bards began strumming lutes and playing pipes. A woman plucked a harp. The guests drank, and conversations erupted around the room, which were soon followed by bouts of laughter.

Jaslin leaned close to Fileena. "Has your son ever been married?"

"Years ago he was," she said. "His wife died when Jaken was born."

"I am sorry to have asked such a question."

Fileena shrugged. "I would ask many more. I am always... curious." She tapped her lower lip as she eyed Jaslin. "Mostly I am curious about your lady. Why is she here?"

"Riscott asked her if she would accompany the king to Galvenstone."

"Oh, he did, did he?" She grinned. "But that doesn't necessarily mean Riscott is interested in the young lady of the Never. The king could have asked Riscott to invite her, or Riscott may have heard of the queen's death and thus feared Cartaya would throw her daughter at Igare in hopes of seizing more power. Riscott could have wanted your lady here so Igare would have an alternative beauty to consider rather than simply accepting Vysoria and unbalancing the power in the small council."

Jaslin drank as the possibilities swirled in her mind. "I had been thinking it was your son who wished to wed Menoria."

Fileena jostled her head side to side and tapped her fingernails against her goblet as she mulled it over. "The ways of the throne are not always easy to discern, and my son tells me much less than I'd like to know."

Neither of them spoke for a minute, and a conversation involving the woman sitting on the other side of Fileena grew louder, highlighting the awkward silence between Jaslin and Fileena.

"Where was the queen when she was killed?" Jaslin finally asked.

Fileena wound a finger around a lock of her hair. "Now *that* is a good question. I've only heard rumors." She stood and spoke loudly over the music. "The handmaid of the Never wishes to know where the queen was when the assassin struck."

Jaslin cowered in her seat, shrinking and trying to hide as the music stopped and everyone looked at Fileena and then at Jaslin.

Igare swallowed his wine and stared at them for a few heartbeats before attempting to speak. "The murder occurred in the queen's chambers. She was taken by a master assassin who employed the use of magic to slip past the soldiers on watch—similar to the assassin who took the life of the queen of Murgare."

Jaslin hung her head in shame, but she nodded in case anyone was looking her way, which most of the attendees were likely doing.

After an uncomfortable minute of silence lingered over the chamber, Igare asked, "Do you have any other questions, Fileena?"

"No, Your Grace," Fileena said.

The music resumed, and conversations slowly returned. Jaslin risked a glance up. No one seemed to be staring at her, although more than a few regarded Fileena with contempt. Jaslin hid a sigh of relief. It was possible that most of those in this chamber knew of Fileena's inquisitiveness and potential for rumormongering and assumed the orator's mother would simply shame someone else in order to satisfy her curiosity.

Across the way, Riscott drank and spoke to Menoria. The orator was attempting to engage the young lady in conversation, although it appeared that Menoria only answered him in stilted replies.

An ill feeling swam through Jaslin's blood. The king's councilmembers did not seem as concerned about Murgare and the coming war as they should, and according to the letters Cyran and the other squires received, one of the councilmembers might not be working toward the kingdom's best interests. Which of them could have wanted the queen dead? The conjuror seemed the obvious choice—to make her daughter the queen of Belvenguard—but one of the other three could have a more secretive objective.

Fileena downed the contents of her goblet and motioned for a servant to refill it with bloodred wine. "Do not worry, handmaid. Although I also always wish to know things before others, our curiosities will soon be satiated. With the threat of war looming, the king will likely make his announcement about a new wife on the morrow."

13

CYRAN ORENDAIN

EIDELMERE'S WINGS FLAPPED, AND BRANCHES SCRATCHED AGAINST Ineri's turret with their wooden fingers. Cyran felt naked without lance or shield around him. Cyran and his comrades swept farther eastward, remaining low over the Evenmeres as they scoured the northern border of the forest. The Ilmoor Sea was probably not many more days' travel away.

They had continued venturing out of the angoias from evenfall until just after dawn. Over several nights, they found nothing more than a few occupied villages and hamlets, which they kept their distance from.

"The lands of Murgare lie dormant." Vyk's braided hair streamed in front of his face as the archer looked out over Eidelmere's back and tail.

"It is as if most of their people and any sentries are distracted by something," Ineri said.

"Or their people have been brought elsewhere." Eidelmere spoke for the first time in days.

Ideas spiraled around in Cyran's mind. *Gathering for war.*

Silence enveloped them as Eidelmere sailed along, only the

breath of the Evenmeres and the slow and steady flap of Eidelmere's wings breaking a mounting tension.

"Look out!" Cyran pointed ahead, where a circle of crenellations rose above the trees.

Eidelmere veered to the side. Cyran held his breath as they passed by the structure, having to restrain himself from drawing his dragonsteel sword, which would cause the blade to glow. Thankfully, he had no lance to instinctively grip and create the same kind of radiance. No silhouettes of men stood out on the battlements. Eidelmere swooped around the tower and glided on for a full minute before the dragon's chest rose and fell again with breath.

"They do have watchtowers hidden in the forest." Vyk remained focused on the crenellations disappearing into the fading twilight behind them. "But they must have so few for such an extensive border."

"We may not have seen others during the times when evenfall fades to moonlight and moonlight fades to dawn," Ineri replied. "That one barely rose above the canopy."

"Belvenguard has only Nevergrace watching its borders along the Evenmeres." Cyran peered downward, searching for any hint of a path as the treetops blurred beneath them. "The outpost is situated where the lone merchant trail emerges from the woods. The trail could wind through this region—hence the watchtower." No less dense areas of canopy stood out. "What worries me even more than the absence of a horn blast during our passing is the lack of soldiers in the tower."

Vyk's stockpile of dragonbolts rattled as he searched through the projectiles. "A kingdom has only so many men it can spare for watching a border that can only be crossed by people in single file or two abreast."

They drifted farther east as Cyran scrutinized the woods they skimmed over.

Vyk's clatter subsided. "You fear that whatever lurks in the forest killed Murgare's soldiers?"

"I fear that the entire north is preparing to unleash the bloody rain of the sky sea." Cyran's heart twinged with the acknowledgment. "That likelihood makes what we do all the more important."

Vyk grumbled something under his breath. "Unless returning to aid the king would be a better use of our bolts."

They flew along in silence for at least an hour, attempting to stay within the shadows created by looming clouds, but at times they were forced to drift through swaths of moonlight.

"To the north." Ineri's voice rang out before she fell into a fit of coughing.

Just beyond the border of the Evenmeres, a few shadows of structures stood in the darkness.

No firelight. "Is it a village?"

No one answered, but Eidelmere lifted his southern-facing wing and dipped the one pointing north. They glided closer to the area in question. Once they reached the edge of the woods, Eidelmere banked to the east, avoiding flying out over open ground. The shadows of houses and huts became clearer, the structures arranged over a typical rectangular area.

"Bring us down as close to the trees as you can." Cyran gripped his sword's hilt. He motioned with his other hand. "A bit away from the village."

After Eidelmere flapped and slowly eased his bulk onto the ground, the dragon pressed himself up against a few pines. Cyran and his comrades dismounted, and Cyran removed the larger pieces of his armor again. The night was quiet and still with only the wind stirring the grasses in the fields beyond. The icy chill of the north stung Cyran's face, again surprising him, as he always expected the nights to still be of moderate temperature. Moonlight stole through the clouds for a moment and washed over a hill and house on the outer edge of the village. A few snowflakes drifted lazily downward.

Cyran placed a hand on Eidelmere's roughened old scales. "You have been quiet these past days, my friend." Eidelmere's bitterness in the other realm did not ebb. "I am sorry about Morden and all I have put you through, including your injuries, but each day brings us closer to the time when I will set you free."

"Empty promises that neither of us shall live to see." Eidelmere's voice echoed in Cyran's head.

"I speak with all the conviction I can muster. I hope you sense my sincerity and the truth of my words in your realm."

Eidelmere did not respond, and Cyran turned to the village. Cyran kept his hand on his swords' hilts but did not draw either blade. The sheen of the Flame in the Forest would give them away to anyone or anything watching the area, and the silver elvish blade would reflect far too much moonlight. He stepped away from the trees, hunching low within tussocks of winter wheat. Most of the crop and their heads were pale, nearly as white as snow. A few insects trilled around them. Other than for the strange color of their wheat, this village was not so different from those in the south.

Vyk and Ineri followed, and together they ascended a few sharp inclines of mounds and quickly descended their far sides. The mounds wound through the area, disrupting and cracking the ground as if they had been formed recently. Ineri coughed but pressed a wadded cloth to her mouth and muffled the sound. Cyran waited a few heartbeats, listening for anything that might have noticed before he pressed forward again. They passed a row of trees laden with apples and approached the first house from the western side of the village.

Cyran darted from the wheat to the wall of the house and pressed his back against it. He held up a hand for Vyk and Ineri to stay where they were. Ineri muffled another cough with her rag. Cyran quickly peeked around the corner of an open doorway. He pulled back. No one had been moving about inside. He slipped into the opening, his hand clenching the Flame in the Forest's hilt and lifting it a finger's width from its sheath. Green light swept across a single room.

Nothing moved. A table sat against one wall, a smattering of molding bread strewn across its surface. Two chairs were pushed back from the table, suggesting someone had gotten up in a hurry and had not returned to tidy them. Cyran poked the bread. Hard as rock. The meal had probably been abandoned at a moment's notice as well. A straw bed, unmade and empty, took up one corner of the room.

Cyran exited the house and moved farther into the village, keeping his eyes keen for any movement, his ears alert for any sound. He feared hearing music more than anything else. Ineri and Vyk trailed him.

A central well waited ahead, and a figure stood near it. Vyk grunted and lifted a hand crossbow. Cyran ripped his sword from its sheath, and its glow flared. The figure did not move.

They approached cautiously. A skeletal form reflected Cyran's green light. It was nothing more than bones—a full skeleton of a man—but it managed to remain standing, staring in the direction of the woods. One of its hands clutched at its neck, as if strangling itself.

Cyran suppressed a chill and sidled forward until he stood within reach of the skeleton. He tentatively raised a finger as he held his breath. The bones still did not move. He was half-expecting the skeleton to come to life and attack him or leap at him and his comrades. He settled the tip of his finger on its arm. Still nothing happened.

"That man is fully dead." Vyk paced around the periphery of the central area, glancing off into the walkways between houses.

Cyran shoved on the skeleton, still intrigued with why and how it was standing and gripping its throat. Bones slid with a scratching sound, and the skeleton collapsed in a heap, creating a clatter that rang against the surrounding houses and a moment later echoed off the forest. Cyran winced.

A shriek of surprise sounded, and Cyran pivoted about, crouching, expecting Murgare's onyx guard or something worse. A child dashed from a shed and plowed into the wheat, leaving only the waving heads of the grasses and their rustling in his wake.

"Stop!" Cyran ran after the child, who shrieked again. "We've come to help."

The child did not stop, and Cyran had to sprint to overtake him. Cyran drove a hand down into the wheat, catching the child's shoulder. A scream sounded, and small feet kicked at Cyran's shin, ringing off the plate he still wore there. He heaved and lifted the child from the grasses. A boy with wild eyes thrashed about in Cyran's grip.

"Who are you?" Cyran asked.

The boy growled and punched at Cyran's belly, but the boy's reach was far too short to make contact. After failing at that, the boy pulled a knife from his belt and swung it. Cyran lurched back with his midsection and rammed his sword's hilt against the knife. A clash of metal rang out, and the weapon fell from the boy's grip.

Ineri approached, lowered her crossbow, and held out a hand in hopes of comforting the child. Vyk paced around them with his crossbow, watching their surroundings.

"What is your name?" Ineri crouched in the wheat so that she did not loom over the boy.

The boy continued kicking at Cyran until Cyran set him down in the grass while maintaining a hold on his arm. The boy's face and skin were streaked with dirt, his hair matted and filled with straw. He might have been around seven years of age.

"You come from the forest too!" He pointed at Cyran. "You come to finish me."

Cyran shook his head and knelt in front of the boy. "I am only here to help. But you say that people came from the forest to your village?"

The boy's eyes persisted in darting about, but his movements settled a touch.

"What happened to your village?" Ineri pointed at the houses.

The boy's voice trembled. "It was not people. They were monsters. And trees. The trees slid closer. Then the monsters came. And the lights."

Cyran's eyes briefly fell shut in disbelief.

"I was returning from picking autumn berries." Tears streamed down the boy's cheeks. "I was... afraid. I hid."

Cyran squeezed his shoulder. "There is no shame in not facing such creatures. Can you describe the monsters at all?"

"Gray. Small. They had knives. They got my father." More tears erupted.

Forest feeders. The creatures of the woods that had wiped out the people of Gernlet had also struck Murgare. Ineri was studying Cyran, and when he noticed her attention, he nodded. "There is little doubt."

"Are there any more of your people here?" Ineri asked the boy.

He shook his head. "The trees and the monsters ate them. They will eat you too."

"The trees ate them?" Cyran asked more to himself, trying to imagine moving trees opening jaws and devouring people. From what he had gathered when unwillingly entering the lower forest, he did not believe it was the trees themselves. He released the boy and stooped over to match the boy's height.

The boy punched him in the face and bolted into the wheat, creating a wave.

The wheat looks similar to the shifting ground that was beneath the moving trees. Cyran rubbed at his jaw. "Come back! We can find help for you." When the boy did not answer and disappeared into the night, Cyran turned to his companions and said, "Whatever lurks in the forest is not controlled by Murgare. Not unless their ancient evil has also turned against them."

"Unless the kings and queens of this realm are truly diabolical and at times do not care if their creatures raid and murder their own." Ineri stood.

Cyran walked back to the village with her and said, "I could believe their monsters do not always obey them or have decided to follow their own leader, but even Murgare kings should only send minions as dangerous as these south—to attack Belvenguard. Anyone sound of mind would not allow such creatures to travel so far north and so close to their own lands."

Ineri nodded. "Then there are two great evils plaguing Cimeren." She coughed several times, her chest rattling.

"You should come see this." Vyk's words carried over the village and fields, too loud for someone currently worried about being spotted by Murgare soldiers.

Cyran hurried toward the archer's voice. He rounded a corner and neared the north end of the village. A pile of skeletons waited ahead. The bones were erected so that they rose toward the heavens and the sky sea like an altar.

Cyran gawked at the spectacle as Vyk wandered about.

Over the next few minutes, they found no other remains and no other survivors. The boy still did not return or answer any of their promises offering aid or respond to their warnings that someday soon, he would freeze to death out here.

Music sounded in the distance, and Cyran froze. It was an old melody, the same one he had heard in the woods and that Tamar and Jaslin had hummed incessantly.

"We must leave." Cyran turned west to where they had left Eidelmere. "Now!"

"What is it?" Vyk raised his crossbow and spun in a circle.

"You do not hear that?"

Vyk shook his head.

"The music?" Cyran asked.

Vyk did not answer.

"We've learned everything we need to." Ineri looked to the sky. "We should return to Belvenguard."

A flash of light whipped past the perimeter of the huts. Vyk bellowed with fear.

"Eidelmere." Cyran reached out along his bond. *"We need you to come to us."*

A noise similar to trees rustling in a gale sounded. Cyran peered into the distant moonlight. The woods shifted. The hair on the back of his neck stood on end.

"I'd rather..." Eidelmere's response faded. *"Something comes. Dragons!"*

A deafening shriek pierced the night, ringing Cyran's ears. The beating of many wings followed, and Vyk roared and loosed a bolt. The clank of the bolt hitting dragonsteel quickly answered as a shadowy figure descended from above.

"Run!" Cyran grabbed Ineri's arm and tugged her along. The floating light was no longer dancing about, and he angled west toward the trees there. Eidelmere would be ready to fly whenever they reached him.

A massive form dropped farther from the sky and landed before them, releasing a screech and flattening the wheat. "Stop." The male voice carried an air of authority. "Our moon dragons can see you much better than you can see us or your surroundings. You cannot escape, dragon riders."

Cyran halted, and three more moon dragons landed in the grass around them. The beasts' maws gaped as they released more shrieks that were too high-pitched for the human ear to hear but which allowed them to essentially see in total darkness.

"The forest dragon has fled into the woods," the guard on one of the moon dragons said to the man who had addressed Cyran and was likely this legion's genturion. "Do we pursue it?"

"Was there a mage upon the dragon?" the genturion asked.

"Not that my dragon could see," a withered voice answered from the back of the moon dragon, from just behind the guard.

"And there is no mage of theirs sitting in the village?"

"No," the moon's mage answered.

"Then there is no need to pursue the forest dragon." The helmed head of the genturion glinted in the moonlight as he shook it. "Whatever lurks in there will finish the creature, and if you attempt to track it down, those monsters will finish you as well. Their mount is no longer under the control of a mage of Belvenguard. It is no threat to us. We have what we need."

The genturion dismounted and approached Cyran, and the moon dragons' heads advanced and surrounded Cyran and his comrades.

The smirk in the genturion's words was clear when he spoke. "We have a dragonknight of Belvenguard as our prisoner."

14

CYRAN ORENDAIN

Cyran tugged at the bonds binding his wrists behind his back, cursing and grimacing as the ropes bit into his skin. An erected cell of bars surrounded him and his comrades, a temporary holding quickly fashioned by Murgare's guard. Flakes of snow landed around the village.

"Our journey was all for naught." Vyk hunched over as he sat with his back against the bars, his head hanging between his knees. "Murgare does not keep prisoners. They torture them to death."

"The Dragon Queen kept the captives of Nevergrace alive for some time." Cyran worked his ankles against their bonds but failed to find any slack.

"Because she was using them as hostages," Vyk muttered. "To trade them for her queen."

"Maybe the north is no longer bound to the Dread King Restebarge's old laws." Cyran glanced at the village around them. A skeleton sat against the wall of a nearby house, facing outward and staring at them. "His passing could have changed things."

Ineri coughed weakly. Vyk did not answer. Cyran studied the

village and the woods beyond under sunlight. Other than the one skeleton watching them, the place looked more abandoned than it had at night. However, somewhere in the vicinity, the Murgare guard, mages, archers, and their dragons were resting or discussing what to do with their prisoners. Chances were good that someone was also watching the cell, even if from a distance.

Their captors had taken both of Cyran's longswords, but he still wore armor on his arms and legs—the pieces he had not left with Eidelmere. He studied the tree line, searching for signs of the forest dragon. The resentful old creature had probably leapt at the chance to flee and find his freedom in the woods. Cyran closed his eyes and felt into the other realm. The brightness of that world shimmered around him, its threads dancing with lights of their own. He reached out and tried to grasp Eidelmere's thread, the one containing the dragon's true name, but he could not find it.

Bloody Assassin's hell.

He struggled harder against his bonds, and the ring he wore —the ring a merchant gave him for assisting the man and his companions soon after the Dragon Queen had claimed the Never—dug into the back of his other hand. The image of a laden burro pressing into his skin floated through his thoughts. The pendant necklace the young lady of the Never had gifted him after he helped to reclaim the outpost still hung from his neck.

An hour or two passed before more dragons flew in from the north, their beating wings throwing gusts through the walls of the cell. Cyran strained to pivot his head and look skyward. He caught sight of a fire, ice, and mist dragon. The genturion who had captured them, and two of his archers, approached the makeshift cell.

"What are you doing in the lands of Murgare, dragonknight?" the genturion asked, his face masked by his spiked helm.

Cyran furtively glanced at Vyk and Ineri, unsure if he should speak to men of the north. This genturion would seek to learn anything he could about them and Belvenguard.

"You can remain silent for now, but we have ways to make you talk." The genturion stepped closer and loomed over them.

Cyran did not doubt that this man would employ tortuous methods.

"You are not welcome in Murgare." The genturion's tone seemed to carry as much acid as the breath of a marsh dragon. "And you have no rights here. You are trespassing during a time of war."

"The sky sea has yet to rain blood." Cyran glared at him.

The genturion scoffed and shook his head in a demeaning manner. "War commenced as soon as your legions came and killed our king and abducted and then murdered our queen." He paused for a moment. "Indeed—we consider our queen dead, unless Belvenguard can prove otherwise."

Cyran swallowed. He had not known how the northern king was killed, but for Murgare, the war had begun some time ago. *We must return and warn Igare.* "We did not come seeking battle or to lead any attack."

"A dragonknight of Belvenguard sent on a secretive errand and to gather information about our legions is an act of war in itself."

"We came only in hopes of determining what happened to this village."

The genturion quickly looked to either side. "The forest's ancient evil has already awoken. And just like we can assume our queen is dead, we assume the Sky Sea Pearl is now in the hands of the Harrowed King. Surely, Belvenguard knows of this. It is your kingdom's forest."

Cyran attempted to hide his surprise. Was the genturion baiting him into revealing things about Belvenguard? "The floating lights fled when you arrived." At the minimum, Murgare still held power over the creatures in the Evenmeres. "The trees stopped moving at that time as well."

"The monsters in the woods have not yet grown bold enough to confront legions or soldiers." The genturion spat. "Not while we remain outside the forest. Thus far, they have only ventured beyond the boundaries of the Evenmeres to attack this village, or travelers. But things will change once whatever they seem to be waiting for comes to pass."

"Then what happened to that other village near the Evenmeres?"

"You found another village decimated by the Harrowed and their minions?"

Cyran paused.

"Do not lie to me." The genturion clutched the barbed hilt of his sword. "The watch will soon discover what you refer to, even if you just performed the deed last night."

Your watch may not be as adept as you think. "I refer to the village that had circular walls and was burned to the ground."

The genturion stared at him. "You are lost, young dragonknight. The torched village was the work of something else—someone who controls boundless bone and earth magic and wanted to kill some of our dragonmages." He used a key to release the lock on the cell and pulled open its barred door. He addressed the archers behind him. "Have the legion bring them to the *other* location. Finding a dragonknight of Belvenguard certainly warrants such action."

The archers slipped into the cell, cut the bonds around Cyran's and his comrades' ankles, and hoisted them to their feet.

"Go." One of the archers wearing a black helm and armor pointed.

Cyran marched outside, where another guard waited and escorted him to the edge of the village. There, an ice dragon dug a mass grave using talons as long as a man was tall. Fire, mist, and storm dragons waited nearby. Other archers worked together, removing the village's skeletons from the heap they had been piled into and toting them to the grave, where they dropped them in.

"To the blood," the genturion said as he shoved Cyran toward a lone dragon.

This dragon turned its massive neck and tilted its head to study them, its eyes dripping tears of blood.

Cyran shuddered and avoided the creature's head, recalling his encounter with the other blood dragon and its crystal comrade. He glanced at the woods, yearning to see Eidelmere there, their last hope to escape this predicament. The boughs swayed and waved under the wind, and shadows danced beneath the canopy. No green scales stood out against the trunks. A sense of deep loss pulled at Cyran's heart as he felt for his bond with Eidelmere but again found only emptiness. His mind conjured up images of the forest dragon's eyes glistening and watching them from between branches. The dragon stared for a moment before casting them one final look of discontent, and then his eyes closed, his head turned, and the last of his scales faded into the trees.

The forest dragon had returned home.

~

The blood dragon landed with a thump outside a city beside mountains, a vast river, and an endless body of water. Cyran had been unable to see much during the flight other than sky and the fire, ice, mist, and storm dragons accompanying them, as he and his comrades had been strapped down to the quarterdeck in a prone position, their mouths gagged. All he could get a sense for was that they had flown somewhat northward.

Was this the northern shore of the Lake on Fire?

An archer pressed a knee into his back and cut the bonds tying him down. Ineri hacked a few times as Vyk cursed. An archer rolled Cyran to the edge of the quarterdeck and then shoved him. Cyran tumbled down a ramp, his hands still tied behind his back. He collided with the ground, and a dull thud rang inside his head, another lancing through his shoulder—the one he had dislocated in his tilt with the Dragon Queen. Vyk's mass hit him like a boulder bounding down a mountain and landed on top of him. Soon after, Ineri piled on top of them, adding a few more stones of pressure.

The others were pulled off Cyran, and a guard yanked him to his feet. The smell of the sea hit him like a slap across the nose. Endless water sprawled beyond a city of stone, but this was not the Lake on Fire.

The guard shoved Cyran along, and the sound of his companions' footsteps followed, along with an entourage of other Murgare guard and archers.

"Where are we?" Cyran tried to speak through his gag, although his words barely escaped his lips, and they were indiscernible even to him.

They were marched away from the mountains and toward the city and sea. Cyran's dragonsteel boots clattered on the cobbles as he paced down streets that narrowed and wound through multistoried buildings. Flags of sea green and violet snapped in the wind overhead. Gulls squawked and circled above, but many more swarmed over an area out to sea. Stalls with merchants and many bartering locals choked the streets leading to a pier. A temple to the Siren of the Sea stood upon a hillside in the distance, a gilded representation of the naked woman gazing out over the eastern waters—the Ilmoor Sea.

A woman in a stained tunic paused while pointing at a dead fish on a table and speaking with the merchant there. She stared as Cyran passed and then muttered something. After Cyran walked another few strides, the woman began shouting and then screaming. The people ahead turned to eye him, and then they crowded the street, gesticulating and yelling at him and his comrades, only making way when the guard approached and ushered them back.

"Filth!" a sharp female voice carried.

"Vermin of the south!"

"May the Assassin take your bloody hearts and the Dragon eat them!"

The first rotten tomato hit Cyran on the side of the head, and its putrid innards splashed across his face. More flying vegetables and fruits followed, pummeling him as he dipped his head and hurried faster. Ineri coughed and gasped. Vyk's string of curses was muffled by his gag, but he ran at another burly man who had thrown something at him. Two of the guard grabbed Vyk by the arms, halting the archer, although he thrashed about in their grips. They shoved him and forced him through the fish market.

Something solid struck Cyran in the temple and rattled his skull. He stumbled along and covered his head as best he could with his shoulders.

After the gauntlet of pelting food subsided and the hollering and jeering died, the smell of sea air struck Cyran again, although this time it was barely able to penetrate the fetid odors circling his nostrils. He glanced back. The townspeople still glared and shook fists at him and his comrades. The armor of the Murgare guard closest to him was also peppered by spots of foul juices.

The people of Murgare are barbaric. Cyran did not allow himself to ponder what awaited him and his comrades in this city. He only wished he could see Jaslin and his friends one last time and share what he had learned—Murgare considered the war to have already begun, and thus they would have long been gathering and preparing to march—with Sir Paltere and Igare before he was tortured to death.

His heart twisted and burned. Thoughts and emotions for his sister, his friends, his home, and his people assaulted him and grew more powerful than his desire for duty. Then guilt attributed to his archers' current situation sank an additional blade in his back.

Light mist sifted down around them. He tried to apologize to Vyk and poor Ineri for where he had brought them, but his gag would not allow for it.

Vyk chewed and spit out his gag, cursing.

Ahead, a dark form blotted out the sea and the horizon. At first, Cyran believed it to be the end of his life, a vision, but the dark form shifted. A wing unfurled and stretched.

Chunks of ice solidified in the caverns of Cyran's bones. Only one dragon was that black and that enormous.

The guard behind Cyran shoved him from his halted position, and the guard said, "Keep moving. The Dragon Queen awaits you."

15

PRAVON THE DRAGON THIEF

"You will have to wait for the king's audience," an attendant of the Yellow Castle said as Pravon sweated in the heat and marched behind a troop of soldiers with Kridmore and Aneen. "Another supplicant is with him at the moment."

Pravon nodded his understanding as they strode down a long hallway. Kridmore ignored the bald attendant completely. Colossal blocks of granite, each the color of bright urine, surrounded them, and tapestries of green and gold hung all the way from the soaring ceilings to the floor. Light carried in through a massive window ahead, its view that of the Barstell Foothills and the towering Mountain of Titans far in the distance.

The Rorenlands.

"So much splendor for a kingdom haunted by so much death." Aneen paced casually along, her red locks jostling against her shoulders. "I feel at home here. I spent a few years in Tablu."

Pravon snuck an uneasy glance behind them. A dozen more soldiers, who carried spears twice as long as a man, followed them. If only he felt as at home in these desert lands with their new—and rumored unstable—king.

A throne sat just below the window at the other end of the long audience hall. The massive chair was carved from an angoia trunk that had supposedly been shipped to Tablu and hauled across the desert to Sarzuth, a gift to the king of the Rorenlands in centuries past. Its seat was big enough for a giant, but only a man in yellow robes sat there, appearing tiny in comparison to his surroundings. A true giant with skin like stone towered over the lines of soldiers on either side of the central walk. The giant leaned against the far wall of the chamber near the throne, its boulder of a head drooping, its eyes closed.

Pravon shuddered as he eyed the creature, imagining the destruction such a monster could unleash.

The soldiers ahead of Pravon stopped behind several supplicants who were waiting below the king's raised throne. The attendant hurried forward and around them, lowered his head, and approached the king before whispering in his ear. The king's expression shifted below his wooden crown that was adorned with bright jewels.

A supplicant before the king spoke. "King Jabarra, I would like to continue with the—"

"An interesting opportunity has just arisen." The king's booming voice shook the hall, and the giant jerked, its eyes slipping open for a moment before its lids fell shut again. Its head drooped farther downward. "Keep your words in your mouth." The king pointed at two supplicants kneeling before him as he stood, and his bulging gut protruded through his robes. His torso was short, but his lanky legs made him stand taller than most men. The king turned to his attendant, who wore robes so thin that light carried through them and revealed the man's figure. "Fetch from the dungeons the supplicants of Murgare, and we shall all discuss the matter at hand."

Pravon's senses spiked as he peered around the soldiers to study the supplicants currently before the king. Their backs were to him, but they were both men who wore fine red tunics with gold trim. *They are from Galvenstone.*

Kridmore huffed and shoved his way forward and through the soldiers. After their initial surprise, the soldiers turned and lowered their spears, angling their weapons' tips at the assassin while surrounding him. Kridmore chuckled as Pravon's palms grew damp and sweat beaded on his forehead. Aneen shifted uneasily beside him.

"King Jabarra." Kridmore raised a hand. "I have traveled from Belvenguard, where I was... currently overseeing events, to make you an offer."

"You will soon have an opportunity to do so." The king's powerful voice echoed through the hall, but the towering throne behind him made him look like a tiny, spindly man.

More soldiers entered the chamber from a doorway to Pravon's right, and they parted, revealing two people in their midst. One was a man dressed in black leathers. He had a short beard salted with gray, and the insignia of three ice dragon scales stood out on his breast. The woman beside him stood hunched over and held a staff, her tawny hair spilling from her hood.

These two are linked to someone in Murgare, but...

The air in the room took on a vast weight threaded with tension, and it pressed down on the occupants. The emissaries from Belvenguard shifted uneasily as they whispered and glanced at the new arrivals.

"Now that we have Sir Vladden and his mage, Quarren, the emissaries from Murgare, here with us"—the king motioned to the unarmored dragonguard and the mage standing in the middle of the soldiers—"and those from Belvenguard, as well as... where did you say you were from?" The king stared in Kridmore's direction and signaled for his soldiers to part so he could see the assassin more clearly. "Belvenguard as well? But surely not Galvenstone. Which city?"

Kridmore cleared his throat and stepped forward. He pushed his hood back, and for the first time, Pravon caught a glimpse of more than just the assassin's shovel chin and ivory teeth. Dark hair tumbled over his shoulders. Pravon stepped closer, more out of curiosity about his companion rather than to address the king. Kridmore's features were delicate and refined, his cheeks high, his skin pale.

"I did not say we were *from* Belvenguard." Kridmore grinned in his arrogantly rueful manner, only the lower half of his face seeming real. Somehow, the rest of him did not belong. "I said we traveled from there." The assassin left it at that.

The king's eyes narrowed with suspicion, but he spread his arms wide, addressing all three groups of supplicants. "Each of you wishes for King Jabarra to bestow upon you the might of the Rorenlands—the power and strength of the sand dragons, as well as our giants." He pointed at the emissaries from Galvenstone. "But Igare has yet to offer me his daughter as a concubine." He gestured at a line of hooded women. "Do not pander to King Jabarra and waste his time. You have already stood here breathing the king's air and eating his food for many hours. Tell King Jabarra what it is that Igare is willing to offer him for his assistance when the sky sea bleeds."

One of the men from Galvenstone bowed his head and spoke. "King Igare Dragonblade wishes to forge a lasting friendship with the new and rightful king of the Rorenlands. He—"

"What does he offer King Jabarra?" Jabarra asked.

The cadence of the emissary's sentences quickened. "He wishes to honor the ancient pacts and alliances between Belvenguard and the Rorenlands, and to remind Your Grace that when the time comes and Murgare sweeps across the Lake on Fire and through the Evenmeres, all of Cimeren will have to choose a side. None will escape the destruction. In order for you and your people to remain free, you must side with the free peoples of Belvenguard. For if the legions of Murgare overtake our kingdom, they will surely come for yours—to enslave all of you."

The king slumped back down into his carved throne. Then he leaned forward, his cheeks reddening. "And so, after all these hours of dining and drinking and waiting for King Jabarra's audience, you still offer him nothing more than threats and a potential friendship with those who will be conquered in such a war!"

The Galvenstone emissaries retreated a few steps. "No, King Jabarra. I-I... Igare is more than willing to continue to trade and offer ports of entry and exit for all your fleets and vessels."

"But no daughter. No woman. No lands?"

The emissary swallowed. "Land? You wish to be gifted land from Belvenguard?"

The king clenched his fist and hammered it onto the armrest of his throne. The issuing thud caused the giant to lurch again, and Jabarra turned to the guard and mage from Murgare. "And what does the Dragon Queen offer King Jabarra?"

Sir Vladden stepped forward, his arms clasped behind his back, his chest puffed. "I wish to thank you, mighty King Jabarra, for hearing our requests and allowing us another opportunity to explain our—"

"*What* does she offer him?"

Sir Vladden fell silent for a moment. "The southern lands of Belvenguard, once the kingdom is dismantled. This will include all of the lands around the Mountain of Titans as well as those reaching all the way to Somerlian. The cities of Progtown, Lynden, and Trasten will be yours, in addition to all the lands between the Merchant's Road and Redwater Bay, including the Folisian Keep, the Constell Islands, and all the ports along those shores."

Jabarra smiled, leaned back, and clasped his hands over his bulbous gut. He faced Kridmore. "And what do you offer... envoys of Oomaren?" He grinned knowingly. "Yes, King Jabarra knows who employs you and where you come from. He is no fool." He motioned to the emissaries from Galvenstone and then to those from the Dragon Queen. "You are not dwarves, and the Weltermores have already sent their messengers. King Jabarra returned only the heads of those men to the burro king. King Jabarra now has Belvenguard's and the Dragon Queen's people before him, so only the new king of Murgare has not yet been represented. Power is taken and deserved by might, not by blood. King Jabarra respects a man who can claim the throne of a kingdom."

Pravon cleared his throat. "We are not—"

Kridmore shouldered past Pravon. "You are wiser and bolder than even the rumors claim, King Jabarra. We could not hope to deceive you."

The king beamed but waved off the assassin's flattery. "As long as you do not represent the rumored guild of dragon thieves"—he laughed but shook his head, his eyes darkening—"I will hear your offer. That guild is supposedly responsible for the recent theft of a few of my prized fighting dragons in Tablu." He cleared his throat. "What does Oomaren propose?"

At least we are not part of that guild, if it even exists.

Kridmore nodded. "If you allow us to lead your armies north, to strike Belvenguard from the south and crush them between us and the legions of Murgare—"

Pravon stepped up beside the assassin again and whispered to him, "That cannot work with what we—"

Kridmore elbowed the dragon thief in the gut, silencing him, and added, "When all is said and done..." He glanced about as if he wasn't sure what better gifts to offer, and Pravon bit his lip, feeling the attention of every soldier in the room settle on them. Aneen huffed, and her hand gripped something beneath her cloak. The tips of the soldiers' spears shimmered in the sunlight that poured through the far window.

Pravon wondered what the assassin's angle was. Maybe Kridmore was simply trying to keep them alive and out of the dungeons, which Pravon should assist with. Pravon stepped forward, interrupting Kridmore's pondering and muttering as he said, "You, King Jabarra, will have the rights to... the Evenmeres. All of it. Every pine and oak and maple and angoia will be yours. You may fashion as many thrones for giants as you could ever dream. Not to mention crowns and castles and merchant ships and vessels of war."

Pravon glanced about. There was nothing else in this chamber made of wood besides the throne and crown of the king, which had to be symbols of extravagance. Other chairs were fashioned from stone blocks. All the soldiers' spear handles were steel. The people of the southern deserts had no wood to spare. Here, wood was more precious than gold.

"Your people could cut down the cursed forest to the last tree and sail every log and branch away to the Rorenlands to do with as you please," Pravon continued.

"You will also be gifted the lands surrounding the Evenmeres, including Belvenguard's outpost—Nevergrace," Kridmore added. "The outpost will no longer be of any importance to our contact—or, uh, the new king, rather."

King Jabarra smirked and rubbed his hands together.

Which new king?

Sir Vladden snarled and gripped his sword, pulling it halfway from its sheath as he stepped toward Pravon and Kridmore. Pravon retreated a step, and his hand found a throwing knife beneath his cloak.

"Blood will not be spilt in the halls of the Yellow Castle!" King Jabarra leapt to his feet. "Not unless it is by my hand or upon the blades of my soldiers." He clapped, and the dozing giant's head jerked upward. Two bulbous eyes unlidded as the humanoid that stood at least three times the height of a man and four times broader raised a club of solid granite. The club's yellow stone was marked by faded red stains. The giant repeatedly patted his open palm with his club in a threatening display.

Sir Vladden gritted his teeth and nodded in Pravon's direction. "King Jabarra, you cannot accept anything from that rogue trio. The Dragon Queen—"

"Do not presume to tell King Jabarra what he can and cannot accept." Jabarra motioned, and the giant lumbered forward, poising its weapon for a sweeping strike that could clear half the chamber of people. "You can always make a better proposal, Sir Vladden."

Sir Vladden dropped his sword back into its sheath as he faced the king. "We will also give you claim to the Evenmeres."

Jabarra chuckled. "It is not good enough to match the offer of your adversary. And King Jabarra does not appreciate the taking of another's idea that was a genuine gesture of good faith."

"We will also grant you *all* of Belvenguard." Kridmore folded his arms across his chest, his expression calm and collected. "Surely you can then crush the Weltermores and rule the entire south."

Pravon leaned in close to Kridmore's ear and whispered, "We do *not* have the authority to offer such things. We should not even be making bargains!"

Jabarra waved dismissively at those in the hall. "The envoys of the Dragon Queen are free to return to her and admit their failure. May she burn them with dragon fire." He adjusted himself in his seat and faced the emissaries from Belvenguard. "You two can return to Galvenstone and inform Igare of the coming tide of sand dragons and giants that will roll through the pass to Progtown. The sand armies of the Rorenlands will crush Belvenguard like a bar of hot metal between the anvil of Murgare and the hammer of King Jabarra."

～

Sir Vladden and his dragonmage strode out from the entrance of the Yellow Castle ahead of Pravon, the two envoys of the Dragon Queen hurrying away toward a single storm dragon as fast as their mage could hobble. The emissaries from Galvenstone walked only a short distance behind Sir Vladden. Kridmore shoved past Pravon, pursuing the two other groups of messengers.

Pravon grabbed Kridmore's shoulder, which was hot to the touch, and the dragon thief said, "We should not kill them. Jabarra may not take kindly to us murdering those he set free."

"That is the second time you've touched me." Kridmore shrugged off his grip. "Never again." He paused to emphasize his threat. "We are supposed to kill any emissaries trying to create peace. As well as every dragonmage we can. We are to create chaos between the kingdoms. Have you forgotten?"

"Things have obviously changed since we started." Pravon gestured to the castle and audience hall behind them, attempting to hide his fear of the assassin as they paced behind the other groups. "I don't know what you're trying to accomplish, but we cannot act against our contact. Surely the Assassin will have our souls if we end up betraying contracts signed in our own blood."

Aneen hurried over and joined them. "Is it betrayal if one of our primary objectives is to create chaos in other kingdoms?"

"I do not see how this agreement with Jabarra will be forgiven or altered or forgotten if the war begins." Pravon stopped beside their storm dragons.

Kridmore marched away, increasing his pace.

"Shit." Aneen climbed onto her storm dragon. "We may need to flee the Rorenlands in a hurry."

Anger flared inside Pravon. "Stop!"

Kridmore did not pay him any mind. The emissaries from Galvenstone glanced back at Kridmore and scrambled up onto their storm dragons with waiting mages, and the dragons woke and stretched their wings.

"If you kill people from every side, along with all the potential peacemakers, Jabarra and Igare and the burro king and any others could grow suspicious," Pravon said in a hoarse whisper, knowing the assassin had heard many things before that he should not have been able to. "That alone may stop the coming war, if the kings question why one group is trying to advance such carnage."

The Dragon Queen's mage could not reach her mount before Kridmore came upon her, the assassin not even hesitant after Pravon's pleading. The mage spun around as fast as she could manage, her tawny hair streaming in the wake of her movements. Her clawed hand reached out, gripping her staff.

Kridmore's fingers parted, and he muttered something. Black and violet light flared and extended outward from his palm, forming an ethereal blade.

Quarren retreated, nearly tripping and falling as Sir Vladden leapt forward with his dragonsteel blade drawn and emitting light as white and pale blue as ice dragon scales.

The dragonguard stood in a defensive posture. "I do not know who you are, conjuror, but the Dragon Queen will hear of what has occurred here. If you are Oomaren's envoy, he and you will be punished."

Kridmore lifted a hand and curled his fingers while muttering. Sir Vladden was shoved back by an unseen force, the guard's sword arm pushed slowly outward, exposing his chest. Vladden cursed, his face contorting with fear and rage. Spittle flew from his lips.

In a flash of movement, Kridmore swiped with his summoned soul blade. The weapon did not strike Vladden's chest but cleaved through his shoulder, slicing the guard's entire arm from his body. The limb and blade he carried thudded and clattered on the flagstones.

Vladden screamed, a sound as inhuman as a ghoul's wail. One of his eyes turned black and then slowly shriveled in its socket. His knees gave out, but Kridmore held him just above the ground and muttered something else, which sealed off the guard's wounded shoulder and halted the shriveling of his blackened eye.

"You won't be much of a guard if you cannot wield a lance." Kridmore laughed.

Vladden continued to cry out, and Kridmore let him fall into a heap.

"I know *who* you are!" Quarren advanced with her staff. "You cannot hide from me. And if you kill us, the world will also know. I will make sure of it just before I die."

Kridmore smacked her with the back of his hand and sent her flying away. She crashed onto the ground as the assassin turned and strode for his storm dragon. Soldiers around the Yellow Castle began shouting and pointing with their spears.

"You should be happy." Kridmore shrugged and pulled his hood up over his face, again leaving only his shovel chin visible as he passed Pravon. "I didn't kill the guard or mage. And I only took part of the guard's soul before curtailing the process.

Seeing what that does to him should be an interesting experiment. A grand idea on your part, thief."

Pravon's mouth worked a few times, but no words came out while Quarren recovered, gained her feet, and slowly helped tug Vladden along in the direction of their storm dragon, both of them stumbling with each stride.

"You two can stay here or fly away." Kridmore strolled back toward the castle. "It makes no difference to me, but I will remain with this new tyrant king and discuss how we should pursue the coming war."

16

CYRAN ORENDAIN

A COLD SPLASH OF SEAWATER HIT CYRAN IN THE CHEST AND sluiced up his face and over the gag in his mouth. Salt rushed over his tongue. The water then ran down his leather tunic and across his remaining armor. The remnants of rotten fruits and vegetables washed away and pooled around his feet. His hands were still bound behind his back as he stood facing a dragonarcher with a bucket.

The soldier of Murgare had removed his helm from his black and barbed armor. His hair was long and straight like his beard, and he dipped his bucket into the sea again as waves rolled in and broke across the shore. "If all the people of Belvenguard smell like you lot, I hope I never have to meet another one of you."

"It was your people who threw—" A bucket of seawater hit Vyk in the face, silencing him and causing him to spit and gag.

Another Murgare archer bellowed with laughter and slapped his knee. "You should have kept your gag in place. Would have saved you from several mouthfuls of salty brine and us from the sound of your voice."

Ineri huddled and coughed, and a third archer dumped

seawater over her head. The water rinsed her leathers and chainmail. Pounding footsteps sounded on the docks behind Cyran, and the archers stood at attention.

"Get them onto Shadowmar," a man behind Cyran said. "The Dragon Queen wants these three."

Cyran suppressed a chill as the archers shared a quick glance and then approached him and his comrades. The archers spun them around and marched them back up to the docks and toward the slumbering shadow dragon. Seawater dripped off Cyran's hair and brow, and his boots squelched as he walked.

When they approached the rear of the shadow dragon, its barbed tail was resting on the stone road between several buildings. The dragon's tail twitched involuntarily, as if the beast was dreaming, and Cyran could not look away from its stinger. Black venom said to be more deadly than any other known to man was held in a sac inside that bulbous portion just behind its barbed tip, and that poison held the ability to kill as well as sever and destroy souls. Any victim would be lost to this world, the next, and the other realm.

Cyran's heart skittered in his chest. This was the dragon who, at first sight, had wanted to roast him alive with its black fire. The beast had even used its breath against Eidelmere in a moment of pure rage when they faced off in the sky over Nevergrace. Like all dragon fire, the breath had no effect on another dragon, and any dragon could simply shield its riders, but such an ignoble use of dragon fire was not tolerated per the ways of the *neblír*. Shadow dragons were more wicked and malevolent than any other of their kind, but this beast's fury had been directed specifically at Cyran. Its hatred stemmed from the incident in the den at the Never. Cyran had hewn its clutch of eggs to shreds, and this beast had found his scent in its nest.

"Put this on him." A Murgare soldier with a red beard

protruding from beneath his helm stood on Shadowmar's quarterdeck and threw down a rope.

The archer behind Cyran looped the rope under Cyran's arms and tied it tight. "Use the ladder." The archer pointed to the quarterdeck's rope ladder and shoved Cyran closer to the beast. The dragon's glistening scales were as black as night and seemed to have endless depths, like a sea of shadows.

Cyran shuddered in horror but managed to use his free legs to ascend the ladder as the archer above kept the rope taut, which held Cyran's body upright as he was hauled and then hoisted up onto the quarterdeck. Vyk came next, and then Ineri.

The shadow dragon beneath them stirred, its body rustling about as a deep throaty sound escaped its lips. Both of its eyes were closed, but one appeared to be sealed shut with dark crusts of blood.

The archers pushed Cyran and his companions down on the rear of the quarterdeck, making them face aft and the dragon's barbed tail, and strapped harnesses around their legs and waists. Afterward, the Murgare soldiers took up their positions at the three mounted crossbows—one forward and one to either side of the deck.

"You put this dragon's eye out," Cyran whispered to Ineri as best he could through his wet and loosened gag.

Ineri did not look up as her eyes closed. She hunched over and shivered. Her gag had also loosened after their bathing, and she managed to mutter some garbled words. "She will likely remember us, if she takes notice of all who ride on her back."

Vyk cursed something related to the Assassin.

The dragonarchers chuckled and talked to each other but suddenly fell silent. The pounding thud of dragonsteel boots on stone sounded below. The shadow dragon shifted and rose, the black scales along its lower back and tail rippling and sliding over thick muscle, the ebony spines running down its midline twitching and crowding together.

"They are here?" a woman's voice asked, and Cyran recognized it immediately as the Dragon Queen's.

His terror amplified. She *had* survived their tilt near Nevergrace, as well as her fall through the trees. Not only did she survive, but she and her shadow dragon had already found each other and, for whatever reason, they were residing in what must be the Eastern Reach of Murgare. Quiet anger sheeted off both the queen and her mount, thickening the air like fog. This woman and dragon were responsible for the attack on the Never, and for Sir Kayom's and Sir Ymar's deaths, as well as many others.

Cyran's wrath flared and strangled his fear, but the emotion could only burn at his insides and smolder like hot coals. More than anything, he now wanted to exact his revenge on this woman and her dragon, but instead, these two were about to take their own vengeance.

"The captives are harnessed and clipped in," the bearded archer's voice answered. "But they are wet. They... were covered in filth."

A moment of silence passed, and the Dragon Queen said, "We fly."

"Turrets are prepared." A woman's voice carried up from the lower turret.

Massive wings thrice as long as Eidelmere's extended, their leathery segments snapping and billowing in the wind. They flapped once and then twice, and on the third flap, the dragon lifted into the air. The beast flew away and spun low over the city and the sea before wheeling west and soaring over the river, a small forest, and rolling hills. The heat of the dragon's body wafted up, as if it rose from an entire chamber full of forges, and embraced them, warming them and their soaked clothing.

Cyran stared east over the endless Ilmoor Sea. A cluster of islands lay off to the north, and smoke clung to the sky above them. To the south, the Evenmeres filled the horizon beyond leagues of grasslands.

Eidelmere. The forest dragon was long gone. He had found his freedom before the wars of man even began, before the sky sea released its first storm of blood. Hopefully the spiteful old beast would experience at least a few years of happiness free from the will of man before he passed. No one would be able to find Eidelmere again in those woods that spanned a region larger than a few of the kingdoms.

As they flew along, the clouds opened up and spit cold rain down on them. The droplets pelted Cyran's armor and leathers, and wind whistled in his ears. After an hour of this, Ineri shivered and pressed herself closer to Vyk, huddling into him. Cyran scooted closer to her as well so that both he and Vyk could shelter her, provide warmth, and hopefully trap some of the dragon's body heat between them.

"Pissing Murgare rain," Vyk muttered. "It's colder than the rivers in the mountains."

The repetitive flapping of wings beat the wind back, but the rains continued falling as the shadow dragon bore them west for hours. The plummeting temperatures numbed Cyran's fingers, causing them to swell and turn less responsive. His cheeks and nose burned with cold, and all of his leathers that had been drenched from the seawater bath were now completely soaked through. Ineri coughed a dozen times in a row and then hacked, which made it sound like her lungs rattled in her chest. She whimpered.

Cyran pressed himself closer to her, fearing she would not survive the trip to wherever the Dragon Queen was taking them. The rain droplets turned to balls of ice that clinked as they struck Cyran's armor and stung when they pelted his head. Ineri coughed again.

Bloody northern hell. What kind of people could fly dragons through the skies this far north and not get cold or freeze to death? Cyran glanced over his shoulder to peer in the direction they were headed. The archers remained at their crossbows, at attention, thick capes of fur wrapped around them. The rain beaded off their dragonsteel armor.

Cyran scanned the quarterdeck and their harnesses. There was nothing else he could do for Ineri but pray to the Paladin and Shield Maiden that this dragon would soon land in a warm spot with a fire or that they would be allowed to lie directly against its hot scales. His eyes settled closed as he hung his head, hoping time would pass quickly. His mind drifted, and a rush of sensations hit him as he almost nodded off. The threads of the other realm rippled everywhere. They were all so close. He wasn't sure if the feeling of the *neblír* hovering tightly around him and seeming more tangible was because they were flying closer to the sky sea than he had before or because they were in the north and in the vicinity of the Valley of the Smoke Breathers. Maybe it was the particular dragon beneath him. He recalled Sir Paltere's warning—not to spend too much time in the other realm no matter how much more enjoyable it was compared to the real world. If Cyran did so, he would become crippled like the dragonmages.

He steeled himself, preparing to act quickly and then leave the place. He felt all around him and his companions. The massive thread representing the shadow dragon or its soul pulsed beneath him. He reached out with his mind, curious, wondering if he could learn this dragon's true name and maybe even command it. He seized the thread and squeezed.

A shriek pierced the skies around them, ringing Cyran's ears.

Ineri and Vyk bellowed with fear and fell over. The mounted crossbows swiveled and creaked in their frames.

Silence then hovered around them.

"What on the Dragon's bloody ass was that?" the bearded archer said.

Shadowmar veered sideways and whipped around beneath them. Her neck snaked back toward her body, her one red eye glaring at her riders, searching. She screeched again, ringing everyone's ears. The archers cursed and trembled.

Cyran's bowels sank lower as he swallowed, and regret filled his core. He never should have tried to make a bond with the Dragon Queen's steed. He didn't know if bonds could be broken or usurped, but even if they could, this bond would surely be one of the strongest of them all. Eidelmere had tried to explain the link between human and dragon, but Cyran never thought to ask deeper questions, such as if an established bond could be taken prior to the death of either one of them. Could a stronger mage take a bond from another? He clenched his numb fists, wishing he would have had the foresight to ask Eidelmere these questions when he had the chance.

A haughty laugh sounded. "The young dragonknight has attempted to sever my bond with Shadowmar." The Dragon Queen's boots punished the quarterdeck as she stepped onto its planks and strode aft. She was not harnessed to the dragon, but Cyran had seen her perform such feats before. She knew exactly when and where her mount would shift and turn.

Cyran winced and ducked his head. A minute passed before he looked up again and over his shoulder. The Dragon Queen stood, glaring at him with dark eyes that flashed within her helm. Ineri tried to stifle a cough, but she couldn't. She hacked loudly.

"Once summer has passed up here in the north, every storm is cold." The Dragon Queen motioned behind her. "Especially when you are dragon bound and soaring through these skies." She turned to the archers. "Get them furs."

"How about having Shadowmar light black fire under their arses?" the bearded archer asked. He reluctantly stepped away from his crossbow and opened a trunk bolted to the planks. After removing a pile of furs, he shuffled to the rear of the deck and dropped them on Cyran, Ineri, and Vyk. He grabbed Cyran's forearm and squeezed it in a crushing grip before cutting the ties binding Cyran's wrists. Cyran jerked his hands free and rubbed at his raw skin as the archer freed Vyk and Ineri.

Cyran helped Ineri bundle up under a pelt so large it had to have come from a bear of some sort. He then draped a sheet of wool over her head and wrapped himself under other skins, allowing only his eyes to remain exposed. A craggy peak passed beside them as Shadowmar soared through a gap between two mountains.

The Dragon Queen presided over them, watching in silence for many minutes. She tapped her boot on the deck and cleared her throat. "Why did Belvenguard send what must be its youngest dragonknight to Murgare? Through the Evenmeres, no less? Igare did not even supply him with a legion for protection."

Cyran swallowed, thinking it would be best not to speak. This woman would want to loosen his tongue with what could be construed as kindness, kindness they only needed because of the situation she put them in. Her objective would be to trick him into revealing information about his kingdom, their defenses, and their king. She might have even tricked Garmeen in some similar circumstance.

The Dragon Queen paced about the quarterdeck behind them, every thud of her boots rankling Cyran's nerves. She asked, "Is Igare preparing to confront our legions on the south side of the Lake on Fire? Or is he betting we will cross the Evenmeres again or pass over the Eventide Sea?"

Cyran sat in silence, staring at the quarterdeck.

"At this time, is Igare even halfway prepared for the war?" she asked. "His banners are slow in moving, or so I've heard." Her words carried a texture that suggested she spoke through a mocking grin. "He should have called his banners and waited for their answer prior to killing our king."

A horrible mistake made by one of the guard during an errand meant for abduction had caused the death of the Murgare king.

"I imagine Igare is now inducting every squire he can into the guard while trying to find them a mage and dragon as he hands them bronze armor." She laughed. "The legions outside of Galvenstone do not seem as eager to gather as ours do."

Cyran's heart twisted. All that the Dragon Queen stated seemed to be true, at least the last time he had heard word on the matter. The other cities of Belvenguard were not answering Igare's summons, their lords and nobles exploiting the situation and its mounting tensions for their own gain by demanding favors and marriage pacts that would benefit their families. The forges of Galvenstone had also been working day and night to try to prepare the guard and their legions before the north's hammer fell.

"Have it your way." The Dragon Queen's footsteps retreated, her tone as sharp as a blade. "I was offering you a chance to talk, when you could use your own free will to do so. Where you are going, we have other methods to get you to speak, to draw the information we desire out of unwilling captives." She stepped off the quarterdeck and strode up her mount's neck as easily as walking a flat battlement, occasionally gripping spines as tall as she was while she moved.

Night eventually settled across the frigid north, but Shadowmar kept flying without showing any hint of weariness.

Twilight faded in the west, and the light of the thousand moons rippled through the sky sea.

"There are fires." The bearded archer pointed into the night, and Cyran wriggled around in his harness and turned to face in their direction of travel.

Off in the west, what looked like a great snake of flames wound through the countryside, although smaller rivers of fire diverged from the primary body, forming what could in essence be tributaries to a primary river. A body of water reflecting silver moonlight lay to the west of the fiery lines, but these waters did not extend far enough to be the Lake on Fire.

"Fire surrounds the Lake of the Lady," the archer added.

Shadowmar angled downward and streaked lower, flinging Cyran back against the end of his harness as its straps pulled tight around his thighs and waist. Wind screamed in his ears. When it seemed like the dragon might spear the earth, the beast leveled off, and the archers and Dragon Queen studied the lines of fire that drew closer.

Cyran strained and squinted. The winding walls of fire were not a diverging wildfire or some dark sign for dragon riders in the sky. Rows of individual torches moved along with the people holding them—a massive pilgrimage of some sort.

"The clans are traveling to Cykar." The Dragon Queen's voice carried back from her saddled area on Shadowmar's neck. "And Cykar marches south."

Each small tributary of the main procession was probably composed of a hundred or more soldiers marching, and there were many of these lines. Shadowmar swooped above them and veered south, passing over the widest and longest line that flanked the lake and moved along its winding shores. Thousands more soldiers traveled within this main area. Masses of spearheads twinkled under moonlight, and armor glinted.

"There must be men from every town and village and hamlet

along Northsheeren Road, as well as all the clans in the Dragonback Mountains." The bearded archer's voice was airy with disbelief.

"There have to be five thousand swords marching south," Cyran whispered to Ineri and Vyk.

"Ten thousand," Ineri answered. "And two thousand mounted knights."

Without aid, that was probably as many swords as Galvenstone could hope to assemble, and this was only one small area of Murgare. Cyran's stomach sloshed with stagnant bile as he stared in horror.

Murgare's armies were already armed and armored, and they were marching to war.

17

JASLIN ORENDAIN

A knock sounded on the door of Menoria's bedchamber. Jaslin dropped her book in surprise and strode for the entry, but she paused and turned to Menoria. The lady of the Never wiped away the hints of anxiety and dread from her face as she sat poised, radiant, and beautiful in a stunning dress sewn in green and gray for Nevergrace.

"You're sure you want to look this beautiful?" Jaslin asked as she tested the handle of the door. "If you dishevel yourself, there's a possibility he could change his mind."

"No matter who stands beyond those planks of wood, I wish to represent the Never to the best of my ability. I owe that to my father, my mother, and my people." Menoria took a deep breath and smoothed her dress. She planted a smile upon her face.

Jaslin turned the handle and swung the door inward. Beyond, a handsome young man with emerald eyes and brown hair waited. *Jaken.*

The son of the king's orator bowed low. Menoria's smile dropped as she gripped the armrests of her chair. Her knuckles blanched.

"I hope I did not disappoint you." Jaken smiled. "I am no king, but I've come to ask you if you would take a walk with me."

Riscott may wish to take away one of the king's chances for a wife and thus a son before the war begins. But Menoria could turn down this young man, and Jaken would eventually have to break off any betrothal with Menoria if he were to wed the princess and become king. Jaslin met Jaken's eye, and she nodded politely. Jaken smiled at her and looked her up and down.

Menoria slowly stood. "No. I am not disappointed. I... will join you for a walk. If my handmaid is allowed to accompany me."

Jaken smirked as he glanced at Jaslin again. "Of course she can."

Jaken turned and led them away from the chamber and down long halls and stairways, keeping ten paces ahead of them before he finally exited the Summerswept Keep. Jaslin twirled her shard in her hands, the sweat on her palm making the crystal slick. Once Jaken crossed a courtyard and reached a grove of trees laden with red flowers, he glanced around to make sure no one else was watching and offered Menoria his arm. When the lady slid her arm into his, he turned and guided her between the rows of trees.

Jaslin trailed silently behind.

"Was it you who had your father ask me to accompany the king to Galvenstone?" Menoria asked, looking up at him.

Jaken shrugged. "It could have been that my father wanted it, but if your version excites you, we will say it is true." He smiled down at her.

Jaslin's stomach turned with disgust.

When they reached the rear of the grove, Menoria stepped as if thinking he would lead her up the next row, but Jaken pulled her behind a tree and spoke quietly. Jaslin rushed closer.

The orator's son pried up a curtain of vines, revealing a small wooden doorway bolted by a rusty padlock. He pulled a key from his belt and unlatched the lock, allowing it to fall. "This is the only way we can escape the keep for a bit." He motioned for Menoria to slide into the opening as he turned himself sideways and slipped through. "Your handmaid can still accompany us."

Menoria glanced back, her face pale. She turned and followed Jaken. Jaslin hurried over and jammed herself into the slit of a passageway, navigating between stones of the thick outer wall of the castle before stepping onto the grounds beyond.

Sunlight broke over rocks that overlooked the Lake on Fire far, far below. The kingswood and the Spires were distant smears on the horizon.

"You brought her?" Princess Nistene's voice was meek as she paced along the jagged rocks lining the edge of the cliff. She wore an elegant dress and held her arms out to either side of her body, as if she walked on a tightrope.

"He couldn't resist." Vysoria sat against the keep's outer wall with her knees pulled up to her face. She gazed out over the lake. "The handmaid, too?" She grinned and nodded at Menoria. "Jaken, you understand that the young lady could be your mother soon."

Jaken grimaced and shook his head. "She will never be my mother."

"If Riscott weds and beds her, she may as well be." Vysoria giggled.

Jaken's cheeks flared, and Nistene dropped her arms and teetered on the lip of the outer stones.

"Your father could still ask me to be his wife?" Menoria gazed up at Jaken, her eyes wide. "Even after this?"

"Or the king may." Vysoria laughed with a haughty air. "Then you will be Jaken's queen, and Jaken will be in a lot of trouble."

"She would be my mother then." Nistene's nearly absent chin folded into her neck. Tears sprang into her eyes.

"She will not be anyone's mother." Jaslin stepped forward. "Not unless she bears a child of her own someday."

The others fell silent.

"This one is prickly." Vysoria stood and joined Nistene on the rocks. "The small council is convening again today. They were already in session when I woke, probably debating who would best be served by the lady of the Never's womb."

"We don't expect them to be done until late." Jaken stepped onto the rock ledge and gazed downward. "We thought you two would like some fresh lake air rather than be trapped in a bedchamber all day awaiting your fates."

"Then Menoria is not to be Jaken's wife?" Jaslin asked as Menoria folded her hands against her thighs, and her eyes closed either with relief or anxiety.

"The handmaid catches on quickly." Vysoria shuffled closer to the edge.

"That is still being decided as well." Jaken shrugged. "You know as much as we do."

Menoria cursed under her breath. "The tension is unbearable."

Nistene turned to face the lake with the others. They stood far too high above the water for anyone to fall or jump and hope to have any chance of surviving.

Jaken motioned to Nistene and Vysoria. "That's why we thought both of you would like to have a bit of fun. We often start here and then venture into the city. We should be back by nightfall."

Jaslin took Menoria's wrist and whispered, "We should return to your chambers."

Jaken looked over his shoulder. "Someone who frequents

one of the taverns we visit claims to have seen Queen Hyceth's assassin just before she was murdered."

Jaslin released Menoria. Thoughts bounded around in her mind. Could the assassin have been from Galvenstone? That wouldn't be likely. King Igare was well loved by his people, and if the killer were someone from Dashtok or the city, someone this person knew could have caught wind of their profession or scheme and alerted the watch. Any man hoping to earn enough coin by killing the queen—so that he could live in luxury for the rest of his days—would have to be a master at his trade. He would need to sneak into the castle, kill a queen, and then flee somewhere far away. Unless he was already living in the castle… but even then, he would likely be caught and recognized, and it could not have been an aged councilmember who had achieved such a thing. Probably only Murgare, or perhaps the Rorenlands, could then be a potential haven for such an assassin and any family he had.

"Was the assassin caught and killed?" Jaslin stepped up to the rocks bordering the cliff and walls of the lower castle below.

Jaken nodded. "The kingsknights hanged him. Just as they did with the first one."

"They couldn't get him to talk, either." Nistene sobbed but stifled herself. "That bloody bastard also had no tongue."

Jaslin's curiosity and intrigue piqued. Something strange was occurring within these walls, and she could try to do more here than just watch over Menoria and help keep her happy and safe. Like her brother, maybe she too could help her kingdom with its coming trials.

"Stop thinking about it." Jaken shoved Nistene, and the princess toppled over the ledge.

Jaslin gasped and leapt forward, reaching out, but Nistene had already fallen. Jaslin peered downward. Nistene's elegant dress billowed like a string of sails, but it did not break her fall in the least.

"She cannot—" Jaslin's mouth hung open as a storm dragon hurtled through the air before slowing to match the princess's falling pace. It caught her and whisked away.

Jaken erupted with laughter.

Jaslin stared at him, searching his expression in shock. "How do you arrange for such antics? Surely there are better uses for one of the king's dragons."

"That dragon's mage is having physical relations with the king's clergyman, Lisain." Jaken said it nonchalantly. "The mage grants favors for us so that Igare never hears of it. He fears what the king would think or do to him."

"We walked in on them one time a year or so ago now." Vysoria waited and then leapt over the edge.

"It's only a storm dragon." Jaken stared out over the lake. "So it doesn't have any better uses if it's not carrying messages back and forth to other cities or kingdoms. And those places are not responding to Igare's letters." He paused. "The downside is also that it is only a storm dragon. It cannot carry more than two of us and the mage at the same time. We'll have to wait for a few minutes."

Menoria stepped up beside Jaslin as they watched the beast soar away and disappear around a turret.

"They say ten thousand elves burned alive in this lake during the Dragon Wars." Jaken revealed no emotion. "The last of the elves of Cimeren."

Cyran encountered a few elves in the woods.

"That is not true." Menoria goggled as she studied the waters far below. "At least it was not that many who died."

"There was an entire city that housed fifty times the number of elves who died in the lake, and all those in the city also burned. Legends say the souls of those who died in the lake are trapped there. Like when one of our people dies and their soul is held in the sky sea." Jaken paused and pointed into the distance. "You will not have to wait long. Storm dragons are swift." He took one running step and leapt over the wall.

The distant spot of a dragon barreled toward his plummeting form, caught him after he had fallen more than three quarters the distance to the lake, and streaked away.

"Do you believe he will catch us?" Menoria asked. "They could be trying to get rid of me—their potential new mother."

Jaslin gazed downward, and the water and cliffs spiraled around in her vision. She heaved for breath, but thoughts of the queen's assassin and of the one Cyran had seen kept forcing themselves into her mind like the song from the shard. She wanted to know, to find out what was happening at Castle Dashtok. She quickly considered if she was simply acting like Fileena —wanting to understand the gossip and rumors of the court... No. This was different. If Cyran could risk his life to find out what happened to a lone village in Murgare, then she could risk her life to try to discover what was occurring in Belvenguard.

The storm dragon returned from leaving Jaken somewhere and circled below.

"I want to, but I will never gather enough nerve to leap." Menoria's feet scuffed and scraped along the lip. "It's too far."

Jaslin grabbed her hand and leapt over the ledge.

~

The storm dragon dived along beside them, and when Jaslin brushed against its scales, the dragon leveled out. She settled into a seated position on its neck, slowing her descent, and her stomach returned to its proper position, rather than in her throat.

Menoria cried out in elation and cheered from her seat. The

mage glanced back at them from beneath a long hood. Half of his face was handsome. A lack of muscle and fat across the other half of his face caused the bones of his cheek and jaw to bulge. "Keep the noise down, or next time I *will* let you fall."

Jaslin swallowed, but Menoria continued giggling.

They whistled through the air, the storm dragon flapping and hurtling above the water, everything around them a blur. Menoria cheered again, although quieter.

After what seemed like only a minute, the dragon slowed and landed on shore—behind an outcropping of rock. "Get off," the mage said.

Jaslin swung her leg over the creature's neck and slid down its side, and she assisted Menoria in dismounting.

Jaken patted them both on the back. "Fun, eh?"

"That was incredible." Menoria's eyes were still alight with wonder.

"How about a drink?" Jaken handed them plain tunics and cloaks to go over the clothing they currently wore, and he followed Vysoria. Nistene hurried up to him and clutched his arm, whispering something. He replied with a quick comment, but the princess kept talking in his ear and only smiled when he looked at her.

Jaslin donned her tunic and cloak and trailed the three young nobles around the outcropping to a wharf that led to the lowest tier in the city of Galvenstone. Soon, they walked the streets, and no one paid them any mind. Two men in brown tunics stumbled as they stepped out of a doorway. One mumbled to the other, the reek of sweat and vomit sheeting off them. Vysoria turned and slipped into the tavern they had exited.

Jaslin tensed, but the others—including Menoria, who walked with a lighter step since the jump from the cliffs—all followed the conjuror's daughter. Jaslin gritted her teeth and trailed behind. Inside the tavern, a few dim torches flickered along the walls. Tables ran in rows, but only a few patrons occupied them. It was still early in the day.

Jaken sat at a table, and Nistene joined him, not so subtly scooting closer to him. Vysoria positioned herself across from them and studied the other patrons. Jaken asked Vysoria something, but she remained aloof. A woman in a corset sidled over, her cleavage pressed against her upper chest and bulging.

"What drink shall you have?" Jaken turned to Menoria. "They serve real mead and ale and wine here. Makes the castle's drinks seem like child's juice."

"A Belvenguard ale." Menoria grinned.

Jaken looked to Jaslin, and she said, "A wine from Nevergrace, if they have one."

After the others ordered tankards of ale, the serving wench departed in a flurry of skirts.

"We are four young women and one young man." Jaslin glanced around. "What if these Galvenstone drunkards try something?"

Jaken shrugged. "It can be dangerous outside the castle, but that is what makes you feel more alive."

Jaslin watched the patrons.

Nistene laughed. "That is only a jape. If we ever find ourselves in real danger, we will simply tell the thugs who we are. No one would accost the princess of Belvenguard."

Unless they wanted to abduct you for coin, or assassinate you.

The serving woman returned and slammed tankards down in front of them. "Here's the piss from Nevergrace." She set one before Jaslin.

Jaslin sipped the warm mulled wine. It was more bitter than any she had tasted at the outpost. Menoria downed the contents of her drink in three swallows. Jaslin's awareness perked up because of the lady's unusual behavior, and Jaslin settled a hand on Menoria's arm while studying the establishment again.

"Be careful, milady," Jaslin said.

"She needs this." Vysoria motioned to the wench to order more drinks. "You would too if you were about to be asked to become the wife of either the king or his orator. Both old men."

The serving woman brought more tankards, and Menoria drank deeply.

Jaslin sucked in a slow breath, her unease escalating. She caught Jaken's attention and said, "You mentioned that there was someone who frequents this place who may have seen the queen's assassin?"

Jaken nodded to the side, indicating a dark corner of the tavern. Two men in cloaks sat together there, conversing quietly. After a minute, they looked up and noticed Jaslin watching them. A tingle of dread swam inside her as she quickly glanced away.

"All this talk of the sky sea raining blood is beginning to bore me." Vysoria drank, and a glint of excitement lit up in her eyes. "We should get out of the castle more often, see the real world, and listen to what the people of the city are saying. My mother has informants all over Cimeren, but it's more fun to learn things yourself."

"There's nothing stopping us." Jaken grinned at her. "Not currently, at least. I will meet you at the cliffs any day."

"I'll come too." Nistene grabbed Jaken's arm, and Jaken furtively rolled his eyes so that the princess could not see him do it from her position beside him.

Vysoria reached out and snatched Jaslin's hand, pulling it onto the table. The crystal shard was wedged between Jaslin's fingers. Vysoria grabbed the shard and studied the remnants of figures and markings on its face.

"Give it back." Jaslin squeezed the young woman's wrist.

"How did you get this?"

"From my brother. He is dead now."

Vysoria inspected it for another couple heartbeats before setting it onto Jaslin's palm. "It is interesting. Ancient looking. You should speak to my mother about it. I'll mention it to her."

Jaslin's insides cramped. She hated it every time someone took an interest in what remained of the decanter Tamar had given her, after Cyran had smashed the object out of fear, thinking it was somehow corrupting her mind.

A shadow passed over their table, and Jaslin glanced up as the two men who had been sitting in the corner took seats around them.

"You young ladies been gossiping about us, have you?" the burlier one with a scrubby beard asked.

Jaken peeked at them out of the corner of his eye but would not face them directly. He shook his head in response to their question.

"Then why is this young lady who hasn't accompanied you before so interested in us?" The first man drank and set a tankard on the table before him. His comrade squeezed in closer to Jaslin, pressing her against Menoria.

The hand of the man who had spoken caught Jaslin's eye. He wore a wooden ring. Strange enough, but on its face was a laden burro—just like the ring Cyran wore.

"You're in the guild." Jaslin kept her voice calm and confident.

The supposed merchant glowered, his eyes boring into her, his breath wafting over and reeking of drink. He slipped his hand off his tankard and hid it below the table. "Watch what you say, young lady."

"My brother is in the guild." Jaslin leaned closer to the man addressing them and pushed back against his comrade. "Or at least he was given a ring after saving the lives of two of your own."

The burly merchant looked to his companion.

"How did you know it was *the* assassin?" Jaslin asked. "If the kingsknights executed the man in private inside Dashtok, after he performed his deed, then you must have seen him before Queen Hyceth was murdered. Before anyone knew what he would do."

The merchant beside Jaslin groaned and slid farther away. "You never should have opened your damn mouth," he said to his comrade.

The burly merchant hammered a fist onto the table, making their tankards jump and spill drink over their sides. He snarled. "Why would I tell you children anything?"

"I thought a guild member would share all they knew with another member," Jaslin replied. "That is what my brother was told by the merchant who gave him his ring."

"You are not a guild member and do not wear a ring. It hardly matters if your brother supposedly carries the burro."

Jaslin continued leaning closer to the burly merchant, her mind racing as she lowered her voice. "I am close to some very important people in the Summerswept Keep."

Menoria gasped and grabbed Jaslin's arm, chuckling awkwardly as she wobbled in her seat.

"Is that so?" The merchant studied Menoria and the rest of them. He nodded at his companion in an I-told-you-so manner. "I have a bit of information I could share with you, but I would need you to do something for me first."

"And what is that?" Jaslin asked as Jaken, Vysoria, and Nistene all sat quietly, apparently only interested in the table.

"We"—the merchant motioned to his comrade across the table—"need a particular cart of goods to make it through the gates of Galvenstone uninspected."

Jaslin leaned back. "I do not have the authority to make anything like that happen. Not with assassins killing queens and all."

The man beside Jaslin spoke in a husky and low voice. "Then we need a particular merchant to have *his* goods inspected. Down by the wharfs. In no more than a fortnight."

Thoughts turned in Jaslin's head. "How do I find this merchant?"

"You will recognize him by the diamond shapes embroidered into his robes. Some say it is an ancient and secret symbol meant to represent a flying dragon."

"I will see what I can do." Jaslin drank and forced down a gulp of wine, acting as if she drank flagons at every meal. "But I need the information first."

The burly one laughed. "You'll have that when the merchant's wares are searched. His name is Keliam, and he is not a true merchant, is not part of the guild and does not pay homage to the Merchant. He's been selling illegal goods down at the wharf here for decades. Pretty much controls the territory."

Jaslin shook her head, and some of the stories she had read and their plots popped into her mind. "Then what happens when I've done my part? You two disappear and take over his stalls? *You* sell fish stuffed with poppy dust instead of him?"

The burly merchant twitched.

"I need to hear what you know about the assassin, now." Jaslin folded her arms across her chest.

The merchants shared a glance before the burly one took a deep breath. "I will tell you that we knew it was the assassin because when he was in here, he did not speak, even when we… tried to make conversation." He leaned closer. "When he drank, his hands were shaking like a virgin boy's before his first night with a whore."

Not an experienced or confident assassin, then.

"He kept gulping down drink after drink," the merchant continued. "The way he was acting seemed kind of suspicious and got on my nerves. We thought Keliam sent him to watch us. My friend and I shoved him out of his seat and held him down." He glanced around and lowered his voice. "But this scarf he wore around his neck came loose as he opened his mouth to shout at us. He had no bloody tongue, and there was a tattoo around his throat. I couldn't make it all out, only saw the top of the tattoo, but it was a shape with a wing or feathers inside of it."

"How does that make him an assassin?" Jaslin asked. "He sounds too jittery to be a master of stealth who could sneak into the castle and kill the queen."

"The queen may not have been in the castle. She slips out at times, like other noble children." He casually motioned to Nistene and Jaken. "This man had a similar appearance to another, who some of the merchants that travel the Scyne Road spread stories about. Those stories surfaced just before the time when the Murgare Queen was assassinated by a tongueless assassin."

Jaslin's blood chilled.

The merchant leaned back and drank. "I will tell you the rest once you have Galvenstone's watch look into Keliam's goods."

∼

Evening settled over Galvenstone and the lake when Jaken finally led Menoria and the others through the gates of Castle Dashtok. The soldiers there cast them questioning glares, but none of them said anything.

After they entered the castle, Nistene tried to guide Jaken down a particular corridor, but he shrugged her off. She hurried away with her head down. Vysoria departed in a completely different direction.

"Until next time." Jaken bowed low to Menoria and strode away, his steps unsteady.

Menoria laughed and clung to Jaslin. "You should take me to my chambers." The lady of the Never hiccupped, blushed, and covered her mouth. "Without attracting too much attention."

Jaslin took her by the arm and whisked her down long hallways, following the only route she knew. They climbed spiral staircases with tapestries of red and gold hanging overhead.

When they finally reached the upper keep and walked down the hallway leading to Menoria's chamber, they found a man waiting for them outside its doorway. The man's back was to them, a red cape with golden trim draping behind him.

Jaslin swallowed. Their footsteps echoed in the hall as they approached. King Igare Dragonblade turned to regard them, and Jaslin's mouth went as dry as poppy dust.

"Ah, lady of the Never." Igare stood straighter and brushed his graying blond hair behind his ears. He did not seem to notice Jaslin.

Menoria giggled, and she hurried past Jaslin and stumbled over to the king. She leaned against him and hiccupped, covered her mouth, and giggled again.

Embarrassment for her lady flooded through Jaslin. "Menoria. I should assist you."

Igare stepped back and recomposed himself. "Lady of the Never, I was wondering if you would dine with me this evening."

Menoria closed her eyes and laughed before shaking her head in what was hopefully disbelief.

18

CYRAN ORENDAIN

FIRELIGHT FLARED IN THE DARKNESS AHEAD. BELOW, THE LAKE ON Fire rippled softly under moonlight, its shores teeming with torches and bonfires.

Cyran stared in shocked awe at the massive number of soldiers who had already gathered along the lake's northern boundary, and dread swarmed his insides. Shadowmar dipped and spiraled lower, swooping across a vast army unlike any Cimeren had seen in this age.

The shadow dragon had flown for several days, taking only short respites on the ground to sleep, before arriving at this location—near to what Cyran overheard was the city of Icetooth and the River of the Helm. During their travels, they had passed over other bands of marching soldiers, but none of them were as large as the masses he had seen leaving Cykar. Nothing he had seen thus far prepared him for the sight of this army.

Shadowmar landed with a roar and a thumping of feet as her talons tore into the earth. The soldiers in the vicinity gasped or jumped. Some even jerked awake and fled. Beyond the masses of soldiers and knights, scores of warships were moored out in the water of the lake. Smaller vessels sailed to and from the shore in passing lines, their lamplight smearing across the waters.

The smaller vessels are loading and preparing the warships for their voyage. Cyran's fingers dug into the belt of the harness around his waist.

Something above them shrieked. A pale creature whose black wings blended into the night sky—a mist dragon—wheeled overhead. Silhouettes of other dragons swirled in the skies, and many more beasts were hunkered down on the ground amidst battalions of armored men. In the moonlight, it was difficult to make out what types all the dragons were, but there were at least fire, ice, mist, storm, moon, massive stone dragons with two sets of wings, crystal, ember, emerald, ash, blood, amber, amethyst, and skeletal-appearing bone dragons around them.

A wash of cold bounded through Cyran's blood and prickled his skin. There had to be several hundred or even a thousand dragons in the area, many more than in Igare's legion at Galvenstone. Cyran had to somehow escape from the Dragon Queen and return home. Igare needed to be made aware of the north's numbers and where they were preparing to strike. Their war would happen soon. All of Belvenguard and beyond would have to answer the calls for their banners if their kingdoms were to have any chance at defending themselves.

"Bind them to the quarterdeck." The Dragon Queen pointed at Cyran and his companions as she climbed from her saddle.

The bearded archer approached, and Cyran remained still. There would be no escaping from this area. The Paladin himself could not cut his way through such a massive horde of soldiers and dragons. The archer tied Cyran's wrists together and placed his back to Ineri's and Vyk's so that they formed a small circle, their bonds tied to each other's. He draped furs over their heads, and his footsteps sounded as he marched away.

Cyran shook his head until a gap opened in the furs and he could see part of his surroundings again.

The Dragon Queen faced a group of soldiers who formed ranks around her. "Where is the genturion of all this?"

"There are many genturions here," one soldier answered.

"Then who is acting as the arch genturion?" Her tone sharpened. "Find him and bring him here at once."

The soldier ducked his head in subservience and ran off. The Dragon Queen waited as her archers milled about Shadowmar, talking quietly until a man in violet and blue armor strode from the ranks that formed a half circle around them.

"Dragon Queen." The man carried his helm cradled against his side. His face was clean-shaven, his hair steel gray. "We did not know you would be arriving."

"And you are?"

"Genturion Ravenscroft."

"Under whose orders did you assemble this"—the Dragon Queen glanced about the area—"army?"

His face paled. "Northsheeren's, my Dragon Queen."

"By Northsheeren, do you mean the deceased King Restebarge or Queen Elra?"

Ravenscroft shook his head. "The new king. Restebarge's brother, Oomaren."

"Oomaren is not the rightful king of Murgare. If anyone was going to take the throne during my absence, it should have been the princess, Kyelle."

"Oomaren is overseeing her rule, given her age."

"Is that so?" The Dragon Queen's suspicion spiced her words. "And Oomaren is still residing at Northsheeren under the protection of the onyx guard?"

Ravenscroft nodded.

"What are your orders in regard to departing these shores and initiating war?"

"We are to gather all the clans and armies and legions of Murgare and stock the warships as quickly and as best as we are able. The command for advancement could come at any time."

"Then I command you not to sail the warships or fly the dragons at least until I have returned. You must only obey orders from the new queen, Kyelle. Not Oomaren."

The genturion swallowed, conflicted as to what he should say or do. "Where will you be traveling?"

"To Northsheeren."

The Dragon Queen turned, but the genturion cleared his throat and spoke. "If you could, you may want to pay a visit to the dwarves of Darynbroad. They are upset over something... again. And not only are they asserting that they will not march to the north shore to join our ranks, they are also threatening that they may initiate the war themselves if no one of significant standing comes to speak with them directly."

The Dragon Queen paused for a moment. Cyran could almost feel her eyes close in regret or frustration, and she might have released a sigh of contempt. She scaled her stirrup ladder and motioned for her archers to return to their stations.

"We fly north."

∼

Stone peaks whipped past as Shadowmar soared along into the northwest, the air's cold bite growing stronger even though it was barely past midday.

The dragon dropped in altitude, making Cyran's stomach lurch, as he was not prepared. The shadow dragon flared her wings and beat them against the wind, flapping faster as she alighted in a ravine hidden within the rocky mountains. A fresh layer of snow dusted the area and its knuckles of protruding boulders.

"What is it, Dragon Queen?" a female archer from the turret shouted up.

"Shadowmar grows hungry." The Dragon Queen paced rearward along the dragon's neck and stepped onto the quarterdeck. "There's something lurking farther up this ravine."

The bearded archer grumbled. "All we've eaten since we departed Northsheeren for the outpost is dried out cheese, smoked meat, and old bread. Maybe there will be enough for all of us."

You also dined on all of Nevergrace's stored foods. Cyran silently cursed them as he studied the ravine. He needed to escape, but out here—even if he found an opportunity—he feared he would only die from the elements. Were they near the Valley of the Smoke Breathers? It all appeared so barren, similar to most of the lands they had flown over since arriving at the north shore of the lake. Rumors that the north harbored vast riches exceeding the imagination seemed exaggerated. Beyond the immediate vicinity of the lake, their kingdom looked desolate.

"Relieve yourselves." The archer cut the bonds tying Cyran to his companions and jerked Ineri to her feet. He pointed to the rope ladder as he retied their hands in front of them. "And be quick about it."

Cyran stood and stretched. Vyk led Ineri to the ladder, both of them watching the archers and the Dragon Queen warily. The archers followed them. The Dragon Queen grasped the mounted crossbow on the left side of the quarterdeck and swung it around, aiming it northward.

In the distance, water as clear as crystal flowed over a lip on the rock cliffs and plummeted into a pool. The blue of the water, the white dusting of snow, and the stark rock created a place of tranquil and striking if not stern beauty. How did such a place exist in the dark and barren north?

Cyran shuffled closer to the Dragon Queen, suppressing his

rage and loathing for this malevolent woman so his emotions would not sheet off him. If he could kill her, even if it cost him his life, he would gladly take the opportunity. Such action could save all of Belvenguard—not to mention fulfill the need for revenge for the people of Nevergrace, including Sirs Ymar and Kayom.

"It flows into the River of the Helm." The Dragon's Queen voice was quiet as she released the tension on the crossbow's rope.

Cyran stiffened. She couldn't read his thoughts, could she? But she could feel the other realm and might be able to get a sense for his emotions, although Cyran thought that was only possible between a person and dragon who were bonded.

"You're referring to that blue mountain water?" Cyran stepped closer. "Then it must also drain into the Lake on Fire."

The Dragon Queen did not face him, but she nodded. "Of course." She pulled a thin training bolt from a stack of projectiles and loaded it onto the arms of the ballista.

The shadow dragon slinked forward, jostling the quarterdeck, her wings tucked as she crouched as low as she could without crushing the turrets beneath her belly. Her massive feet lifted, advanced, and settled in slow movements.

Cyran froze. Across the landscape in the distance, a creature crept between brush standing as tall as it. It paced away from the waterfall. Cyran squinted and leaned closer. It was an elk, but its coat was as black as night. Cyran's hair blew from behind him and across his cheeks. He stepped nearer to the Dragon Queen.

"The wind blows from the south," Cyran muttered. "This creature will catch your dragon's scent and flee up into the valley away from us."

Shadowmar crept farther along, her talons punching holes in the fresh snow, creating nothing more than a whisper. Cyran held his breath, and in less than five minutes after he last spoke, the brush obscuring the elk rustled in the wind. A plume of snow dust streaked from branches, and the elk froze in mid-step. Its eyes grew wide as it glanced about and sniffed the air. Cyran couldn't help but smirk.

The elk turned and bolted, making bounding leaps through the snow and over the terrain. But the creature did not flee directly away from them, nor did it run at them. It ran at an angle along the steep walls of the ravine, trying to pass between them and the ravine's entrance.

The Dragon Queen barely twitched, but the rope of the massive crossbow snapped forward and its arms thrummed. The bolt streaked away in a blur. A thud sounded, and in mid stride, the bounding elk went limp and collapsed in a heap. The Dragon Queen descended the quarterdeck and paced away after her quarry.

Cyran hurried down the rope ladder, trailing the Dragon Queen, his footsteps much louder than hers. When she reached the elk that was three times the size of any elk Cyran had seen, she easily rolled the creature onto its side, as if it weighed only as much as a dog. The exit wound from her bolt gave the impression that some creature had been birthed inside its chest and torn its way out.

The power of the mounted crossbow and the wound it created imprinted itself in Cyran's mind. Such ballistae could hurl projectiles with enough velocity that even a simple training bolt would butcher any creature not protected by dragon scale.

And she hit it directly in the heart. The Dragon Queen had handled a crossbow with masterful accuracy, but only against a fleeing elk, and her dragon had not been flying. Maybe when flying, she had difficulty hitting targets. As far as Cyran had seen, she never manned a crossbow in battle and left that up to her archers.

"That is a blade tree and its creeping tendrils." The Dragon

Queen nodded toward the falls as she pulled out a knife and began dressing the animal, starting with an incision along the middle of its belly. A snow-covered tree resided in the only gap leading north from the falls, its trunk surrounded by brush. Vines ran from the tree into and through the bushes at its base. "The tree and its tendrils came to Murgare no more than a decade ago. It crept out of the Evenmeres and spreads northward."

Cyran remained silent, unsure if she would blame Belvenguard or the Evenmeres for the tree's appearance.

"Its leaves are like blades, and the wild animals have learned to never run through it," she continued as she worked, not facing Cyran. "Not even if a dragon is about."

She knew the elk would not flee into the valley beyond. Cyran swallowed any smugness he had experienced when he predicted that the elk would flee northward.

The Dragon Queen cut off a forelimb and stuffed the entrails back into the elk's abdomen, making Cyran wonder why she had done any of it. She grabbed its two hind limbs, muttered a word under her breath, and began to drag the carcass back to Shadowmar.

"The beast is massive," Cyran said. "I could help you pull it." He held his bound hands out.

The Dragon Queen didn't seem interested in taking him up on his offer. "How is your shoulder?"

My shoulder? His thoughts trailed back to their last encounter and their tilt in the sky. Afterward, his shoulder had ached immensely until one of the guard performed what he called the Bleedstrom technique and reduced his dislocated shoulder. The Dragon Queen knew she hit him hard, even though she was not prepared for him to be immune to the magic she called up from the dragon realm.

"It is fine," he finally answered, concealing his rage. "How is your body? After the fall through the trees?"

"Healed." She slowly turned to study him. "I will not make that mistake again."

Now that she realized his abilities associated with the *neblír*, he would not have any advantage over her, and he lacked her power and experience. "My shoulder is healed as well."

"If you dislocate it once, it is easier to dislocate again."

Another emotion bit into her last words, making her statement seem like a threat suggesting where she would focus any torture on him. Cyran remained silent. Since the battle at the outpost, his shoulder had mended, but the thought of her twisting his arm until his shoulder popped out again made the roots of his teeth ache.

"Your dragon's eye will not heal," Cyran muttered.

The Dragon Queen whipped around and grabbed him by the throat, hurling him into the snow and frozen ground with the strength of a giant. His back smacked into something hard, and the air in his lungs burst from his mouth with a huff. He lay there and groaned before trying to roll about and climb to his feet.

"Do not believe for one minute that I will not eventually kill you." The Dragon Queen resumed dragging the elk's carcass away.

Cyran's back throbbed, but he found a knee and faced her. "What did you expect to happen? *You* took over the outpost. My home!"

She didn't respond.

"My sister and friends were still there," Cyran said, "and you were sacrificing them."

She stopped and stood straighter but still faced away from him. "Your people ambushed and killed many of my people, including my king and queen."

"The queen was taken to Galvenstone." Cyran's cheeks felt as if flame scorched them. "*Your* kingdom's assassin killed her."

The Dragon Queen dropped the elk and turned around, studying him. The black horns on her helm made her look demonic and threatening, and he feared she might kill him here.

"Then it is confirmed," she said. "Queen Elra is also dead."

Cyran cursed the Assassin under his breath. He shouldn't have let his anger get the best of him. The Dragon Queen still had not known for sure that her queen was dead.

"The lies of kings." She shook her head. "We could all be subject to them." She paused for a breath. "I recall that not long ago I encountered you when you were in a turret below a forest dragon, then on the quarterdeck of another. Next, you were stationed as an unarmored guard. Most recently, a dragonknight. Yours is the fastest rise I've ever witnessed."

"I did what was necessary to save my outpost and my people. And I'd do it all over again if I had to."

"But that is not the only reason why your advancement has been rushed. Belvenguard is worried it will not be able to defend itself from our coming legions. They must induct new guard and archers as quickly as possible." The tilt of her head made it seem likely that she was smirking wryly beneath her helm. "If only your king could find more mages and more scaly mounts now that the hatcheries are empty and Belvenguard and Galvenstone have lost the ability to breed and raise dragons in captivity."

A jolt of shock struck Cyran's heart and rumbled through his chest before a cold stillness followed. *No more dragons?* He shook his head. It was probably a lie meant to further frighten him.

The Dragon Queen said, "And now that the Sky Sea Pearl is in the hands of the vile Harrowed, we shall see if either of our kingdoms will survive, if either of our methods of commanding dragons shall allow us to prevail and live on in Cimeren. The survivors of the Dragon Wars once made such promises of triumph and long life to all posterity. At least until the day comes when an elf rides a dragon and the world ends, so they say."

Cyran was too stunned to speak, and he didn't want to give away any more information. He feared he had already been baited into revealing that the Murgare queen was indeed dead.

"The Harrowed King may rule us all before long." The Dragon Queen turned and dragged the carcass away again. "The legend of his curse, from the time of the Dragon Wars, insists he cannot be killed except by the hand of one of his own." When she reached Shadowmar, she placed the dead animal before her dragon and held its limb out to the bearded archer, who had built a fire. "Yenthor. For the crew."

The archer grinned and took the offering. He fashioned a spit out of a downed branch beneath the snow and began roasting their meal. The other archers gathered around.

A roar sounded, and black fire spewed from the shadow dragon, engulfing the remainder of the elk carcass. Vyk shrieked from somewhere nearby and leapt back, tripping and stumbling before crashing into the snow.

The dragon lunged out and snatched up the carcass with her teeth, chomping on it as she lifted her head and swallowed several times, working to get the entire thing down her gullet.

As night descended around them, Cyran waited in silence, considering running off over the walls of the ravine or up the valley, but if the blade tree's leaves didn't get him, the cold surely would. He also didn't want to sacrifice Ineri and Vyk by leaving them to the Dragon Queen. However, if he found an opportunity to potentially warn his kingdom and save it, he would be a fool not to take it. He would probably suffer with guilt for his comrades the rest of his life, but his friends, his people, and Jaslin might then survive.

The Dragon Queen removed her helm, and her long brown hair fell around her shoulders as she watched the fire. She was beautiful and only appeared to be in her late third decade of life, an impossibility considering the tales surrounding her.

"For the time being, it does not matter as much to me what the Harrowed King holds, dragonknight," she said without looking back at him. "The murdered souls of my king and queen must be avenged so they do not continue to suffer within the abode of the sky sea. Until justice has been served, Belvenguard is still my primary enemy."

19

SIRRA BRACKENGLAVE

Shadowmar crested the snowy peaks and sailed on into Darynbroad. The Stonelands spread out below them in a massive swath, extending all the way to the Eventide Sea, which glittered with morning light and mist.

The land of the dwarves. Sirra did not want her captives to see more of Murgare nor her kingdom's gathering armies and dragons but, at best, those three would live in the dungeons of Northsheeren until the war was over. Then they would only be freed *if* Belvenguard somehow won such a war and found them. Even more likely, they would be sentenced to death or would reside in their cells for the rest of their short lives.

Shadowmar's simmering rage roiled through the other realm.

"We must keep these prisoners with us." Sirra laid a hand on the dragon's ebony scales. *"Even the one who destroyed your eggs and whose archer took your eye."*

Shadowmar shrieked, and her blast rolled out over the Stonelands.

"Keep your wrath in check, my beast. I do not trust any others to

watch over a dragonknight. He could escape. I would also rather not succumb to my emotions and kill him. He could still become a great ally... if we could train him in the art of the elder magic. I doubt there are many, if any, still alive in Belvenguard who can control and wield it. If he desires its power, I could tempt him in the process—change him. He is young and still malleable."

A memory of herself wearing the white armor and riding her snow dragon of old lanced through her thoughts, but the armor quickly crumbled and broke away, revealing the black steel beneath.

Shadowmar swooped north. The glow of vast forges shone from inside the ice-armored mountains ahead, spewing their orange light across a valley.

"But if the time comes and he resists, I will allow you to finish him," Sirra continued to her mount.

"More legions?" Disbelief bit into the young dragonknight's hoarse whisper, but his words carried distinctly to Sirra's ears. "Surely Murgare cannot have so many dragons still waiting to join its ranks."

"The firelight is from the Mines of Skorlar." Sirra did not turn around. "The dwarven stronghold."

Cyran fell silent as they swung lower. A mass of soldiers filled the snow-dusted valley. Hundreds of small brown and white speckled dragons with curled horns drifted about the cliffsides, freighting a dwarf or two to various locations. Sirra angled Shadowmar into a steeper dive, and the ranks of armored dwarves shifted, creating an area for them to land.

One of the pygmy dragons fluttered its wings and zipped away from the cliff, heading toward Shadowmar. Sirra waited, feigning patience until the dwarven genturion arrived. A dwarf seated in front of his dragonmage stepped up onto platforms in his short stirrups, his silver armor and helm appearing radiant in dawn's light. He stood proudly, and Sirra had her mount crouch lower so the dwarf could appear taller than her.

"Dragon Queen." The genturion briefly dipped his head in acknowledgment but not subservience, his braided brown beard dangling past his waist.

"Genturion King Westfahl." Sirra bowed her head respectfully. "I received word that the dwarves of Darynbroad have requested to speak with the Murgare king or someone of close ranking."

"It would be truer to say 'demanded to speak with the king.'" Westfahl turned his head and spat over his dragon's side. "We were asked to prepare our legions for the ensuing war. That was all the message said." He paused. *"What bloody war?"* A sliver of exposed cheek above his beard purpled. "The dwarves of Darynbroad will not be jerked around by Northsheeren. We are our own kingdom and are not under your king's rule."

"Indeed, Genturion Westfahl. No one would assume otherwise."

He huffed. "We better not have amassed all of our soldiers for simple training. Dwarves do not need additional training. The regimens we uphold for our kind are very strict. So if the southern kingdoms march, we must know. No more of these secretive messages being passed along by storm dragons!" He reached to his belt, yanked out a parchment, and tore it to shreds. "We dwarves *must* also be privy to the full extent of Murgare's knowledge and understanding of any situation if you expect aid from our mighty warriors."

Sirra glanced about the ranks of dwarves standing at attention but pretending not to be interested in their conversation. Behind the nearest ranks, a dark gray dragon with two sets of colossal wings waited. The dragon was of the largest type of all the land dragon species.

"She is an absolute beauty." Sirra nodded toward the cave dragon. "And she makes her distant stone dragon cousins pale in comparison."

Westfahl stuttered a few times before he also turned to regard the dragon. "Well, that she is." His chest swelled as he ran a few fingers along the braid of his beard. "It took us over a decade to dig her out from the lowest caverns of Skorlar. Finally freed her no more than a year ago. The finest cave dragon we've ever released from the mountain. She must be several millennia old—spent most of those years growing and sleeping and digging new caverns."

Ten dwarven crossbows with immense metal arms were mounted on the dragon's quarterdeck along with twin catapults. Probably another five crossbows were fitted into the turret below the beast. "She is utterly massive."

"And strong and bold. The legions of the south will fold before her. She is *my* new mount."

"In her shadow, any would become weak with fear."

Westfahl beamed.

"It is beneficial that the largest of their kind can nourish themselves with nothing more than rock," Sirra said.

Westfahl's face darkened. "It is more than simple rock." He motioned around him. "You cannot wander about Cimeren, pick up any old rock, and throw it to her like the bone of some sheep to a mine wolf." He took a deep breath. "It is only the heart stones of these mountains that feed and satiate her. She could never have grown so large otherwise." After a brief pause, he muttered, "Perhaps the boulders of the Stonelands could feed her as well. When needed. But surely nothing else."

Sirra concealed her amusement. Thankfully, she was still wearing her helm. "You have done well, Genturion King Westfahl. How many cave dragons are at your disposal?" She had counted at least five in the area.

Westfahl folded his arms across his chest. "That information is privy to only the dwarves. For now. But I believe you are here to tell me more, which must happen long before I shall disclose any more of our great strengths."

Sirra nodded. "You deserve that, the king and his free peoples of Darynbroad."

"Damn right we do. We try to remain on friendly terms with Murgare and the barbarian Smoke Breathers who occasionally wander over the mountains and into our lands, but I am finding it more and more difficult to do so in these past years. I am not suggesting we will commence war with Murgare, but we have earned our respect and must be kept abreast of any matters we are asked to assist with."

"You certainly deserve respect, and I apologize on the part of Northsheeren for not informing you sooner."

"Indeed we do deserve..." The king's harsh expression relaxed as much as could be expected for this particular dwarf. "What did you say?"

"I understand your concerns. I have been away on other matters but will travel to Northsheeren as soon as we are done speaking. I will meet with the..." She nearly mentioned Restebarge's and Elra's deaths, but Westfahl had probably not heard of either. How would he react if he found out that his correspondence with Northsheeren had been with an illegitimate king? "I will meet with the queen upon my arrival."

A second pygmy dragon flew up beside the dwarf king's. A taller dwarf holding an axe and dragonbolt across his shoulder stepped onto the raised footholds in his guard's saddle so that he stood over Sirra. The dragon beneath the dwarf wavered a little to one side, and the dwarf wheeled an arm to maintain his balance, almost dropping his axe in the process.

"I told you to hold position, you stubborn beast." The dwarf glared down at the pygmy, his cheeks reddening as he shifted in his stirrups and slowly straightened again to his full height. The dwarf then looked up and scrutinized Sirra for a moment before speaking to the king. "Some of the mountain dragons"—no dwarf referred to their small mounts as pygmies—"grow uneasy with this shadow dragon lingering about. They fear it was sent in a vain attempt to intimidate us rather than for respectful negotiations."

"I apologize for my dragon's appearance, master dwarf." Sirra bowed her head to the new arrival. "I was the swiftest emissary Murgare had, and I shall be leaving soon enough."

The armed dwarf glared at her. Resentment burned beneath his red-bearded cheeks and dark eyes.

"This is Genturion Master Dahroon." Westfahl gestured at the dwarf. "He is our first-ranked battlemage. A dwarf to be feared."

Sirra nodded. Then this dwarf was a conjuror, but he was also strong and skilled with weapons and in combat, something akin to a dragonknight but without the dragon. The elves had even managed to teach some of the dwarves the ways of their magic before they were nearly all wiped from the face of Cimeren.

"He is our most experienced and adroit battlemage when fighting on dragonback," Westfahl added.

"I will surely not prod him into a duel." Sirra removed her helm, and her locks tumbled over her shoulders.

The two dwarves stared at her in surprise, and the battlemage's posture faltered, his knees buckling. Dahroon's mage and dragon remained completely still, but Dahroon folded his thick leg on top of his saddle and rested his shin there as he partially sat. The dwarves looked upon Sirra for nearly a minute before recovering and clearing their throats and grumbling awkwardly.

Sirra hid her escalating amusement. Most dwarves were fools for beauty, perhaps because their kind carried so little of it.

Dahroon cursed, "My damn beast won't allow me to stand properly. Keeps shifting around... in this wind—probably because he's nervous being next to this shadow dragon." He cursed again, but this time more quietly, and then said, "I am sorry, Dragon Queen." He bowed. "I did not intend to insult a lady such as you this day."

"You did not," she replied. "And I am no lady."

The dwarves shared a glance.

"King Westfahl," Sirra said as gently as she could manage, "I hope you and your legions will join us at the north shore soon, as Belvenguard prepares for war, but I must clarify one detail before I fly to Northsheeren. You said you received word of war from the king." She paused.

Westfahl slowly nodded in confused acknowledgment.

"Were the messages signed by the king, with his name?" Sirra asked.

"I believe so. There were some scribbles at the bottom of them along with the word 'king.'"

"But you could not read whose name was signed?"

Westfahl scoffed and then sputtered. "You are asking *which* king signed the parchments? By all the bloody rivers in Murgare, the dwarves are not so far out of earshot from your kingdom. Restebarge is still king of Northsheeren." His confidence fluttered. "No?"

Sirra allowed her eyes to settle closed. She should not lie to him or, soon enough, she would have to start all over with appeasing him. "King Restebarge was killed when Belvenguard dragons ambushed his legion, attempting to abduct him and Queen Elra. This all happened"—she paused, thinking about the duration as well as hoping to ease the surprise of how long it had really been—"perhaps two or three months ago now."

"Buggering shit on the Great Dwarf's bloody anvil!" Westfahl's upper lip curled.

The battlemage beside him huffed and fumed, smacking a palm down against his mount's neck. The pygmy lurched, throwing Dahroon back and causing the dwarf to struggle to maintain his balance.

"Murgare and Northsheeren have not officially appointed our new king or queen," Sirra said. "Not as of yet."

"A bloody lying bastard has been sending us orders?" The words spewed from Westfahl's lips as he resumed a spittle-laced rant. "This would-be king lied to me and my dwarves through a messenger." He shuffled his feet about on the small platforms, acting as if he wanted to storm around and pace but could not. "Who is this man?"

"Oomaren. King Restebarge's brother. His ascension to the throne would only become legitimate if Kyelle were also dead. She is not, or better not be. I apologize for any deception. That is why I am here and why I will soon be on my way to Northsheeren." Sirra paused for effect. "But before I fly, I must know—if Princess Kyelle is appointed as the new queen of Murgare, will the dwarves honor her rule?"

Curses continued to rain for several minutes before the king regained a shred of composure, his face still flushed. The battlemage clenched a fist, and violet flames spurted from each end of his hand. He lowered the weapons he carried on his shoulder and lit the tip of the dragonbolt with his flames, the flames of a conjuror. The broadhead snapped and crackled with eerie fire, and suddenly the amusing dwarf's appearance swung across the spectrum and seemed utterly dangerous.

"I cannot make any promises to Murgare now." Westfahl's shoulders heaved along with his chest. "But I do wish to have a talk with this Oomaren. Face-to-face."

"I will arrange the meeting." Sirra gave the dwarves a

promising grin. "Have only a bit of patience, if you can. I will ask nothing more of you. But if you join Murgare's legions outside of Icetooth before it becomes time to fly south, you will have your best chance of speaking with Oomaren. Otherwise, I swear to you, I will make sure you meet each other when the war is over."

20

CYRAN ORENDAIN

The keening wind hurled balls of ice at Cyran's cheeks and eyes as he attempted to watch the lands below. Ineri coughed and sputtered. She shivered and pressed herself closer to Cyran, tugging their furs tighter around them.

Days of flying had already passed as they crossed the mountain range of the dwarves, heading east beyond the Lake of the Lady and then following the Dragonback Mountains north. They were supposedly heading to Northsheeren, the heart of Murgare and its ancient evil.

Cyran studied all he could of the lands whipping past, although much was blurred by rain and sleet, and what he could see was speckled or fully covered in snow. However, he would take every opportunity to learn what he could about this kingdom—how to find his way back to the Lake on Fire, and to Darynbroad, and how they traveled to Northsheeren. All these things could become important when the war on the lake was over and Belvenguard had hopefully defeated their enemies there and could then march north and crush the last of the infamous dark legions and lords of the north.

Cyran's teeth chattered. Either the shadow dragon's body

heat hardly carried over the quarterdeck at these speeds, or the cold was so severe it did not matter. Sleet pelted him, pinging off the planks around them and off the dragon's wings. Twin curtains of rain loomed ahead, and Shadowmar bore straight through them, the icy precipitation striking and washing over the deck, soaking everything.

This will all be worth it once I discover any weaknesses that Northsheeren has.

Ineri moaned and fell over, collapsing in the wash of water rippling across the deck.

"Ineri?" Cyran asked as he shook her. "Ineri!" He glanced at the archers. "She will die in this storm."

The bearded archer seemed to snarl at Cyran from beneath his helm, equivalent emotions radiating from his demeanor and the words he shouted over the storm. "Prisoners and spies from Belvenguard do not dictate how the Dragon Queen travels." He returned his attention forward. "Help her survive for another half hour, and then she may find relief."

Cyran's fury sizzled anew inside him and beat at his heart with fiery fists. Damn these coldhearted Murgare bastards. But what had he been hoping for? Once he was in their clutches, he did not expect to survive. Even if they were to be held captive at Northsheeren, they would remain there until they died, if Murgare continued to hold power in the north.

Cyran hunched over Ineri, and Vyk pressed himself against her other side, both of them enshrouding her in as much warmth as they could manage. The sleet and rain pummeled them.

Eventually, Shadowmar circled and descended. Cyran lifted his head and peeked over the dragon's sides. A gush of white smoke rose from somewhere below and melted against the sheets of rain.

When Shadowmar landed, her talons grated against wet rock.

"Dead captives are no good to us." The Dragon Queen trod across the quarterdeck and untied Cyran and his companions. "We cannot learn anything from them. Go. Follow Yenthor and Zaldica."

Cyran and Vyk hefted Ineri to her feet and dragged her along as she wheezed for breath and sputtered a few times. Together, they used her harness and a rope to lower her from the quarterdeck.

When Cyran and his companions stood on the ground, the Dragon Queen pointed off to one side. "Take her into the water."

A sense of wariness burgeoned inside Cyran. "Then she will surely freeze to death." The white smoke he had seen earlier plumed from the area the Dragon Queen was indicating.

"The water is hot."

Cyran's brow wrinkled. He had never heard of any natural water being hot. It seemed more likely this was a Murgare trick meant to deceive them and then destroy their resolve by tricking Cyran and Vyk into essentially killing their own comrade.

"On the coldest of winter days, I've seen the river breathe white smoke," Cyran said. "It occurs when the air is at its coldest and driest. Such fog does not mean the water is warm."

The Dragon Queen began stripping off her armor and dropping its plates onto the rock around her. Her archers followed her lead until they wore nothing more than their leathers, then only their undergarments. Without hesitation, they even removed those. The hairy chests and muscled backs of men stood out against the pale and lithe female figures as they all strode toward the smoke, acting almost as if they were undead beings immune to the cold.

Cyran stared dumbfounded at the scene before his attention

settled on the Dragon Queen's backside just as that portion of her body slipped below the surface of the water.

"You should get your archer into the water, or she will not survive the last leg of the journey north." The Dragon Queen motioned over her shoulder to them.

Vyk tugged Ineri along, and Cyran blinked to dispel his surprise as his companion said, "We have to get her in."

Cyran assisted Ineri with walking, and when they approached a second steaming pool almost touching the one the Murgare soldiers had entered, Cyran grasped Ineri by the hand and helped guide her in.

"Do not put her in the water with her leathers on"—the Dragon Queen did not turn around, staring directly away from them into the steam—"or she will have no dry clothing to change into and, once we are in the sky again, she will freeze."

"Her leathers are already wet," Cyran said. "It should not matter."

"They will dry here." The Dragon Queen waved nonchalantly. "Just remove them and get her in the pool. Your stalling is making her all the weaker."

Cyran glanced about as Ineri hunched over and wheezed. There were no fires around, nothing to dry wet leathers that would be sitting out under the rain.

Vyk grunted and hesitantly began untying Ineri's tunic. Cyran forced a deep breath before working on her leggings, keeping his eyes closed as much as he could until he had to tug and work the rumpling leathers over her waist and thighs. The wet clothing bunched but slid off her emaciated frame without as much of a struggle as he was anticipating.

When Ineri was stark naked, the slats of her ribs stood out like rungs on a ladder, and they heaved as she coughed. Her breasts were nonexistent, the knobs of bone along her back protruding from lack of fat and muscle. She was even paler than the people of Murgare. Cyran realized he was staring with a sickly shock, and he looked away. He stepped into the pool, his foot sinking until the water rose to his knee. Heat drove itself against his skin as the water bubbled. He stared at the pool in wonder. How could water residing in the frigid regions of the world carry such warmth?

He held Ineri's hand and arm as he and Vyk eased her in. After everything but her face and head were submerged, she sighed, closed her eyes, and leaned back against the lip of the pool. Vyk's hairy legs, chest, and back appeared like an animal's before he dropped into the water in front of Cyran, creating a small geyser and propelling waves out over the rocks around them.

Cyran stepped out and shed his armor and leathers before reentering the pool. An almost scalding heat enveloped his legs, wrapping them in an uncomfortable and yet welcoming embrace. He lowered himself in, and the water rose beyond his waist and chest. Its warmth pounded against his flesh and rippled through his cold limbs and muscles. His eyes settled closed, and soon, the only unpleasant sensation he noticed was a smell of rotten eggs that hovered above the water. The voices of the Murgare soldiers faded to a murmur, one that was barely discernible over the roar of the rain as it struck rock. Cyran strained his ears, attempting to eavesdrop on their conversation, but he could only pick up a word here and there, not enough to learn anything of importance. His muscles relaxed, and he may have drifted off to sleep.

A slurping gurgle sounded nearby, and one of Cyran's eyelids slipped open. Vyk stroked through the middle of the pool, sucking in mouthfuls of water.

"What are you doing?" Cyran lifted his head to get a better look at the archer.

"Drinking." Vyk wiped at his mouth with the back of his

hand. "I've been dying of thirst since the day after we were taken. Been limiting how much I swallow from what they offer us. Theirs is probably some concoction meant to make us spill our guts or go mad enough that we'll want to leap straight off a quarterdeck."

Cyran sniffed at the odor rising from the water. "Does it taste fine?"

Vyk shook his head. "It's got an unpleasant aftertaste, but it goes down fine." He took another guzzling drink.

The walls of Cyran's throat felt parched, and the sensation intensified the more he watched Vyk drink. Cyran lowered his lips into the water and took a sip. The rotten egg smell permeated his nostrils as he forced a swallow. He grimaced at the foul aftertaste.

"You should not drink water from the pools." The Dragon Queen's voice carried over.

"You see?" Vyk's eyebrow crept up his forehead. "They want us drinking only theirs. I've already ingested enough that a little more won't hurt me, and I feel fine."

Cyran considered the possibilities.

"This water may make you sick," the Dragon Queen added. "If you are not used to drinking it. Things you cannot see could grow in it, and the sulfur content can make those who consume it ill. We have clean water for you, and you may have some once we mount up again."

Vyk raised a hand over his head and waved, acknowledging her advice, but to Cyran, he whispered, "I'd rather take my chances with this water."

Cyran allowed the rain to run down his hair and face and sipped at that, but it was not enough to quench his thirst. Since becoming captives on Shadowmar, they had only been offered water with their small meals around dawn and dusk. He took another sip from the pool.

"Do you think we have any chance at escape?" Vyk asked.

Cyran hesitated before glancing at Ineri, who appeared to be sleeping, and slowly shook his head. "They will use us to learn what they can. If we give them nothing, they should keep us alive. If we cannot resist their tortures or magical manipulations and tell them everything we know, we are as good as dead."

Vyk pursed his lips. A roar and crackle blasted behind them, and Vyk leapt from the water, flailing with his arms before falling back down and plunging beneath the surface. The bubbles of his scream erupted over the area where he was submerged.

Not far away, the massive shadow dragon blew out a breath of black fire, but her target was not clear. The flames gushed through the air and over the rocks behind them, but nothing was there.

Cyran's lungs burned with the need for air as he stared, wondering if the beast was threatening them or might try to boil them alive in the pool. The black fire sizzled and then snuffed out, leaving only billowing clouds of smoke. The rains swept past them and carried north, leaving nothing more than scattered drops. Cyran absently gasped to relieve the burning in his chest.

"Do not fret, captives from Belvenguard," the Dragon Queen said. "Now that the rains are passing, my beast heats the rocks and air to dry all of our leathers and armor. It is the quickest and most effective way of accomplishing the task."

Cyran's nerves settled, and Vyk's eyes surfaced. After glancing around, the archer lifted his head from the water and heaved for breath. Ineri had barely cracked an eyelid.

Several minutes passed before Vyk calmed down and leaned back against the wall of the pool. Cyran studied his companions as the uncertainty of their future and his role in landing them in this situation piled up inside him. He tried to shake the thoughts, but he could not. Tiny blue lights from glow flies erupted and sizzled out around them as the insects danced about the area after the rain.

"I drink before battle." Vyk's eyes were closed, but he seemed to be making a confession.

Cyran waited a few heartbeats. "You did so prior to our attempt to reclaim Nevergrace?"

Vyk nodded.

"I smelled alcohol on you," Cyran said.

"Drinking helps me find my immense rage." He shrugged. "Rage that is usually buried too deep for me to call up. It's the only way I know to face battle. But I won't ever be needing it again."

"Doesn't drink affect your ability with the crossbow?"

"Probably. But not as much as when I do not drink."

Cyran's forehead wrinkled in confusion. "And how does that make sense?"

Vyk sucked in a deep breath and slowly blew it out. "I've never told anyone this, but as we won't be seeing Belvenguard again, I don't know how it matters. I was a young lad when I was thrown into my first battle on dragonback. I had proven myself with the bow and had trained hard and did not get motion sickness even during the most aggressive flights and maneuvers. Then I was placed with a legion that was to voyage north for a small surveying expedition. Once we crossed the spires, a Murgare battalion showed up almost immediately." He paused, and his tone turned distant, as if sounding from years ago and he told what he saw before him. "The dragons... Fire. Ice. Mist." His lips trembled, and his eyes rolled around beneath their lids. "Turning. Twisting. Diving. Bolts raining all around." He shuddered. "I shit myself, I did."

Cyran laughed once before he could stop himself.

"It's no jape, and no laughing matter," Vyk continued. "Not

when evil dragons hurtle toward you at enormous speeds with teeth and claws and a lance all bent on tearing you apart. No amount of training can prepare you for real war." He swallowed. "We fled, and my comrades and I survived, but I had to toss my leathers. I think they all knew what happened, as the old guard soon told a story of his first dragon battle in the skies and how he pissed himself."

The glow flies popped with light as a quiet settled and dragged on.

"I was also terrified." Cyran recalled his first experience—being ordered into the turret and having to remove the body of an archer who had been killed, and then taking the dead man's place. He had never flown on a dragon before, not even for training. He had to quickly pull himself into the harness and bootstraps, and he proceeded to shoot out one of the poles of the turret's frame, making the turret even more wobbly than it had already been. "I never wanted anything more in my life than to be a guard or archer, to join the ranks of legendary men such as Sir Bleedstrom, but suddenly I found myself disoriented and I almost vomited."

"Consider yourself lucky. Before every battle or archer venture I've been part of since that day, I drink. And I drink heavily. It's the drink that's allowed me to unleash a fury I didn't know I had. When I am intoxicated to a good measure and focused on decimating the evils of this world, I do not know fear."

Cyran mulled that over. The archer's explanation certainly fit with what Cyran had experienced beside Vyk. None of it seemed like a good idea, but the alternative could be worse, if he was so terrified he could not even man a crossbow. The potential reasons why these two archers were placed with him ran through his thoughts again.

"I believed I wanted the same things you did—to be an

archer or a guard." Vyk eyes squeezed shut. "Now, only something deep inside of me can handle the grimness and horror of war upon dragons. Don't have enough Smoke Breather blood in me, I guess."

Another stilted silence followed before Cyran said, "We must have flown near to the Valley of the Smoke Breathers on our way here."

"Mad dragon worshippers, those lot are." Vyk didn't move. "I don't know that I want to meet any of them, but I'd like to have laid eyes on Frozen Fist Mountain and the site of the first taming before I die."

Longing tugged at Cyran's heart as he imagined what it might have been like to go on a quest in the icy north to locate and tame the first dragon. *The men who altered the fate of all of Cimeren and beyond.*

"Did you notice the other forge fires on the far side of the dwarves' mountains?" Vyk asked.

Cyran absently nodded. "I assumed it was more dwarves within another stronghold."

"Nay. Dwarves stay in Darynbroad. Those were Murgare forges, likely working all hours of the night and day arming and armoring their warriors and dragons."

"The fires seen from the other side of the mountain range come from the mines of our kingdom." The Dragon Queen glanced over at them from behind a curtain of steam, her hair soaked and clinging to her flushed cheeks. "The dwarven mountains are rich in minerals and wealth. We mine them in areas that rightfully belong to Murgare."

"I've heard they use dwarven slaves to do their quarrying," Vyk whispered to Cyran.

"There are dwarves inside our mines, but they are not slaves," the Dragon Queen said, and Vyk flinched. "Their kind have grown too plentiful in Darynbroad, and many seek work in Murgare."

Vyk scowled in disbelief as he shook his head but remained quiet. After the Murgare soldiers returned to their own conversation, Vyk added in a hushed voice, "That is why the north is so wealthy. They quarry riches—gold and silver and platinum—from vast sources. Murgare's side of the mountains are said to carry three times more ore than the other."

Cyran imagined the mines burrowing into the roots of the mountains, their forge fires blazing in the deeps, melting and purifying ore. No wonder Murgare had so much—people, dragons, wealth, food, and other resources—in a land so barren. Theirs was ancient wealth. They could trade with any kingdom overseas that did not know of their vile ways. And for all he knew, they could trade with Darynbroad and possibly even the Weltermores and the Rorenlands.

Vyk belched, long and loud, and a sulfureous odor wafted over the pool. He paled. "I... uh, don't feel so good." He clamped a hand over his mouth and belched again as he turned his head and spewed a gush of vomit across the rocks. It splattered when it landed. He heaved and clambered from the pool before vomiting several more times.

Cyran's stomach turned queasy and gurgled as he climbed out and settled a hand on Vyk's back. "Are you all right, my friend?"

Vyk nodded, wiped his mouth, and straightened a little from his hunched position on his hands and knees. "Still better than shitting myself."

"It is because of the hot spring," the Dragon Queen said as she lifted herself from the pool, water cascading off her naked body in shining droplets. Several glow flies flashed their blue lights as they spiraled around her. "He drank far too much of it."

Cyran furtively released a rank belch as he straightened but covered up his groin. He tried not to notice her glistening flesh, but her nipples were hard and steaming. He abhorred her, hated her more than any person in all of Cimeren, and one day he would kill her.

The Dragon Queen looked him in the eye as she paced closer. She stopped just before him, the steam from her body wafting up over his face. He almost retreated a few steps, but he did not want to give her the satisfaction of thinking she had intimidated him and that he was afraid. Her breasts were too close, and although he fought off the temptation to look again, he could almost feel them against his skin. The glowing insects hovered around them, creating a sense of beauty and mysticism. How could such beauty be part of such a cold and dark kingdom?

A twinge of excitement tingled somewhere within Cyran, and he silently cursed himself as he focused on staring into her eyes. His stomach sloshed with a sickening wave of nausea, but he hid any appearance of discomfort as best he could.

The Dragon Queen's lips parted only slightly as she said, "These lands are not the same as those south of the Evenmeres and the lake." Her gaze rolled across his face, studying him. "You may not understand everything you believe you should. Not up here."

Unsure of what else to do, and to hide his true emotions and desire to relieve her of her life, he slowly nodded.

"When I took Nevergrace, my legion used a mist dragon to hide the fires in your beacon towers," the Dragon Queen said, unblinking. "But even mist cannot hide all light, and a beacon was lit before we could reach it. We risked Galvenstone knowing of our attack. It was a mistake." She seemed to search through Cyran's eyes and sought out his soul, causing him to tremble inside. "There was probably a better way to go about it. Your soldiers there are attentive and swift. I should have pursued another means, another way to make sure that Galvenstone would have had no chance of seeing the fires."

Cyran tensed his jaw and met her gaze while trying to ignore the presence of her nakedness nearly pressing against him. Her nipples brushed his skin. Vyk, still on all fours, retched again.

"I would have had my dragon who breathes black fire use that on the last beacon tower along the stretch. The closest one to Galvenstone. At night. Those flames would burn up any fuel meant for a true fire, and no one would ever see the blackness of..." Cyran paused, realizing he was distracted and speaking hypothetically about the past, but she might be seeking information for the future—for when the sky sea rained blood.

One corner of her lips lifted in a subtle smirk.

Cyran belched, and his stomach rumbled. He doubled over and heaved, spewing a slosh of liquid across the rocks.

The Dragon Queen said, "There are many dangers lurking up here in the north, ones you cannot possibly understand unless you have lived in these lands. You should listen to me, before we reach Northsheeren." She motioned to his queasy stomach and paused. "You also hold a power over the other realm that even the mages and most dragonknights do not. You surprised me during our tilt—caused me a moment of weakness —as I did not expect you or anyone to have the potential to harness such abilities. You will not surprise me again. And if you seek it, only *I* can train you in the ways of the elder tongue and its magic. Your only chance at true power lies with me."

She strode past Cyran as he turned his head and watched her walk away, his mind reeling with thoughts and a flood of conflicting emotions.

21

PRAVON THE DRAGON THIEF

The dim flicker of torchlight surrounded Pravon as he hunched over a table and his tankard of ale. Aneen sat across from him, staring into the rippling surface of her brew.

"We should leave him." Pravon sipped at his earthy drink. "I am almost to the point that I would rather betray a blood contract and the Thief and Assassin than stay with that man. Whoever he is."

"He is mad." Aneen did not look up.

"Or I may stab him in the back before he kills me with whatever dark magic he wields." Pravon sipped. "I could not face him and hope to survive when he is prepared and ready for my strike."

"No one I know could confront and kill him." Aneen ran a hand along the short red hair on the side of her head. "Have you noticed that man staring at us?"

Pravon's hackles spiked, but he released a slow breath and remained calm. "I've noticed several people watching us. It started soon after we sat down. There's one in the corner with a pipe." Pravon nodded in the direction. "Another standing by the hearth. And a man in a cloak in the far corner."

Aneen's eyes darted about, but she did not turn her head. "We entered without drawing too much interest, but after we were given our first drinks, I felt someone watching us. I was hoping it was only my paranoia."

Pravon downed the last of his ale. "Finish up. We should go. But keep it nice and slow, and don't let them think we suspect anything."

Aneen threw her head back and chugged, the cords of her neck working several times. When finished, she slammed the tankard on the table. "Best ale I've had in Sarzuth. Not that that is saying much." She swung one leg over the bench she sat on and stood.

A hunchbacked man in a dingy cloak slid onto the end of Pravon's bench and set a tankard down before him.

Pravon slowly rose to his feet. "The table is yours. We were just leaving."

"So soon?"

"I'm afraid we have somewhere to be."

"Can I show you the cellar here first?" The man's head hung and lolled as if he were intoxicated, but his words were clear and distinct.

Pravon's hand slid under his cloak and found one of his daggers' hilts. "Maybe next time."

"But you came here for a reason."

"Indeed. For a drink."

"And how did you find this particular Sarzuth tavern?" The man's head drooped low over the table.

"We asked a..." Pravon caught himself, remembering that they had asked a man outside King Jabarra's castle where he would recommend getting a drink.

The man on the bench slowly nodded. "You are not the only hunter stalking your quarry."

Aneen lunged over and rammed a dagger into the man's

back, and the man collapsed onto the table with a thud, spilling his drink and flinging his tankard onto the floor. She grabbed Pravon's arm and pulled him toward the door.

The tavern fell silent, and everyone stared in attentive but calm silence. Two burly men in cloaks stepped before the doorway and crossed their arms over their chests.

"I have powerful friends in Tablu." Aneen flashed her dagger, its blade surprisingly clean of any blood.

"Sarzuth is not Tablu." The hunchbacked man at their table stood and dropped his tattered cloak onto the floor. He released a strap at his chest, and a pile of folded leathers that had been made to appear as a hump on his back—and which acted as armor—fell to the floor. He stood tall, his face shadowed beneath black hair, and he wore a mask over his mouth and cheeks. "And I insist that we talk."

Beneath his cloak, Pravon gripped a throwing knife in each hand. All of the other patrons in the tavern stood and took a step closer, encircling him and Aneen.

"What do you want?" Pravon glanced about, hunting for the tavern's windows. Both were closed and located behind a few cloaked men.

"That is far too complex of a question to answer on this side of the streets." The man at their table turned and gestured for them to follow him. "You should both be made aware that a poison, yurthgrane, was placed in your drinks. It comes from a desert weed of the Rorenlands and is not only deadly in minute quantities, but it is also believed to be the most painful way to die that is known to man."

Pravon's fingers crushed the hilts of his daggers as he glanced back at their tankards. "You lie."

The man tilted his head in a strange manner. "The poison is odorless and tasteless and dissolves instantly in liquid. Within the hour, you will grow ill and start vomiting blood. Diarrhea will quickly follow. Your intestines will cramp and convulse as if they are having seizures of their own while you writhe around on the floor in pain. Then your muscles will lock up and you will develop a fever. At this stage, there is no cure, but you will not die. Not for a fortnight."

"I will kill you before I go." Aneen stepped closer, but the man did not retreat.

"Then you will not be offered the antidote." His vacant expression did not shift. "Which comes from a parasitic fungus that attacks the weed."

Pravon shook his head. "Why are you doing this?"

"To offer you your lives back," he answered.

"After you attempted to take them?" Pravon glanced at the men all around the tavern.

"As I asked earlier—would you mind visiting the cellar?" He gestured at a dark hallway. "You will find the antidote down there."

"Do we have a choice?"

"There is always a choice." The man's eyes nearly closed when he grinned and his cheeks lifted. With his back still half-turned, he held a glistening dagger aloft and studied its blade under torchlight in a nonchalant but obviously threatening display. "If you take the antidote, you can then leave the tavern through a tunnel that leads back up to the streets."

"I don't understand the point of all this."

"Nor should you at this stage."

A wave of panic surged through Pravon's chest, replacing his alarm. "I will accept your request, but I need to inform you that it must be our third companion who you are probably most interested in. He is the one responsible for the maiming and killing of emissaries. We"—he motioned to Aneen—"cannot control him."

"If you ingest the antidote and survive and wish to tell him of the matter, I will leave that up to you."

Aneen snarled at the men around her. She did not remove her hands from inside her cloak, but she spun about to follow the masked man and said, "I hope you're wearing yet another wad of leather on your back. You will probably need it."

The man chuckled as he led them through the narrow hallway and into a back chamber. "I do not think you will try that again. Not tonight, at least. Knowing your prey is the most important aspect of any thief's dealings." He patted his back where he had worn the folded leathers and paced to the rear of the room. "And we have studied your work, Pravon and Aneen."

Pravon scrutinized the men around them, but he did not recognize any of them.

Two men in cloaks stepped around Pravon and dragged a pallet stacked high with barrels off to one side. Beneath where the pallet had been lay a rug that the leader of these men lifted a corner of and tossed aside. A bolted door was fashioned into the floor below, and the leader picked its lock and lifted the door by a metal knocker.

Below the doorway, a winding staircase led down into the darkness.

They do not even blindfold us. Either we will give them something they want, or we will not leave this tavern alive.

"You may enter." The leader's grin was concealed beneath his mask, but the expression dusted his words with false cheer. "Find the antidote you seek and live another day."

Aneen and Pravon shared a glance, leaving the notion that neither of them would return unsaid.

Pravon descended, the darkness enshrouding and swallowing him like the throat of a shadow dragon. He reached out with his feet to feel every step, not trusting anything about this place or the people here. Aneen's footfalls scuffed on the stones behind him. After a dozen steps, the doorway in the floor slammed shut behind them, and a lock clicked. Pravon's stomach dropped into his bowels, and he worried the poison was starting to make him nauseous.

Aneen's foot hit his leg as she bumped into him, and she said, "Keep moving. I don't think I'll like what I find down here, but I don't think those men were going to let us leave the tavern alive."

Once Pravon reached what he believed to be a landing, he strode more quickly into the darkness, realizing if there had been any escape from this situation, it had long passed. Beyond a lengthy passageway, firelight danced, and after they passed through the tunnel, they entered a circular chamber. A bonfire blazed in the center of the chamber, the flames ringed by stones and skulls that were not human. Two empty chairs both faced the fire, and Pravon stopped before one. Aneen soon stood before the other. A table holding three cups made of bone waited beyond the chairs, each cup filled with a different color liquid—midnight blue, blood red, urine yellow.

A parchment on the table had writing scrawled across its surface. *Two cups are filled with different poisons that do not have antidotes. A third contains the antidote you seek.*

"Blood Thief's hell," Pravon cursed.

"This is nothing more than a trick." Aneen glanced around that chamber. Opposite the fire, another tunnel led away into darkness. "Should we just flee to the streets?"

"And potentially die from this yurthgrane poison?" Pravon sniffed at the liquids held in what he thought could be small skulls. Ripples rolled through the yellow drink, and a bubble seeped to the surface of the red. The blue remained completely still.

"How are we supposed to know which is which?" Aneen

searched about the room, hunting for other clues, but she uncovered nothing else.

Pravon cursed again. He didn't even get to witness a man placing the cups on the table to determine if the bearer gave a slight tell—holding two a touch more tentatively or more carefully placing them compared to the one containing the antidote. "You are the one who has spent significant time in the Rorenlands. I was hoping you would know more about its poisons."

"I was studying certain dragons held in the cities and how best to steal them, not wandering about the desert inspecting plants and fungus."

"Well, we are still thieves, even if we do not deal in as many poisons as common thieves and assassins."

"You hope to detect the poison?" Aneen leaned over the blue and sniffed. "I smell nothing. You can sip from each of them and let me know if something tastes off."

Pravon released a dry chuckle.

Aneen scrutinized the other two. "If I were to drink one by its looks, I'd take the blue. Much better than drinking blood or piss."

Pravon eyed the red. "And that is why it is probably not the blue." He paused and sniffed the liquid before him. "This one has a very faint odor."

Aneen leaned closer, her lower lip wrinkling with disgust as she breathed in the air above the red. "Almost nonexistent, but it's something fetid. Although I get the feeling the smell is being masked by some other ingredient."

Pravon nodded. He sniffed the yellow and wrinkled his nose. "And this one carries just a hint of the scent of a blossoming flower."

"Then it probably comes from a plant." Aneen reached for the yellow and wrapped her fingers around it. "I knew it had to be the piss that they would make us drink."

"I do not think it is piss, or it would reek." Pravon snatched her wrist and held it down against the table so she could not take the cup. "What do we know about most poisons used to kill?"

Aneen hesitated and pulled her arm back as she pondered it. "That they must not be easily detected by the person meant to consume it—little if any taste, and no odor. Or the taste and odor must be masked by something palatable."

Pravon bit his lip. "Aye. That fact alone makes me think poison lies within the blue, which has no smell, and the yellow, whose scent is minimal but pleasant."

Aneen waited in silence, glancing at the cups while Pravon took the one holding the deep red liquid. He sniffed it again. The odor was faint but again discernible. He lifted the cup to his lips and took a small sip before pausing with fear. At first, it carried no taste at all, but a moment later, as the liquid dribbled across his tongue, a foul metallic flavor emerged. He closed his eyes and drank half the cup before handing it to Aneen.

"You believe you are correct?" she asked.

He shrugged. "There is only one way to find out. We should run out that far tunnel and see how long we live, before the men above change their minds and decide to come check on us."

Aneen glanced at the two cups on the table and sniffed them all again.

"Hurry." Pravon glanced back at the passageway they had come through. It was still dark and silent.

Aneen downed the remainder of the red liquid and wiped her lips with the back of her hand before flinging the cup into the bonfire. "Shall we?" She rushed for the far exit, and Pravon followed.

Cloaked figures filtered out from the shadows around them, carrying hooded thief lamps, surrounding them and blocking their escape. Pravon cursed under his breath and retreated a step, his anger flaring. This entire ordeal had all been a ruse. But why?

The masked leader then emerged from the darkness and circled around the bonfire before pausing in front of them, his hands folded beneath his cloak.

"Is this your guild's hideout, thief?" Aneen asked, her tone defiant.

"Please, sit." The leader nodded at the chairs.

Aneen remained standing. "I do not sit for mere thieves."

"This is no simple thieves' guild," he snapped and swung an arm out to indicate the chamber and the people gathered around them. "You have entered the realm of The Guild of Fire and Shadow."

Aneen glared at him, unimpressed. "A thief is still a thief, no matter what impressive name you mount over your doorway."

"Is that true for you as well, Aneen, *dragon thief*? You both drank the dragon's blood from the cup of one of its eye sockets."

Aneen folded her arms across her chest, her disgust revealing itself in her contorted expression. "So that is why we're here. You want us to sign a blood contract with you, to bring you some dragon you can in turn sell to a lord."

"We seek something different." The leader paced with his head down. "As well as something along those lines. We would be most delighted if you would join us, but"—he held up a finger—"even though you have passed one introductory test, you still have another that you must complete in order to prove you truly belong here."

"Why would we do such a thing?" Pravon asked. "Perhaps I look forward to slipping out of here alive, but once I find a way to do so, I will hardly want to return."

"You will do so because you are one of the rarest of breeds—dragon thieves—and The Guild of Fire and Shadow is the only guild for your kind."

Pravon's heartrate escalated. Had he finally drawn the rumored guild's attention? A sense of awe and honor and pride radiated through him and heated his face and chest, but these men were dangerous and they would probably try to ensnare him and use his abilities to garner coin for themselves.

"The dragon thieves of the guild are the elite, the commanders, the genturions of our world," the leader continued. "If you become one of us, you will be looked upon with reverence and wonder, and you will be treated as gods."

Pravon shook his head, considering if he and Aneen had really even ingested poison to begin with and if any of the three cups had actually contained other poisons or even an antidote. A new rush of anger bubbled beneath his pride. "You mean *if* we agree to steal dragon after dragon for you so that you and your friends can sell them to the highest bidders. We will be forced into contract after contract and will hence be your servants. We are already under contract with a man who is far more powerful than the likes of you."

The leader paused his pacing. "The dragon thieves of our guild are the coin producers, and that is why when you join us, you will be granted immediate status and power. There are fewer than a dozen of our kind in the guild, although we range across all of the kingdoms. We are always attempting to train more—the quickest and most agile of our young members—but few trainees survive their initiate testing. And it is not at all uncommon to lose a thief during an attempt to purloin scales."

Scales? He means dragons. "There are fewer than a dozen dragon thieves in your guild and you say it spans the kingdoms?" Pravon glanced at the cloaked figures surrounding them, incredulous. "Then as soon as I join your guild, I should have a plethora of underlings to do my bidding."

The leader clasped his hands together and steepled his fingers. "Once you prove that you are worthy of the guild, it will be so. You will find that we employ what you consider underlings—our footmen—in every major city in every kingdom. We also have such people in many of the villages across the lands. As a dragon thief, once you are initiated into The Guild of Fire and Shadow, you will have protection, resources, informants, watchers, and people at your fingertips who are paid well and will die if they must to make sure you escape whatever troubles pursue you. There will always be footmen at your disposal, wherever your travels bring you, and while you will not know them, they *will* know you."

Pravon's confusion and curiosity mingled with his ambition and cautiousness, all spiraling around inside him. "Why would we believe that this lot makes up some of the fabled guild? You look to be nothing more than an average city's cutpurses."

The leader threw his head back and laughed. He pivoted to showcase the skulls around the fire, all of which were inhuman. "These are some of the skulls of the creatures who lost their bouts in the pits and arena games. They are the smaller and weaker beasts some would-be dragon thieves brought to us in hopes of joining our ranks." In a blur of movement, he reached beneath his cloak and withdrew a vial, holding it in his clenched fingers. Black fluid filled its interior, and a few bubbles erupted from the liquid's surface.

Pravon took a step closer, inspecting the vial. He tentatively touched it with his fingertip. It was warm but not hot enough for any common liquid to be close to boiling. The contents of the vial resembled the poison he carried but was not yet wealthy enough to own. His heart fluttered. If these people were who they claimed to be, they could be his route to finding true power. He could become wealthy and influential and face his father again before living as a king of thieves... but the fact that the possibility could finally be within his grasp frightened him and cast more doubt over the entire affair. Over the past few years, he had begun to accept that he would never acquire such power, and a ploy seemed far more likely than a true offer from a mythical guild.

"If this is truly shadow dragon venom diluted by a master alchemist, you could sell it for enough coin to purchase you and your guild a small kingdom," Pravon said.

"We do not desire a small kingdom." The leader paused and looked directly into Pravon's eyes. "We wish to be part of *all* of them—to infiltrate without drawing attention or the notice of the lords. To remain beneath the streets and beyond the castles while molding all of Cimeren to our ends."

"Then do so. You do not need us."

"We need coin from dragon sales and arena battles to employ so many and ensure that our footmen throughout the cities and kingdoms remain only in our coffers. Our work is precious and expensive, and those of us who are dragon thieves wish to live like kings. We are the richest scoundrels in the known world."

Pravon swallowed his desires, afraid they would reveal themselves on his face and make him appear weak and lustful. "And so you offer us positions of high standing, but your guild will also force us to steal dragon after dragon for you. We will remain the toiling workers who risk our lives daily. I hardly consider that a position of power."

"Other than for your first abduction, when and where you act will be your choice. It is in all of our interests to make sure you only take what you can and are never caught. When we lose one of our thieves, the guild suffers greatly. It is not so with the footmen. You will have times of luxury between events, and you can study your targets for months or years prior to taking them. You can do whatever you must to best ensure you will not be caught or killed. As you are probably aware, all of the kingdoms' punishment for stealing dragons is death. Many also first include mandatory and immense torture."

"I know of the laws but, as I mentioned, we are already under blood contract. We cannot work for the guild and also fulfill the obligations we have promised to see through."

The flames raged behind the leader. "In your circumstances, you will only have to satisfy your initiation tasks. After that, you will be thieves of the guild and you will have a say in whatever you do. You can pursue your current affairs while still having access to the protection and aid of the guild."

Several minutes followed when no one spoke, the crackle of the fire echoing around the chamber.

Pravon glanced at Aneen and asked in a hushed voice, "What do you think?"

She shrugged. "Do we have a choice?"

"I think they may not let us leave this place alive—not unless we join them—or we would otherwise be their competitors."

She nodded. "I have the same feeling."

The leader returned his vial to somewhere beneath his cloak. "Would you two like us to have your third companion—the other thief—brought here as well?"

"No." Pravon said without having to think that part over. If he and Aneen truly became members of the legendary guild, when the time came, they would have assistance when they needed to avoid or contend with Kridmore. Pravon's answer to this riddle of a proposal was suddenly clear. "Our other companion is a dragon assassin, not a thief."

The leader considered that for a few moments. "Some kings and nobles pay as much coin to assassinate the dragons of their enemies, or even those from rival cities, as they do to steal them. We have many fewer dragon assassins even than we have thieves."

"But this man cannot be trusted. Not at all. He will kill in broad daylight and draw attention when it should be the last thing any typical thief or man of sound mind would want. If he desires blood in a certain instance, he will do as he wishes. No orders would supersede his yearning for it, and he would uncaringly expose the guild and pretend his actions are of no consequence."

The leader slowly nodded. "I see. Then it will just be the two of you?"

Aneen gripped Pravon's arm and squeezed his flesh as she scrutinized the leader and asked what she and Pravon both feared the answer to. "What is our initiation?"

The leader beamed.

22

CYRAN ORENDAIN

Silhouettes of castle spires loomed over the mountains in the vast distance, jutting above many peaks helmed in ice.

When Shadowmar soared past a rocky outcropping, a colossal beast nearly as massive as the shadow dragon erupted from a hiding spot and streaked at them. The white of its mummified flesh appeared like bones. Pinpoint lights glowed red in its otherwise empty sockets.

Cyran lurched in horror as he instinctively tried to reach for a weapon with his bound hands. The bone dragon rammed into Shadowmar, throwing even her bulk about as Cyran and his companions flew into the air and jerked against the ends of their tethers. The attacking beast sank its teeth into Shadowmar's leg, and Shadowmar roared and spun about, snapping at her assailant.

"Careful!" Ineri said. "Bone dragons breathe a poisonous gas, which cannot always be shielded by the wings of your mount."

The bone dragon shrieked, an ear-piercing cry, and its guard adjusted a lance with dangling icicles. Several crossbows on its quarterdeck and its turret thumped, propelling bolts into Shadowmar's flesh. The bone's jaws gaped, and green fog swirled in its throat.

Many crossbow ropes around Cyran thwacked, and projectiles screamed away, plunging into the flesh of the bony beast. The Dragon Queen uttered a sharp word and flicked the mechanism that capped and uncapped her lance's tip. Shadowmar veered and uncoiled in a swift and explosive burst that contained many small adjustments, and the Dragon Queen's lance slipped past her adversary's shield, plunging through his armored chest and impaling the mage behind him. Both bodies sagged on the shaft of her weapon like carcasses on a spit.

The points of light in the bone's eyes blinked and darkened as it shrieked, folded its wings, and dropped like a plunging bolt. Shadowmar whipped about to pursue the beast, but the Dragon Queen held her mount back.

"Your rage would be wasted in trying to kill that creature," the Dragon Queen said. "And bone dragons are not easily defeated, not even by us. Your true attacker lies ahead, at Northsheeren."

They flew onward and in silence as the Dragon Queen appeared more wary and veered away from other potential sites of ambush. Over the following hour, Cyran's nerves slowly settled, and leagues were eaten away by the shadow dragon's wingbeats.

The spires on the mountaintops neared, and Cyran stared in horrified wonder. *Northsheeren.* The black castle was built into the cliffs and sprawled across many of their faces. Only those riding dragons would ever be able to reach it or hope to siege the stronghold. The area around them was as desolate as any Cyran had seen, but the castle's natural defenses were far superior to Castle Dashtok's, which was situated at the top of the hill at Galvenstone.

Torches burned along numerous walks and inside an assortment of windows, giving the castle the appearance of a cavernous skull with many flickering eyes. Far below, beyond a league of plunging cliffs, snow-covered pines reflected moonlight, and a frozen river wound through the trees. Beady-eyed moon dragons swirled in the skies overhead, screaming their silent shrieks with jaws agape.

Shadowmar soared toward a gap between crags where a bridge spanned an abyss, connecting towers. The shadow dragon then veered toward the peak on their right, one with a flatter summit. Dozens of beasts perched on the walls around that area, and the creatures stirred and flapped wings or hissed at Shadowmar, but these beasts did not attack. None of them were shiny silver or sun dragons, and there were no obvious forest dragons in their ranks, either.

Scores of soldiers along the walls shouted and pointed with their spears. Others dashed off across the bridge, probably to inform those who needed to be made aware of the Dragon Queen's return. Mounted crossbows of enormous size, as well as catapults, dotted the battlements.

Shadowmar circled the flat area on the summit before descending, and Cyran studied Northsheeren's legions under moonlight, trying to determine which types of beasts they had, where they were positioned, and their total numbers. Most of the creatures were fire, ice, mist, storm, blood, moon, amber, crystal, or amethyst, although there were a few skeletal bone dragons and several other types he was unsure about.

Shadowmar landed with a shriek and a flapping of wings that beat back the winds roaring across the peaks. A contingent of soldiers in full black armor marched across the bridge toward them.

The onyx guard. The legendary immoral hand of the Murgare king.

Scores of soldiers in typical steel armor and helms, who bore spears and crossbows, marched from the battlements around the peak and encircled Shadowmar. The Dragon Queen dismounted, uttered a word, and quickly removed the bolts that had pierced her mount's flesh, tossing them aside as if they weighed no more than spears. After she was finished, she stepped away and onto a stone platform, looking over the soldiers, who parted and made way for the approaching onyx guard.

"I demand an immediate audience with Oomaren, the brother of our late king," the Dragon Queen said to the soldiers around her.

No one responded.

She strode over, grabbed a soldier by the lip of his breastplate, and yanked him close to the face of her helm. "Go find Oomaren or his orator or whoever is up at this hour and inform them that I have arrived and will be speaking with the late king's brother within the hour."

When the Dragon Queen released the soldier, he stumbled back before rushing off, skirting around the approaching onyx guard. The archers on the quarterdeck freed Cyran and his companions from their harnesses and motioned for them to stand and climb down the rope ladder.

Cyran led the way, with Ineri walking between him and Vyk. Ineri moved more fluidly than she had since they were taken, and she didn't cough. In fact, she hadn't been coughing nearly as much after leaving the steaming pools.

The Dragon Queen paced toward the onyx guard, whose ranks of booted feet stamped the stone bridge as they marched. A tall guard at their forefront held up a closed fist, and the contingent halted and rammed the butts of their spears onto the walk, creating an echoing din.

"Genturion," the Dragon Queen said, "if Oomaren is amassing all of the banners across Murgare and commanding them to gather along the shores of lake, why is he still hiding up in Northsheeren?"

The onyx guard's words rumbled inside his concealing helm, his voice as resonant as a trumpet but much deeper. "The king regent watches over and keeps the young queen safe here. Oomaren will journey south when the war begins."

"The king *regent*?" The Dragon Queen scoffed. "Why is Oomaren even needed for the war? All he will do is fly above Murgare's legions and attempt to instill a sense of pride and duty and bravery. But he will fail. The people do not trust and respect him as they did Restebarge."

The genturion remained silent as an archer shoved Cyran from behind. "Move." A mist dragon along the battlements roared.

Cyran shuffled toward the Dragon Queen as her archers flanked him and his comrades, escorting them onto the bridge spanning a chasm.

"I will speak with this king regent and discuss why he appointed himself to such a position before we even knew Queen Elra was dead." The Dragon Queen gestured at the onyx guard, and their ranks parted as one, each soldier stepping aside and creating a path between them. "We will take our Belvenguard prisoners to the cliff cells."

The onyx guard smashed their spears against their shields, creating a metallic bang. Cyran lurched, but the Dragon Queen led them onward. These guard seemed to be attempting to intimidate the queen and instill the notion that they were loyal to this king regent.

Cyran followed her across the bridge, his companions and the Murgare dragonarchers at his heels. They passed under an archway and entered a wing of the castle where soldiers stood at attention. Dim torchlight spilled across the walls and walk. They passed more soldiers and descended a winding stairway that had been cut into the mountain. At the bottom of the stairs, a hallway that had one wall created by the irregular stone of the cliffs led onward. Oak doors with steel frames dotted the stonework along the opposite wall. A gaoler in a black cloak hurried up to the Dragon Queen and whispered to her. His long and crooked nose poked out from beneath his hood.

The gaoler opened a door, and the Dragon Queen stepped back, making way for Cyran. Cyran shuffled through the doorway and into darkness. Vyk and Ineri joined him before the door slammed and locked behind them.

~

Cyran lay on cold stone that sloped downward toward a waiting ledge and the open night. A stone wall made up the back of their cell, the same with either side, but nothing other than leagues of empty air and cliffs waited beyond the floor directly ahead. Moonlight highlighted gusts of snow and rain or ice pellets that howled past.

Ineri had covered her head and body in furs and angled herself so that if she rolled down the incline in her sleep, she would hit one of the walls rather than tumble out into the abyss. Surely such a thing had happened here before.

"What the fuck do we do now?" Vyk huddled and pulled his knees up to his chin as he sat staring out into the wild night. He scooted closer to the back corner of the cell and pressed himself against two walls. "They mean to make us desperate or drive us mad with all of this—looking down into the nothingness."

Cyran clenched the fur wrapped over his shoulders and tugged it tighter about him as the wind skirled and its cold fingers pulled at his hair and stung his cheeks. "So it seems. I do not think there is anything we can do, other than wait."

What felt like hours passed before the lock at their cell's

door grated and clicked. Cyran slid away from the door as it swung inward.

The gaoler, only his protruding nose visible beneath his hood, held out a lamp and studied them. At least two soldiers with spears waited in the hall behind him, silently watching. "How are the accommodations? Do you find them fitting?"

Vyk sneered. "I wouldn't mind a fourth wall, or for you and your lot to take a long walk across the chamber."

The turnkey chuckled. "It will be one of you who first walks off the edge. The more days you spend here, the more appealing the option will become." He dropped three buckets on the floor with a clatter and then let a round of bread fall onto Vyk's lap. "You might also end up fighting each other over food. Always plenty of water though." He exited and retrieved another bucket from near the doorway, waddled in, and set it down. "Not the cleanest water, but better than water from the geyser springs." He guffawed. "Not that you would be fools enough to make that mistake again."

Cyran hid his scowl of irritation.

The gaoler kicked at Ineri's side. "You alive?"

Cyran leapt to his feet, and the soldiers lunged into the cell. One jabbed the butt of his spear into Cyran's face while the other drew a club and swung it at his stomach. Both weapons struck him with painful thumps. Cyran doubled over, his forehead throbbing, ears ringing. They hit him again and again until he fell onto the stones and lay there.

The turnkey chortled. "You shan't try to do anything to me, or you'll be punished." He cleared his throat. "There is one last thing though. It pains me to mention it, but the Dragon Queen insisted that each of you make a single request for comfort."

Cyran lay still, clutching at his midsection and his pounding head.

"Then, if there is nothing, I will take my leave." The gaoler turned. "See you again in a few days."

Cyran sat up, glancing around, his thoughts still impaired by his pain. "A lute would be nice."

"A lute?" The gaoler scratched his head. "Not sure if we have such a thing at Northsheeren, but the Dragon Queen would become upset if I do not at least try to find one."

"I'll take all the ale this castle has got." Vyk glared at the turnkey, who wagged a finger in reply.

"I will bring you a flagon." He turned.

"Ineri?" Cyran shook her.

Ineri uncovered her face and spoke, and her voice sounded strange. Not odd for her, but Cyran realized she had not said much of anything over the past fortnight or so. "I will take a warm fire."

The gaoler's nose twitched upward, and firelight reflected off his nearly concealed grin. "I'll bring you a few logs and light them." He exited with the soldiers and slammed the door behind him. A key turned, and the lock clicked.

Cyran sighed as he hugged his shins to his chest and stared into the night, attempting to ignore his pains.

Something sounded over the howling of the wind. Cyran's senses prickled. It came from beyond their cell. Something faint. He stood and crept closer to the void, keeping one gloved hand pressed against the wall to steady himself. He tilted his head, straining to listen.

A voice carried from somewhere beyond, but he couldn't make out the words.

"Hello?" Cyran leaned his head out beyond the walls.

A rush of wind hit him like a spiked mace—the brunt of its force taking him by surprise, its sharpened points grasping at his furs and flesh while threatening to drag him over the lip. He teetered before collapsing onto his knees and lurching back into the cell, heaving for breath.

"Where do you hail from?" A man's voice reached Cyran's ears, barely audible over the wind.

Cyran steadied himself and glanced back at the cell door before shouting into the wind, "Not from these forsaken lands."

The reply was muffled, but Cyran caught most of the words. "No need to yell and alert the turnkey. I can hear you fine. You are the one upwind."

Cyran glanced to his right, where the snow flurries came from and barreled past. This man must be in a cell to their left. Cyran spoke without hollering. "We are from Belvenguard. You?"

"Aye. Me as well. Been trapped up here for bloody months."

"How were you captured?" Memories of the Dragon Queen's hostile takeover of Nevergrace rolled through Cyran's head. Some of her legion had survived and fled, but they had not been able to take any captives with them.

"Our legion came north over the spires. We snuck into Murgare with the objective of capturing their king and queen."

Something in the back of Cyran's mind tingled. "Did something go wrong during your errand?"

"The Dread King Restebarge"—the wind roared, silencing the prisoner before some of his words returned—"killed."

"Did you see what happened to the king?"

"It was all a curious situation. We had a new mage guiding our rose dragon. The guard's lance skewered the king, although the guard had been targeting the royal dragon."

"How could that have happened?"

"It was the mage's doing. He veered Renorrax at the last instant."

"Do you remember the mage's name?" Cyran asked as Vyk and Ineri crept up behind him, listening.

"No. Never seen him before. Always wore a hood. Had a shovel-shaped chin and teeth like ivory. I don't know if I'd ever be able to recognize his entire face."

An image of the description flashed in Cyran's mind, planting itself somewhere deep so he could recall it later, if the opportunity ever arose.

"The whole incident smelled like a fresh dragon carcass—of treachery and deceit," the man said.

"Are your other comrades here as well?" Cyran asked. "Your guard? Others from your legion?"

"No." A few moments of pelting ice followed. "I was the only one who survived Renorrax's crash after she was shot down. Didn't escape without injuries though. Can barely walk. Those of us on Renorrax stayed behind to help make sure that the last of our other survivors in the legion could return home. Only Sir Paltere and his men escaped the incoming legions, and they had the Murgare queen as their captive." A heartbeat of silence passed. "Is she still being held prisoner in Dashtok?"

Cyran slowly shook his head before realizing what he was doing. "No. She was killed. By an assassin sent from Murgare."

"From Murgare?"

"That's what the small council believes—an assassin was sent by this new king regent here at Northsheeren." Thoughts about this prisoner's account of their raid and how its turn of events initiated the attack on Nevergrace floated around in Cyran's mind. It was why the Dragon Queen had come to his outpost with a legion. This Oomaren was probably the culprit behind it all, but it was also likely that one of Igare's small councilmembers was working with the king regent of the north.

Memories of the sealed messages he and his squire friends and Dage and Sir Kayom had received spiraled around in the storm raging inside his brain. One message hinted that a councilmember did not want the squires in Galvenstone. But how could any squire from Nevergrace foil a plot overseen by one of the king's four closest advisors? Cyran tucked his jumbled thoughts into different pouches in his mind. He would sort them later, if he learned more or ever found the opportunity to confront the small council again. Or maybe he could sift through all of the possibilities slowly, during the long hours of boredom that lay before him.

"What is your name, dragonarcher?" Cyran asked, assuming the man's position as he had mentioned a guard and mage.

"Turin Bolenmane."

Cyran wasn't sure if he had heard the name, but something about it all—a lone survivor from a rose dragon that was left behind at the pass to make sure Sir Paltere could return to Belvenguard with Queen Elra—struck him as familiar.

"Have you any notion at all about how we can escape this place?" Vyk shouted over Cyran's shoulder.

"There is only one potential route. A hundred dragons and ranks of onyx guard and other soldiers and knights fill this monstrous castle. In all the days I've been here, I've found no other option."

"What is this route?" Vyk nearly leapt over Cyran's shoulder as he screamed into his ear.

"You either roll down the length of your cell and over its edge in your sleep, or you eventually go mad and run and take a flying leap into the sky. I've considered each choice over a thousand times. I do not know if I'll ever be brave or mad enough to leap. So someday soon, I will sleep sideways near the edge, and I pray to the Great Smith and the Shield Maiden and the Siren and anyone else who will listen that when I turn over and fall, I will not wake up before I crash into the cliffs or the treetops far below."

23

JASLIN ORENDAIN

Menoria walked beside Jaslin with her head down as they approached the king's dining hall.

"Why did I make such a fool of myself?" Menoria groaned with disgust. "I dishonored Nevergrace."

"Igare still seems to want you to become his wife." Jaslin paced along. "I'm sure he's seen similar behavior from women, at times. He's been married before and has a daughter. And Nevergrace is not dishonored because in one instance you were a little drunk."

Menoria sighed in frustration and shook her head. "These dinners have not gotten any less awkward. What will this be now? My fifth with the king? Maybe he is doing the same with a few other women—deciding who would make the best queen of Belvenguard."

Jaslin pondered that as they approached two kingsknights in gilded armor who guarded the doorway ahead. It was possible that the king was considering more than one woman. Jaslin leaned closer to Menoria. "This time, can you ask him if he would send a few of his soldiers or the city watch to look into the merchant Keliam? Down by the wharf?"

"I've made a fool of myself and of my home, and you already want me to start asking the king for favors?" Menoria folded her hands and shook her head. "I do not understand why this thing you pursue regarding the assassin interests you so much. I just assume what everyone else does—the assassins were the vile servants of Murgare and this new king of theirs. I am sorry. You are my best friend, and I wish to help you with what I am able, but I cannot ask the king to act on something trivial. Not yet."

"It could reveal what kind of sway you will hold with the king in the future." Jaslin tried to sound reassuring and optimistic before adding her teasing tone. "He may even want to impress his new queen, such a young and nubile woman, him being a middle-aged man."

"Stop." Menoria did not say the word like they were friends but with a definitive manner as a lady did to her servant. "He is forty and nine. I will be ten and nine soon. I've heard of much larger age gaps between kings and nobles and their ladies." She swallowed and changed her tone to a more friendly one, the timbre she typically used with Jaslin. "Besides, it is not as if I have a choice or could ignore or rebuke the king of Belvenguard."

They neared the doorway, and the kingsknights stamped their heels, pivoted, and opened the double doors wide. Menoria stepped inside, and Jaslin followed with her head down as the doors were shut behind them.

Igare stood from his spot at the middle of a long table covered in plates that were piled high with duck and dark meats, strawberries and grapes, potatoes and asparagus dripping in butter and red sauces.

"Lady Menoria." King Igare bowed his head. "I am delighted that you are willing to attend another droll dinner with me. I enjoy your company so. Please." He stepped to the side and pulled out a chair. "You help ease my mind and let it drift away from all the other matters of the kingdom."

Menoria smiled at him. "Thank you, my king." She sat, and he helped scoot in her chair.

Jaslin hovered off to the side of the chamber, and a servant darted forward, offering Menoria a choice between two flagons. "Mulled wine or honeyed mead?" the servant asked. "Or I could fetch you a light ale."

Menoria smiled politely as her cheeks reddened. "No more ale for me for a while. I will have only a splash of wine."

The attendant poured as the king cleared his throat and said, "I hope the Summerswept Keep is treating you well, and that you are not growing bored here when so many are preoccupied with readying for... for what may come."

"Your castle is finer than any in the kingdom." Menoria swung an arm out to emphasize their surroundings and knocked over her goblet. Red wine splashed across the table coverings and splattered her sleeve and the king's robe. Her eyes grew wide as she stared in horror. "I-I am so sorry, Your Grace."

Igare chuckled. "I prefer wine over blood."

A half-dozen servants rushed forward to stem the tide of wine rolling across the cloth, and one dabbed at the king's robes.

"I am fine." Igare shooed the servant away.

Menoria's head drooped. "I must excuse myself for a moment." She stood before the king nodded and rushed to the doors where they had entered. The kingsknights standing on the inside pulled the doors open, and the lady of the Never darted between them.

Jaslin hurried after her, but the kingsknights had already shut the doors by the time she approached them. The knights eyed her, and she almost demanded they open them again and allow her to attend to her lady but, instead, she paused and turned to regard the king.

Igare took a long drink from his goblet.

"I apologize for my lady, Your Grace," Jaslin said.

Igare studied her then nodded as he waved off her remark. "If I didn't fear that she was disrupting our conversations on purpose—to avoid me—I would not be so worried."

Jaslin scoffed. "She is only nervous. Very nervous. She has not dined alone with a king before, but I can assure you, she is not trying to avoid you."

Igare knitted his meaty fingers together. "I once acted the same way. With my previous wife. My stomach felt like rats scampered around in it whenever she came near. I made a fool of myself around her many times, especially when I was young."

Jaslin smiled, a sense of empathy for the man and the king he had to be twining within her. "She fears she made a fool of herself when you awaited her outside her chambers, and now she is more agitated because of it."

"It is I who should be agitated, a middle-aged man trying to claim a young beauty because my small council convinced me I must do so and as quickly as possible, before Murgare... Before there is no time to conceive a son." He sighed and shook his head. "I feel that I am the fool, and I feel it all the greater whenever some trivial incident like this happens. I couldn't care less about my robes." He swiped a palm down across the stains coating the gold trim of his garb as if they meant nothing. "If it were blood instead of wine, then there would be reason for concern."

"I will speak with my lady and let her know how you feel." Jaslin bowed and pivoted halfway to the door before pausing. When she returned her attention to the king, he held the offending goblet in his fist and stared blankly into the distance. "There is one question I was humbly wondering if I could ask you, Your Grace."

Igare blinked and focused on her. "If you can help the lady

of the Never understand that there is no need for embarrassment or any other unwanted emotion relating to our interactions, I would be indebted to you." His smile pushed his cheeks back. "I only wish for her to feel comfortable in my presence and to speak to me as she would with you or anyone else she has known for years."

Jaslin returned his smile. "I will try to help her with that and ease her worries." She swallowed. "In regard to the other matter, I... had overheard that there is a merchant along the wharfs who may be smuggling something into the city inside his fish."

Igare's eyebrows rose. "From whom did you hear of this? Fileena?"

Jaslin shook her head. "From a merchant who noticed something suspicious."

Igare brooded on that for a minute and then drank.

"The merchant in question—his name is Keliam," Jaslin said.

"In my own city?" Igare looked over a plate of duck but did not eat. "One can never stamp out all the dark dealings of people. Not even a king. Not in a city whose population numbers in the hundreds of thousands."

Jaslin waited another minute, but the king did not add anything else, so she asked, "Will you send soldiers to look into the matter?"

Igare slowly shook his head. "I wish I could. And I would if this were any other time, but with the threat of war brewing, Galvenstone cannot spare a single man to investigate the hunch of some other merchant when we are preparing arms and legions." He sighed. "Every trusted man in each tier is working themselves to exhaustion for this cause—to save their city and kingdom from the evils of Murgare."

Jaslin's stomach sank as she struggled to compose herself. She opened her mouth to protest before realizing this was the king of Belvenguard. She should not press him, not like she did with her brothers. He had made his decision, and asking again could annoy him. She bowed her head. "Of course, Your Grace. I will go after my lady."

Igare nodded, and the kingsknights pulled the doors inward. She paused again as the knights watched her, waiting for her to exit.

"Do you believe that Menoria should be accompanied by any kingsknights?" Jaslin asked before facing Igare.

"Pardon? Kingsknights?"

Jaslin nodded. "It may seem like a strange proposal, but at a time when assassins murder the queens of Cimeren and yet spare some of its kings, do you at all fear for the safety of a potential queen? That she could become their next target?"

Igare's face paled. His mouth worked a few times before he spoke. "I... did not even consider it. I figured whoever is behind the murders is ultimately after me, but I understand and recognize your concern." His eyes drifted side to side, across something in his mind. "I am an old fool. It shall be done. As soon as this dinner is over, I will appoint two kingsknights to inspect and guard any chamber that the lady of the Never is occupying. They will also accompany her wherever you two must travel."

"Thank you, Your Grace." Jaslin bowed.

"Thank *you* for bringing this matter to my attention before it is again too late. I am humbled by your insight. This is something no one in my small council has addressed."

Jaslin smiled and rushed out into the hallway. Menoria was not about the area composing herself or preparing to return. Perhaps she was changing her dress and having difficulty doing so by herself. Jaslin paced along, headed for the lady's chamber.

After whipping around a corner, she almost ran straight into someone in mauve robes. The conjuror before her held out a hand, pushed her hood back, and smiled. White hair framed an eerily young face. "Ah, there you are. You are the lady of Nevergrace's handmaid?"

Jaslin nodded as something inside her cringed and pulled back into a corner. "I am."

"Your lady said you would be coming this way. And my daughter tells me you hold a crystal of some type that drew her interest."

"I... do?" Jaslin's hand instinctively clutched at the shard hidden in a pouch at her waist.

"May I see it?" Cartaya's fingers uncurled to reveal her open palm.

Jaslin hesitated, her fingers gripping the object tighter. She never wanted to part with the last piece of the decanter. Tamar had given it to her as his final gift before he passed in that bizarre event involving a falling tree.

"I need to see the object." One of the conjuror's fingers curled in a come-hither motion.

Jaslin clenched her jaw as she glanced around, hoping for a distraction, hoping Menoria would come sweeping past them on her way back to the dining hall. When nothing happened, Jaslin slowly eased the shard from her pouch.

"You do not wish to part with it, do you?" Cartaya asked.

Jaslin shrugged, as if it were of no significance. "It is the last piece of a gift that my dead brother gave me. That is all. It carries sentimental value."

"Do not worry. I will return it to you in the same state in which you give it to me." Cartaya's lips twitched, and Jaslin tentatively placed the fragment of the decanter on the conjuror's palm and released it. Cartaya's finger snapped closed around it as she held it up to her eye and inspected its contours. She rubbed her fingertips across each surface and muttered a few things to herself before saying, "It is ancient, indeed. The artwork of the elves of old Cimerenden. That is what this is. Where did you get it?"

"I told you—my brother gave it to me. It was from a decanter that was broken. I saved only the single largest fragment."

"And where did your brother find this decanter?"

"Somewhere in the Evenmeres."

"After all these years?" She said the words more to herself than to Jaslin. "Unblemished and intact. Now a shard." She contemplated something for a minute. "Does this relic call to you? Tempt you into following its will?"

Jaslin attempted to appear nonchalant. "I have wanted to visit the woods more often since I've had it, but that's only because I wish to look for more items."

"And does it influence you and make you not want others to see it? Does it make you want to keep it for yourself alone?"

Jaslin did not immediately answer.

"You were hesitant to hand it over." Cartaya studied her.

"It is the last gift I will ever receive from one of my brothers."

"That is only an excuse. It is similar to claiming that you only wanted to venture into the woods to find more artifacts. But"—she held up a finger—"you have arrived at Galvenstone without falling prey to its requests."

Jaslin's insides tingled. This conjuror was probably not going to give the shard back as readily as she promised.

Cartaya's other hand shot out, and she squeezed Jaslin's arm in a tight grip, which made Jaslin jump as the conjuror said, "There is something within you that allows you to resist it." She studied Jaslin from head to toe. "You carry a hint of power. You must—to have made it this far. You are like your dragonknight brother, but you... are vastly different."

Jaslin gawked at the woman, unsure of what she was claiming.

Cartaya dropped the shard into Jaslin's hand and said, "I

would tell you to be wary of the crystal of the elves, that it carries more power than most any magical item of this age, but it seems that while you may still be tempted by it, you are not completely obedient to its will. Come and see me in three nights from this. I would like to investigate this matter further."

Jaslin could not think of any kind of response.

"Before the time when the sky sea rains blood, anyone with even the slightest potential to harness bone and earth magic should determine what they can and cannot do. To aid us all against the coming darkness. We need all the help we can get. Better to do so now rather than wait for the beginning of the end of all things." The conjuror smiled, patted her arm, and whisked past her, hurrying down the hall.

24

SIRRA BRACKENGLAVE

Dim torches guttered along the walls and sent shadows rolling and twisting about the floor of the audience hall. A lone man stood in the center of the chamber.

"Oomaren." Sirra strode forward, removing her helm and looking him in the eye. She could kill this man here and now, although she might die during the act, as he would likely be keeping the legendary conjuror of Northsheeren and many other protectors close by. Also, if she killed Restebarge's brother, she would probably fail in her primary objective, which was to keep Murgare from fracturing apart. Killing Oomaren with the intention of halting the war of the kingdoms would likely lead to war sweeping across a divided Murgare. However, Shadowmar would not be pleased with her decision to let him live.

A contingent of onyx guard stepped from multiple entryways and into the chamber in an attempt to display strength that could in turn lead to intimidation. Sirra gritted her molars and silently cursed them. They should only be loyal to the true king and queen of Murgare.

"Sirra Brackenglave." Oomaren lifted his head and smiled. He stood taller than Sirra, his scarred cheek and lips holding his expression in a permanent snarl below one scarred and milky blue eye. "It is an honor to greet you after your long-awaited return to Northsheeren." He tapped his chin. "I also recall sending you messages with orders to leave that waste of an outpost in Belvenguard much earlier and to aid us in preparing for the coming war."

"I recall that we did not have a king sitting on the throne when I departed Northsheeren for Nevergrace, and that Princess Kyelle is still Restebarge's rightful heir."

A short man in mauve robes shuffled into the chamber using a staff for assistance, his head bowed and hooded. He opened a fist, and a cone of purple flames sprouted from his palm.

Luminsteir. He was no dragonmage, rather the legendary conjuror of Northsheeren—Restebarge's former conjuror. Sirra reached into the other realm, preparing to call upon its power.

"No one misses or grieves more for Restebarge than I," Luminsteir said in a crackly voice, "but, as you know, Kyelle is not of the age to govern Murgare."

"Did either of you ask her consent for Oomaren to rule as the king regent in her stead?" Sirra scrutinized them. "Or to assist her in her rule?"

"Of course." Oomaren folded his arms across his chest. "We have not done anything that would challenge the laws of the kingdom, Dragon Queen. Kyelle can still sit on the throne and rule one day, but this is what the people of Murgare wanted. It is what the kingdom needs right now."

"And who informed you of what the people wanted?" Sirra took a step closer, and the onyx guard advanced in an enclosing circle, their dragonsteel armor clanking and ringing as their boots struck stone.

"The people did not want Murgare to fall into anarchy and split apart after Restebarge's untimely death," Oomaren said. "Not after Belvenguard's assassination of my brother. An ascension ceremony has already taken place and was witnessed by the people of Northsheeren. I was named the king regent before them all."

"A ceremony was witnessed by the people of Northsheeren?" Sirra glanced around and frosted her words with an icy skepticism. "You mean by the onyx guard and some soldiers? The vast majority of the people of Murgare do not reside here."

"You may not have consented, should you have returned and placed the needs of Murgare above your own emotions and need for vengeance, but again, you chose to leave and remain at that outpost." Oomaren sighed. "I wanted you here, Dragon Queen. You are one of the pillars of Murgare and Northsheeren. There is nothing to be done now without confusing and dividing Murgare and weakening us all further."

Rage boiled inside Sirra. He had only summoned her here prior so that he could try to control her.

"The princess is too young," Oomaren said, "and any others are too weak to rule the north during this time of conflict. Too many weak rulers have presided over Murgare in the past, but they will not do so now."

"I presume you also had nothing to do with a bone dragon and its team ambushing me on my way to Northsheeren?" she asked, distrust weighing heavy in her words. "Perhaps in hopes that I would never arrive?"

Oomaren's expression did not budge. "I know nothing of such a matter, but we should look into it for certain. A rogue bone dragon with riders is not something we should simply ignore and hope goes away. If you left the creature alive, that is."

You sent them after me but I cannot prove it, and you believe they are dead because I am here. "There is also the matter of your war that we must discuss." Sirra took another step toward Oomaren, and the onyx guard advanced again.

Oomaren raised the scarred eyebrow above his milky eye.

"You sought retaliation and battle as well, and do not pretend otherwise. The king of Belvenguard and his legions killed my brother and his queen in cold blood. Such heinous actions will not go unavenged. Their souls now reside in the sky sea and face unrelenting torment. They must be freed."

"I was aiming for something much less encompassing to avenge my king and reclaim my queen. You have always wanted this war. Ever since you were a boy. A war that will burn and destroy all of Cimeren. A war that will change the rule of Murgare so you can claim its throne without Kyelle's consent."

"I will have Igare's head on a pike!" Spittle flew from Oomaren's lips. "And then will we occupy all of Belvenguard."

"Even if we crush Igare and all of his legions"—Sirra met his gaze without blinking, allowing her cold anger to meet his fiery hate—"we will lose tens if not hundreds of thousands of lives and crush the five kingdoms while turning them into something that is no longer recognizable by current standards."

"There is no other option. Your attempt at negotiating with the immoral of Belvenguard has only caused death and has not reaped any rewards."

"I will call the banners back to their homelands and stop what is about to unfold." Sirra stood in his face. "Unless a queen or king is appointed in proper fashion and they have consulted with all those necessary before unleashing something that cannot be avoided." She glared at the onyx guard. "So please tell me where the princess is currently residing."

"In her chambers, as usual."

"Not the queen's chambers?"

Oomaren did not respond.

"And Sir Trothen?" she asked.

"Sir Trothen has been relieved of his command as genturion master of Northsheeren."

"Where is he?"

"Confined."

"In the cliff cells?"

Oomaren shook his head. "To his quarters."

Sirra snarled and stepped back, tearing her sword from its sheath. Black fire erupted along its length. The onyx guard lunged forward.

"*Vördelth mrac ell duenvíe!*" Sirra's dragon voice blasted through both realms and pounded the approaching guard like battering rams, throwing them across the chamber and against its walls. Metal rang, and most of the guard collapsed in heaps. However, at least a half-dozen of them remained standing, only shaken, and they drew long black halberds—weapons that could act as either axe or pike against charging horses or dragons.

Luminsteir knelt on the ground. Oomaren trembled, and his knees buckled but he braced himself against a pillar and smirked. "The onyx guard are not all susceptible to your magic. You are no longer the ultimate power here, *Dragon Queen*."

Sirra marched up to him, looming over him in his weakened state. "I will go to war if I must—to avenge Murgare—but I will not do so for a false king. I will speak with Kyelle and Trothen. And for your sake, I hope they support what you have told me. If the princess did not willingly allow you to oversee her rule, then you will witness much more of my wrath, and I will stop this war."

"The war cannot be halted now. It is too late. Its recipe has already been brewed and set forth. Ships depart the north shore as we speak. The legions will fly before either of our messages could reach them. It would be in Murgare's and your best interest to side with those you love and hold dear. Fight alongside them."

Sirra glowered and shoved past him. "*Dramlavola.*" An onyx guard stepped toward her with his halberd raised, and she swung her sword at the weapon. Her blade cleaved through its handle, and she used her hilt to smash the guard's breastplate with a vicious blow. The guard was hurled away, and he landed atop another who had resisted her first magical attack.

∽

Sirra ignored two onyx guard standing before a doorway and rapped on the door's planks with her fist. Wood banged against stone.

No one answered. Sirra beat on the door again and tried the handle, but it didn't turn.

"Why is this locked?" Sirra asked.

"The young queen prefers it that way," one of the guard answered. "For her safety."

"She is not being kept in here against her will, is she?"

The guard shook his black helm, which was encrusted with small spikes, his entire face covered.

"And who keeps the key?" Sirra asked.

"The young queen."

Sirra released a sigh of relief and knocked again. "Princess Kyelle. It is Sirra Brackenglave. I am sorry to disturb you at this early hour, but I must speak with you. At once."

The strength of the *neblír* still coursed through Sirra's bones and tendons. She reared back, preparing to kick the door down while fearing what she might find inside. Her muscles coiled and prepared to spring.

Metal grated against wood, and the door clicked. Sirra quickly curtailed her blow, visualizing Kyelle being crushed under or behind the heavy door if she were to strike it. Hinges creaked, and the door crept inward, creating only a crack of an opening. Two bronze eyes peered out and reflected firelight.

"Princess." Sirra bowed her head. "You are alive and well?"

"I was told to be wary of you. If you returned here looking for me."

A jolt of surprise lanced through Sirra's chest. "Of me?"

"Indeed. And now you arrive at a strange hour."

"I have always been faithful to your father and mother. Why would you believe you should be wary of me?"

"Oomaren said you did not comply with my wishes when we asked you to return to Northsheeren. He feared that when you finally returned, you would try to claim the throne for yourself."

"Kyelle." Sirra, imagining herself in white armor once again, genuflected before this young woman who would now be ten and two. "The power of rule has never been my desire. I could have taken it long ago and ruled for centuries. I did not. My people... I would not want to make the same mistakes." She paused and steadied herself. "Why are you locked in your chambers?"

"Out of fear. Fear of you."

Sirra glanced up in surprise. Someone had been molding Kyelle's mind and thoughts during Sirra's absence. "You never have to fear me. My treatment of you shall be the same as it's always been."

"Can you prove that I can still trust you?" Kyelle asked.

"I nearly just severed Oomaren's head from his body because he informed me that he was crowned during an ascension ceremony when you were not. I support you. That is why I have come. To make sure you are all right."

"The words of the Dragon Queen can be deceptive."

"Who has put this in your head?" Luminsteir's face flashed in Sirra's mind. Maybe Oomaren had even become a conjuror of sorts or had learned some of the art while she was away. "Your father and mother never would have warned you of such things. Remember our days on the dragons."

Kyelle's swift inhale followed.

"*Desirité*," Sirra whispered. "You wanted nothing more than to soar through the clouds on Brexenior—or rather Shadowmar." She had misspoken, referring to her snow dragon of old, and she was surprised to have made such a mistake after so many centuries.

"But my father never knew of it. He would not have condoned such actions." The princess's tone lightened, and her door opened a little more.

Something akin to a cloud of shadows was weighing on Kyelle's mind. Sirra felt it now in the other realm through the power she had called upon. Tendrils of that blackness started to lift from their wrapped positions around the princess. "Your mother did not know either, but it was no betrayal. You were safer on Shadowmar than within the same castle as Oomaren."

Silence followed.

"Dispel whatever magic has enshrouded you, Kyelle," Sirra said. "I am your friend and faithful servant." The onyx guard shifted uneasily beside her. "I can feel its hold on you, but only you can break it."

Hinges creaked as the door budged, but it did not fully swing open.

"Remember Restebarge," Sirra said. "Remember his name. His sword. His face. And with all your might, remember your mother. Queen Elra. Powerful and just. Let the sound of her voice, the memories of her words comfort you now. I am still her servant as well as yours."

The door opened, and Kyelle blinked repeatedly, glancing about. Sirra stepped across the threshold and swiftly closed the door behind her, bolting it. Kyelle backed away as a new wave of fear lit up her eyes. She held her hands up before her as she nearly collided with the bed.

"Do not fear me, child." Sirra eased her way forward and took one of the princess's outstretched hands, squeezing it.

"Please, tell me what has happened, and if you consented to Oomaren acting as your king regent." Every muscle in Sirra's body tensed.

"I... I did." Her head hung, and her black hair curtained her face. "I believed no one would heed my rule or commands."

Sirra's heart sank into her bowels. "Did you feel like yourself when you did this?"

Kyelle's lips pursed. "I am not sure."

"Then your right to rule may have been taken from you by deception."

Kyelle shook her head. "I do not believe it was. One day, I do desire to rule over all of Murgare, but I am not yet ready. I am young, and I've been told that I must experience much before taking on such a task."

"Then you already have the conscience of a good queen, and a preferable one compared to Oomaren's. Every decent ruler I have ever known questions themselves and their decisions. Solely the arrogant and blind trust only their gut and judgment."

Kyelle looked up into Sirra's eyes. "Is there anything you can do to prevent the coming war?"

Sirra shook her head. "Probably not, but in its aftermath, all kingdoms shall be redrawn, and I will still stand by you then."

25

CYRAN ORENDAIN

CYRAN PLUCKED AT A LUTE'S STRINGS WITH NUMB FINGERS, OFTEN hitting wrong notes that rang out dissonantly and carried off over the cliffs. He partially hummed and intermittently sang a song of longing and of waiting for a lost love to return home.

Vyk whistled absently, and Ineri stared bleary-eyed out into the daylit skies. She coughed and hacked as she kept her furs wrapped tightly around her and huddled up against Vyk. At least she was coherent and was not attempting to sleep—how she spent almost all of her hours. The fire she requested as her item of comfort had died as soon as the gaoler lit the logs. Immediately afterward, the turnkey had laughed derisively, shaken his head, and made a comment about how fire had been a terrible request but he had nearly completed his duty. Then he dropped a few warm stones for them to tuck under their furs, which were only warm enough to keep them from freezing to death, and departed.

Vyk's flagon of ale sat beside him, the last of its droplets frozen in his mustache and beard. Out of their three granted requests, only Cyran's lute remained.

A gale hurled a flurry of snow against one wall, and a sheet of frozen rainwater lay thick along the floor, creating an icy slick near the edge of their cell. This made venturing too close to the opening to make conversation with their comrade from Belvenguard treacherous.

Turin Bolenmane. He had once been a quarterdeck archer on a rose dragon, but Renorrax had perished on their quest for the Murgare king. Cyran cursed under his breath, wishing he could have shared what he had learned with his people before he died in this cell or was tortured to death. His heart twisted and burned.

Perhaps even more so than upholding his duty, he longed to spend one more day with Jaslin and Smoke as well as Brelle and Laren and Dage. Not Garmeen the traitor. *Emellefer.* He swallowed as tears surfaced and burned in his eyes. He imagined Jaslin sitting in the grasses out beyond the outpost, her back against the old oak as she read one of her stories. Cyran would be practicing sparring and loosing bolts, but this time he would stop training. He would stroll over and sit beside her, take up another book, and read as well. He would laugh and cry, and he and his sister would discuss the stories—what they loved, whom they hated, and what they desired to happen. The day would last for an eternity, and still he would not grow tired of it. He would enjoy every moment, every second of the time spent with her, doing what she loved, what made her happy. Did the promise of a safe and happy sister or family matter if in the end war would destroy them? Maybe instead of preparing himself the best he could for something that could not be stopped, he should have enjoyed more of his life. His situation was the price of his interests, his desires, his duty, and his becoming a dragonknight.

Where was his little sister now? Probably back at the Never trying to help rebuild before Murgare launched their attack and the world of Cimeren came crashing down around them.

Tears rained from his eyes like droplets from the sky sea. He imagined these tears as blood, resembling those of one of the north's dragons that had borne him on this fateful journey. He glanced upward. The sky and snow whipping about appeared darker than typical, ominous. The time had come, the last days of Cimeren. He swallowed and forced himself to look ahead at a future that would not last much longer.

At least soon enough I will be reunited with Tamar in the sky sea.

He tried to say he was sorry to Vyk and poor Ineri, whose bony cheeks made her appear like a prisoner who had been starved for months, but the words would not escape his throat, much less his numb lips. It was because of him that they had ventured into Murgare and because of him they had found what they came for but still failed. Igare knew war was coming, but Cyran was unsure if the king knew that Murgare considered the war to have already begun.

Vyk's voice sounded beside Cyran, his tone far more hollow than normal. "You know what the point and hell of all this is? All that matters is who you are with. That's it. That is all life is about." His voice wavered and cracked. "But when you're alive, you cannot spend all your time with the people who matter. I love my daughters, but they do what interests them and those things bore me to tears. Same with my son. I try to entertain them, but after a few hours, that's it. I'm done. My wife—we mostly argue if we're together for more than a full day at a time." He laughed loudly, the sound drowning in the wind. "But in the end, they are all that matters. Nothing else does. Nothing." He sobbed and laughed at the same time, shaking his head. "That is the crux of life. When I imagine doing it all over again, right now I'd want to do things differently, most of it, but if I was actually given the opportunity... I don't know that I would." A bellow escaped his lips, and then a wail.

Cyran's heart sank into some bottomless deep.

Ineri coughed weakly.

A drawn-out creak sounded, and the door to their cell swung inward. The gaoler clutched his hood tight to his head as the frigid wind blasted him. He stepped into the chamber, followed by the Dragon Queen and two of her archers.

"You play without gloves." The Dragon Queen nodded at Cyran's pale fingers. "That is not wise at this elevation and this far north."

"Gloves make my fingers too thick to play well." Cyran finally allowed his hate for her to seep from his pores. "I cannot hit individual strings that way."

She gave a slight nod of understanding. "A man who slays enemies not only with his blade but also with his heart. The most dangerous kind of all."

Cyran almost dropped the lute as he studied her, but her face was hidden by her ominous helm and visor.

"A strange man, indeed," the wiry woman archer Cyran remembered as Zaldica said, and the bearded archer, Yenthor, nodded his assent. "Men of Belvenguard must be weak, needing to appease themselves in such a way."

"They would probably be better fighters if they did not have to be consoled like babes," Yenthor said. "And learning such a skill surely takes up too much of their training time and softens their hearts."

Defensive anger rose inside Cyran, but he held his tongue. Vyk shifted uneasily.

"Better to follow our ways than have cold hearts packed full of hate," Ineri said, steel-eyed as she watched them.

The Dragon Queen studied Ineri. "How do you find the hospitality of Northsheeren?"

Ineri scoffed.

"I thank you for the lute, but I've seen nicer accommodations in the deepest dungeons of Belvenguard," Cyran replied.

"Oh?" The Dragon Queen tilted her head. "Have you spent time there?"

Cyran did not answer.

"Will you play us a song of Belvenguard?" she asked.

Suspicion bloomed inside Cyran, and he made no move to reposition the lute on his lap for playing.

The Dragon Queen motioned. "Lighten the mood of this chamber, Yenthor. Give us a taste of your craft."

Yenthor strode forward. "For us heartier men, it is a lyric or poem." He cleared his throat, his chest rising to full breath. "Once I was a lad along for glory." His voice belted out over the roaring wind without care for pitches. "Found a clutch of eggs the size of barrels. Evil hid inside, that's the story. I hewed and rendered their shells to pieces, then realized the mother's coming quarrels. I slipped into the shells to hide within, but the dragon waited for me to hatch. This dragon was blind on one side, they said was the catch. She could not ever discover her offspring were all dead, so I crawled out to pretend—to suckle a teat. Then I remembered she was a dragon and, instead, she'd be waiting for me to leap from the peaks." He stared out over the edge of their cell and guffawed.

Cyran's confusion whipped around inside him. The story had to have been based on something he had done with Shadowmar's eggs in the dens at Nevergrace. Did the archer compose it prior and recite it for a purpose? Or did he only want to crystalize the part about them waiting to jump to their deaths?

"It is the custom of the north for you to then attempt to top Yenthor's lyrics." The Dragon Queen folded her arms across her chest. "Then the spectators declare the winner, who is usually bought drinks by the loser."

A shout of warning sounded in the back of Cyran's mind. These soldiers were trying to bewilder him and his companions, to set them off guard. Then the Dragon Queen would seek what it was she wanted. Cyran smiled as amicably as he could manage. "I can play a song of Belvenguard, but I could not possibly top such fine lyrics on the spot."

Yenthor nodded, planting his hands on his hips.

Cyran positioned his lute and strummed a few chords.

Vyk leaned close and whispered in his ear, "Be wary, my friend. They play to you, hoping you will open up to them and spill yourself."

Cyran nodded, and his smoldering rage flared. "I will give them nothing more than music." He sang the only song he could recall at the moment that was reminiscent of a poem, although it was much more tasteful than the archer's. He sang as powerfully as he could in the setting, his voice ringing and one verse standing out against the gale more than the rest.

In the new age, not all that grows has life
    Not all that is buried has gone to rest
    Time and deeds are counted nothing more than strife
    Those who speak otherwise have not seen the iron crest

Yenthor chuckled derisively and shook his head. The Dragon Queen remained silent before slipping off her helm and cradling it against her chest. Her bronze eyes bored into Cyran, reminding him of his past encounters with her, but now there was a softer, more inviting emotion shining back at him. Her long brown hair, tossed by the wind, swirled about her beautiful features. She could be no more than thirty years of age.

"The women of the north often sing," she said. "It is the way of the Shield Maiden and her warriors, as well as the Siren of the Sea. Your song reminds me of another, one I have not heard or sung in centuries. It is from the old world, first told in the elder tongue. I shall sing its words to you." Her eyes closed, and after she drew a deep breath, a hauntingly beautiful hum and then tone streamed from her lips.

In the night, there's a shining star
    When you look, you'll see how far
    From the dragon's back, we soared away
    And the deeds we dealt, few can say

The long ago still haunts our steps
    Till the paths we've seen have been laid to rest
    Steel and scale, flame and shadow
    War and wrath when all's been hallowed

Wings and breath will bear our cross
    In the frigid lands, all's been lost
    Some roots are never reached by fire
    Though the time calls for us to defy her

Darkness is where to stow your heart
    Because in the light they'll tear it apart
    Upon that star we look from afar
    'Cause here now is where we all are

Cyran shivered, a haunting chill coursing through him. The winds and storms had nothing to do with the sensation. Her words and emotion alone created the feeling, and something inside him melted and released its contents. He struggled to maintain his composure, fearing this woman had used some of her magic from the other realm on him. He would have to be far more careful in dealing with her.

"It is time for you to decide if you wish to leap over the edge of this cell or be freed." The Dragon Queen spoke only to Cyran. "If you yearn to understand the *neblír* and unlock its secrets, the only way is through me. I am the *only* path to such power. You should not allow your life to be wasted. Together, we could change the fate of Cimeren." She held out her gloved hand and flexed her fingers, offering to help him stand.

Temptation pulled at the strings of Cyran's heart and twined with his loathing for her as he imagined delving deeper and discovering more of the dragon realm, something so few humans had done. But it would be a betrayal. To accept aid from and be taken under the wing of the Dragon Queen, he would have to turn against his king, his kingdom, and his people. He glanced at Vyk and Ineri, who regarded him with fear. There was probably nothing the Dragon Queen wanted from his companions. If he left the two archers here, they might be forgotten in this cell—unless he could use his position with this woman to beg for their release.

Potential outcomes of accepting her offer flashed through his mind. After negotiating with her, the Dragon Queen could open the cell door and allow his friends to exit and find some comfort while she took Cyran away to a dark chamber to bend his mind and manipulate whatever powers he might hold. However, after Cyran was gone, the soldiers of Murgare could simply use Vyk and Ineri as targets to practice their archery. They would be riddled with fletching, lying on the walk of Northsheeren, blood pooling around them, and Cyran would be on his way to losing himself.

"Maybe after another few days… or weeks, or months, you will change your mind." The Dragon Queen made for the doorway and exited along with her archers. "Perhaps when the war has started and Belvenguard is being destroyed, or after the war has ended and there is nothing left of your kingdom."

The gaoler followed the Dragon Queen and slammed the door with a bang that shook the stones beneath the prisoners' feet.

Cyran stared out into the empty sky, his mind and guts churning.

26

PRAVON THE DRAGON THIEF

Pravon slipped through the night without a sound. Aneen was hidden somewhere in the shadows nearby. A third contender for a spot in The Guild of Fire and Shadow hurried away under a gray cloak, headed for the sand pits outside the Yellow Castle. The king's sand dragons should be kept there, but the place would be heavily guarded, likely by giants as well as soldiers.

Moonlight cast rivers of silver along the dunes as they crept on, and the silhouette of a lone dragon emerged, a storm dragon outside of the pens. Pravon paused. He and Aneen had turned their acquired storm dragon over to the guild so the scaled steed could be kept behind gates after the poison they had stuck it with was negated, which had to be done eventually or the beast would die, and after neutralizing their poison, they retained no control over the creature.

The creature waiting ahead was probably Kridmore's storm dragon. The assassin was still visiting the Yellow Castle, and in King Jabarra, Kridmore might have finally found a man who viewed the world the same way he did—as something you could violently attack whenever you felt the urge.

The third contender for admission to the guild, a promising young thief named Hassellstaff, rushed toward the pits. Pravon cursed and silently trailed him. When they neared the storm dragon, it became apparent that the beast was slumbering, and the gem glinting behind the dragon's head confirmed that this was Kridmore's beast and it was still bound to the assassin.

Hassellstaff veered from his current direction and padded toward the storm dragon.

"Stop!" Pravon said in a harsh whisper. "That is our comrade's mount."

Hassellstaff halted, and his hooded face partially turned. His tone was cold and quiet. "To pass initiation, the guild master only said we had to steal a dragon from the Yellow Castle. He never specifically said it had to be one of the king's sand dragons. That is just what you two assumed. And I do not care if your companion made a mistake in leaving his mount unattended and beyond the castle's walls."

"It is not even that." Pravon stalked closer. "I do not give two farthings if you steal his steed or not. I despise him. But because we could become guild brothers, I feel obligated to let you know of Kridmore's claim. Our comrade is a dragon assassin, and he uses magic and enchanted items"—he nodded at the gold-hilted dagger protruding from the base of the beast's skull—"in ways I've never seen or heard of before. He has warned us that we should never try to remove that dagger, as doing so will kill anyone but him."

Hassellstaff glanced back and forth between Pravon and the storm dragon, mulling over his options. "That sounds like a simple deterrent tactic meant to scare you with his supposed magic. Then you would not turn against him. You have the spine of a water lily, and I fear we will not become brothers."

Pravon shook his head. "I do not consider us competitors. All three of us could enter the guild if we fulfill the requirements and survive."

Hassellstaff stood straighter in the moonlight. "It is much wiser to take the easy pickings rather than face legions of sand dragons and giants. My mentor said that accepting too much risk is the primary reason why so many trainees die during initiation."

"Aneen and I have stolen dragons many times. The more of us who work together, the more likely we will all succeed."

"Then that is the true reason why you do not want me to take this dragon, so I may aid you and then you can use me as a decoy to assist with your own escape. No. I will seize this opportunity and enter the guild as one of its prestigious dragon thieves, and I doubt I will be seeing either of you again."

"Kridmore is a man who does not hesitate to kill. I've seen—"

A hand settled onto Pravon's shoulder and squeezed. "Let him go," Aneen whispered in his ear. "His actions should offer us two pieces of information—if Kridmore was indeed telling the truth, and how powerful the assassin's items and bonds truly are."

Pravon opened his mouth to protest, but Aneen silenced him with a look.

Hassellstaff darted over to the storm dragon and then slowed just before approaching it, keeping within the narrow angle of its blind spot. The would-be thief crept closer in a heel-to-toe manner. In an instant, he sprang onto the beast's neck and ran along its scaly length as the dragon's eyes fluttered and it blew a massive breath out of its nostrils.

Pravon tensed and crouched behind the crest of a dune, watching. Aneen dropped down beside him.

Hassellstaff dived for the dragon's head, and he grasped the shimmering black gem and the dagger's hilt. He rose to his knees and heaved at the dagger as he muttered something. The storm dragon's head jerked upward along with its neck. A foot with dark talons lashed out from beneath its bulk. Hassellstaff grunted, and his fingers erupted with violet flames. His jaw dropped in horrified shock as he tore his hands from the hilt and turned them over before his eyes. Then his arms ignited, and the flames raced up across his chest and down his back and legs. His head was engulfed. He collapsed and fell from the dragon in a smoldering heap.

Pravon's heart bounded around inside his rib cage. The storm dragon glanced about, sniffed at the charred corpse, lumbered away a few steps, and lay down again. Pravon scooted down the far side of the dune.

"Do you think our chances are ruined?" Aneen asked.

Several heartbeats passed before Pravon could answer. "I… the storm dragon is not too concerned, and it didn't create much noise." He exhaled slowly. "I've been considering all of this more since the guild forced us to hear their offer. If we had such an organization backing us no matter where we were, we could still fulfill our contracts and have a way to escape or even a means of fighting Kridmore, if it comes to that. Otherwise, we will remain at his mercy." Images of violet flames enshrouding Pravon's own hands and body haunted him. Kridmore had no love for him. "I will steal a sand dragon this night."

"Then we should do so quickly." Aneen crawled over the dune and hunched as she veered away from the storm dragon and dashed for the sand pens.

Pravon followed her, moving much more cautiously than Aneen as he glanced around. Soldiers were stationed at regular intervals ahead, around the outskirts of the pits. Four of them had gathered together, discussing something and pointing in the direction of the storm dragon. They had probably seen the light of the purple fire.

"Do we kill them or try to get them to wander off?" Aneen asked when Pravon neared. She pressed herself low in the sand.

"It could be difficult to kill four soldiers at once, but then we won't have to worry about them spotting us later."

Aneen nodded. "I thought even you would want to just dispose of them." She pushed herself to her feet, her torso remaining horizontal as she shuffled toward the soldiers. Her hands moved under her cloak.

Pravon trailed behind her, his fingers finding his throwing knives that were strapped to his tunic. He tested their weights and shapes, feeling the difference in their lengths as he gauged the distance to his targets. He switched one out for another.

Aneen rose from the desert night like a wraith sculpted from the shadows. She loomed under moonlight. One of the soldiers gasped and pointed, his eyes widening as Aneen's arms flicked out from her cloak. She hurled two objects, and two soldiers collapsed with hilts protruding from either their throat or chest.

Pravon flung one of his knives backhand. It twirled end over end with a sharp whistle that died abruptly in a thud as its blade sank into a soldier's eye. Pravon's other knife was already flying, and the blade punched into the last soldier's throat, silencing a shout of warning with a bubbling sputter.

Aneen waved Pravon onward. The massive walls of the pen were directly ahead, the gates towering farther off in the distance. There would be many more soldiers at the gates than around the walls, and the area ahead appeared unguarded, the sentries from there likely the four who were now dead. Aneen darted to a section of wall without torchlight, and she pulled out her climbing blades and strapped others to her boots. She leapt upward and began to scale the sandstone blocks, primarily using the gaps between stones. Pravon attached spurs to the front of his boots and pulled out his climbing blades, following her lead while glancing about to either side and keeping watch for patrolling soldiers as they ascended. He weaved about as he climbed, seeking out slats of shadow to move through.

Near the top of the wall, Aneen lunged upward and over its edge, impaling a patrolling soldier with a dagger to the underside of his chin. She caught the man and directed the path of his falling body before it plummeted through the darkness. Pravon pulled himself up onto the walk and joined her. They both crouched and studied the interior below. The sand pit stretched away into the night, and bulky, tan-scaled bodies rested in groups here and there. Soldiers stood atop the walls in the vicinity, all of them facing outward.

"How do we get a couple of beasts out of there?" Aneen asked.

Pravon shrugged. "I've never stolen a sand dragon. I thought you were familiar with the Rorenlands."

"These muscly beasts cannot fly well, and unlike most of their kind, they lumber along on four legs and can only glide short distances over the desert. They do not soar in the skies. Their wings are far too small for their bulk. None of them could fly high enough to even make it over these walls." She patted a sandstone block beside her.

Pravon swallowed. Was this all a setup? To have them caught and imprisoned? He had not considered all the angles there. He and Aneen could be the guild's primary competition, and maybe the guild wanted them disposed of. He wished he had considered that possibility sooner. "Can these dragons climb well enough to scale the walls?"

Aneen shook her head. "There." She pointed at the gates in the distance. "But sand dragons are large enough that when they charge or stampede, they can easily smash through steel. We will just have to move swiftly and get away before any mages and guard mount up and chase us."

Pravon's eyes fell shut for a moment. "I do not steal dragons when I am not familiar with the terrain, have not studied the plan, and when there is so much risk of being caught. King Jabarra will have us tortured to death."

Aneen nodded. "We could turn back. But then the guild may hunt us down, and we will have no way to contend with Kridmore."

"Damn the day the Thief stole the first dragon," Pravon cursed.

"We have no other means of flying away from this kingdom, either. The guild now houses our storm dragon."

Pravon sneered and cursed again. "This is going to be a mistake, and I will regret the rashness of it for as long as I live. I never attempt a heist if I am in such an unprepared state."

"You did it at Nevergrace. When the Dragon Queen occupied the place."

"True, but she only had a few soldiers for the entire outpost. And the dens there were not full of dragons that the king's mages and guard could use to follow us."

Aneen shrugged. "We do not practice our art because we hope to live forever. Live for the moment, the thrill, and the Thief will guide you." She swung her legs over the far side of the wall and scaled downward, using her knives as stabilizing tools to slide down gaps between stones. She descended at a rate many times faster than their ascension.

Pravon briefly lidded his eyes again and pressed his fingertips into them. He took a deep breath and then quickly followed, concealing himself in a swath of shadows near a corner. When he was close to the bottom, he dropped into the sand beside Aneen.

"We circle around and take the two beasts closest to the gates, hitting them at the same time." Aneen gestured for him to follow as she stalked along the periphery of the interior, headed toward the gates. Their feet sank deep into the sand with each stride. "Two should be able to break open the gates."

"*Should*? I thought you said they could do it. Just a bit ago, you even made it sound like one dragon could accomplish the task."

Aneen shrugged. "Two should be able to."

Pravon's stomach clenched, and his anxiety rushed from some internal paddock as they crept along. The snoring of beasts sounded all around. Some repositioned themselves or paddled with their feet or wings in deep sleep, their scales scraping against the sands.

As they snuck along, a wingtip shot upward, poking above the sand just to the left of Pravon's foot. He lurched and flung himself against the wall, smacking his shoulder. Aneen quickly shushed him.

"There are some sleeping under the sand," Pravon mouthed.

Aneen cast him a I-thought-you-knew-that look. "There are probably thrice as many creatures under our feet as those sleeping atop the sand pit."

Pravon's bounding anxiety spilled down into his limbs as he took a quick look at the sand he stood on and swallowed. Aneen pressed on, and he tentatively followed.

Once they finally neared the gates, Aneen pointed to two dragons, both of them probably as large as any in the entire pen. "Those two should do."

Pravon pulled out his vial of poison and dipped his spine's tip into the liquid.

"I should also let you know that sand dragon skin is tougher and thicker than the hide of most other dragons," Aneen said. "Ram your spine deeper than you think you'll need to."

Pravon shook his head in disbelief. This entire errand was riddled with more uncertainties than any ten contracts he had fulfilled. It had better pay off for the rest of his days.

"But they do sleep sounder than most other kinds." Aneen darted from the shadows, her spine in hand as she angled for the smaller of the two beasts—the one to the left.

Pravon headed for the one on the right, his feet sinking deeper with each step. Once he neared his target, he lost any focus on Aneen and allowed his instincts and experience to guide him. His heartrate slowed. The beading of cold sweat on his forehead ceased. His hands settled. He took a few springing strides and reached the dragon's neck before gripping the edge of a scale and lifting it. Once a patch of skin was exposed beneath the scale, the steady pulse of blood trundling beneath the surface showed in waves—the jugular vein. The vessels of these beasts must be fatter than those of many other types of dragons.

The dragon grumbled and shifted its head. Pravon rammed his spine into the exposed area.

The creature inhaled with a startled gasp as Pravon rushed to its head, leapt up, and found his position on its snout and between its eyes.

"The diluted venom of a shadow dragon courses through your heart and veins," Pravon whispered. "Any bond you held with another human has been severed. The poison is causing you pain, and for that I am sorry. It is also causing the muscles of your heart to cramp, and your soul is being cut off from your realm. But your heart will not fail. Not yet. And your soul may still endure. You know what I speak is true. Your soul's existence now depends upon my survival."

The creature shook its head, further awakening. Its short wings unfurled.

"I hold the antidote," the dragon thief said. "I will release you from the pain, let you live, and allow your soul to wander both realms *if* you do exactly as I ask. But you must protect me, or the antidote will never be found or administered properly."

The dragon's body heat seethed from its face as if it were a hearth, and its rage bubbled up from somewhere deep within. It roared.

"Thieves!" a voice shouted from the walls above.

"Fuck." Pravon closed his eyes and held on tighter as the dragon rose, his mind attempting to convince him that he must have hit its jugular despite its thick hide.

A horn blasted over the pits.

The sand dragon's escalating tension seemed to crash into a wall, and the beast quickly relaxed.

"Thank you." Pravon climbed up over the dragon's face and head while unwinding his leather strap. He flung the length of the strap around the beast's thick neck, tied it off, and slipped his feet into its makeshift stirrups. "Now is your chance to be free. Run for the gates."

The dragon bellowed, and a gust of wind and sand exploded from its maw and tore across the grounds, stirring up more sand and hurling it about. The beast lunged forward, and metal links clattered. It hit the end of a line, and its neck whipped sideways.

Pravon glanced over in horror. The beast was chained to something, the links having been hidden in the sand. A muted bellow from a dragon sounded under the ground nearby, and many answering calls carried up from around the vicinity.

"Sand dragons are often chained to other members of its legion," Aneen shouted as the gates rattled and soldiers overhead yelled. More horns blared. "Especially those at the Yellow Castle. I should have remembered that and picked their locks first."

The front gates burst open, and two giants with stone skin lumbered into the pen, each holding clubs the size of oxen.

"Buggering bloody Thief's hell."

A few bolts screamed through the air around Pravon, and he ducked.

They would shoot their own dragons? One projectile struck his new steed's flank and bounced harmlessly away. These bolts had not been launched from mounted crossbows and were only meant to harm a person.

One of the giants rushed toward Pravon, swinging its club at him. The sand dragon shrieked and reared back, pulling its head and neck away from the incoming attack. The club blew through the chain links binding the creature, causing metal to snap. The sand dragon lurched and barreled forward.

"The chain!" Pravon pointed to his dragon's smashed chain, hoping Aneen had seen what had happened and could attempt something similar. These soldiers and giants were obviously inexperienced in their encounters with dragon thieves.

Pravon's dragon lowered its head and raised its shoulder, charging and smashing into the giant with a thunderous crash. Scale hit stone, and the giant grunted in surprise as it was launched from its feet and flung into the wall. Sandstone bucked and shuddered, and the soldiers above hollered. One fell, screaming as he plunged downward, and he hit the pen's floor with a thump, his cries silenced.

The dragon charged through the gates, trampling a score of soldiers and driving them into the sand. A battalion of other armed men came running from the castle, along with a contingent of knights. Pravon's dragon blew another breath, and wind and sand swept over the expanse between them and the approaching ranks. A thousand little pings sounded as the breath of the beast pummeled armor and shields, its wind moving with such force that it scraped at and tore through metal.

The dragon veered and hurtled into the night, heading away from the castle and the blaring of horns.

When Pravon glanced back, the soldiers and knights who had been rushing from the castle were either kneeling or lying in heaps on the ground. Most did not move, although some shook their helmed heads and rubbed at their eyes. The horses were screaming as they tossed their heads and bucked and kicked, bolting in all directions and stumbling as if they could not see.

A second sand dragon tore through the open gates of the pen as two more giants lumbered closer. The dragon humped its back and leapt, knocking one giant aside with its neck while whipping the other down with its tail.

Pravon's breath rasped in his throat, his heart banging against his ribs as he turned to face forward again, a grin of relief and exhilaration pulling at the corners of his lips. His sand dragon spread its wings, and a hot wind billowed its leathery segments, lifting them from the desert floor.

They glided off into the night.

27

CYRAN ORENDAIN

The door of the cliff cell swung open, and the gaoler glared at Cyran as he said, "The Dragon Queen again requested me to ask if you've decided to meet with her. I personally do not know why she wastes her time or gives two rat shits about you, but I must fulfill her demands."

Cyran glanced at Ineri, who barely peeked through a slit in her furs. Vyk's jaw bulged as he clenched his teeth. Cyran leaned closer to them and whispered, "I could try to find a way for us to escape, or talk our way out of here. We have no other options, and none on the horizon. If we remain as we are now, we will never leave this place, and soon, we will surely die from the elements."

"As long as she doesn't turn you against us and Belvenguard." Vyk shook his head, flinging bits of frost from his beard, animosity and suspicion ripe in his words.

Ineri's eyes closed, but she only shivered, coughed, and nodded.

"She will never be able to turn me against my people." Cyran patted Ineri's back and slowly rose. "I despise her more than anything in Cimeren." He faced the gaoler. "I will meet with the Dragon Queen."

The gaoler cursed under his breath before ushering Cyran out the doorway. A dozen soldiers waited in the hall beyond, all of their spear tips angled at the dragonknight.

Damn. Finding a way to escape from Northsheeren would not be easy.

The gaoler pointed at a half-dozen of the infamous onyx guard, who waited in the shadows ahead, and those guard led Cyran onward while the soldiers' spears and footsteps followed at his back. They wound through halls and up several stairways before stopping outside an oaken door. One of the onyx guard rapped his knuckles against the door, then opened it and marched into the chamber beyond. The other guard followed the first and made way for Cyran to enter.

Once Cyran stepped inside the chamber, the onyx guard lined the wall near the doorway and watched. The Dragon Queen waited in the distance, and three men—one in a silver robe, one in a mauve robe, and a taller man with a scarred face and eye—stood nearby.

"Young dragonknight." The tallest man waved Cyran forward, and Cyran tentatively trod across the stone floor. "I welcome you to Northsheeren. I am the king regent, Oomaren."

Hate smoldered in Cyran's heart. This man was the epitome of evil. If there were anyone viler than the Dragon Queen, it was a king of Murgare. Such men found their way to the throne only through heinous deeds.

"Sirra Brackenglave, the Dragon Queen of Murgare, has spoken highly of your abilities." Oomaren paced around Cyran. "I must admit that I am doubtful, but I would like to be proven wrong."

"Who are your friends?" Cyran eyed the robed men.

"My orator, Astor." He pointed at the man in silver robes and then to the one in mauve while adding, "And my conjuror, Luminsteir."

Cyran stared at the king as an awkward silence lingered.

"You realize what awaits Belvenguard, do you not?" Oomaren asked.

Cyran swallowed. "I've seen the legions amassing at the north shore of the lake."

"Then you must realize that Belvenguard has no hope." Oomaren stopped pacing, and his scarred and blue-tinged eye bored into Cyran. "I do not say this to bring you sorrow or incite your anger. It is simply a certainty. Belvenguard cannot withstand what we have prepared for them. Not unless they find significant aid, which is not coming."

"You could call it all off. Save Cimeren from fire and destruction."

Oomaren shook his head. "Our prior king—my brother—was slain in cold blood, his soul lost to the sky sea and enduring torment until justice has been served. Such an incident cannot go unavenged. Igare must face retribution for his actions. We have granted your king enough leniency many times prior."

"Then why am I here?" Cyran's words flew past his lips as his rage mounted. "Surely, you do not believe you can offer me anything that would make me turn against my people."

Oomaren pursed his lips and rubbed his jaw. "You are here because Sirra claims you have a gift. One not seen in even most of the dragonknights. You were unaffected by the threads of the other realm, its magic, when she aimed to use it against you. There is no one else who can teach you what she can. If you do not pursue such a path, you would be forfeiting most of your potential."

"I would only use such magic against you." Cyran's fists clenched.

"We understand that is a likely outcome." The Dragon

Queen marched forward and stood in a pool of torchlight, her helm removed, her brown hair shimmering, and Cyran's wrath erupted in his chest. "But it is a chance we are willing to take to assess your abilities. If you must, you can decide to learn what you are able while still clinging to the hope of aiding your people. Or you may become drawn to your teacher and the *neblír*, and you could discover that your mind has become changed—forever altered."

I could never *not despise you and Murgare.* Cyran studied her. She seemed willing to risk such a thing. Could it even be possible that his powers could one day challenge hers? Then he would be her greatest adversary and could kill her, for good this time. "And if I refuse all of this?"

"You will remain in the cliff cell with your companions," Oomaren said. "Until the end of your days, or until Belvenguard defeats our armies, occupies Northsheeren, and frees you. But we both know that is a fool's hope."

Cyran mulled everything over. Spending the rest of his life in confinement with nothing but abyss and cold around him and his comrades seemed like a life from the Assassin's hell. If he outright refused here and now, the king might give up on any hope of him changing his mind, and if that happened, he and his comrades could be killed outright. If he pursued their offer, perhaps in time, he could grow closer to the most powerful people in Murgare and convince them he was one of them. Then he could turn on the north, hopefully before its war with Belvenguard was over.

But something in the back of his mind rattled bars of confinement there. These people would not easily be fooled or manipulated. An inkling of fear coursed through his veins. If they were to train him in the ways of the other realm, they would also be working to undermine his resolve and corrupt his understanding of his world. If he accepted their offer, he would have to always remain on guard and wary. Very wary. He forced a deep breath, burning the scene of Sirra and Oomaren and the robed councilmembers into his brain.

"Train me in the ways of dragon magic, as quickly as you can." Cyran folded his arms over his chest, concealing his true emotions. "And then maybe one day I will join you." *In death at each other's hands... if my abilities can ever rival the Dragon Queen's.*

A grin slowly lifted the unscarred portion of Oomaren's lips as he faced Sirra. "I told you I could convince him this would be in his best interest. He just does not trust you, Dragon Queen. It is the same with all outsiders. They fear your power. And your demeanor."

Sirra did not acknowledge the king regent's words. She donned her helm, and her voice echoed inside it as she addressed Cyran. "I must know what you understand at this stage—your beginning. When did you first learn you could link with a dragon?"

Memories rolled through Cyran's mind. "When I was called into a turret to act as an archer, and we lost our dragonmage. Our mount was preparing to throw us and flee the battle."

Sirra's head dipped. "At a time of utmost need. Much is the same for conjurors." She gestured at the man in mauve robes. "When you are forced to try, you fail. When you must, you have a chance of succeeding."

"How do I wield the magic of the dragon realm?"

"It is not magic. No more than dragons are magic. Their realm is as real as ours, is just as tangible to them, only our minds are not as open or imaginative enough to always see it. But their lands always reside around our world. The threads of their domain are always here."

Cyran closed his eyes, remembering his experiences with the throbbing strands of light. "I've seen it. And I've used it to command the dragon, but what else can it do for us?"

"It doesn't do anything *for* you," she snapped. "It is simply there. But if you can feel it and see it, then you can try to pull a part of it into our realm, to bridge the gap. There are several elder words that I have found which can affect our world."

Cyran clamped his eyes shut, but he could not see the threads. "I have only witnessed its fibers when my dragon is near."

The whisper of steel running against leather sounded, and when Cyran opened his eyes, the Dragon Queen held a sword that crackled with black flames. She swung the blade at him.

Cyran gasped and fell backward, landing on his backside as the weapon whistled just above his head. It would have cut him in half. He scrambled away, reaching for a weapon he did not carry. He did not stop fleeing until his shoulder hit the far wall.

Sirra advanced slowly. She was angry with him after all for what he had done, and she meant to kill him.

He quickly stood and retreated along the length of the wall, holding his hands up. "Why kill me now? You could have just let me rot in that cell, or let me freeze to death." He glanced at the king and his councilmembers, hoping for aid, but they simply watched with interest.

"A dragon does not have to be near you in order for the *neblír* to exist." Sirra stalked him. "As I told you—it is always around us." She angled the tip of her blade at his chest and lunged forward.

Cyran dived aside and rolled across the stones. The orator gasped as Cyran came to a stop near his feet. Violet flames leapt from the conjuror's hands. Cyran stood and slipped behind the two men in robes, placing them between himself and the Dragon Queen.

"You use others to protect you when you should rely solely on yourself." She strode closer, and the conjuror and orator parted.

"I cannot even see the other realm." Cyran backed away. "When you used your powers on me in the tilt, I was riding Eidelmere. I cannot see any threads to grab in this chamber."

"Then you will die here." Oomaren motioned for the Dragon Queen to finish Cyran with a slice across his throat. "You are of no use to us."

Cyran's heart tumbled in his chest. What seemed like a tense but not hostile meeting had turned deadly. This was no test. He must perform or die.

He slipped an intangible hand into what he thought could be the *neblír*. He scrabbled around and clutched at everything he could, but he could not grasp anything solid.

"You evaded not only *opthlléitl*, the dragon's voice, but also *aylión*." Sirra coiled her arms holding her blade, preparing to strike. "If those specifically did not affect you, then you have seen them. You already have the ability to grasp their threads."

Cyran tried again, straining, and temptation pulled at his core. Something dark surfaced inside him. He could grab that something and nurture it, but somehow he knew if he did, this woman would use it against him here and now as well as in the future. He ignored the sensation, and he found nothing around him to take hold of.

Sirra swung her flaming sword, and Cyran leapt aside, colliding with one of the chamber's columns and issuing a dull thud. The impact forced the air from his lungs. He held a hand out. "I cannot do it! My dragon abandoned me, and I can no longer find the other realm."

Sirra shook her head in disappointment as she lowered her blade. "Then you are nothing more than a guard."

"We do not need any more members of the guard." Oomaren waved to the onyx guard near the doorway. "Return him to his cell with his comrades. They shall be used as a bargaining tool. They are worth nothing more."

28

JASLIN ORENDAIN

MENORIA PACED ALONG THE BATTLEMENTS WITH HER HEAD hanging, and Jaslin trailed behind her. Soldiers around them carried bolts and beams and metal to fortify and build more mounted crossbows and ballistae along the walls facing the Lake on Fire. Nistene, Vysoria, and Jaken paced ahead, the three of them lost in a conversation of their own. Menoria's two newly appointed kingsknights followed them.

"Igare has asked me to another dinner," Menoria said and groaned, and Jaslin caught up with her.

As they passed a mounted crossbow, the archer pulled its trigger handle, and the rope snapped forward, making Menoria jump. The metals arms blurred as they vibrated, and a bolt streaked away toward its target—a flag waving behind a soaring storm dragon. The bolt passed wide of its mark, and a few soldiers groaned. A commanding officer shouted at them, his tone riddled with disappointment.

"You will be fine," Jaslin said to her lady. "You're only nervous because of what happened during your first encounter. If you try to imagine starting over and acting like yourself, the past events will soon become something you two can look back on and laugh about, together."

Menoria paced along quickly as a man pulled a cart laden with dragonbolts beside them. "What if I do not want any of it?"

Jaslin faltered before recovering and catching up with Menoria again. "I thought you felt that you had to come here and go through with this, for Nevergrace. Surely you prefer Igare courting you over Riscott."

Menoria scoffed. "Indeed. Of course I do not *want* to wed a much older man, but I realize it is something that must be done. For Nevergrace and all of Belvenguard. I cannot turn down the king. I could have declined the orator."

"We could run away," Jaslin said, and Menoria glanced over and studied her adventurous grin, "and find a place where kings and war cannot reach us. Maybe the Weltermores, or we could hide out in the Sivwood for a time."

"There is no place this war will leave untouched."

They paced along behind their three friends, and the king's conjuror and nyren both stepped onto the battlements ahead. Tiros waved to Menoria, and the lady of the Never stopped and quickly bowed her head.

"Tiros," Menoria said. "Can I be of any assistance to you or the king?"

"Actually, we were hoping to speak with your handmaid." Tiros studied Jaslin. "May I see the shard that Cartaya has told me about?"

Jaslin's skin prickled like needles. They all wanted the fragment, but how could she say no? She hesitantly reached to her waist and removed the shard from a pouch before holding it out.

Tiros's fingers wrapped around it, and he took it from her. He squinted and held the shard closer to his eyes and then up into more direct sunlight. "It dates back to the days of Cimerenden," he said to Cartaya, who nodded, her face shadowed beneath her hood. "Your powers of observation, or your sense for the arcane, have not deceived you." He shrugged. "But it no longer harbors any magic. That potential died with the last of the elves."

"The young dragonknight, her brother"—Cartaya indicated Jaslin—"claimed to have encountered a few elves in the Evenmeres, and everything else he told us turned out to be true."

"But if there truly are wicked creatures and monsters lurking in the woods and attacking villages, they surely would have slaughtered a few elves who remained under the canopy."

"That does seem likely." Cartaya opened her fist, and white fire bloomed on her palm. "But I still sense the shard's power. Pass it over the flame."

The nyren did so, and the crystal flashed violet. A cracking sound burst out and rang Jaslin's skull. Jaslin covered her ears with her palms and winced, but no one else seemed to have noticed the noise.

Cartaya pointed a finger at Jaslin and said, "Then the power I sense must lie within the handmaid. She heard the testing of the elven crystal."

The nyren shrugged and handed the shard back to Jaslin, who quickly took it and tucked it away.

"The shard's magic is gone." Tiros's fingers worked at the curls in his beard. "That fact is irrefutable."

Cartaya nodded slowly but apparently in agreement.

Jaslin pondered their conclusion. She had never wanted to accept that the shard might hold some power over her, but she was not convinced that it was purely sentimental value making her feel the way she did about it. She faced Tiros. "How do you know for certain?"

The old man grinned. "I am a nyren, remember? I studied the lore of Cimerenden decades ago, and a trained nyren does not forget anything they have read or are taught."

"What if you remembered something wrong?" Jaslin asked. "Even in just one instance? There is no other nyren here to refute you."

Tiros chuckled. "In all my years, I have not been proven wrong on a concept I have learned. Nor has any other master nyren. Our order still convenes and tests each other's mental capabilities to ensure none of us are succumbing to the effects of age. When we do, we may no longer wear the chain." He jostled his belt made of links.

Jaslin capitulated and simply nodded.

Cartaya wagged a finger at her. "Remember—come see me tomorrow night in the conjuror's chamber. If it is not the shard, then we must delve into this power you may carry as soon as possible. You are a sibling of the young dragonknight, and a similar ability with magic could also flow through your veins."

The conjuror and nyren strode away, walking along the battlements, watching the soldiers prepare and practice loosing bolts at flags that streamed behind dragons.

"I had no idea there was anything strange going on with you," Menoria said with a crackle of suspicion in her tone, which pulled Jaslin's attention away from the two councilmembers. "You should obey Cartaya's request. I can attend one dinner without your assistance."

Jaslin nodded. "But first, I promised to take you to the wharf." She waved the two kingsknights who were following them onward.

∽

"What are we doing in this slum?" Jaken asked as he trod along, trying to keep up with Vysoria, who walked confidently around bustling locals bartering for fish, nets, seaweed, shellfish, and pearls. Nistene hurried after Jaken. The kingsknights trailed behind Menoria in silence.

"I thought the future queen needed to see the wharf market of her city," Jaslin lied as she glanced about, searching for the vendor whom the merchants in the inn described. *Keliam.*

They wandered about the crowds for nearly an hour, the screeching of gulls and smells of the sea wafting around them. People haggled and shouted, shook their heads, and smiled toothless grins of welcome. Pairs of soldiers patrolled the area or stood at attention within patches of warm sunlight.

After passing along the entire length of the wharf and not finding anyone with a diamond pattern on his robes, Jaslin feigned an air of excitement and turned to head back through the merchants' stalls again. "Now that we've gotten a quick glance at everything, we can stop and have a look at a few things that interest us."

"You're acting strange." Menoria cast her a bewildered expression. "I did not see any books for sale here."

"I thought it would be good for you to get out and purchase a few frivolous things." Jaslin started back along the walk. "To take your mind off everything else. If there's anything you like, please let me know."

"This is the last time I'm walking through this throng," Vysoria said to Jaslin. "And only because I must in order to head into the area of the city where I want to go. After that, we'll leave you and our future queen and her kingsknights to do whatever you want."

Jaslin flashed her a friendly smile, and they strolled along the wharf again. Menoria browsed around but did not approach any vendors. There were so many of them, so many people selling fish and a multitude of other goods while shouting, it rattled Jaslin. This place was as far from the likes of Nevergrace as she could imagine. She did not spot her quarry and reached the end of the walk without stopping at a single stall.

"Then we are done here?" Jaken asked, interrupting Nistene as she was whispering in his ear.

Menoria opened her mouth, but Jaslin spoke first. "We'll join you, but first, we'd like to visit a tavern we saw that was past the far end of the pier." Jaslin pointed back through the market.

Nistene groaned. "Suit yourself. I'm leaving." She turned and stalked off.

Vysoria almost followed her but then seemed to realize she would be following Nistene's lead. The conjuror's daughter stopped. "One last pass so we can all have a drink together."

Jaslin nodded. "Thank you."

Nistene returned, her mouth hanging open in protest, but Jaken remained beside Vysoria, ignoring the princess. They entered the crowds one last time, and Nistene sheepishly joined them.

Jaslin stopped, eyeing a fishmonger directly ahead. They had already passed by this man twice, and she had not noticed him. He did not have diamonds standing out on his clothing in gold or some other flashy trim, but the pattern was sewn into his black robe—subtle. Jaslin grabbed Menoria by the wrist and led her to an adjacent stall. As Menoria looked over bright pearl earrings and necklaces, Jaslin watched the merchant in question.

Two people arrived at his stall, paid coin for trout, and then departed. A third man hunched as he neared the table. The merchant who must be Keliam smiled and motioned to the displayed fish while discussing something with the patron. After a minute of hushed conversation, Keliam pulled a bass from between stacks of fish and passed it to the man. The patron accepted it and hurried away.

Two of Galvenstone's watch stood across the way in a splash

of autumn sunlight, their spears leaning against a pillar. Jaslin casually strode over to them, and they glared at her from behind helms and breastplates.

"There is a merchant here who is selling goods in violation of the king's laws." Jaslin kept her voice low.

The soldiers' gazes rose over her head as they peered around. "How do you know?" the one on the left asked.

"I saw something very suspicious." Jaslin quickly described the details, embellishing much of it. "I think I even saw something *inside* that fish. Something was stuffed in there."

The guard squinted as he watched Keliam. "We've been watching this area and that merchant for years. He is not a smuggler."

"I saw it."

"I believe you think you saw something you wanted to believe. That man is a simple merchant."

The way the soldier said the words, with a rising animosity, made Jaslin suspect he already knew about Keliam. Maybe the merchant bribed the watch and even had certain men he trusted stand in his area to settle any issues that arose when selling his illegal goods.

"Menoria, the future queen of—"

"Be off, little girl." The soldier sneered at her and shooed her away. "You know nothing of the wharf, not if you live in some noble's manor or inside Dashtok."

Jaslin retreated a step, a burst of surprise rising within her before she slowly accepted defeat and returned to Menoria.

"Find anything you like?" Jaslin asked the lady. Jaken, Nistene, and Vysoria browsed the goods beside her.

Menoria held up a blue pearl necklace. "I purchased this."

"It's beautiful." Jaslin took Menoria by the wrist and guided her toward Keliam's stall. "Now, just one more thing."

"Then will you stop acting so strangely while trying to occupy my mind with jewelry?"

Jaslin nodded as they approached Keliam's stall.

The fishmonger grinned and studied them, all of his teeth intact and white. His gray hair and beard were cut close to his skin. "Can I help you two young ladies find something in particular? Today, I have lake trout, perch, giant sturgeon, and scrapper bottoms." He waved a hand across the table.

Jaslin looked past the offered fish to another table stacked with oysters, clams, and shrimp. "What about those?"

"You prefer shellfish? I have plenty. What would you like?"

A man in a stained apron gutted fish behind Keliam and slapped one down on a table then hung another using twine that ran between its lips and through its gills.

What shellfish could best be used to hide something? "I'll have a look at the clams."

Keliam turned and plucked two from the table before displaying them on his palms. "I sell only the best clams of the lake."

"Would we be able to pick out our own?" Jaslin asked, tapping her chin and studying the shellfish, putting on the act of a discerning eye.

"Certainly." Keliam grinned again. "I appreciate women who know their fish."

He is not afraid of us choosing any of those. She sauntered behind the fish table and examined the clams, then the shrimp. Her attention wandered to the man gutting fish. A massive sturgeon dangled from a beam, twisting ever so slightly on a rope. "I would like this one." She took two quick steps toward the hanging fish.

Keliam's voice rose an octave. "Those are not for sale." He hurried after Jaslin and reached for her. "They have just been cleaned."

Jaslin avoided the merchant's attempt to snatch her arm, and she grasped the tail of the hanging fish and gave it a tug. The rope holding it creaked, and the sturgeon spun, its head and gills bowing, but it didn't break free or slap down onto Jaslin's forearms as she was hoping. The merchant shrieked. Jaslin quickly dug her fingers into the opening that had been created when gutting the fish, a cut that ran along its lower margin. It was partially sewn shut. She yanked at its edges.

"Leave the merchant's stall!" one of the soldiers across the way shouted as both of them marched closer, and Keliam again tried to grab her.

Jaslin circled the enormous fish, placing it between her and the merchant. She opened its cut and rammed a shoulder into the fish's side, expecting bags of white poppy powder to spill out —like in one of her favorite stories. Instead, two black scales the size of a man's torso hit the ground.

Menoria yelled in surprise.

Keliam shrieked again. "What are you doing?" He stared in horror at the scales. "What are those?"

Jaslin glanced back. The two soldiers shouted and ordered her to desist, but they did not come any closer. However, the two kingsknights—the kind of men Jaslin had wanted with them in case the events at the wharf played out like this and they needed someone on their side for protection as well as to apprehend any questionable people—came sprinting. Their hands clenched their sheathed swords, and their golden capes fluttered behind them as they drew their blades.

"Dragon scales?" Geniar, the tall and thin knight, arrived and used the tip of his sword to push the scales about, inspecting them. "From a moon dragon? Why?"

"Or are they from a shadow dragon?" Farsten, the muscular one, said in shock.

Jaken, Vysoria, and Nistene advanced along with a crowd of spectators.

Keliam turned and bolted, knocking over the shellfish table and strewing his goods across the wharf before crashing through the onlookers. The kingsknights turned to pursue him, but the merchant had already slipped away into the masses. Instead, Farsten grabbed the man gutting the merchant's fish and shoved him up against a wall, holding him at sword point. Geniar searched all of the fillets on the tables and cut down the rest of the hanging fish. He dumped out white powder, black pearls, foreign coins, and gems, forming a pile near the man they had detained.

Geniar reached inside an unassuming perch that had been hanging and slowly pulled out an object—a vial. It was filled with liquid as black as the deepest shadows. A few bubbles roiled along the vial's glass walls and rose toward the surface.

"And what is that?" Farsten kicked the fish gutter, who whimpered but did not respond.

"It looks like something abominable." Geniar held it up to his eye and then into direct sunlight. "Like poison."

As the perch in question spun around on its line, something else inside the fish caught the sunlight. While everyone watched the kingsknights interrogate the suspect, Jaslin crept closer to the perch and furtively slipped her hand into the slice in its belly. She grasped another vial. This one was smaller, and it had fallen toward the tail. After quickly glancing over at her friends and the kingsknights, who did not notice what she was doing, she slid out the vial—which also contained black liquid—and tucked it beneath her belt.

She took in the scene around them. The two soldiers who had been standing across the walk were no longer around. For an instant, she thought she caught sight of Keliam's face leering at her in the crowd, but then it was gone. A chill swept down her spine. She had done all of this to learn what the guild merchants knew about the queens' assassins, but she had not foreseen her target escaping and becoming a vengeful enemy.

Her fist closed around her belt where the vial was hidden, and a tingle of dread spiraled about inside her as she imagined what Keliam might want to do to her in retaliation.

29

CYRAN ORENDAIN

"If you move around, you won't freeze up." The gaoler kicked at Ineri.

Ice crystals spiked her fur blankets. She was lying across the incline of the cell so that if she rolled too far or slipped, she would plummet over its edge.

Cyran gritted his teeth while glaring at the soldiers just beyond the doorway. "Do not kick her! She is ill."

"She would be better off if she'd move around." The turnkey dropped buckets of water and a plate loaded with dark breads and hard cheese onto the ground. He nudged Ineri again with his toe, threatening to send her rolling out into the sky.

Cyran stood, battling against the skirling winds that swung into the cell, whipped around in the interior, and threatened to push anyone inside out of the gap in the walls. The soldiers stepped into the chamber and advanced with their spears lowered.

"I am only looking out for her health." The gaoler held up his hands in feigned innocence and smirked. Several of his teeth were missing, and a few others dangled by only one root. "And I have not caused her any harm."

Cyran pointed at himself and Vyk before indicating Ineri. "You can torment either of us as much as you'd like, but not her."

The wind howled, and the turnkey clutched his furs tightly about his neck. Another type of cry rang in the distance—the blaring of horns across Northsheeren. The gaoler's eyes lit up as he stared out through the absent wall. The clatter and jostling of armor sounded from within the halls beyond the doorway. A louder commotion arose in the halls, and faraway voices shouted across the castle. Cyran whirled around as a legion of dragons streaked across the sky beyond their cell.

Whatever was happening was not part of some distant war preparations. *They hunt something near.*

"The Dragon Queen said something is coming." A voice echoed in the hall outside.

Cyran spun to face the gaoler and the doorway as he flexed his fingers on his lute, preparing to use the instrument as a weapon if the opportunity arose. The beating of massive wings sounded behind him again, and these noises did not fade. Instead, they drew closer. Cyran slowly turned to face a dragon as it rose over the lip of their cell. Green scales and wings. It squinted its yellow eyes against the gale and snow.

Eidelmere... Cyran's heart stopped beating for a moment and then raced faster.

The turnkey shrieked, and more soldiers poured into the cell. Eidelmere's spined wings battled against the wind. Other larger and darker dragons dived from the spires of Northsheeren and hurtled toward Eidelmere. The forest dragon's jaws parted, and he breathed a gush of water across one side of their cell. The deluge smacked into the gaoler and the approaching soldiers, blasting them back. Almost instantly, the water froze, creating a wall of ice that held its victims still and in cringing poses, making it appear as if they were still alive.

"Do not stand there looking like the simple boy who once fed me in the den," Eidelmere barked at Cyran. "The only chance you three have is to escape."

Eidelmere was hovering too far from the ledge of their cell, still fighting the harsh wind. Cyran would never be able to leap onto his snout. Cyran glanced back at the doorway of the cell.

"But not through there," the dragon said. "I cannot save you in the midst of Northsheeren. You must run over the edge."

A legion of Murgare dragons barreled closer, the beasts screeching and roaring.

"Dive from the cliff." Eidelmere turned to face an ice dragon and blood dragon that hurtled toward them, their talons and teeth extended. "It is your last and only chance." Eidelmere roared at the approaching adversaries.

Crossbows thrummed on the decks of the Murgare dragons, and bolts streaked across the gap, screaming toward Eidelmere's vital areas. Cyran raced to the ledge of the cell, and Ineri and Vyk joined him. Beyond leagues of stark cliffs waited a patch of snow-covered conifers and a winding river of ice. They would never survive such a fall.

Voices rose behind them as steel clashed with ice. Soldiers chopped through the walls of Eidelmere's frozen breath, which stood in front of their doorway.

Eidelmere spewed another river at the approaching legion, breaking the oath of the *neblír*. The blast did little more than fling icy pellets and chunks through the tempest, although it did freeze and drop some of the bolts flying at him. The forest dragon bared his teeth and raised his talons in defense.

"I could not leave you to be tortured to death, but do not make my efforts all for naught," Eidelmere said, his voice rasping in his throat as his rage and fear flooded the other realm. "Just this one time, *trust* me. By the Dragon, take the last bloody step!"

Thoughts of the Dragon Queen's offer of training Cyran and her supposed friendliness toward him and his companions surfaced as he glanced down at the treetops again. If he did not join Murgare or did not harbor the ability to call up the other realm, he and his companions would never leave this place alive. Murgare did not keep prisoners—unless they had an ulterior motive.

A massive black dragon barreled in from the side, crashing into Eidelmere and sending both creatures tumbling through the air as the dark one lashed out at Eidelmere with its barbed tail. Shadowmar roared and sank her teeth into Eidelmere's neck, and her tail plunged through the scales of the forest dragon's chest.

Cyran bellowed in surprise and anger, flinging his lute at the beast and clenching his fists as the last of his breath streamed from his lungs.

Eidelmere's head pivoted slightly in Cyran's direction. "Leap." The light faded from the dragon's eyes, and his scaled body went limp. Shadowmar released him from her grip and let his body fall.

"NO!" Cyran's heart felt like it burst as he grabbed Ineri's and Vyk's wrists and pulled, launching himself and them over the ledge.

Cyran's stomach sucked up into his throat as he plunged downward, the snow and ice and wind assaulting him and striking his face like ghostly whips. His companions screamed from somewhere beside him. Another cry accompanied theirs as a figure dived from another cell and began falling.

Time slowed as Cyran watched the beautiful scene of snow-laden trees rushing up to meet him. At least Murgare would not be able to torture them for information or to death, and Cyran would not end up using any power he had against Belvenguard and his people. His eyes closed as the gale tore at his hair and tunic.

A sense of stillness settled over everything, and the world transformed into a place far more serene than reality. Cyran's senses dulled, and tranquility and a sense of peace and happiness blossomed inside his core. Pulsing fibers of light arced around him. He released a single dry chuckle. Little good any of the Dragon Queen's magic would do him now. Even she could not fly, or she would not need a dragon. A breath of air filled his lungs as his heartrate slowed.

Beating wings sounded below, and Cyran opened his eyes just in time to see three dragons the likes of which he had never encountered before swooping out of the treetops. Their brown bodies and tan spikes made them appear like bristling balls of scales. *Thorn dragons.* Cyran recalled them only from drawings. These creatures soared upward and then angled themselves so Cyran and his comrades could latch onto some of their spines with their hands and feet.

The thorn who caught Ineri pivoted and flapped away before catching what must have been Turin's plummeting form. Then the creatures streaked downward toward the forest's canopy.

A massive crash rang out above. Eidelmere's spiraling body, his descent slowed by his limp wings, smashed into the cliffs, sending several avalanches plunging down into the valley and forest below. The forest dragon bounced off the rocks, his wings folding inward, and he fell much faster, soon crashing into the valley and flinging up a cloud of snow that resembled white smoke.

Murgare's legions shrieked in outrage and swirled in the skies and around the spires overhead.

∽

Green pines whipped past as Cyran soared through the forest on the thorn dragon, disturbing branches, which sent showers of snow crashing down upon his companions behind him. Pain lit up his heart, but the sensation was not nearly as severe as the suffering he had felt pulsing within the *neblír* when Eidelmere had lost his bond with Morden. Cyran worried there was something wrong with him and his lack of deeper emotion, if he was not as affected or hurt as another one of the *sïosaires*. Surely he had lost Eidelmere, their bond severed... Or was it possible that his friend was poisoned, his bones crushed, but he was not quite dead yet?

"I have to turn back." Cyran looked at his companions and Turin, whose blond hair and beard made him resemble Vyk, although Turin's were not braided, and his lower leg and foot appeared disfigured in his boot and leggings.

"We cannot." Turin pointed upward. "The legions of Murgare swarm the skies. If they see us, they will kill us. The forest is our only cover."

"You three continue on. We will catch up." Cyran urged his mount to turn, but the dragon resisted. He said to her, "I must find Eidelmere and see if he is still alive."

"The old dragon could not have survived that sting or his fall," his mount said. "The errand is foolish. And dangerous."

Cyran reached into the other realm and immediately found the thread of this thorn dragon's soul. He grasped it gently. *"Milluriumillen. I must see if Eidelmere still lives."*

The dragon braced against him and flinched. *"Eidelmere told us to be wary of humans, but he thought you were different. We have remained hidden in the smaller trees of the Evenmeres and away from man since before the Dragon Wars. Would you truly risk your own life for nothing more than hoping to comfort a dead or dying dragon?"*

"I would. And I apologize for this, but it must happen. I will release you when Belvenguard is safe and the war is over, and then I

will never speak of your whereabouts." He gripped the thread to initiate his command, and Milluri swung around a broad trunk, beating her wings and racing for the massive plume of snow hovering over the northern margins of the forest. Her disbelief inundated the other realm, but she no longer resisted his commands and even flew of her own accord.

They soared as fast as Milluri could manage under the boughs as she weaved and ducked before emerging in the swirling cloud of ice dust and snow that had been dislodged and thrown into the air during Eidelmere's crashing fall.

Cyran pointed. "He is somewhere over there. I can feel it."

A dark form emerged in the churning white ahead, and when Milluri landed, Cyran leapt off her, wading through deep snow toward Eidelmere.

"I lied to you." Eidelmere's voice was raspier than normal, and it sounded far away, fading. "But you came anyway."

"You saved us." Cyran gripped a segment of his broken wing and held it tenderly. "You somehow traveled all the way to Northsheeren to free us." Tears stung his eyes.

Eidelmere shifted and grunted in pain before lying still. Both of his legs jutted away from his body at strange angles. His other wing was crumpled beneath his body, and black veins branched and flowed across his flesh, their dark shade even showing through his scales. These veins pulsed with each of the dragon's heartbeats, and they spread across his chest and along his limbs, crawling up toward his neck.

Cyran suppressed his horror, forcing himself not to think about what the dark veins would do.

Eidelmere coughed weakly, and a spurt of black liquid shot from his mouth and splattered the snow. "I used a distraction." His chuckle died almost as soon as it started. "A few other thorns drew off the watching legions of Murgare so I could come out of the forest without being spotted right away. I had been waiting for many days and realized there would be no good opportunity. I knew one of us would have to fight some of them off, and none of the thorns were willing to take that position."

Cyran's heart buckled and collapsed like a smashed crate, spilling its emotional contents through his chest and out into the rest of his body.

"I said I lied to you," Eidelmere added. "Even though so many of the oaths of the *neblír* do not allow for it, I still did it. Just once. I said your father was one of the dragonguard. That was not true. The only reason I said it was so that you would be more inclined to take up Sir Kayom's sword and become a dragonknight. Your kind also do what they are told not to. I essentially told you not to take up the sword and join the guard to further encourage you."

A quick laugh escaped Cyran's lips as tears burst from his eyes.

"You are all a conundrum," Eidelmere said. "Another aspect I cannot comprehend is that you are all taught that ability and rank can only be granted by ancestry and blood or by a king's will, and you all fall for it. For your entire lives. Never believe that. Such things are almost always accomplished through utter need and pure desire."

Cyran could only nod, the dragon's words barely registering in his mind. "You should have stayed in the Evenmeres."

Eidelmere shook his head, his movements slow and weak. "The forest will be destroyed soon. I saw it—the dying trees. A great evil is coming. That is one reason why the thorns agreed to help my cause. This evil is not what we all feared but more. Far more. You must find it and stop it. Such things are beyond me." He took a few shallow breaths. "The Evenmeres are no longer my home, and my desire for such a life could not create that reality. The woods are foreign. I did not know the other forest dragons in the woods. They did not know me. What I longed for over so many years was no longer there. The home I yearned to return to lies somewhere in the past of this world, and none of us can go back to those times."

Cyran fought off a sobbing wail and wiped at his eyes. "We must get you back to the Evenmeres. I truly mean to free you, my friend—*Eidelmerendren*—once this is all over. But I should have done so earlier, when I had the chance, and for that I am utterly sorry." He could not hold back a sob before clamping a hand over his nose and mouth.

"I know you would have freed me, *Cyranorendain*." Eidelmere's closest pupil narrowed a bit as he attempted to focus on Cyran, although his eye remained cloudy. "And I have met no other who would have done so. That is why I came for you. Once you earn the loyalty of a dragon, my kind will not abandon you. You were not my ideal choice, but you are the best option I know of to become someone who will try to save my kind." He shifted his back, groaning in an immense pain that blinded Cyran in the other realm. One of his talons extended. "Take it."

In his grip, the dragon held a sheathed sword. *The Flame in the Forest.* "How did you...?"

"It was still on the Dragon Queen's beast. I took it from her when her tail pierced my scales. But I could not retrieve both of your blades. The silver elvish sword is still hers. The rest of your armor that you left with me is also here." He motioned to his side.

Cyran squeezed Eidelmere's wing tip tighter, his heart tearing apart, its ribbons floating through the slats between his ribs as he tried to hold on to Eidelmere in this realm and in the other. This old and most bitter of dragons had made the ultimate sacrifice for a boy he might not have even liked and surely did not love.

Cyran spoke the words from the dragon realm when it was

time for one of their kind to die. "*Mörenth toi boménth bi droth su llith.* Till the end of days we soar. *Mörenth toi boménth bi nomth su praëm.* Till the end of nights we reign. *Röith moirten íli. Ílith ëmdrien tiu gládthe.* You honor me. My soul sees yours."

Eidelmere's pupil widened in surprise but abruptly transitioned to a look of solace. His dying breath was faint. The ravaging black veins covered his body and ensnared his throat, their darkness throbbing. Cyran wasn't sure if he heard the dragon's last words in this world or somewhere else, but they echoed within the vault of his skull. "Forget the boy you were. Find the man I pray to the Dragon that you can one day become."

"If I could, I would lay all the glacial roses in the world around you, my friend." Cyran's vision of the dragon and his sword blurred through his tears as the weapon's sheath slid off and fell. Its blade glowed green with the scales of the forest dragon.

From this moment onward, the sword shall be called Eidelmere's Flame, and it will find vengeance.

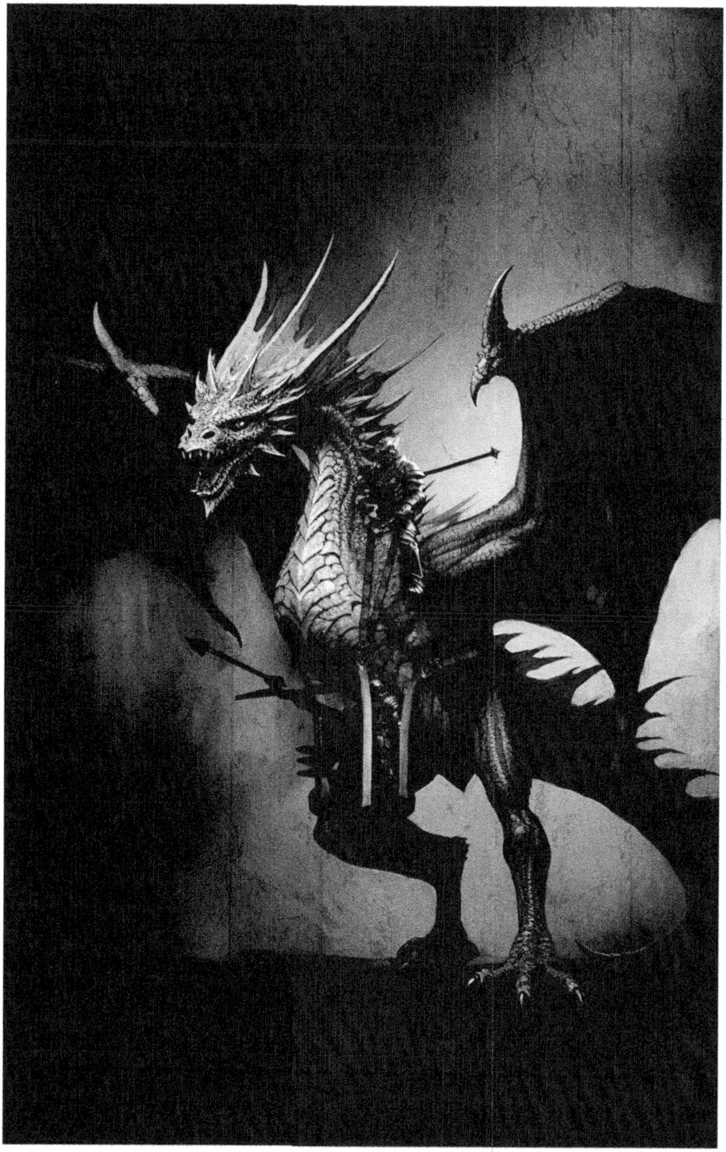

30

CYRAN ORENDAIN

Curtains of green needles whipped past Cyran, flinging and dropping snow in his and the thorn dragon's wake. A massive weight of pain and anguish had settled over his heart, seeming to want to crush the beating organ.

Eidelmere. The dragon was truly gone from this realm and from the *neblír* as well, his soul lost to existence—the only outcome after dying from the venom in a shadow dragon's stinger. Cyran's head sank, and his heart lit with fire as his chin rested against his chest. The blurring surroundings barely distracted him, and soon they faded into nothingness.

Shrieks rang out overhead, and Cyran lurched. The rattling echoes from the shrieks rolled off the cliffs above the forest, making it hard to pinpoint their origins. Milluri rolled and twisted her body so she soared on her side, positioning Cyran parallel to the ground and her spiny wings vertically, one above the other. They whizzed between two trunks and hurtled out into an open expanse. The tree line ahead was many dragon lengths away. A roar blasted behind them, and the thrum of crossbow arms sounded.

Cyran glanced back to find a dark bolt streaking toward them.

"*Barrel roll.*" He gripped his dragon's thread—her soul and will—and imagined the movement.

Milluri dipped her right wing farther beyond its vertical position, and her left wing snapped upward. She twisted and spun as the bolt screamed past Cyran's head.

"*Fly like the wind on the mountains,*" Cyran added.

Milluri leveled out and flapped faster as the beating of more wings sounded in the distance. A blood and an ash dragon raced to join a mist, whose archer had already loosed. Cyran repeatedly glanced ahead and then behind them, judging how long it would take for them to reach cover again versus how long it would take for the archer to reload and for the other two dragons to join the first. He did not carry a lance or shield, and there were no archers on this dragon. Their only weapons were Milluri's teeth and claws, which would not be useful unless they were forced to engage in close combat.

"*We may die because you wanted to go back for Eidelmere,*" Milluri said in Cyran's mind.

"*I would do it again... but I am truly sorry for involving you.*"

"*Initially, I was skeptical, but now I trust your feelings for our kind. Because of what you were willing to sacrifice for a dragon.*"

A small weight lifted from the walls of Cyran's collapsing heart as Milluri raced on. Roars erupted from the sky, and the whistling of bolts followed. Cyran maneuvered his dragon in a haphazard pattern across the open field, hoping to avoid any incoming projectiles. Bolts rammed into the ground around them with sharp cracks, flinging plumes of snow and ice into the air.

Cyran ducked low and clung to his dragon's neck as they streaked past the far tree line, finding cover again under a canopy of pines. Milluri darted and weaved around trunks and branches, barely slowing her pace. The pursuing dragons' cries of protest faded but did not vanish completely. Murgare's legions would be flying the length of the forest, watching from above, waiting for their prey to emerge from any gap, their archers poised and ready to loose their deadly bolts.

More wing beats sounded from within the forest and drew closer. Something flanked Milluri, and Cyran's guts churned as he cursed and glanced over his shoulder.

"You survived long enough to find us," Vyk called out from the back of his dragon. "Although I don't appreciate the company you brought with you."

Cyran released a sigh of relief as he spotted Ineri and Turin on another dragon behind Vyk's. "If we stay beneath the canopy, we may be able to avoid them."

"And how do you hope to do that all the way to Belvenguard?" Vyk's tone rose with skepticism. "There were not forests in the south of this kingdom."

"We will deal with that difficulty once we run out of trees," Ineri said and hacked a few times.

They flew along, whipping around conifers and boulders, and within minutes, the crushing sensation returned and sat on Cyran's chest. His sorrow sheeted from his bones and blood and flooded the other realm. The magnitude of his pain was comparable to Eidelmere's after the forest dragon had lost Morden.

The despair of the sïosaires. Cyran's bond with Eidelmere had been forever severed. It was his first broken bond, although he speculated that he might form and lose many more. He had experienced young love with a couple of women in years past, and his parting from them—with the breaking of their relationship—was nothing compared to the pain raging inside him now. This grief ran so much deeper. It seemed as if he had lost his soulmate.

Bitter old Eidelmere was my soulmate? Emellefer would not be happy if he ever used that term to try to explain the emotions burning inside him. The thought gave him a brief flicker of humor, and he released a half-hearted chuckle.

"You retrieved your sword." Vyk pointed to the weapon strapped across Cyran's back. "At least one of them."

"And the rest of your armor," Ineri added.

Cyran nodded.

"How'd you manage all that?" Vyk tried to scratch his scalp, but his helm curtailed his attempt.

"I have them only because of the actions of the bravest soul Cimeren has ever known."

∽

Over the following days, Cyran and his comrades flew through the shrouded daylight within the forest, and they stopped and rested at night while the thorn dragons clung to pines and seemed to become part of their trunks and branches. At first light, they raced on again.

At some point, Turin had recognized Ineri either from her nearly concealed face or her cough. "The greatest archer in all the kingdoms," he had said and bowed to her. Ineri smiled but dismissed his attention with a wave.

After many days of using snow or creeks for water and, with the aid of the thorn dragons, foraging and hunting for meager food sources, they arrived at the southern border of the forest. A vast expanse of open terrain extended beyond its boundaries, the Lake of the Lady to the west, the last of the Dragonback Mountains to the east. Rolling hills carried on to the south.

"The Evenmeres await us." Turin pointed over the hills, his beard whipping across his face under the shrill wind. "Across that gap."

"How far?" Cyran asked. They had flown over the region

after being captured, but their travel had taken them east to the sea and then back west. He could only guess how long such a crossing would take with thorn dragons flying as fast as they could.

"Leagues." Turin shook his head. "Many leagues. On the backs of these dragons, I'd wager"—he bobbled his head and hands—"it will take much longer than we could ever hope to fly in Murgare without being noticed. And we will not have any cover close at hand."

"Then we remain here and continue hiding in this cursed kingdom?" Vyk grunted. "We will die here as sure as the sun will set."

Ineri coughed. "These lands hold a tempting but treacherous beauty. Like all of Murgare. They are far too harsh. We will not survive alone in these wilds. I suggest we risk the crossing."

"I already lost one bollock to the cold of that cell," Turin said. "I'm not about to lose the other hiding in this forest through the dead of winter. Nor will I risk losing the greatest archer in the kingdoms."

"We will find no more cover passing over the Lake of the Lady or racing east to the sea." Cyran's eyes lidded in defeat, his despair still rippling through him. "But we should wait for nightfall. Then we fly low, and we race for the first line of angoias." He glanced down at his mount. "Do you know how to travel across the Evenmeres using its angoia canopy?"

"I've seen forest dragons pass through the copses using such means," Milluri answered in his mind. *"We thorn dragons only use the angoias to hide in when needed. We have never had the desire to make such a crossing."*

"Then you three will be the first of your kind to do so."

They waited for nightfall, their conversations few and far between.

Cyran cleared his throat. "Besides for the coming darkness

Eidelmere mentioned, how did he ever convince three thorn dragons to aid him as well as three humans who were being held in Murgare?"

"The old forest dragon knew and understood an obscurity about the two realms, and he shared it with us in return for our assistance," Milluri answered. "And he convinced us that we would be pulled into the brewing war either way, that our home would be lost if we did not offer aid."

Vyk shifted uncomfortably about on the scales beneath him, and his hands trembled. Ineri sank into her furs. Turin pressed himself closer to Ineri, his boot and lower leggings on one side flopping about as if he had a stump around the area of his knee.

"What happened?" Vyk gestured at the archer's disfigured limb.

"I took a bolt during the errand to capture the Dread King," Turin said.

When darkness finally swept out of the east and crawled westward, Vyk tugged at his beard, his eyes wide with fear. Cyran wished they had an entire barrel of ale for the archer now. Lines of torches glowed somewhere far to the east, appearing like a winding dragon on fire.

More Murgare armies travel to the north shore. "It is time." Cyran adjusted and braced himself, and Milluri launched from the trunk of a pine and hovered just within the edge of the forest. The other two dragons joined her. Torches burning in towns far to the west created pockets of light. *We will avoid those areas as well.*

The dragons beat their wings, emerging from the woods as tentatively as a premature dragonet from an egg. No roars or shrieks greeted them as they glided through the open night, the companions and their mounts keeping their eyes out for stray trees or mounds they could potentially use for cover.

Cyran held his breath as he watched the sky, but too often he turned to the dark lands before them, willing the Evenmeres to arrive. The moonlight grew brighter, painting the sky sea overhead and frosting the grasses and brush that blurred beneath them.

The wind whistled in Cyran's ears as they soared along. A league passed without incident. Then another and another. Cyran's heart lifted with hope as an hour burned away. More and more hours followed without incident, and eventually they began to near the once distant line of the Evenmeres. Then the songs of moon birds and the chirring of winter insects died out. The night became quiet. Too quiet. Snow fell lightly.

Cyran glanced skyward. A dark cloud passed between him and the illuminated sky sea, a cloud with many flapping wings. Cyran's heart iced up in his chest and thumped against his burning lungs.

"They come." He pointed, his finger trembling.

"Fly on!" Turin's voice cracked. "I've already been taken once. Never again."

The thorn dragons screeched and beat their wings faster, propelling them over hills that passed in flashes of moonlight and lakes of shadow. The cloud of pursuing dragons drew closer and dived. Roars belted out. Leathery segments of wings throbbed in the wind.

"We have too far to go." Ineri shook her head, her hands reaching out, as if she hoped to grip her ballista's handle and wheel about. All that her fingers found was empty air.

Cyran faced forward, his breathing fast and shallow as he waited for the silhouettes of the Evenmeres to grow larger on the horizon. The Murgare dragons swarmed closer, and those on either side of their legion broke away from the others, racing off at angles.

More shrieks erupted ahead. A wall of dragons appeared in the southern sky, curtaining off their escape route, although the

Evenmeres lay just beyond them. Their pursuers closed in behind. The outlines of a few small storm dragons darted back and forth between the Murgare legions, probably passing commands and organizing their guard.

"We have to separate," Vyk said, "and hope that at least one of us will be able to slip around them."

Cyran glanced about, seeing no other option.

"Death itself rides on the dragon's neck behind me." Turin lowered his head and nudged Ineri. "It has chased me ever since that fateful raid. Pass yourself along to your comrade's dragon. I shall lead some of those before us away—create a distraction."

"No." Cyran gripped his sword's hilt more for support than for any use. "I will try to draw them off. I am a dragonknight and can react faster than any of their mage and guard teams are able to."

"That's why Belvenguard needs you to return alive," Turin said as he hoisted Ineri from where she sat and assisted her as Vyk's thorn dragon neared. She climbed over to sit with Vyk. "Your mounts should both continue on, but one should travel far to the east, the other to the west. I will head straight for them."

"You just escaped Northsheeren," Cyran said. "I will not allow you to die before you have returned to Belvenguard."

Turin grinned. "You are not in charge in these lands, and you were not around when I was an archer. It will be far better to be killed in battle in Murgare than to have wasted away in that bloody cell."

The dragon beneath Turin wavered, and its spiny lips trembled.

"We will also not ask you to further risk your life, my friend," Cyran said to the dragon, although he felt responsible for whatever outcome was about to happen. There was no easy escape now. "You can try to avoid the coming legions by any means you think best."

"I am in this situation because I already made my choice," the dragon answered in a throaty whisper, the sound of her voice reminiscent of something that had not spoken aloud in centuries, if ever. "To aid my kind in spite of great risk. I do this for Eidelmere and all the others who live in our forest." She flew along and motioned at Vyk's dragon with her claw tips. "Nithinix is the fastest of us and has the best chance of evading them. I do not look forward to what is to come, but I would not flee, even if there were somewhere to flee to."

Cyran slowly nodded. "Lead that archer on your back to safety and glory, and Milluri and I will attempt the same. For Belvenguard and the dragons of our kingdom, *and* for those of the Evenmeres."

"For Belvenguard and the dragons!" Vyk shouted, and Ineri repeated it.

"But I beg of you," Cyran said, "no one try to create any distractions. Just aim to get to the forest by any means necessary."

Turin cast Cyran another wry grin, this one carrying a more haunted look, and his dragon tore away, streaking south.

"Ineri"—Cyran gestured as his stomach clenched—"use the approaching army from the east as protection. The legions may not shoot at you if you fly close to their soldiers."

Cyran veered Milluri sharply to the west as Ineri and Vyk headed east. The beasts of Murgare descended from the skies ahead, some of them breaking off to pursue Cyran while others bolted after the swift Nithinix, who hurtled away into the night.

Milluri's thread throbbed in Cyran's intangible grip as he steered her, watching the hills and mounds and boulders and trees emerge and whip past them.

"I may be able to see better in the night than you," Milluri said. "Perhaps I should guide us."

Ballistae arms thrummed, and Cyran found the other realm and its shimmery light. Both worlds blended together, moonlight and shadow twining with the luminous threads. "I can see in both worlds now."

The bolts arcing toward them stood out in the night. He dived Milluri, avoiding the incoming projectiles that screamed past, and he ascended in quick bursts as more archers loosed at them. They soared close to a few dragons that roared and tried to block their route, but Cyran and Milluri wheeled about and flew below their adversaries, angling out to the west. Crossbow arms creaked and groaned as windlasses cranked, and dragons swung around to maintain pursuit.

Several thuds rang out louder than others. In the distant moonlight and threads of the *neblír*, Turin's dragon wobbled. The fletching of two bolts protruded from the creature's neck and chest. She listed to one side as more bolts flew from the majority of Murgare's legion, who had remained directly ahead of Cyran and his comrades' original location.

"No!" Cyran's throat clamped shut, stretching his word and contorting it into a hoarse shout.

More bolts hammered into the thorn dragon's flesh, releasing muffled thumps. She veered as she fell out of the sky and smashed into the ground, her forward momentum causing her to skid and roll, which flung Turin—who was no more than a dark speck—out over the fields and into a hillside. His body smacked into the earth with a definitive cracking of bones.

Cyran hurtled toward the Evenmeres. He glanced over his shoulder, hoping against reason that he could somehow still save Turin and the archer's dragon, but a score of Murgare beasts were right on Milluri's tail, streaking after them.

"*Preamithis is no longer of this world,*" Milluri said in his mind. "*I can feel it.*"

Cyran looked farther to the west, and the blurred radiance of the other realm again superimposed with the moonlight and shadows of his world. He could not see Nithinix, but he hoped the dragon had been swift enough to reach the Evenmeres before the north's legions had shot them down.

The adversaries pursuing Cyran clattered as archers reloaded and swung their ballistae around in their mounts. Beasts roared. More bolts screamed toward them, and Cyran studied the projectiles and their trajectories, maneuvering Milluri in each instant—left, right, down, diagonally upward, barrel roll. One bolt punched a hole through a leathery segment of Milluri's wing.

Milluri flew as fast as she could, her heart thumping in her chest and inside Cyran's head like a percussion drum with a beat faster than any song Cyran had heard. They tore through the shadows clinging to the border of the forest and barreled into the pines of the Evenmeres, snapping off droves of branches while trunks hewed scales from Milluri's body.

31

SIRRA BRACKENGLAVE

SIRRA RIPPED THE DOOR TO THE CHAMBER FROM ITS HINGES AND slammed it up against the far wall. "And how did all of our Belvenguard prisoners manage to escape Northsheeren?" She paused before glancing into the chamber she had opened.

"A dragon came for them," Yenthor said, his tone uncharacteristically submissive. "It was the young dragonknight's beast. And it had help—several thorn dragons."

"Thorn dragons?" The pitch of Sirra's voice climbed. "I have not seen one of those in an age."

"They must have come from the Evenmeres," Zaldica said from behind Yenthor. "For whatever reason, the beasts of Belvenguard still wish to aid their tormentors."

"Some of them may." Sirra glared at several onyx guard, who stepped closer, but none of them moved to stop her.

"You must have sensed other dragons approaching"— Zaldica kept a hand on her sword's hilt as she eyed Oomaren's minions—"given the horn blasts that sounded before their arrival."

Sirra did not respond.

"No one else but you could have known what was coming." Yenthor studied her.

Sirra did not feel as if she had to confirm or deny their suspicions. She entered the chamber she had torn the door from. Yenthor and Zaldica strode after her. Inside, Sir Trothen sat with his back against a wall.

"Then the war has begun?" the prior genturion of Northsheeren asked as he slowly stood and straightened his short gray beard as best he could. He was much thinner and more disheveled than when Sirra had left to fly south and claim Nevergrace. Although Sirra had visited with Trothen inside this chamber soon after her return to Northsheeren, she had not yet attempted to release him from confinement. But after the loss of her potential trainee—a rarity even among dragonknights, and a young man she was hoping to mold and turn against Belvenguard while introducing him to the abilities of the other realm—she no longer cared for Oomaren's capitulation or assent on any matter.

Sirra shook her head at Trothen. "The war has not begun yet, but the tide is rising, and the first ships are sailing south. I have come to release you."

"You cannot release this man," an onyx guard waiting just outside the chamber said. Several of his comrades stood at attention at his side. "Oomaren's orders are for him to remain in his chambers."

Sirra ignored the guard, facing Trothen as she spoke. "Igare and Belvenguard are not moving nearly as swiftly as Murgare with their preparations for what is to come, but once they assemble, I have no doubts they will sail to us if we do not reach them first."

"Why do you suspect this?" Trothen asked.

"We captured a dragonknight of Belvenguard. I believe that is what he thought his king would do."

Trothen nodded. "Then Oomaren has taken control of Northsheeren and Murgare, and all of Cimeren will bleed." He rubbed at the back of his neck. "Is there anything that can still be done?"

Sirra shrugged. "That is what I've come to ask you, and why I'm releasing you. I seek your aid. The banners and cities across all of Murgare have united under Oomaren. They already camp at the north shore of the lake or are marching there. Everyone except the dwarves of Darynbroad may believe that Oomaren is now the rightful king. I could still sway the dwarves to consider other options, and the people of the Eastern Reach should prefer to follow me instead of him."

"Then it is only me and the three of you who would be resisting Oomaren's rule?" Trothen looked to Zaldica and Yenthor.

"And one other." Sirra shouted over her shoulder, "Come in, Princess."

Kyelle glided into the chamber, her posture rigid as her dress swept across the stones. She nodded to Sir Trothen. "I will not pretend to have learned everything there is to know of war or ruling Murgare or even about Northsheeren itself, but I think the time draws nigh when I shall announce that I no longer require a king regent. Once that happens, I will request your counsel, genturion."

Trothen chuckled. "Restebarge's bloodline should overrule his brother, but it will be difficult to convince some. The usurper has asserted that Kyelle is too young and inexperienced to rule, and he has already been witnessed and named king regent."

"What would you consider the best route for bending the ear of the people?" Sirra asked. "Especially those already riled and ready for war?"

Trothen shook his head. "I have no clear advice."

"Are there any I have not already named who are resisting Oomaren's orders?"

Trothen paled before his expression brightened. "There is one. I did not consider them before, but, yes, it would be a wise move to speak with them. One of the key peoples of Murgare—those most revered and feared—have not acknowledged his rule."

Sirra tensed. "The brotherhood did not answer Oomaren?"

Trothen nodded. "They had not responded or mobilized when Oomaren ordered me confined."

"Then we must fly to the valley." Sirra pivoted about and strode for the exit.

"The Valley of the Smoke Breathers?" Yenthor groaned. "Those barbarians scare me more than any dragon ever could."

"Then you are no fool," Sirra said. "The taming of the first dragon was no small feat. The brotherhood is cunning and manipulative and quick to violence. And ill-tempered. I should know."

Yenthor and Zaldica exchanged a quick glance of confusion. As Sirra stepped through the doorway, the onyx guard formed a half circle in the hall around her, blocking her passage.

"You cannot escort the traitor from his chambers." One of the guard pointed at Trothen as the prior genturion emerged. "And we of the onyx guard are not all susceptible to your dragon magic."

"You will part, or I will cut you all down." Sirra pulled her sword a handsbreadth from its sheath, and its black flames crackled.

None of the guard advanced, but they did not part either.

"*Aylión*," Sirra whispered, and ethereal images representing the future movements of those around her formed ghostly scenes. She paced, and the *neblír* revealed that only one of the guard would draw his weapon and attempt to duel with her. She spun her head in the direction of the offending guard. "*Opth-lléitl.*" Then, just as the guard started to take his first step, she roared, "*Vördelth mrac ell duenvíe!*"

The full brunt of her power struck the one guard like a storm atop Northsheeren's highest peak. The guard was flung backward against the far wall as he grunted in surprise, his armor clashing with stone and ringing. He fell in a heap onto the floor.

The remainder of the guard simply watched Sirra and the others depart.

After they exited the castle and crossed the outer bridge to the dragon landing area, Sirra approached Shadowmar. A storm dragon slept near Sirra's beast, and its proximity to her dragon seemed odd. Shadowmar did not usually allow other dragons to venture so close.

Two people sat near the storm dragon and rose as Sirra approached. The guard wore three ice dragon scales as his sigil. The mage's tawny hair stirred beneath her hood.

Quarren and Sir Vladden—her previous mage and guard, whom she trusted more than any others in her legion. But she had sent them away from Nevergrace to negotiate with the southern cities and kingdoms.

Quarren hobbled closer, her staff clacking on the frozen stones, the fierce wind streaming her cloak beside her like a banner. Vladden's figure was partially obscured by the mage's cloak as he marched along behind her, his gait as stiff as that of a green soldier who wished their bones were composed of dragonsteel.

"Sir Vladden?" Sirra asked. "How were the negotiations?"

Vladden took off his helm, his salted beard longer than typical. Quarren paused, and he stepped around her. His other arm —his lance arm—was missing.

Sirra stifled an inhale of surprise.

"Negotiations at the Weltermores had progressed and were

continuing along an amicable path, both in person and through messages, before a mysterious trio arrived there and sabotaged our diplomacy," he said without any hint of emotion in his words, his voice stilted and forced, almost inhuman. "Afterward, the burro king would not speak with us or return our letters."

"What happened to your arm?" Sirra asked.

Vladden stared, but not exactly at her, rather past her, unblinking, as if his mind were corrupted and he was one of the walking dead.

"He is the half-souled now," Quarren said. "And he has been acting this way since the day the vile deed was dealt upon him. In the Rorenlands, one in the trio we mentioned—the one with enough power to summon a *luënor* blade—took his arm, severing his soul. This attacker also commanded enough power to curtail the process and stop Vladden's soul from shriveling and fading completely."

Confusion spiraled in Sirra's mind. "I have never heard of such a thing happening. The soul is either consumed or it is not."

Quarren released and then clenched her staff again, her knuckles blanching, her claw-like fingernails digging into its shaft. "If anyone could understand what has happened and may be able to help him, I believed it to be you, my Dragon Queen."

"I..." Sirra slowly shook her head.

"At least it seemed that neither the Weltermores nor the Rorenlands were keen on assisting Igare and Belvenguard," Sir Vladden said with staccato words.

"Then this trio does Oomaren's bidding?" Sirra asked.

Quarren shrugged. "It seems likely, but we have no proof."

"And at least one of them can summon a *luënor* blade?" Worries strummed a thread in Sirra's heart as she speculated on whom such a man could be. "There are very few who can accomplish such a feat."

"May we reclaim our ice dragon?" Vladden asked.

Sirra glanced to him and then the storm dragon she had sent them away on, her attention finally settling on Vladden's missing arm. As a guard, he would probably no longer be as helpful as he once was. "For the time being, a swift storm dragon would aid us more so than an ice. When the war is over, both of you may return to your true mount." She scaled her stirrup ladder. "But if either of you feel obligated to obey Oomaren's rule, remain at Northsheeren. If you wish to follow me, we depart for the valley at once."

~

Days later, Shadowmar soared over the icy tundra lands in western Murgare. Early winter's chill clawed at Sirra's eyes, even though her dragon's heat radiated around her. She was also used to such climate, conditioned to it since she was young, when she had worn the white and ridden a snow dragon. Long ago, she had adapted to the cold, something rarely needed in the lands occupied by her ancestors.

"Breather's Pass." Yenthor motioned downward with a bob of his helmed head.

"The very site where King Restebarge was murdered." Trothen was anchored to the quarterdeck behind the archer. "And where Queen Elra was abducted. It is here that people will point a finger and lay blame when all of Cimeren burns."

On his storm dragon and unarmored, due to the weight restrictions of such a creature, Sir Vladden released three bursts of stilted laughter. He had done so one other time in the preceding days, in response to a comment that would not have brought humor to any normal man.

To the north, the Chasm that had opened when the first dragon was tamed cut through the valley, a rift between the two realms. The Smoke Breathers disrupted both worlds that day long before the Dragon Wars, and Cimeren would never fully recover. On either side of the Chasm were the Ruins and the Gravelands—abandoned towns of the people of this valley, areas they would never visit again out of fear of what they had unleashed and what dark forces and horrid memories might lurk there.

"They are a miniature of Cimeren," Trothen said. "The Ruins and the Gravelands and the Chasm. And they are portentous of what Cimeren will become. The tales claim that the structures on each side were once part of a single city of the Smoke Breathers, their capital, if such people ever had a capital. But the city was ripped apart and divided by the rift, most of its structures falling into the abyss. The city was divided into bickering factions—those of the newly formed brotherhood who embraced the beliefs of Gregor Borgensen and his son, Rakar, and those who opposed them."

"Legends claim a great secret still lies hidden in those ruins," Zaldica shouted up. "A secret pertaining to all that was lost and all that will be."

"Sages claim something similar." Kyelle shifted on the quarterdeck behind Trothen. "And the old writings tell of something there, although the descriptions are riddled with vague words and metaphor. No one claims to have ever found anything of immense interest."

"But no sane men venture to the Chasm or its ruins," Yenthor said. "It is cursed beyond even the darkness of the Evenmeres and the brutal history of the Dragon Wars."

"The binding and splitting of two realms cannot be undertaken without great cost." Quarren gazed out into the distance at the massive canyon running away to the north. "Things roam within the Ruins and Gravelands and lurk in their shadows. No one in their right mind has traveled there in centuries."

Sir Vladden bellowed with laughter and then released a series of whimpers.

A chill crept through Sirra as her attention was pulled to the Chasm. Whenever she traveled this way, she attempted to ignore the jagged scar on the land and pretend it did not exist, but every time she failed to do so. One day, someone would have to answer its mystery, if Cimeren and Murgare and the realms and humans and dragons were to ever heal. Maybe Sir Vladden would now understand something there that no one else ever could.

Shadowmar spiraled lower and lower toward Darkwater Lake and the Pronged River. Gilth, the major city of the valley—although the Smoke Breathers referred to it as only a village—waited ahead. Beyond, far in the distance and at the edge of the world, the Sky Sea Falls plunged down to the earth, its waters shimmering under sunlight.

Sirra tore her attention away from the beauty of the falls. She had seen them before, had seen this entire valley many, many times in days long past. She had spent years here, her formative years, and although the Smoke Breathers distrusted her and had since shunned her, she was one of them. But none currently aboard Shadowmar knew of her upbringing.

For what would be one of only a few visits over the past centuries, she was returning home.

32

CYRAN ORENDAIN

MILLURI VEERED AND TWISTED BENEATH CYRAN BEFORE SLOWING and weaving around pines and oaks, her wings moving slower, her pain from the impacts with the trees and her fatigue lancing through to the other realm. Shrieks of rage from many dragons rang in the distance.

The thorn dragon glided along as Cyran steered them eastward. The pain of the *sïosaires* shoved itself down on his shoulders and heart until his worries about his companions blurred and melded with images of Turin and Preamithis being shot down.

Could Eidelmere really have lost his entire soul to the venom in Shadowmar's tail? Cyran did not want to believe it now, but that was what the nyrens and guard said happened to such victims. Even dragons agreed. The prospect seared Cyran's heart and drew a rush of hot tears and a guilt that would never leave him. The cantankerous old dragon had given and done more for him than anyone, and Cyran would never be able to reciprocate that. Cyran deserved every ounce of his *sïosaires* pain. Now, thorn dragons who owed him nothing were still aiding him and his comrades, only because of Eidelmere. Someday, he would have to find a way to repay them.

His mind turned to Jaslin and Smoke and his friends from Nevergrace, wondering where they were and what they were doing, and then to Tamar and who their parents had been before they died when all their children were young. For a brief time, Cyran believed his father had been one of the guard, but that was only a lie Eidelmere conjured up to help send Cyran down his current path. What did the old dragon care if he became a guard? And what did Eidelmere expect him to accomplish now? Once the war began, none of it would probably ever matter. Belvenguard would be crushed.

An hour of weaving through the trees crawled by as he relived memories.

"You made it!" Vyk's voice carried through the woods as he and Ineri emerged from a few pines, still riding their dragon.

Cyran's elation at seeing two of his companions and their mount alive was quickly drained by his pain. "As are you. Milluri took a bolt to the wing, but that was all we suffered."

Vyk patted his dragon's neck. "Nithinix outran our pursuing legion and got us into the forest. A bunch of bolts whizzed past us, but we avoided taking any hits."

"Where is Turin?" Ineri asked as the dragons pulled alongside each other and flew southwest toward the nearest copse of angoias.

"He and his dragon went down in their last and greatest sacrifice."

～

Days later, Cyran flew over the southern border of the Evenmeres. They had kept their distance from the lower forest as much as possible, afraid of the flaming Harrowed and the other monsters lurking there. The weight in Cyran's heart for Eidelmere and Turin and Preamithis, and his part in their deaths, had not lessened.

Milluri soared upward so Cyran could take in the area and assess their whereabouts. The Scyne Road lay to the south. Nevergrace would be to the east, Galvenstone to the west.

"I must fly to Galvenstone as quickly as possible." Cyran studied the area. "To warn the king of what is coming, of what awaits Belvenguard and could already be sailing south across the lake."

Vyk and Ineri nodded as Nithinix angled westward.

"But, please, you two should fly to Nevergrace." Cyran pointed east. "We must also warn the outpost that the Dragon Queen could be traveling over the angoias and could arrive any day. She may try to flank Galvenstone and take the city from two sides. I would rather take your route to my home, but Igare will want me stationed in his legion and helping to defend Galvenstone as soon as possible. I implore you to find Jaslin, my sister, and tell her she must take Smoke and the other wolves and Emellefer and flee the outpost. I would rank that task as a higher priority for myself if I thought she would ever listen to me, but she is more likely to heed your warnings than mine."

Vyk clenched his jaw, and Ineri nodded in understanding.

Nithinix vocalized in a throaty rumble and rubbed his neck against Milluri's. The dragons shared a moment, speaking in a tongue Cyran could not comprehend, but their grief flooded the other realm. Tears even welled in Nithinix's eyes and rolled down his scaled lids in large droplets.

Cyran's heart trembled anew. Their new mounts had lost one of their own while attempting to save a few humans they did not even know. Eidelmere's powers of persuasion must have been unmatched, and Cyran had been such a fool. He rubbed the spiny scales on Milluri's neck and closed his eyes, embracing his despair and pairing it with hers.

"You lost a dear friend, one of your kind," Cyran said. "For that, I am utterly sorry. In my sorrow for the loss of my bonded dragon, I did not fully realize your pain."

Milluri and Nithinix spoke in the *neblír*, only clicks and grumbles carrying through Cyran's world. Cyran allowed them their time but uttered the appropriate words. "*Mörenth toi boménth bi droth su llith*. Till the end of days we soar. *Mörenth toi boménth bi nomth su praëm*. Till the end of nights we reign. *Röith moirten íli. Ílith ëmdrien tiu gládthe*. You honor me. My soul sees yours."

A sense of gratitude seeped from Milluri and wrapped itself around Cyran, embracing him in a tender but pained warmth. After another few minutes passed, the dragons spun about and flew their separate ways. Vyk and Ineri held their hands up in farewell, and Cyran returned the gesture.

Milluri streaked southwest, skimming over the fields just beyond the forest while following the brown ribbon of the Scyne Road. Within the hour, one of the beacon towers—a signal between Nevergrace and Galvenstone—passed by on their right. The stone tower soared upward, a mound of logs and kindling waiting at its summit to become a pyre at a moment's notice. A forest dragon was perched near the top of the tower, and its guard and a few soldiers walked around the periphery of the logs, studying Cyran and his strange dragon.

Cyran raised a fist into the air to greet those at the tower. "The party that departed in hopes of seeking information in Murgare has returned to Belvenguard!"

The soldiers and guard flashed spears and a sword in salute.

Cyran whipped past, his thoughts simmering and replaying a conversation with the Dragon Queen while her naked flesh was exposed. He had let something slip about the beacon towers. He had been a fool, allowing his defenses to falter with her distraction. If only it had eventually all culminated in him learning some of the magic from the other realm, but he could not command such power, could not even see the *neblír* without a dragon nearby.

Another thought started as a spark and then bloomed into an idea, causing a deep tingle of wonder to spiral around inside him. *The shadow dragon's egg...*

He could try to hatch it and use it as a weapon against the enemy, a powerful beast that could potentially contend with Shadowmar. Doubts quickly followed. The creature would be a hatchling, and surely it would not be strong enough to offer much of a challenge. Not for years. Still, the possibility and potential use for such a dragon simmered in his head and would not leave him.

There was also the problem that Belvenguard had outlawed shadow dragons for a reason.

～

"So, at a minimum, there are already at least thirty thousand swords with enough fleets to carry these soldiers to our shores." Igare stared at Cyran, the king's face pale as he stepped down from his throne of red and gold dragon skin, a gold wing extending to one side and the red of a rose to the other. A massive dragon skull sat atop the throne. Igare approached the dragonknight. "As well as several hundred dragons of all types imaginable, legions far outnumbering our own, gathered and prepared. *And* the Dragon Queen lives, as does her shadow dragon."

Cyran glanced about. One of the kingsknights at the periphery of the audience hall shifted uneasily. The four members of Igare's small council waited at the base of the throne's dais. Riscott glowered. Cartaya's eyebrow arched.

"And our esteemed archer, Turin Bolenmane, survived his initial ordeal and escaped confinement only to sacrifice himself for his kingdom once again." Igare rubbed at the bridge of his nose and shook his head with sadness. "Such a great man and his family will be justly honored."

A clatter of metal sounded from the doorway behind Cyran, and Sir Paltere and a few other guard rushed into the chamber. The older dragonknight's hair waved in his wake, his look austere as he advanced and stood beside Cyran, regarding him. Paltere clapped Cyran on the back and then crossed his wrists, making fists and bumping them against Cyran's. "Mir," Paltere said in a low voice. "You have returned."

The mention of that word from the man Cyran revered more than any other brought only a spark of warmth. Cyran's relief because of his and his comrade's return had faded to a grave somberness. Cyran nodded to the dragonknight and voiced the same word to Paltere for the first time. "Mir."

"And the village that you were originally sent to investigate, young dragonknight?" Tiros stepped forward. "Did you discover if the rumors were true or myth?"

Cyran nodded. "That was where the legion captured us. But we were able to determine that what had happened resembled what Orinia described in Gernlet." He turned to Paltere. "Did you discover anything else at the hamlet?"

"Nothing to dismiss Orinia's account of what occurred there," Paltere said. "I found remains supporting the notion that something came from the woods, and there were many skeletons. Mounds also weaved about the area."

"The Shield Maiden does not skulk behind her defenses." Lisain spoke, but his eyes remained closed, his head bowed. "There is no more that is hidden."

"Then Murgare is likely *not* responsible for what happened in Gernlet." Tiros pursed his lips and dragged fingers through his curly beard. "That is interesting."

"But of no consequence to what they are now plotting." Riscott strode forward. "We *must* assume that Murgare is already sailing. If Cyran saw what he did a couple fortnights or more ago, before he was held captive, it would be folly to believe that the legions of the north are not already moving."

Cartaya paced about. "But the implications that Murgare has so many forces north of the lake and could also send more through the woods may change how we approach the coming war."

A minute of silence settled over the chamber, connecting each person's tension and a sense of dread that rose from all those present.

"Surely the Dragon Queen interrogated you while you were her captive." Riscott's gaze bored into Cyran, a dangerous smirk playing at his lips. "Tell us what she wanted to know."

"She asked me about Belvenguard's defenses and our stage of preparations."

"And what did you tell her?" The orator's smirk contorted into a snarl.

Cyran swallowed as he pondered stating everything that had occurred. "I... let something slip."

The clergyman gasped.

"Sirra Brackenglave, the Dragon Queen, had just saved one of my archer's lives by taking us to a hot spring," Cyran said and explained the situation.

"He refers to her by name." Riscott shook his head. "One who takes you captive does not save a life by removing you from the danger she placed you in. Do not begin to think that way. That is how the heinous corrupt young minds. What did you tell her?"

"I... she mentioned a mistake during her attack on Nevergrace. She allowed a beacon tower between Galvenstone and the outpost to be lit for a moment before her mist dragon could conceal its firelight. I said something about"—Cyran's shoulders sagged—"if I had a dragon who breathed black fire, I would arrive at the beacon towers first and burn their wood at night. No one would ever see such flames destroying all that tinder."

The chamber turned silent, and not even the sound of a breath inhaling or exhaling broke the quiet.

"You betrayed us." Riscott's face purpled. "You were not even under distress when you said this? You were not being tortured?"

Cyran shook his head.

"But he was distracted," Cartaya added. "And thankful for the warmth. He said nothing the Dragon Queen has probably not already considered. Perhaps the sole purpose of her questioning was to make the young dragonknight appear the traitor in our eyes if he ever escaped."

Riscott pointed straight at Cyran's chest. "You should have been near to death before letting anything of the like pass your lips. Some of the guard have spent their lives in the dungeons for less."

"I am sorry, my king." Cyran genuflected.

"But what he brings us has far more value than a few slightly questionable words he spoke to the enemy." Paltere stepped forward a pace to place himself between Cyran and Riscott. "He risked everything—took on an impossible errand and brought us information. He was captured in the process and escaped from Northsheeren. He has seen Murgare's fortress. He knows where it resides, and he knows some of its defenses. He is one of our few dragonknights, and still he did not lie to us and claim he let nothing slip to a beautiful and manipulative woman who was naked at the time. The Dragon Queen is no fool. She has ridden

Shadowmar for centuries. Surely the fact that her dragon's fire cannot be seen at night is something she has known since long before any of us crawled from our mothers' wombs. I find that his minimal mistake, if you can even call it that, does not shadow all he has brought us in return."

Igare scratched his scalp, the crown he once crushed still not replaced. His eyes settled closed as he pondered it all.

"Is there anything else you should tell us about your interactions with *her*?" Riscott asked.

Cyran stood and sidled around Paltere. "She claimed that only she could teach me about the magic of the elder tongue and the other realm. She offered to train me. I did not accept at first—"

"But then you did?" Riscott's pointing hand fell limp at his side.

"I believed doing so might create an opportunity for us to escape and return here with all the information we gathered. At that point, we had found no other possible options to free ourselves."

"Except all it took was for your dragon to come for you," Riscott said.

"I did not foresee that happening and never dreamed a dragon would take such a risk of their own volition." Cyran folded his arms across his chest. "I was a fool." A biting pain twisted in his heart. "To find aid and travel the length of Murgare only to face Northsheeren and certain death... I did not understand the depth of the bond between me and Eidelmere. Not until he was killed."

"Then let the anger that such an event should unleash drive you," Riscott snapped. "If the Dragon Queen attempts to turn you against us, you turn against her!"

"Even I cannot harness the magic of the other realm," Paltere said. "After Cyran told me he resisted her magic during their tilt at Nevergrace, I've been asking every nyren I can find, but none know a suitable mentor for him. There is no one in Belvenguard who can help him harness such power."

The councilmembers and the king brooded on that for several minutes.

Igare pushed past Riscott, elbowing the orator to the side as the king spoke. "Then, if there is nothing more on the matter of this brave dragonknight's errand and slight slip of the tongue, I will speak of some ill news that has transpired here." He shared a glance with everyone in turn. "The Rorenlands and the Weltermores have fallen silent, neither responding to any messengers or emissaries. They do not gather their banners for war. We have also sent ambassadors into Darynbroad and even Murgare. None have returned. I fear they have been hunted down and killed, like those I sent to the Rorenlands and the Weltermores."

A sinking feeling began pulling at Cyran's stomach as the implications of what the king said grew and gained weight.

Igare slowly marched up the steps to his throne and thumbed through a stack of parchments. He cleared his throat and picked up a couple of them. "These are the most recent messages I've received." He shook them in his fist.

A broken red seal on either end of the parchments caught Cyran's attention. The seal appeared the same as the one on all the furtive messages he and his friends had received since this ordeal began. The letters had not come from Galvenstone after all.

"Rumors claim that a new king sits on the Rorenlands's throne," Igare said, "and his kingdom now marches to war. But *not* to support Belvenguard. They have declared themselves allies of Murgare."

The uncomfortable pressure in Cyran's stomach tripled, feeling like someone kicked him.

"A contingent of the Rorenlands's army have begun to invade the Constell Islands." Igare's tone turned dour. "Others have landed on Stormwatch and are sailing across Stormark Bay to Silverbow and southwestern Belvenguard. But the majority of the new king's forces march north to Progtown with legions of sand dragons. They already wage war on our outer lands." He shook his head in disbelief or dismay. "And a growing faction of the Constell's people—*our* people—are defying us in hopes of making the islands their own kingdom. They have openly declared themselves free of Belvenguard and have even mentioned seeking peace with Murgare. This rogue faction, along with the Rorenlands's soldiers, have separately been making landings in eastern Belvenguard and the Weltermores. They sail in, raid and pillage and burn villages before fleeing back to the islands only to regroup and strike again." He gesticulated with a fist in the air, this typically calm and reserved king finally revealing deeper emotion. "My own people are turning against me when we need them most!" What looked like a wisp of smoke slipped past his lips. "Only if they all join us do we have a chance of winning this war. I fear that the hammer strike will land all at once—from Murgare in the north and the Rorenlands in the south and west. If the Weltermores fear our enemies' amplifying power and join them, or if Nevergrace is again taken, we will be crushed on all sides here in Galvenstone. All routes out of our city will be cut off. Then, after we fall, the dark armies will spread across Belvenguard and wipe out its remaining cities."

"I should return to Nevergrace." Cyran wheeled about.

"No." A redness stood out in Igare's eyes. "I am very sorry for this, Cyran, but Nevergrace will not remain standing simply because it has one dragonknight at its disposal. We have to think logically in times like these, not with our hearts. If it brings you some comfort, know that your sister now resides here in the Summerswept Keep with Lady Menoria."

Cyran swallowed, attempting to absorb all the information while experiencing a battery of emotion and rampant thoughts. "My archers ventured to the outpost, to warn my people."

"The farthest watchtowers in the lake, and our storm dragons, are yet to report sighting any incoming fleets." Igare paced. "From this moment onward, we'll be preparing as though Murgare could reach our shores at any time, but at the minimum, we still have a few days. Fly to Nevergrace, young dragonknight. Reclaim your archers, warn your people, and allow them to decide if they want to attempt to defend the outpost or travel here and help us fortify the city. Then you must return to Dashtok and face the legions of Murgare. Go, quickly."

Cyran slowly nodded. *Belvenguard is doomed.*

33

JASLIN ORENDAIN

Jaslin entered the conjuror's chambers. The inner expanse was filled with tables and books and bottles, but there was no one else about. The door had been left open, and she had been asked to arrive at this time.

"Is anyone here?" Jaslin called out.

No one answered.

After waiting a few minutes, she began to wander about, glancing at the drawings in open books—a sleeping dragon, a white elk, an angoia copse. She was interested in the possibility of being able to control magic, but she didn't want to give up her shard. Being invited here could have been the conjuror's ruse to take it. She plucked the shard from its pouch and twirled it around between her thumb and forefinger.

Memories of all that had transpired at the wharf and with Keliam and the vial she still possessed, as well as the unspoken threat of the merchant's revenge, swarmed her thoughts. She would rather be searching for those guild merchants to learn what she could about the queens' assassins and potentially aid her brother and her kingdom. However, Cyran had hinted that one member of the king's council could be behind the murders. She should take time to learn about each of those four, especially when the conjuror offered her an easy opportunity.

A drawing of a black dragon with a barbed tail caught her attention, and she froze. The elegant script beside it appeared like a story with an elaborate decorative initial, which made that letter appear like a serpentine dragon. The section was titled *The Outlawing of Shadow Dragons.*

"It is a sad story."

Jaslin jerked away from the table and looked around.

"I am sorry to have startled you, young lady." Tiros had entered the chamber, and he smiled as he tugged at one of the curls in his beard. The chain around his crimson robes rattled. "I was referring to the tale of Belvenguard's shadow dragon."

"You know it?" Jaslin recovered and glanced down at the page, furtively tucking away her shard.

"I am a nyren, remember? I can recall all that I've studied. I no longer need books. I've learned from the masters who passed down knowledge from the first books without alternation or error."

Jaslin's incredulity surfaced, enlivened by her love of books and her need to find a reason to possess them. *How can that even be possible?* "What if your masters taught you something they interpreted incorrectly, and it has been passed down to you?"

"There have been no errors since the elder nyrens perfected the skill. No errors in centuries. And I have read that story"—he nodded at the book before her—"once. I can recite it word for word, although I have not picked it up in more than three decades."

"Show me." Jaslin lifted the first page of the shadow dragon tale. "What is at the top of the following page?"

Tiros closed his eyes and hummed a nearly silent melody. "'The dragon waited until the king's boy fell asleep. Then the beast crept from its abode of shadows, its red eyes gleaming, and—'"

"All right." Jaslin waved him off, her skepticism and surprise twining within her. His every word was exactly how it appeared in the book. Still, there was a need for books, no matter what this man said. "How do I know that you haven't read this story just yesterday or even today? It was sitting open on the table."

"Because these are my chambers." Cartaya's robes swished as she entered, her white hair bouncing around her shoulders. "Tiros seldom steps inside these walls, and he has not done so anytime recently. I can attest to him not having read from any of my books in many years."

"What about his own books?" Jaslin asked.

The conjuror and nyren exchanged a rueful glance before they both chuckled, and Cartaya said, "Nyrens do not carry books beyond their citadels unless they are for pleasure reading, and even then, such books are discarded after one reading."

Jaslin emotionally clutched her memories from scores of stories and books she loved, holding them like a talisman over her heart. Those tales did more for her every time she reread them. Discarding a great book after only the first pass through would create an unnecessary deprivation, an abstinence without benefit or meaning. "But there must be so many books stored in Dashtok and the Summerswept Keep. Surely you find time for reading and learning something new."

"Rarely," Tiros said. "And only when I wish to undertake the learning of a new discipline or a dash of history. I do not claim to know all areas of study. No nyren could possibly recall and comprehend everything that has been written. That is why we have the citadels—to train different nyrens in all aspects of our world. Then we carry our knowledge with us when we disperse across the kingdoms. The citadel is the only place where books are needed."

Jaslin's defensiveness sprang up like a wall of shields. She ran her finger across the drawing of a dragon. "Why does Belvenguard no longer keep shadow dragons?"

"Would you like me to recite you the entire story?" Tiros grinned at her. "Or would you rather hear a summary?"

Jaslin forced a friendly smile in return. "A summary would be fine."

"You see, Premraine, Igare's father, sought to claim the kingdom's first dragon from the shadows." Tiros paced in a tightening circle. "So many, including myself, apprised him of the potential dangers, but he would not heed our warnings. He longed to own a dragon that was one of the most powerful of their kind, believing that if Belvenguard did not, we risked losing all of the shadow dragons to the dark riders of Murgare. The idea that every one of those dragons would be enslaved by our enemies—for all the years to come—frightened him. Premraine pursued the idea that we could balance the power between our kingdoms by having a shadow dragon head up our legions. He thought this would ensure that Murgare could not completely destroy us in any coming war." The nyren sighed. "Premraine was wrong. Some beasts and men are made for each other. It is a pity that the dragons who are the strongest are also the most diabolical. That dragon did what even our enemies could not."

Jaslin cringed. Then dragons of specific breeds were all born evil? It was not only certain individuals—like with people and every other kind of animal she had known? That notion did not ring true in her mind, but she told herself she was young and naïve.

The nyren continued, "The king's dragonknight, along with many of the guard, captured a shadow dragon in the wild. Premraine kept the beast alone in a den, but the king's son—Igare's brother—was an adolescent at the time and was wonderstruck by the might of such a creature." Tiros paused, lost in memory. "Gerraine would often sneak down to the lair and attempt to speak with that monster of a dragon. No one knows all they discussed, but rumors say Gerraine was plotting his vision for the kingdom and the beast, Shannowmere, corrupted his mind. Days faded into weeks and then months, and Gerraine turned reticent and would no longer speak with his father or brother, only to his mother, the queen, and only in private. That was when the kingsknights were placed on watch outside his door and window. They discovered that the young man was sneaking out of his chambers at night and visiting the den. The first time they witnessed this, the knights followed Gerraine until he disappeared into the darkness of the lair. One ventured forth while the other was about to return to the keep and inform the king. That's when they heard the screams."

Jaslin's heart scampered around in her chest as she recalled the dens of Nevergrace and having to walk through the fog of a mist dragon's breath without knowing if the monster was waiting to devour her.

"The kingsknights charged into the lair of the beast." Tiros shook his head. "First they found a pool of blood, then the queen's body after Gerraine had plunged a sword through her chest while the dragon held her. The dragon was still speaking and convincing the young prince that by killing her, Gerraine was actually helping to ease her suffering. This was after the beast must have already deceived Gerraine into luring the queen into its clutches." The nyren exhaled slowly. "Belvenguard has a long and dark history of murdered queens."

All the moisture in Jaslin's mouth dried and then seemed to pool on her palms as she thought of Menoria's future.

"Shannowmere struck again without warning," Tiros said, "killing both kingsknights with the venom in its barbed tail, the act witnessed by a soldier. The venom of a shadow dragon has the ability to sever and mangle and then consume the souls of its victims."

"Does their venom bubble?" Jaslin asked through a parched throat. Images of the dark liquid Keliam had been peddling haunted her, and she unintentionally reached for the concealed vial at her waist.

Tiros remained silent for a few heartbeats before humming something quietly. "If the venom has been extracted from the bulb and is held in a vial, then it is considered a poison, and it can appear to bubble." He studied her closely and cleared his throat. "But that was not all that happened during the last king's reign. Shannowmere escaped the den and headed straight for the hatchery towers. He bit and clawed soldiers in half and broke into the chambers to destroy dragon eggs, flinging their shells and contents out into the city. The legions were called in, and they surrounded the dragon. The genturion challenged Shannowmere and bade him to come out. When the dragon did not answer, they flew in. No one could see for certain what happened, but stone shattered and burst. Dragons fell from the skies. The evil beast's barbed tail worked like an assassin's dagger, jabbing and poisoning those of the legion. Belvenguard lost a score of its best silver and rose and sun dragons before the beast was slain. We lost as many guard and mages as well. They say the monster's corpse was pierced by fifty lance strikes, his hide spiked with a hundred dragonbolts. Gerraine's mutilated body, without its head or arms, was found in the carnage as well, the slashes of dragon claws upon his corpse. Premraine soon outlawed the shadow dragons from Belvenguard forever."

A disturbing chill slipped along the back of Jaslin's neck as she pictured the shadow dragon in the story and then the Dragon Queen's mount that was as abhorred by people in the present as Shannowmere must have been during his time.

"What is shadow dragon poison used for? If people were to use it?"

"Dragon thieves use it to steal dragons." Cartaya approached her. "You have seen this poison?"

Jaslin nodded, afraid her thoughts or demeanor would give away that she carried a vial. "Down at the wharf. A merchant was hiding it inside fish." Her eyes went wide. "Does that mean there are dragon thieves here in Galvenstone who are plotting to decimate our legions?"

Cartaya ran a hand through her white hair, her young-appearing face contorting with thought. "It is possible. There could be thieves here who are employed by Murgare. But what you saw must then be the same vial that the kingsknights brought to Igare."

"Then we have already discussed the matter," Tiros said, "and begun our counter. We have further elevated our inspections of merchant wares."

Cartaya nodded. "And you, handmaid, did not come here to discuss such things." The conjuror strode toward an opening in a side wall and motioned for Jaslin to follow her. "You are here about magic."

Tiros trailed the conjuror, and Jaslin followed.

"Can shadow dragon poison be used to kill another shadow dragon?" Jaslin asked.

Tiros mulled something over as they walked. "There is one instance in an ancient tome I read that says it can."

They entered a chamber as sprawling as the previous one, but this room was completely devoid of clutter. Only a few tapestries hung on the walls.

"Bone and earth magic was discovered and harnessed by the ancient elves." Cartaya faced Jaslin and pulled her mauve hood over her forehead. "In ages past, the elves entrusted humans with some of their knowledge and powers, but men feared what the elves could do. In the Dragon Wars, the legions of Murgare turned against the elves not only by riding their newfound steeds of scale and fire but also by harnessing the magic that the elves had shared with them. As you know, the elves were decimated and are no more. None of us can command all the powers of bone and earth as they did, as many of their secrets were lost, but particular humans who were trained by them then trained others and experimented. More power and knowledge have been uncovered since. However, no human knows the depth and abilities that once existed or that can potentially be obtained." She whispered something and opened her fist with a flourish. White flame sprouted from her palm. Her hooded face lowered toward the flame, she blew, and the flames flew off her skin and streaked toward Jaslin's feet.

Jaslin released a cry of surprise and leapt aside. The fireball struck the stone floor where she had been standing, and its flames flared and died out. "Why did...?"

Cartaya did not move, but she spoke calmly. "The power lying in bone and earth can be pulled from your own body or from the soil and roots beneath you. Then you can channel and harness it."

"You could have killed me." Jaslin retreated, glancing over at Tiros, who merely observed without concern.

"I was hoping you would react on instinct and summon magic of your own," Cartaya said.

Jaslin frowned, suddenly distrusting these two councilmembers much more. "I do not know any magic. I have not even heard talk of it other than in stories and myth. Can it make anything besides flame? Maybe a shield that can protect me from fire?"

"Bone and earth magic is only limited by your imagination. Its power can be fashioned into whatever you want it to be. That shard you carry was created with its lattice. You have resisted its call, and so there is something more than stubbornness inside you. Its pull is fierce. I can feel it even now."

Jaslin's hand clutched the pouch that her crystal resided in. "It calls to me often, tempts me to enter the Evenmeres—which killed my brother Tamar and which Cyran asked me to avoid."

"It is fortunate you have not listened to it. The Evenmeres are restless. A wildness grows there, lurking in its depths, breathing behind its curtain of leaves and needles."

"I want to help in any way I can." Jaslin tentatively stepped closer. "I've already lost one brother, and the other may never return. I should help fight Murgare as well. There is also the matter of the assassins…" She let the thought trail away. In case the conjuror or nyren or both of them were the traitors, she did not want to give away that she suspected anything with the queens' murders.

"Make a fist." Cartaya leaned closer and clutched Jaslin's wrist, squeezing until her bones hurt. "Now, use your imagination, story connoisseur. Start simple. Picture your flames in whatever color you choose. It was only the ancient elves who always used violet, but current conjurors use what is to our liking. Call up the sensation from the ground, from these stones around you. Hear their voices and allow them to listen to the melody of your bones. Pull the substances you need through your boots and up into your legs, making each particle of magic spin and rotate faster and flare with light as it races along the track of your bones and through your blood. Command them to coalesce and form something tangible, but"—she squeezed Jaslin's wrist tighter—"also allow them free rein to work on their own. Do not control or force any of it, or you will never succeed."

Jaslin's bewilderment twisted her lips. "I do not understand."

"Nor will you until you master the art. Even after all my years, I do not understand it all, especially the particles. Now, say whatever ancient word you feel inside your mind. Do it!"

Jaslin closed her eyes and imagined her soul extending out of her body and into the stones beneath her feet, delving into the earth. She grasped at fragments of magical particles in the area and scooped them together, drawing them back with her as her soul reentered her body through her feet. She released the particles into her bones, where they spiraled around shafts like dancing fairy lights and ascended her legs to her pelvis. After they reached her chest, the particles hurtled out along her arms and adhered into a ball in her hands before erupting on her palms. She muttered a strange word she might have read somewhere.

Her eyes shot open in wonder, inspiration thrumming through her as she fully believed she had summoned magic... but her skin was cold and bare. A sinking disappointment swirled in her stomach. "It didn't work."

Cartaya shook her head. "No. It did not. You could be too old to begin training in the ways of bone and earth magic, your mind too hardened to the realities of this world and not the other. Try again."

Jaslin attempted the process a second time, mentally diving deeper into the earth and scooping up more particles while speaking quietly. Again, she failed to create any flames.

"Again," Cartaya said.

After an hour of repeated failures, Tiros sighed. "She does not hold any power that would be useful to us." He departed the chamber in a clinking of chain links.

Cartaya studied Jaslin. "What the nyren says may be true, but the shard tells me otherwise. Keep trying."

Jaslin practiced her mental imagery another dozen times until she was sweating and trembling, feeling as if she had hauled bushels of grain all day and night.

Cartaya pursed her lips, shook her head, and left without a word.

Jaslin stared after the conjuror, bemusement raging through her. Was she supposed to give up now? Cartaya's footfalls withdrew into the other chamber and exited that room as well, the sounds fading and then disappearing in the hall beyond.

"Damn this false hope and chance to be something more." Jaslin slumped onto the floor against the wall, and a few tears slipped from her eyes as she thought of Cyran traveling into the north while the kingdoms were on the brink of war. "Bloody Siren, you've once again let me down."

Cyran would never survive on his own. Murgare was too powerful and evil. She had to do something, somehow. Maybe it was time to find the merchants and look into the assassins as best she could. Stopping another assassin could save Menoria's or someone else's life and potentially unmask a traitor in their midst, a traitor who would sabotage their kingdom from within and weaken them during Murgare's attack. Investigating this was something she could do, and after several difficulties, she had accomplished what the merchants demanded of her. Cyran had never struggled so much with defeat prior to achieving knighthood, entering the guard, and then becoming a dragonknight. He worked and trained hard for many years, but he always seemed to be met with success, advancement, and acknowledgment. Jaslin often tried whatever she could to rival her brother, but before she helped the captives at Nevergrace and earned Menoria's trust, no one had ever recognized her actions.

She stood and cursed the Siren again, wiping her sweaty palms on her legs and then quickly making sure her fragment was safe in its pouch. She froze. When she brushed her palm against the area where the crystal was lying, heat radiated through the bones of her pelvis. She lifted her hand away.

A wisp of amber smoke rose from her fingers and dispersed into the air.

34

PRAVON THE DRAGON THIEF

Pravon pounded on the tavern door again. Wood thudded against stone. No torchlight showed through the windows, and no voices carried out.

"It looks abandoned." Aneen cupped her hands against the sides of her face and pressed her nose to the window. Then she rubbed at the glass with the heel of her palm and tried again. "It's of no use. All the grime is on the inside."

Pravon's memories of him and Aneen racing away from the pens with their stolen sand dragons and gliding far away into the desert flashed in his mind. Per the guild's orders, they had left the beasts at a predetermined location in the desert and returned to Sarzuth seeking the specific tavern where they had been confronted. Returning here was not part of the original plan, but Pravon assumed it had to be the next step. Where else would they be expected to go? "Were we complete fools to do what some cloaked man acting as a guild master asked of us?"

"Right now, it doesn't seem like the wisest move I've ever made, but it is still not the most reckless thing I've done."

"It is the most reckless raid I've been involved in." Pravon pulled his hood lower over his face and glanced about. The street around them was empty.

The tavern door behind Pravon creaked open, and he lurched and spun about. The door had only parted a crack, and complete darkness shadowed whoever was inside.

"Be off," a voice said. "Why are two hooded persons at my door at this hour?"

Pravon recovered and pushed his hood back a little so moonlight could land on some of his features—his hooked nose and long brown hair. "We have returned from our initiation victorious."

"Be off, filth. I do not know you, and you have no business here," the person inside said.

Pravon sidled closer. "It is us, Pravon and Aneen. Hassellstaff did not make it, but we did. We are here—"

"Be off before I call the night watch! At night in Sarzuth, they kill any questionable characters before seeking answers." The door slammed shut.

Pravon hesitated as shock rattled through his bones.

"We were fools." Aneen spun about and paced down the street. "That is the tavern we were in, and yet it is not always a tavern. The dragons we left for these scoundrels will be long gone, as well as our storm dragon. The same with all the coin we could have gotten for them."

Pravon's stomach clenched into a hard ball, and anger flared in his chest and climbed, heating his cheeks. He raised a fist to pound on the door again, but he paused and glanced around. He would have a difficult time tracking down the people who tricked him. All he could think to do would be to wait here or visit the tavern again at another time, and returning when no one was expecting him would probably be wiser. If they pushed it tonight, there would likely be many dangerous people here who were prepared to deal with him and Aneen.

He could hold a grudge for months or even years. It was much safer that way, and probably the only reason he was still alive after a prior incident or two. One day, he would return to this very spot, once those men considered him long gone. Then his vengeance would take them by surprise. Blood would splatter the walls of the tavern.

Aneen vanished around a street corner, and Pravon strode after her, glancing back at the tavern one last time. He wasn't sure, but the ghostly image of a face might have been peeking out one of the windows just as he turned.

When he rounded the corner, Aneen stood still, grasping something. A dark form slipped into the shadows of a side street and disappeared. Pravon's hands found two of his throwing knives, and he joined his comrade.

Aneen lifted a parchment with a broken seal up to the nearest torch and let it burn. She watched as orange flames crawled along one margin and turned the parchment around to allow the fire to creep up its other side. The broken seal of the message—which appeared to be red, although the fire was already melting it—dripped onto the street.

When the parchment was nearly consumed, Aneen dropped it onto the cobbles, and the last section curled up into a petal of black ash. Then she stomped on it.

"It said to recall nothing of this night other than drinking at a tavern and imbibing too deeply." Aneen gestured for Pravon to follow her.

"Someone gave that to you?" Pravon hurried after her.

She shrugged. "More like appeared out of nowhere, slipped it into my hands, and vanished."

"Did the message mention anything else?"

"It said we should return to our prior duties, unless we want to tempt the Assassin into taking our souls for betraying a blood contract."

"Then you mean to head back to the Yellow Castle? To find Kridmore and see what other chaos we can create?"

"I do. If we are indeed members of The Guild of Fire and Shadow, we may no longer have to fear that assassin or anything he does. And if he wound up in the castle's dungeons or has been beheaded or worse, then we can pursue our contract using our own methods."

They walked through the vast city and its shadows, moving as silently as they could. After a couple hours, when dawn's light stole over the deserts around them, they wound up the long trail on the hill to the Yellow Castle. Near the top, soldiers barred their way.

"Emissaries are no longer allowed inside the castle." One of the soldiers crossed his spear with another who stood on the opposite side of the roadway. "Per King Jabarra. No exceptions. Not even for the friends of the king's newly appointed third orator."

Pravon shoved his hood from his head, a little confused. "We have only come here to find Kridmore, a man we arrived with, but we are not friends. If he has done any wrong in this city, we will leave him with you."

The soldier simply glared at Pravon.

Aneen strode forward. "Kridmore is King Jabarra's third orator."

The soldier nodded. "But the third orator no longer resides here in the Yellow Castle. He travels with the first legion. The king prepares the rest of his legions to follow in the wake of the first."

"Where is this legion going?" Pravon asked.

"You can join your friend if you hurry north and reach them before they enter Belvenguard. They travel the road to Progtown."

Plumes of sand billowed into the air, rising from the road just south of the Mountain of Titans.

Pravon wrapped a scarf around his nose and mouth and veered his hoofed steed around ranks of plodding sand dragons hauling massive carts. He squinted against the stinging dust, the suffocating heat of the southlands causing sweat to drip down his forehead and back. He wished he still had his storm dragon, but his mount had to be released from its poisoned bond, or by this time, the beast would have died and been lost to the realms. They had purchased desert horses instead, the thought of stealing more dragons not tempting either of them as much as usual.

Giants marched on either side of the lines of sand dragons, the dragons at least ten abreast and stretching on as far as Pravon could see. The beasts were bound like oxen with metal yokes around their shoulders and necks, and each was chained to other dragons on either side of them. Soldiers with long spears and pikes eyed Pravon and Aneen as they passed, but the soldiers did not move to stop them.

The reek of all the rotting fish and other marine carcasses the dragons in the rear carried in their carts almost caused Pravon to retch. While all dragons could slumber for years and needed little nourishment during that time, sand dragons were known for their ability to go even longer without sustenance. Their kind required much less food than other dragons, even during times of prolonged activity, so they didn't have to haul enormous quantities to sustain their army. Sand dragons needed little to no water as well.

Pravon and Aneen slowly passed each rank of the lumbering beasts. The creatures must have been over one hundred strong, each accompanied by their mage and guard. This legion was surrounded by a few thousand foot soldiers and hundreds of mounted knights riding desert horses.

After a few hours of riding along, when he and Aneen finally neared the forward ranks, they spotted Kridmore's dark cloak. The assassin rode on one of the largest sand dragons, and three other men in armor, who sat atop similarly sized beasts and headed up the entire legion, rode alongside him.

Pravon drifted closer to the ranks, the dust storm they flung up in their wake minimal near the front lines. The armored leaders regarded the dragon thief for only a moment before returning their attention north.

"You've decided to try to fulfill your contracts after all." Kridmore's lips and shovel chin were all that jutted from beneath his black hood even though he sat far above Pravon. The stifling heat did not seem to trouble the assassin as much as it did Pravon and Aneen. The gilded dagger with the black jewel on its hilt protruded from the base of his mount's skull. "I did not want you two to lose your souls to the Assassin's hell simply because we had a disagreement." A sarcastic smirk pulled at his lips.

Pravon's anger smoldered. "We've joined you once again to determine what else must be done in order to fulfill our contracts. One contract cannot bind us together through many more events." He tried to swallow his rage, but some of it spilled out. "And I, for one, would have been content if we discovered that King Jabarra had you killed."

Kridmore's smirk twisted before it lifted into a smile. "You have not yet been introduced to Genturion Master Ristanus and his two genturions of the first legion—Cavius and Nortimus." He motioned at the rigid man in tan dragonsteel armor at the forefront and then the two men whose dragons flanked the genturion master. The master had a tapering black and gray beard. The other two were both helmed. The claim that sand dragon scales held the power to keep those who wore them cool in immense heat must be true.

"We ride to Belvenguard, then?" Pravon asked. "To create as much chaos as possible by initiating the war in the south?"

Kridmore gave him a noncommittal shrug. "I did not have to convince King Jabarra or his genturions of anything, although I may have given them a bit of a nudge. I am excited to witness what will happen in Progtown."

Pravon's stomach sloshed with an uneasy dread. For an instant, he thought he felt a few droplets of liquid hit his exposed wrist. He glanced upward, but the skies were clear. It could have only been saliva from Kridmore's dragon, or the premonition of blood falling from the sky sea.

35

CYRAN ORENDAIN

Cyran hurried down hallways, rushing around a corner and out past flickering torchlight. The open walk of a battlement lay ahead, and soldiers gathered in groups around an amber dragon and a rose dragon that perched on the merlons.

The amber dragon's head drooped, its back and wings hunched, its scales not as translucent as typical for its kind. The pain of Eidelmere's loss lanced sharply through Cyran, the disheartened look of the dragon before him a bitter reminder of his severed bond. Cyran forced himself to stand straight despite the pain, and he neared the soldiers encircling the creature. A group of younger people hovered nearby.

Jaslin. His sister stood with Lady Menoria and three young nobles of Dashtok. Cyran weaved his way toward them.

"Her pulse is thready." A gray-haired woman in red robes had her arm jammed under the dragon's scales on its rear leg. She slipped her hand out, the chain around her waist rattling. "Another one."

"What is causing it?" Sir Paltere paced within the ring of soldiers, rubbing at his scalp.

A hunched old man in blue robes shuffled around the dragon's other leg, squeezing a handpump attached to a bottle and misting the creature's scales. The mist fell across its lower leg. The man leaned his flat nose closer and sniffed. "Tatter farthing sickness." He tapped a scale, and the mist coating it gave off a purplish hue. "It spreads via the humors of the beasts and is contagious."

The nyren woman glowered at the old man and shook her head. "The truth is, we cannot know what is causing it. Not without more knowledge." She turned to a dragonmage sitting on a crate. "Can you have her lower her head? I'd like to have a look in her mouth."

The dragonmage nodded as Cyran stepped up beside Jaslin, who turned toward him. Her eyes grew until the whites were visible around her entire irises, and she lunged over and threw her arms around him.

Cyran grinned and returned the hug. "I heard you were here. But why?"

"Have you heard that Lady Menoria is betrothed to the king?" Cyran's blank look filled a gap in their conversation, and Jaslin clarified, "Queen Hyceth died, and Menoria asked me to accompany her here."

Cyran swallowed, trying to recollect himself as he gestured at the amber dragon. "And what happened to that creature?"

"Nothing happened to her. That's the problem. There are many in the legions who are falling ill from some affliction."

"I did not know dragons were susceptible to mortal illnesses." Cyran watched as the nyren woman stuck her head into the beast's maw, reaching deeper and pulling at its teeth. The old man tapped what looked like a utensil against a scale and then touched the utensil to a crystal he suspended on a thread. "This cannot be happening. Not now. Belvenguard may not even be able to defend itself against what is coming, but if our legions are filled with sick dragons, we will all surely be wiped from the face of Cimeren."

Jaslin's smile dropped. "You have seen some things, haven't you?"

Cyran slowly nodded. "I'd like to tell you everything, but I must visit Nevergrace. Quickly. I'm only still here because I heard you were as well, and I couldn't leave without seeing you."

Jaslin squeezed his hand. "You found me."

"Her breath smells of degeneration," the nyren said, "but all of her teeth are sound, and there are no lesions in her mouth."

"This one's third eyelids are thickened." The old man had moved on to inspecting the hunched rose dragon, and he rolled back a pale flap of skin that was beneath the creature's outer eyelids.

"That one is a rose dragon." The nyren sidled around to that beast's eye and inspected the membrane. She shook her head with obvious disdain. "All rose dragons have a much thicker third eyelid, so they are not blinded by their own breath. They can still see through the membrane in the midst of their glaring light and fly on without being hindered, unlike all the dragons around them."

Cyran recalled scenes from the outpost when the rose dragon had breathed blinding light, which the guard and mages referred to as starlight. The mist dragon there had used its breath in a similar manner, but those beasts were said to have a much more acute sense of smell and hearing compared to other dragons, which helped guide them through the haze they expelled.

"A fortnight of rest," the old man said, "and then she can return to her duties."

"We do not have a fortnight to rest any dragon." Sir Paltere paced around in a circle, his hand clenching and unclenching on his sword's hilt.

"I believe we do not even know if these two creatures will recover or slowly grow more and more sickly." The nyren turned to Paltere. "The old diseases of their kind are few and far between. Such afflictions seldom arise, and each disease has a lot of the same signs as the next. The only way to tell them apart is to look at the body after it..."

"You are suggesting that I sacrifice one of these dragons so you can examine its body even though they may recover?" Paltere stared in disbelief.

"I am not suggesting sacrificing any dragon." The nyren shook her head. "But if one is to finally pass on and return to their realm, then we should take advantage of the situation. To learn."

Paltere's eyes fell shut, and his chest slowly expanded with breath.

Cyran took Jaslin by the elbow and guided her away. "Jaslin... I've seen the legions of Murgare. I... you probably don't want to stay in Galvenstone. You can come with me to the Never and from there run away to a village with Smoke and Emellefer, a village that is so small it will not concern the legions of Murgare."

"Do you really think I will be any safer at a village? Or even at the outpost?"

Cyran exhaled in frustration as they strolled along the walk, staring at the assortment of dragons perched at their stations. Forges burned down in the baileys, releasing clouds of black smoke. A half-dozen soldiers wheeled a harnessing cart over to a sun dragon, but instead of a quarterdeck, a dragon pauldron was suspended by the cart's rope. They aligned the piece of armor and settled it into place on the creature's shoulder, positioning the pauldron so it left a gap for wing movement. Others rolled up a golden helm of dragonsteel, and the creature lowered its neck, preparing to accept its new armor.

More soldiers ran around them, stacking an assortment of bolts—thick broadheads, spined, spiraling, and oil-soaked in preparation to use as flaming projectiles.

"What are those?" Jaslin pointed to a stack of bolts with a flared style of head where the steel had been pounded outward, leaving an empty space inside. "Wouldn't those be weak and break on impact?"

"I believe those are the Galvenstone projectiles that conjurors can cast their magic on, summoning fire or ice or whatever other power and placing it inside the empty space just before their archers loose. I've heard they choose what magic to summon based on what type of dragon they are trying to bring down, but I've never seen the bolts used in battle. Nevergrace doesn't have them, probably because we don't have any conjurors."

Jaslin fell silent. "I..." She reached for something at her waist.

"Do you still have that shard?"

She hesitantly nodded.

Cyran tried to hide his disappointment. "I think you should get rid of—"

"Can you tell me about the assassin you saw? The one who murdered Queen Elra?"

Cyran glanced over at her as they walked. "I've told you about the tattoo on his neck, and his missing tongue. I do not recall any other distinguishing features. The assassin was supposedly magically clinging to the rafters when the kingsknights found him in the chamber where the queen was being held, but without a tongue, a conjuror cannot use magic."

Jaslin was silent for a few heartbeats. "There was a second assassin found here who looked similar. And this assassin murdered our queen."

"The Assassin's bloody hell! How are such men sneaking into Dashtok?"

Jaslin's eyes glazed over as they wandered across some memory. "And you've told me everything about the letters the squires and Sir Kayom received?"

"Everything I know about them, which isn't much. I never saw Sir Kayom's message. He only told me about it." Cyran studied her. "Are you concerned about one of the king's councilmembers?"

"Weren't you?"

"Indeed, but they are all questionable. Riscott is by far the worst, but I could not prove he is evil or working against his own kingdom, if that's what the warnings were meant to imply. But you seem to know or suspect something."

She sighed. "All I have is suspicion, and it is probably the same as yours."

"This place is not safe. Come with me."

"No place in Belvenguard is safe, and I am trying to find out who works against us. I will not be able to do that in a small village or at Nevergrace. The assassins and the letters raise a lot of questions, and they probably could not have all come from outside kingdoms and slipped into Galvenstone."

Cyran turned and grabbed her by the shoulders. "And how do you intend to figure this all out? No one in Dashtok is going to tell a handmaid—even if she is the handmaid of the future queen—their traitorous secrets."

"I will have to work like the dragonguard of old and use my head as well as my might. Use limited knowledge to arrive at the truth through reasoning, and then prove what needs to be proven. I will ask myself who benefits from these events and why."

"That approach likely works best in old legends."

"At least we no longer have to worry about that other myth I used to remind you of when we were children—that when an elf finally rode a dragon, the world would end."

A deep dread and disbelief twined inside Cyran. Jaslin had not mentioned that in years, and he only faintly recalled her ever doing so. But the Dragon Queen had also mentioned it to him. He had encountered a few elves in the Evenmeres, but their people were supposed to have been wiped out completely during the Dragon Wars.

"I just have to understand each person's motivations, what drives them," Jaslin said, as if this were something as simple as counting coins.

"And how far have you come in your pursuit?"

"Not as far as I'd like, but I know a place I need to visit, one that could hold some answers."

"And where is this place?"

She hesitated and glanced off toward the lower tiers of the city.

36

SIRRA BRACKENGLAVE

Darkwater Lake sprawled into the icy distance, the city of Gilth—more of a massive village composed of huts covered with animal skins—hugging its shoreline. Plumes of smoke drifted from the huts but seemed to float and smear the air just overhead rather than rising. Shadowmar grumbled and stretched her neck, eyeing Mount Frozen Fist, a towering peak on the far side of the lake that jutted toward the sky sea. The site where it all began, where this world had changed forever.

Sirra descended her stirrup ladder and landed on the snowy tundra, her boots punching through a brittle top layer with a crunch. She strode boldly forward in her black armor. Yenthor's rotating platform creaked.

"I'll put a dragonbolt through the chest of any barbarian that threatens us," Yenthor said. "That should knock him back into the past age."

"We did not come for violence," Trothen said.

Sir Vladden howled in a series of unintelligible sounds.

A man laden in furs shuffled through a gust of ice dust just ahead. He did not turn or even acknowledge them, although he surely could not have missed the landing of a shadow dragon just beyond the city. The wind keened and blew harder, obscuring him completely.

When the gust died and the storm of snow crystals drifted away and faded, several score of similarly dressed men appeared, all of them fanned out and waiting.

Sirra paused. The ways of the Smoke Breathers were sometimes still a mystery even to her. "We have come to speak with the Claw of the Dragon. I am Sirra—"

"We still know you here, Dragon Queen," one man in the middle of the group said, although his face was concealed, the furs he wore spiked with frost. "No matter how much you wish to forget your heritage."

"I have forgotten nothing." She stepped forward and pried off her helm. The cold wind whipped her hair around. "But the weight of kings hangs over Cimeren now. There are matters beyond the valley that must be considered and dealt with."

"Then follow me." He turned and walked toward the city, and all the men around him closed in and formed a narrow path between him and Sirra. They waited.

Sirra marched forward, keeping her helm at her side in an attempt to show she was unconcerned and unafraid, although something about these people always made her wary. She strode between the two lines of people and kept her attention directed forward, but all the sunken eyes above every beard watched her closely, hunger seeping from their expressions. They did not attempt to hide the axes and mauls clutched beneath their furs. Some even patted the palms of their other hands with their weapons.

The man leading her to the edge of the city stopped cold, and those around him angled their two lines farther away from Sirra. Their leader slowly pivoted about to face her and threw back the fur over his head. He was bald, his scalp riddled with scars, a thick gray beard ravaging his face, his eyes as pale as snow. "The Claw says that matters of others are of no concern to the Smoke Breathers. You only seek to goad us into war. To help you fight the battles of Murgare. You believe that man for man, the strength of the clans is unmatched anywhere else in the kingdoms."

"I have never doubted the savagery of your people, Claw." Sirra spoke as loudly as she could, hoping her archers on Shadowmar would be able to hear their conversation. "This war will require all the peoples of Murgare, or it will take all of Murgare's people with it."

The wind skirled and threw ice at the Claw, but he did not even blink. "We have learned that your king is dead. Do not try to deceive us. We are not without ears or knowledge, tucked away in the valley. The Dragon still speaks to us. We are her children."

"There is another king."

"Not one we acknowledge. A usurper. A man who stepped in for the queen."

"The queen has come to the valley," Kyelle shouted as she strode to the edge of the quarterdeck and overlooked the Smoke Breathers, revealing no fear. "I am Kyelle, the rightful queen of Murgare, and I am here to speak with my people."

The Claw looked over Sirra's shoulder. "Then speak, Queen."

"The time is coming when the sky sea will rain blood." Kyelle slowly turned to look at each man in the distance as she yelled over the wind. "No one can stop it now. You are still part of Murgare and have sworn oaths to my father. I hold those oaths in my palm now." She squeezed her hand into a fist.

"We care little for oaths and even less about the workings beyond the valley," the Claw said. "It is the same for the rest of the clans. Even if I wanted to support you, I hold no authority over the others. You would have to journey to each clan and try to convince them as well. The war would be over before you could accomplish such a feat."

Shadowmar reared back and roared, the dragon's impatience and wrath deluging the *neblír*. Her cry echoed over the lands and rolled away.

The Claw's eyes had closed, and they slowly opened. "Dragons and their riders do not impress or frighten us. We created them, remember, Dragon Queen? Without us, the world would still be ruled by the elves of old Cimerenden."

"Till the day when an elf finally rides a dragon and destroys the entire world." Sirra shifted, the snow crunching like brittle bones beneath her feet. "That is your divination, is it not, Claw?"

"Not mine. The saying came long before me, but it was from a Claw. And it may become true yet."

"If there are any elves left in this world." Sirra smirked.

"I pray to the Dragon that there are, or her children and their riders will destroy Cimeren first."

"And you would sit here safe in this valley while wars rage around you." Sirra motioned in a circle. "When blood flows in rivers and plunges from the sky. You—the people whose ancestors were savage invaders—would take your leisure as the world devours itself. You, whose ancestors are responsible for humans commanding the most powerful mounts and weapons the world has ever seen." She pointed south. "A legion from Belvenguard skewered King Restebarge on Breather's Pass, at your very doorstep. The king was traveling for his annual visit with your people. Igare mocks your complacency now, your weakness. Your people have grown soft in your seclusion and worship of the Dragon. I wonder what the Dragon thinks of you now."

Several of the Smoke Breather's around her shifted. At least one grunted in outrage.

"Belvenguard seeks to raise an army that spans their entire kingdom by bringing all the legions of their cities together alongside all the legions of the Weltermores and the Rorenlands," Sirra said. "A force like it has never opposed Murgare, and they will sail and march north if we do not first meet them in their lands. And if they come, they will not stop at the north shore. They will storm the southlands and they *will* advance into this valley. They will destroy your divided clans and raze your villages to the ground. Then they will capture every free dragon in the valley and turn the beasts into engines of war."

"So they will do the same with the dragon as you and Murgare have done?"

Sirra exhaled with annoyance. "We are not the same, but we have done what we must. If this war is lost, there will be no more of the Dragon's offspring to worship and share this world with. None will remain. Not one. They will become the steeds of mages from Belvenguard and will also be ridden by their guard and harnessed and mounted by archers. They will become infertile, and out of what little eggs will be laid, none will hatch. The Dragon would not be content with such an outcome for the last of her children."

The Claw gazed into the distance as the wind gusted and whipped at his furs. He appeared to be pondering all of it. "I will call a meeting of the clans."

"Then Murgare will fall while your savage brotherhood dines and engages in idle gossip." Sirra turned away.

Sir Vladden began sobbing uncontrollably.

"What plight has affected the one-armed guard?" the Claw asked.

"He is the half-souled," Sirra answered, as if that would explain everything.

The Claw did not respond, but two of the Smoke Breathers nearby stepped closer, as if intending to cut off Sirra's return to Shadowmar. She glared at each of them as they towered head and shoulders over her, her mind racing to reach into the other realm. They did not make another move or swing weapons. They simply stared, unblinking.

"Live with wonder," the Claw said.

Sirra glanced over her shoulder at the leader, who held a hand up in farewell. "Die before you've lost it all."

She marched for Shadowmar.

37

JASLIN ORENDAIN

The tavern's lamplight burned low as Jaslin sat at a table by herself. Several of the patrons leered at her over their shoulders.

Would any of these people remember her from her prior visit? She hoped her association with the young nobles would give her some kind of protection, as Menoria and her kingsknights were currently attending a midday meal with Igare. Jaslin had not been able to convince Menoria to return with her to the tavern, and Jaslin's impatience had been eating at her. She couldn't wait any longer. She also did not want to visit the tavern after nightfall, so she snuck away when Menoria was distracted by the king.

Jaslin took a sip from her tankard, letting the wine of Nevergrace pool in her mouth before slowly swallowing. She would not allow herself to become intoxicated. This place could be dangerous, especially if Keliam were to come after her. Only the thought that the merchant should not know she was in the city at this time and that he should not be able to reach her inside Dashtok comforted her. She pulled her hood lower over her face.

A few hours slipped away, and there was no sign of the merchants who wore the burro rings.

They better not have tricked me into getting rid of Keliam only to disappear and never fulfill their end of the bargain.

She waited, dismissing the serving wench whenever she stopped at her table. Nervous anxiety ate at her with each passing minute, and eventually she stood, laid a few halfpennies on the table, and strode for the exit. A boy of about ten years stood beside the doorway. When she neared, he grinned at her.

"Have you seen the burro?" He held up a hand. On one of his fingers was a wooden ring similar to Cyran's.

Jaslin froze and glanced around. No one seemed to be watching her.

"If you want to find the burro, follow me." He turned and opened the door, which threw a blinding beam of sunlight onto Jaslin's face, and he hurried down the street.

Jaslin rushed after the boy as he passed several buildings and turned down an alleyway. Jaslin paused, remaining at the main road. The boy waved her on and slipped around the back of a building and disappeared. Jaslin took a deep breath and considered her options. Following him might be a bad idea. She gripped the hilt of a knife she had sheathed beneath her cloak and drew the blade. Cyran had risked his life to protect his people and all that he held dear. Why couldn't she do the same? Other than for Cyran and Menoria, no one would be too badly affected if she died.

She exhaled and hastened down the alleyway and into its shadows, watching a stack of crates to make sure no one hid behind them. After passing the crates unharmed, she approached a cross alley just in time to see the boy step through a doorway. She darted after him but slowed as she neared the opening. The chamber inside seemed to be unoccupied.

"Hello?" She stepped across the threshold and glanced

about, crushing her knife's hilt. It was a single room with nothing more than an armoire placed against the wall to her left, but the armoire was askew. She approached the furnishing while taking quick glances over her shoulder. Behind the armoire, a door in the stone wall had been opened inward. She pressed herself behind the furniture.

"The burro is in here." The boy's face emerged in the doorway, a dim light shining behind him as he grinned again. "Come."

Jaslin held her knife before her as she crept through the doorway. Once she was on the other side, the boy reached out with a closed fist, showing off his ring again.

"Tell the man outside the Sparrow's Den of the burro," the boy said. "And may your travels always bring you joy, wealth, and new experiences."

Jaslin cocked an eyebrow as she studied the ring.

"It's their saying," the boy added.

"And where is the Sparrow's Den?"

"In the underground city. Away from the lake. It's not far, but if you have any trouble, just ask around."

"The underground city?"

The boy nodded and gestured her onward. After she took a few tentative steps down a hallway, the boy slipped back out through the doorway and bolted it closed. The rumble of the armoire juddering across the stone floor of the chamber sounded on the other side.

Jaslin cursed under her breath and swallowed before following a passageway that must have been located inside the adjacent building. After a few horse lengths, its floor sloped downward into the earth. She descended below the lowest visible tier of Galvenstone, and the air grew musty and cool. When she reached the bottom and the floor leveled off again, a longer hallway like an underground street ran in two directions.

The ceiling arched overhead, and torches burned against the walls.

Several people wandered past and did not even seem to notice her. She turned in the direction of what she believed would be heading away from the lake and paced along as if she belonged here beneath the streets of this city. Lone people or those in groups of two or three wore cloaks or tunics and traveled in the opposite direction as her. They passed without a word, moving as casually as those who walked the streets above. Most didn't even bother to hide their faces, apparently unafraid of their association with this place.

Jaslin sheathed her knife and paced on, and over the next half hour, she slowly started to feel more comfortable. She reached a square where passageways entered from at least eight different directions. People milled about, but no one spoke, or if they did, it was not above a whisper. She neared a lady in a brown tunic and caught her eye.

"The Sparrow's Den?" Jaslin murmured.

The lady studied her until Jaslin furtively flashed her hand, pretending to be wearing a ring but then concealing her fingers so quickly the woman would not have been able to see much. The lady pointed at one of the passageways. Jaslin nodded her thanks and hurried on. She passed several shops that lined the square and appeared to be selling nothing more than clothing and bread and jewelry, like any shop in Galvenstone. One had many potions in vials sitting outside, their liquids ranging from yellow to blue to deep red.

Jaslin angled into the appropriate passageway and flowed with and against several other people who were coming and going. Once she reached the end, another square opened up. The signs hanging outside the shops here caught her eye, and on one there was a painting of a small bird lying on its back beside a tankard. She veered for the establishment, and a large man in a cloak stepped before her, blocking the doorway.

Jaslin quickly flashed her hand again, but the man didn't budge. He folded his arms across his chest.

"May your travels always bring you joy, wealth, and new experiences," Jaslin whispered.

The man studied her for several heartbeats before stepping aside. She entered what appeared to be a tavern not too different from the place where she had first met the merchants. She took a seat at an empty table beside a hearth, trying to get a look at the patrons without making it obvious she was doing so. None of the three closest people appeared familiar.

"What will it be?" a man in a bright green tunic asked as he approached her table.

"I'm here to meet someone. Two men actually. But I'll have wine. One of Nevergrace's vintages, if you have that."

The man cocked his head before nodding and stepping away. Before he returned, two men in cloaks sat down across from Jaslin.

"You shouldn't keep ordering the same wine everywhere you go," the burlier of the men said, his voice familiar—the merchant from the tavern. His hand rested on the table, revealing a wooden burro ring on his thumb. "After what you did to Keliam, there are probably people hunting you."

Jaslin's blood turned icy. "You should have warned me about that before sending a young woman after such a man."

"I didn't think you'd be able to pull it off this side of a decade." The man's teeth shimmered beneath his hood and above his scrubby beard. "No one has been able to touch Keliam in years. But you somehow managed to get the kingsknights involved. Then the bribed watchmen could not simply ignore what was happening."

Pride swelled inside Jaslin, but she suppressed it, fearing this man was playing to her for reasons she could not yet fathom. "It's time for you to hold up your end of the bargain."

"Indeed." The merchant drank from a tankard. "You wish to know everything we do about the assassins?"

Jaslin nodded.

"It would be best if this conversation is never repeated," the merchant said. "Ever." He waited. "Do you understand?"

Jaslin nodded again.

"We do not know all of the potential repercussions," the merchant continued, "but I fear more assassins will become involved. The *only* reason we are here is because the Merchant requires all of his people to uphold the bargains they make."

Jaslin wiped her damp palms on her cloak.

"I can tell you that the assassin you were wondering about came from the same place as the previous one who murdered the Murgare queen," the merchant said in barely a whisper.

"And how do you know this?" Jaslin gripped her tankard tighter to stop her hands from trembling.

"Because of the tattoo on his throat. I lied to you before. We actually saw it in full, but I would have preferred not to share that knowledge with anyone. It could get a person killed." He took a drink. "It was an image of a raven inside a triangle."

"Is that the mark of some thieves' guild?"

He glanced at his partner before shaking his head. "But Keliam could belong to one such guild—The Guild of Fire and Shadow. Does that name mean anything to you?"

Jaslin slowly shook her head, attempting not to appear naïve.

"Best hope it stays that way." The merchant swallowed. "The raven in the triangle is a brand placed on men who have been shipped to a group of isles far in the south. It is a penal colony beyond Belvenguard. The Southern Isles of the Rorenlands."

"What does the penal colony have to do with assassins?"

The merchant shrugged. "That is the real question now, isn't it?"

"So that is all you know? I unknowingly risked my life for you to tell me that the assassins both came from the Rorenlands?"

The merchant nodded and drank again. "You wished to know as much as we did about the assassins. The only other thing I can add is that we saw someone sit down with the assassin in question and mention his name—Burren, former member of the guild. And I know the guild the other man was referring to was certainly not the Merchant's Guild." He downed the rest of his drink. "Now I have told you everything, and this includes what we already divulged—that both assassins had their tongues removed, which we do not believe is a requirement of the men shipped to the isles."

Jaslin's anger stewed. What was she supposed to do with this knowledge? Assassins being trained on some isles in the south was hardly something she could deal with. She could never even hope to visit the place to learn anything more. The Rorenlands probably worked to undermine Belvenguard. That would make sense with their lack of response to Igare's calling of their banners. The only thing she could do with this knowledge was pass it on to Igare so he could better prepare for the Rorenlands siding with Murgare, which was already the rumor. What she had learned would not help prevent any more assassinations.

She silently cursed herself. Igare and his council probably already knew all of this, all of it except for maybe the assassin's name. They just did not want to inform everyone in the castle. She had been a fool to risk her life for such a cause, in her naiveté believing a simple young woman like herself could help swing the pendulum of war away from Belvenguard and thus protect her people. *I am too much like Cyran.*

The merchants rose. The burlier one placed more than

enough coin down to cover their drinks and then dropped a ring that rolled about the table. He and his companion exited the tavern.

Jaslin took up the wooden ring and studied the laden burro on its face before slipping it on her finger. After a few minutes, Jaslin departed the establishment, her mind churning as she retraced her steps along the passageways, headed for the area where she had entered the underground city.

By the time she finally returned to the inclined hallway she had followed to the underground, she was alone. The shadows seemed thicker and denser than she remembered as she paced along, hoping the doorway could be opened from the inside. How else would she return to the conventional portion of the city?

A dark figure rose up from the shadows before her, a man in a cloak. He lunged at her, reaching out and catching her around the throat.

Jaslin attempted to scream, but her air was cut off as her assailant squeezed. A stench of smoldering alcohol and old sweat hit her nostrils with a burning sting as she grabbed at his wrist with both hands, trying to pry his fingers from her flesh. Pain erupted along her neck as she gasped and clawed at her attacker's hand, her mind racing for any means of escape.

His mouth opened, as if to speak, but only a few guttural grunts escaped his lips. He had no tongue...

Jaslin lurched, her vision darkening as the assailant pulled a blade from his belt and jabbed it at her chest. She yanked back and shouted something, and the man's mouth opened again, emitting a strange shriek, his blade tearing into her tunic but only nicking her skin. He jerked his hand from her.

Amber flames crackled along his forearm. His eyes widened, and he screamed as he stumbled back, staring at his arm. The flames crawled up his flesh, racing toward his neck and head as he turned and fled down the passageway.

Jaslin braced herself with her hands on her knees as she heaved for breath, her head spinning. Something at her waist vibrated, and she felt along until her fingers found the shard in her pouch. When she touched it, it sent a jolt through her marrow cavities. Her bones were already humming and shaking beneath her muscles.

She stared at her attacker's parting trail, in the direction of his cries, until it dawned on her. Her swirling head and the tilting walls around her steadied as she uncurled her fingers and looked at her smoking palm in horror and awe and shock.

The shrieks faded and died, and something thudded in the distance. Jaslin trembled with fear, but after a minute, she crept onward. A smoking body lay near the doorway where she had entered the underground city. She hesitantly approached, a line of blood dripping from the prick to her upper breast.

The body was curled into a fetal position, its clothing charred, its skin blackened. The odor of burned flesh engulfed Jaslin, and a wave of bile hit the back of her tongue. She retched, spewing her stomach contents against the wall with a splatter.

After taking a few moments to recover, she forced herself to inspect the body. There were two potential things she had to know. She leaned over and peered into the corpse's open mouth, confirming that there was indeed no tongue inside. Then she used the flat of her knife's blade to tilt the body's head back. Much of its skin was blackened, but only in patches. A tattered and burned scarf was still tied around its throat. Jaslin cut the scarf away. Beneath, a partially burned and distorted tattoo was visible—that of a bird inside a triangle.

Jaslin exhaled as her feet quickly carried her to the exit, where she unlatched a few bolts and shoved on the door. The door opened a little before banging against the armoire, leaving barely enough space for her to slip through. She squeezed into the gap, and the edges of the door and frame dug into her hips and breasts. After she forced her way into the other chamber, she hurriedly unbolted its front door and stepped outside into the streets of Galvenstone, her head spinning with all that had occurred. Through all the images and smells assaulting her and the sensations running through her bones, the picture of the tattoo clarified in her mind.

Maybe she would have to find a way to travel far into the south and discover what those tattoos and men with missing tongues had in common.

38

CYRAN ORENDAIN

The crumbled keep of the Never waited ahead, along with the outer curtain, which had holes the size of seize engines punched through it. Only the twin towers overlooking the Evenmeres appeared as Cyran remembered everything prior to the Dragon Queen's occupation of the outpost. Pain from the loss of Eidelmere's bond flared again, and memories of the spiteful old dragon who slept in the den exploded in his mind and tore at some fabric of his soul. The dragon's soul had been lost, and Cyran could not do a thing about that fact.

Milluri flared her wings, cupping the wind and circling lower as evenfall neared. The puncture wound in her leathery segment had been stitched closed by a nyren and would heal. Her newly placed quarterdeck and turret creaked, and Cyran's lance, which was mounted on his saddle, glowed with green light. Igare had made sure his dragonknight and thorn dragon were well equipped.

Three forest dragons and a thorn dragon waited either in the bailey or atop the sturdier sections of the curtain walls. One of the forest dragons hooted when they spotted Milluri. Nithinix trilled and arched his neck.

"Dragon!" A voice rolled over the outpost, and a horn quickly answered—only one blast for a single approaching dragon, one considered friendly.

Milluri landed in the outer bailey, and Cyran dismounted.

"You've returned, brave dragonknight." Brelle leaned her thick hips against a stone, grinning, although a haunted look played in her eyes. "Murgare hasn't killed you yet."

Barking sounded, and three wolves came tearing through an archway. Smoke leapt at Cyran, tail wagging, tongue licking. Milluri gasped and beat her wings, eyeing the animals nervously.

Cyran pet Smoke's head and allowed the wolf to lick his cheek. "Brelle, I'm glad you're the same as ever. Have Vyk and Ineri warned everyone of what is to come?"

"If you want to call what they told us a warning." Her chin jutted out as if she was recollecting the affair. "It sounded like the same kind of thing we were already preparing for and have far too few soldiers and knights and dragons to defend against."

"I fear the time is nearly upon us. I've... seen much. Where are Laren and Dage?"

"Shitting themselves is my best guess. These archers of yours scared everyone more than they helped rally us together."

Cyran's heart twinged. "That was not my intent, but everyone needs to be prepared and waiting."

More people rounded a corner of the bailey, moving quickly.

"Our brave friend has returned!" Laren spread his arms wide, his typical boyish grin spreading across his lips, although the expression seemed to take more effort than usual.

Dage grumbled something and brushed his long blond hair behind his shoulder. "Was Murgare responsible for the village?"

Cyran stepped closer. "I hoped you would have heard the answer to that from Vyk and Ineri."

"We could have, but we want to hear it from you." Dage

folded his arms across his broad chest. "From a real dragonguard—or knight, no less."

"There are creatures in the woods that are responsible for the destruction of our hamlet and a village in the north." Cyran lowered his gaze as he approached his friends.

"So it is all of Murgare that is coming to wipe out our kingdom, and the monsters in the woods may join them." A sour frown crossed Dage's face, and he shook his head.

"The monsters do not seem to be on Murgare's side." Cyran stopped before Brelle, and Smoke trailed behind, panting at his heels. "We can hope that the monsters will kill any legions the north sends through the woods."

"Maybe the Assassin will fly up from his hell on a legion of rainbow dragons with unicorn horns, the Paladin and the Shield Maiden at his side, and together they will smite the Dragon Queen and all of her legions for us as well." Brelle spat on the ground.

"What a sight that would be." Laren's grin broadened.

"Cyran!" Renily, the little redheaded girl, tore across the bailey carrying a lute, hers the only human eyes here that were not riddled with fear. "You've returned." She brushed her tangles of hair behind her ears. "Will you play us a song?"

Emellefer walked behind Renily and smiled when Cyran's gaze met hers, although she carried an unfamiliar tension in her spine and hands as she absently picked at her fingernails. Cyran dipped his head to her.

Three guard in green dragonsteel armor arrived just behind Emellefer, each of them holding torches as the sunlight vanished. Their firelight cast dancing shadows across their faces and blackened their eyes. Vyk and Ineri accompanied the guard.

"The legions of Murgare are now moving?" the guard in the lead asked.

"As I'm sure Vyk and Ineri told you, we saw them along the

north shore of the lake, preparing." Cyran swallowed a lump of dread. "That was before we were flown to Northsheeren and held there."

A jolt of emotion shot across the guard's face. "Then we should expect to see hordes of dragons flying across the lake at any time, hiding fleets of ships in their shadows."

Cyran simply nodded as Renily held the lute up for him. He tousled her hair and forced a smile. "Unfortunately, I cannot play because I must return to Galvenstone straightaway. But I will play for you soon. Once I return. At that time, the war will be over." He could almost hear Jaslin's voice in his ears, telling him not to allow his duty to take control of every aspect of his life.

Renily's lower lip protruded, but Emellefer wrapped her arms around the little girl's neck and pulled her back a step. "He will play all night once this madness is over," Emellefer whispered to the girl.

"What says the king?" Ezul, the nyren of the Never, strolled up behind the genturion of the new guard at the outpost. The nyren's chain belt clinked.

"King Igare asked me to offer the brave people of Nevergrace a choice." Cyran glanced around as soldiers and knights and farmhands and woodsmen and women and children gathered in the bailey. "You may decide if you wish to remain here and defend our legendary outpost, or if you would rather travel to Galvenstone and provide aid for the king's city."

A hush fell across the bailey. Somewhere nearby, a dragon shifted over its straw bed.

"I suggest that we stay," Ezul said. "If the legions of Murgare pass through the Evenmeres and take the outpost, they will flank Galvenstone and crush the capital between their armies."

"Do you really believe we can stop them?" The genturion

wheeled on the nyren. "With three forest dragons and a fraction of the soldiers and knights this outpost once held?"

"You suggest we run with our tails tucked between our legs?" Ezul asked.

The genturion's face flushed. He did not acknowledge any fear, although the emotion seeped off of everyone around them. "All we can hope to do here is watch the skies and the woods and wait for death to come take us."

Cyran's stomach clenched. Would everyone at Nevergrace be killed? Or would Murgare pass over this decimated outpost along the border and turn toward Galvenstone? Cyran's brief ideas on how he could try to stay here or stop any attack at the Never flashed and burned out as soon as they appeared in his mind. No option seemed plausible.

"I will leave the decision up to each of you." Cyran slowly spun in a circle. "This castle is also my home, and I long to defend her, but King Igare has ordered me to return to Dashtok." He faced Vyk and Ineri. "Please gather whatever you need and prepare Nithinix. Meet me at the first beacon tower in no more than an hour. There's something there I must look into. Once we've returned to Galvenstone, we'll fly together on a single dragon again, as comrades and companions." He crouched and took Renily's hand as tears streamed down the little girl's cheeks. "If you leave Nevergrace, please take Smoke and wolves with you. They will need you to look after them."

Emellefer nodded and silently mouthed, "We will."

Renily burst out in a long wail. She flung the lute on the ground and sprinted away, crying. After several strides, she tripped and sprawled across the ground, sobbed louder, and scrambled to her feet. "He'll never play for us again." She dashed off and disappeared behind an archway.

Cyran's eyelids fell like dropping portcullises. Perhaps he should have taken the extra few minutes to play for her, for

Nevergrace, for his home. Regrets piled upon him as he reached for the discarded lute. The king had ordered him to leave the outpost and his people to assist with Belvenguard's primary defenses, but protecting the Never was the only thing he had ever known. It was in his blood. If even a single one of Nevergrace's people died when he was not here to offer assistance, he would be ridden with more guilt. The only comforting thought he found was that Jaslin was no longer at the outpost.

Something thudded into the ground in the distance and thrummed. Another similar sound followed, and another and another.

"Take cover!" the genturion shouted, and everyone ducked and ran. Several screams echoed around them.

Cyran held a hand over his head as he grabbed Emellefer and pushed her up against a wall, shielding her. He glanced skyward. Winged silhouettes blurred against the backlit sky sea, but these creatures were very far away, at an altitude near the sea. Only one kind of dragon could fly so high. The creatures split ranks, and some sailed back to the north while others continued south.

"Storm dragons." Cyran pointed upward. "This is not an attack."

The thuds ceased, and Cyran glanced around. A score of steel arrows used by storm dragon guard were buried into the ground around them, their fletching waving like flags.

Messenger arrows. Cyran hurried over to one and unwound a parchment from its shaft.

To all those of Nevergrace,

. . .

Each of you who does not stand against the coming war will be spared. But that is not all. If you do not resist the coming legions, you will be rewarded when the war is over. A sword's weight in gold will be gifted to your family, gold mined directly from Murgare's vast resources. Your family will also be granted lands of their own, and unowned lands will soon be bountiful in Belvenguard. You will be accepted into your new kingdom with open arms. Look around you, and make your decision now. This may be your last opportunity. The fields you till and sow could one day be yours. Your family and friends could survive.

Oomaren, King of Murgare

Cyran glanced up in horror. How could his people resist such an offer? It was what everyone but the past lords and ladies of the outpost could have desired—freedom, riches, land of their own. Nearby, Dage was reading over a message, his eyes wide. Vyk looked over Ineri's shoulder as they, too, read from a parchment.

Cyran crumpled the message into a ball, and he hurled it at a distant wall. He kissed Emellefer's dark hair. "Do what you will, but please be safe. I must return to Dashtok."

He whipped about and hurried for Milluri.

39

PRAVON THE DRAGON THIEF

The city of Progtown emerged on the horizon as the legion of sand dragons marched onward. Pravon had given up his horse and now rode on one of the beasts behind Kridmore's, Aneen on the back of the same creature with him. There was no guard on this particular dragon, and although there was a mage, the man probably wasn't even needed. The beast simply followed the ranks, guided by its yoke and chains that were linked to the other beasts in its row, this one on the outer end with no dragon to their left.

Horns blared in the distant city, and silhouettes of winged creatures leapt from the walls and swarmed the skies ahead.

Aneen shifted uncomfortably behind him and tapped his shoulder. "This city has long been aware of our coming."

"Who wouldn't be with all the dust we create?" Pravon asked. Surprise would not be their ally.

Genturion Master Ristanus led their steady march, Kridmore flanking him with the two other genturions from the Rorenlands. None of them appeared frightened, Ristanus's posture as rigid as ever.

The legions of Progtown circled outward beyond their city's walls in enlarging spirals. The hair on the back of Pravon's neck spiked. He had never been a sitting target on the ground before, in a position where he was supposed to be outwardly brave and protected enough to face something head-on without cover. He always used subterfuge and stealth. His nerves felt as if a dull blade dragged along their tracts.

"I do not like this." Aneen squeezed his shoulder. "We should find cover."

Shrieks sounded in the sky and rolled out over the sands.

Pravon gripped his spine tool and found his vial of diluted shadow dragon poison. If he were to be thrust into war, he would need a beast he could control. Silver fire arced overhead in a threatening display, although the opposing legions were still far away.

The archers on all the ranks of sand dragons swiveled on their quarterdecks and sighted upward. The beasts from the Rorenlands did not have turrets or archers below them since their only type of flying was gliding over the ground, but they did have multiple crossbows mounted on each quarterdeck.

Pravon's legs tightened around his mount's scaly neck.

"If this is our end, I will be pissed that we never got to enjoy any of the benefits from joining The Guild of Fire and Shadow," Aneen whispered in his ear, her breath warm against his skin.

"I do not know if we would have ever benefitted, but I will... I... it was not the worst thing I have done to have traveled and shared a contract with you."

Aneen guffawed. "So touching. If only we did not have to share the task with Kridmore."

The legions of Progtown formed ranks in the sky and soared toward them, apparently realizing that the Rorenlands's army was not intimidated and would not be turning around.

Genturion Master Ristanus raised a fist and punched it into the air. The sand dragons bellowed, spewing breaths all around them. Dust whipped around Pravon in blinding sheets, swirling and thickening until the sunlight was muted. He wrapped a cloth over his nose and mouth as his eyes stung and teared.

"Here." Aneen shoved something around his side.

He took the item, barely able to see it—some kind of wrap with clear glass to shield his eyes.

"The Rorenlands's soldiers all have them," Aneen said. "They fire and make glass out of sand. I got them from our mage."

Pravon slipped the strange visor over his head and tightened a strap at its back. He blinked several times, and his eyes stopped burning and weeping. The haze around them was dark brown with tinges of yellow. He prayed to the Assassin that this concealing cloud covered them as well as the land all around them so the attacking legions would not know exactly where they were and where to aim.

They marched on, and dragons roared and blew sand, some of the rows taking flight together and gliding along to either side. The foot soldiers and knights, and even Kridmore and the genturions, soon vanished in the thickening storm. Pravon could not even make out their own dragon's head or their mage. Their archers behind them were also completely obscured.

Bolts screamed and tore through the storm, thudding into the sands around them and burying deep. Pravon lurched, instinctively trying to roll to the side and find cover on the ground, but he hung on once he realized that if he fell, he would be trampled. These beasts were disciplined and well trained, and they seemed to know where to go.

Bluish flames exploded in the murk above, lighting up the area around them and backlighting the billowing sand. These flames also revealed the silhouettes of enemy dragons and where the attacking creatures flew overhead. Someone nearby screamed.

"I say we take out our mage and control our own dragon," Aneen shouted over the roar of the wind.

Pravon swallowed, unsure, but feeling more and more like he had no control over any outcome. "We risk being found out by the genturions and punished."

"The Assassin can judge me. I don't give a pygmy dragon's ass about the Rorenlands's mages or genturions. Or their new king."

Pravon lifted his wetted spine above his shoulder so Aneen could hopefully see it. "I will take the bond. You take the mage. He cannot live to tell the genturions."

Aneen did not hesitate, clambering around him and disappearing into the haze. Pravon worked himself around to the side of the dragon's neck, gripping onto scales and planting his boots in the stirrups of his makeshift saddle. He found the groove for the jugular vein and impaled the dragon. The dragon stiffened and shuddered, and a few shouts came from the archers behind them. They should have no notion of the takeover, as Pravon would ensure as best he could that they did not experience any change with the new bond.

The sand dragon lurched with pain, and Pravon spoke his typical introduction for its understanding. The brain of this creature was not robust nor as capable of the degree of comprehension as most others of their species were. The dragon's rage rolled off its scales, but the beast quickly acquiesced.

Pravon climbed back onto the top of the beast's neck as he patted it. Then he crawled his way toward its head, finding that Aneen had already taken up her new seat where the mage had been, her demeanor as calm as or even calmer than before this confrontation with Progtown had started.

"I removed the chains from its yoke," she said.

Pravon nodded. *A wise move.* He veered the dragon slowly at first, driving it to the left where no other dragons had been marching. "We will create some distance between us and this army."

"They are strong and numerous and fight based on those factors, but I do not wish to become one of the many who will be decimated."

Pravon agreed. He commanded his dragon to breathe in the direction they were traveling as they angled away from the ranks.

Fire and bolts blasted and buzzed around them, most of the projectiles hidden in the murk, but the majority of the attacks sounded to their right. A dragon bellowed in pain, and the tumult of its thudding collapse followed. Men screamed. Pravon's archers loosed along with hundreds of others, ballistae arms thrumming as bolts hurtled skyward through the storm. A tromping giant nearby raised its club, and a spark of blue flames shot from the weapon and arced overhead, creating the display that helped their legion locate their enemies while their legion remained obscured.

A rush of wind howled overhead, and a massive cloud of darkness emerged, blotting out the sunlight. Pravon spurred their dragon on. "Fly!"

The beast lunged forward with a surprising burst of speed and beat its wings. It lifted from the ground and glided through the haze. The dark form they had seen grew, and in an instant, the colossal body of a sun dragon smashed into the ground behind them with a thump that shook the earth. The dragon's wings and legs were twisted, its head partially buried into the dirt, blood flooding the area around it. Several bolts protruded from its chest and flank. The archers on its quarterdeck were flattened against the frame, having taken the impact of the fall in full even though they were on top.

The beast's corpse faded to a dark outline and then quickly disappeared in the swirling murk.

"By the blood of the Assassin's own contract." Aneen's voice was hoarse.

Their dragon landed and marched onward in silence as the onslaught and chaos raged. The outlines of fallen sand and enemy dragons and scrambling men emerged at regular intervals in the haze but quickly vanished again. After what felt like an hour of nervous tension and narrowly avoiding flaming breaths and bolts while their archers loosed projectiles, the flat ground beneath Pravon and Aneen's mount's feet turned to a steady incline.

The outline of a wall suddenly emerged in the storm before their dragon—a wall that had been breached.

"Progtown!" Pravon pointed.

To their right, a hole gaped in the wall, and their beast ambled through it. Inside the walls, the dust settled some. More figures of marching beasts appeared around them, continuing their slow and steady progression, tramping through streets and destroying buildings with their feet or wings or heads or tails.

People screamed and fled before them, hurtling through the streets, most racing away, although some weaved around incoherently or ran directly at them without even bearing a weapon.

The number of bolts raining from the sky and the fiery breaths of the attackers above dropped sharply.

"We are safer in here," Aneen said. "Their legions do not wish to assist with the ruin of their own city."

A sand dragon battered through a building as large as the beast was, and stones flew through the air as the creature roared and flung wreckage aside with its wings while ramming the structure again with its neck. The din of other collapsing buildings and walls echoed around them, and the streets became littered with debris and bodies.

Bolts from their army's dragons sailed skyward, and occasionally an enemy dragon fell, taking out more of the city and smashing soldiers and townspeople. Pravon covered his head as stones pounded the street and skittered beneath their dragon.

After another hour of what Pravon could only think of as obliteration, the dust cleared further. The outer walls along the northern edge of Progtown rose into view. Pravon steered his mount out of the far side of the city. Beyond the walls, ranks of sand dragons waited in rows as others poured out from the city behind them, knocking the walls flat and roaring as they went. The archers and guard of the Rorenlands did not cheer or celebrate. They simply sat or stood rigid.

Genturion Master Ristanus waited on his massive steed of scales, facing Progtown. Kridmore rode a dragon beside him.

Damn it. A sinking feeling pulled at Pravon's guts. He had hoped that if anyone were to die, it would be Kridmore.

The genturion master wheeled his mount around and indicated for the ranks to continue their march northward. A cloud of dust hurried away from their army—the trail of the fleeing survivors of the city. Less than a score of remaining Progtown dragons soared off in the same direction.

"Shit." Aneen's voice sounded far away, although she was still right behind Pravon.

Pravon's limbs turned sluggish and cold as realization of what the army had done vexed him. "Do you think the firebreathing Dread King will be happy with the path we've taken?"

"Only Kridmore seems to know what that path now is. Maybe our contact and his master wanted to punish the people of this city specifically to initiate the war."

"Or perhaps the king will unleash his wrath and breathe fire upon us like a dragon."

Aneen chuckled. "Like the rumors and legends claim."

Pravon glanced back as the Rorenlands's legions resumed their steady advance deeper into Belvenguard.

Progtown was nothing more than smoldering ruins littered with bodies of dragons and men, including many more sand dragon carcasses than other kinds. Clouds of dust swirled silently around where Progtown once stood, marking the passing of a great city of Belvenguard.

40

JASLIN ORENDAIN

The hallway leading to the chamber was empty as Jaslin rushed along.

She glanced down at the message from Cartaya again, a brief letter summoning her to the chamber ahead, but only if she wished to again attempt to summon magic. When she reached the closed door, she paused and lifted a hand to knock. Voices carried out from inside—someone giving orders. She pushed on the heavy plank door, and it creaked inward.

Inside, Cartaya and Tiros and a dozen people in mauve robes paced about in front of groups of people in tunics.

"Jaslin, join us at once." Cartaya waved her in. "You are late."

Jaslin swallowed as she strode into the chamber and closed the door behind her.

"You invited the handmaid?" Tiros asked the conjuror. "I thought we discussed her ineptitude."

Cartaya silenced him with a glare and gestured at Jaslin. "Join the others."

Jaslin headed for two people she recognized—Vysoria and Princess Nistene. The other half-dozen people in their group varied in age from adolescents to old and hunched and included men and women. Each person in the group held a dragonbolt before them, the butt of the projectile placed on the ground, the open-style tips extending above their heads.

"Galvenstone has only used conjurors atop dragons in times of utmost importance—great wars—and such a time has come." Cartaya placed her hands behind her back and paced before the people in tunics, her hood lowered, her white hair waving about her shoulders. "Your kingdom may only survive if some of you can help your guard and archers. What we do here is not unimportant. It is true that most of you will not fly with the legions, but anyone who can control any amount of power *must* do so. Some of the worst estimates suggest that Murgare's soldiers and knights and dragons outnumber ours by ten to one. And we only have enough conjurors—our new battlemages—to assist fewer than a quarter of our dragons. Any advantage we can give our legions could save you and your families." She faced Jaslin. "You do not have a bolt yet?"

Jaslin glanced about. Projectiles were lined up and leaning against the far wall. She hustled over to one and wrapped her fingers around its shaft, attempting to lift it and return, but the bolt was much heavier than she expected. It probably weighed half as much as she did.

"These are real projectiles that the archers will be using in war," Cartaya said. "Made of Dragonsteel. You may need to use both hands or drag it back with you."

Jaslin lugged the thing across the floor, its end scraping against stone and grating and bumping. She winced as the superficial cut on her chest from the assassin stung.

"Are you all right?" Cartaya asked.

She nodded. "It is nothing."

When she returned and faced Cartaya, the conjuror began speaking again. "Now, keep trying to call out whatever name or elder word you hear and summon anything you can. Place the essence of it into the empty space in the broadhead above you. Do not worry about appearing like a fool or if you can only call forth the scent of roses. *If* you can evoke something from nothing, that is the hardest part and all I require from you. Altering what that something is shall be much easier."

Cartaya paced away, and the other conjurors in mauve strolled about, watching the groups.

"How did you end up here?" Vysoria asked Jaslin, eyeing her bolt.

She is Cartaya's daughter. Of course she would be able to harness bone and earth magic. "Your mother was interested in a piece of broken glass I carry, and she thought I must have some ability because I'm not susceptible to its temptations."

One of Vysoria's eyebrows climbed her forehead, and Nistene scrutinized Jaslin.

"I do not believe I hold any amount of magical aptitude either." Nistene shook her head as she glanced up at her projectile's tip. "But Vysoria's mother asked me to come along as well."

A middle-aged man in their group gasped. A faint green light glowed inside the open space in the broadhead of his bolt.

Tiros shuffled over to the man and began speaking with him, indicating the light and encouraging him. Then the nyren spoke loudly to all in the chamber. "The light you all see here is a fine start. Some of you may be working under the assumption that magical fire or ice will inflict more harm upon our enemies. This can be true, depending on your adversary, but the most desired effect a battlemage can impart on a dragonbolt is to bestow it with an ability to seek its target. Imagine that scenario when you attempt to summon anything here. If you can aid an archer by accounting for some of the effects of the wind and the dragons whipping about during flight, and give him or her a better chance of hitting their target, that is the biggest win. Other, flashier, magic can inflict more damage and drop a beast from the sky, but *only* if the bolt actually strikes its target. Otherwise, all the power you place upon a projectile—which takes its toll on your body and soul—will be wasted."

Murmurs of discussion followed as the people in the chamber shifted their bolts around and studied them.

Vysoria closed her eyes, and concentration lines deepened on her forehead. Nistene watched and mimicked her. Jaslin stifled a sigh of frustration and glanced upward. She focused on feeling the stones beneath her feet and imagined them stoking something in her bones and blood. Her eyes settled closed.

"Without some ability, you could not have resisted the call of that shard."

Jaslin opened her eyes to find Cartaya watching her. Jaslin said, "I cannot summon any magic... unless it first flows through the shard."

Cartaya's expression narrowed with skepticism. "Then you have accomplished something?"

Jaslin shrugged, not trusting this woman or any of the councilmembers. She also feared that they might take her shard if they knew what she had been able to do while bearing it.

"But if not, you have returned to try again," Cartaya said. "Desire is the first and strongest step."

Jaslin forced a grin. "I also came because I wanted to speak with you about something else."

Cartaya's suspicious look became more exaggerated.

"It is known that you have informants around the kingdom." Jaslin's most pressing worries sprang forth, and her fingers clenched the shaft of her bolt as Cartaya remained silent. She would never be able to do much in a war made up of thousands of dragons and warriors. Her energies would be best spent tracking down a traitor in their midst. "I heard about Nevergrace's impending situation, and I wish to travel there and speak with my old friends," she lied. "As swiftly as possible. I will return before anyone notices. Do any of your informants or others you know have access to such means of travel?"

Cartaya pursed her lips. "I know how it could be done. We are not without storm dragons here at Dashtok and, while some of the messengers are not being utilized at the moment, with the situation rising around us, the dragons should probably not be venturing out of the city. They may be needed at some point in the near future."

Jaslin feigned a deep pain. "I must see my friends before... I never have the chance to speak with them again. I must tell them some things that I was never able to before."

Cartaya sighed. "There is one mage I know of who occasionally steps beyond his orders, but"—she paused and glanced over at Tiros, who casually walked around the would-be conjurors, watching them but saying nothing—"he would charge heaps of coin to fly you anywhere. And he is only trustworthy when he is getting paid. Otherwise, he is dangerous and should be avoided."

Damn. Jaslin had very little coin to her name. "Who is it?"

"One of the storm dragon mages."

"It's the man who caught us when we jumped from the cliffs," Vysoria said, and her mother tried to silence her with a glare. "He's one of the king's swiftest messengers, and he secretively takes on questionable ventures. If the coin is right."

Memories spun in Jaslin's mind.

"I'll make you a promise," Cartaya said. "If you can focus and place a wisp of magic into the bolt in front of you, I will see if I can set up a meeting between the two of you. But I cannot guarantee that he will take you anywhere. Not with war brewing on the far side of the lake. And if you do somehow manage to go for a quick visit, you must return as soon as we receive word of the initial sighting of the enemy's fleets."

"It would mean the world to me if I could spend even an hour there."

"Then show me what you can do." Cartaya pointed at the bolt.

Jaslin gritted her teeth. She closed her eyes and tried again, focusing with all of her willpower. After she felt a warmth rise from the ground and rush into her body, the heat spiraled around her skeleton and then trundled out along her arm into the bolt. She muttered some word that popped into her mind and furtively cracked an eye open to see if anything had happened. The open area in the bolt remained empty of light and fire. She cursed the Siren under her breath. Maybe she needed to... She slipped her other hand into her pouch. When her fingers contacted the cold surface of the shard, a flicker of amber flame flashed inside her bolt's open broadhead. The light quickly died out.

"You see, if your desire is strong enough, you can control the bone and earth magic." Cartaya grinned at her. "Keep practicing. When this is over, I will speak with the person I mentioned. But do not say I did not warn you about him."

A chill crept up Jaslin's spine. Cartaya observed as Vysoria created a white flame around her bolt's tip. Nistene attempted the same, but nothing happened. The conjuror nodded her approval to her daughter and wandered away to another group.

"Damn this thing." Nistene squeezed and then released her bolt in frustration, and it teetered before toppling over and smacking into the ground with an echoing clang.

"Do not fret," Vysoria said to the princess while wearing a mocking grin. "Maybe I will be sent up on a dragon and killed. Then Jaken will marry you."

Empathy in regard to the insult hit Jaslin in the heart with a twisting pain. Did these two young women really despise each other? Because of a young man? Instead of the traitor being someone in the council, could one of them be working against the other and the kingdom? Nistene's face flushed before she stormed away, flung a door open, and exited in a huff.

"You do not have to wait for that meeting," Vysoria said, pulling Jaslin's attention away from Nistene's fiery trail. "But you are only a handmaid. Not to mention a handmaid from Nevergrace. I suspect you do not have much coin. Not enough for the man in question."

Jaslin tentatively nodded.

"If you happen to get ahold of any coin," Vysoria said, "this mage meets with his lover every third day. In the same place. And today is one of the days they will see each other."

"Where?"

~

Jaslin knocked, and after receiving no answer, she entered her and Menoria's chambers. The lady was probably out walking off her anxiety over her coming marriage. Jaslin strode through her sleeping area and grabbed her coin pouch. Only a few farthings, pennies, and halfpennies jingled together.

She glanced around. Menoria's coin purse sat in the other chamber beside her bed. If Jaslin did not uncover who was behind the tattooed assassins, more of them could come for her and Menoria. She swallowed and crept into the other room. She did not ever want to take anything from her lady, but she suspected that what she might discover could alter aspects of their understanding of the war and reveal the traitor in their midst. And she did not want to delay by having to convince Menoria to lend it to her.

Before she knew it, her hand was reaching for the pouch. She paused, briefly closing her eyes and taking a deep breath. After a moment, she glanced around. Her fingers slipped into the lady's coin purse and felt around. There were many bits and marks and other smaller coins along with a few large ones.

She withdrew her hand, and in her fingers, she held a single gold crown—more coin than she had ever owned in her life. Her palms grew damp, almost making the coin slip from her grasp as she stared at it. Menoria would understand. Her lady was from the Never, not a noblewoman of Dashtok, and Jaslin would replace the coin as soon as she was able.

Her hand shook as she glanced around the empty chamber again, stuffed the coin into her pouch, and hurried out of the room.

41

CYRAN ORENDAIN

"Here." Cyran pointed at the ground on the far side of the old oak south of Nevergrace. He kicked at a patch of bare dirt and dead grass as the sun rose over the eastern horizon. Then he scraped at the ground with his gloved fingers, clawing a few shallow lines through the area. "Can you please dig it up? It will take me far too long to do so."

"You buried a dragon egg here?" Milluri's closest eye flicked back and forth, first gauging him and then assessing the ground. "Why?"

"There was a sudden... need. It would be much faster if you could just dig it up and we do not have to discuss the prior situation."

Milluri grunted and reached out with a hind foot. She sank her talons into the earth that had been firmly packed by Eidelmere, and she raked up a mound of soil. After scooting the mound behind her, she dug again. "How far down is it? I do not want to crush it."

"The hole was about as deep as I am tall."

The thorn dragon dug quickly, and the hole grew to the estimated depth before she worked more cautiously. Her foot drew back, an ovoid object clutched in her talons.

Cyran's heart lurched, and he reached out as the dragon released the egg into his arms. Its scaled shell tugged at his sleeves, releasing clods of dirt. The egg was about half the size of a barrel, the smallest of the clutch that he had decimated out of fear. The others had all been the offspring of Shadowmar, the malevolent shadow dragon, but this one...

He set the egg down and brushed as much dirt from it as he could. Forest-green scales were intermittently mingled with black ones. Perhaps the only way to defeat Shadowmar was with another shadow dragon, or a dragon that was at least part shadow dragon.

"What kind of dragon egg is this?" Milluri asked.

"A..." Cyran swallowed, considering the implications and laws of Belvenguard. "It is the egg of a moon dragon. But Eidelmere believed it could have been fathered by one of the last forest dragons to remain at the outpost."

"A hybrid? An impure dragon?"

Cyran shrugged. "It seems so."

Milluri studied it closer. "Moon dragon, you say?" She squinted. "My kind do not lie to the *mëris*, but your kind are not so trustworthy. I have seen moon dragon eggs. Once. They were much smaller."

Cyran bit his lip and did not reply. "I do not know if a dragonet will be of any assistance in the coming war, but I cannot help but think of this egg as an opportunity. Every single dragon we have on our side could help tip the scales."

"A moon dragonet will be useless. If it is indeed meshed with a forest dragon, it may be an interesting hybrid but hardly powerful enough to fight a full-grown dragon. You do not really think it is a moon dragon, do you?"

Cyran still did not answer. He simply stared and then ran a

hand over its textured shell. "There must be a way to hatch it. Can you breathe fire on it?"

"Dragons cannot be hatched before they are fully developed, and even then, they can only be freed by the breath of their own kind."

"As in—only a moon or forest dragon could hatch this egg?"

"Precisely."

Cyran glanced up, his forehead furrowing. "Even in the king's hatcheries?"

"I do not know of such places, but what I tell you is the only way."

The hatcheries were probably more of a place to rear and protect the young when they were most vulnerable, not a place that held special magic to release the creatures from eggs. But trying different breaths should not hurt the egg, and they might work. This was a potential hybrid, after all.

"Will you breathe on this egg?" Cyran asked.

Milluri chuckled. "I could do so, but it will probably not hatch." She inhaled, her chest expanding, and Cyran ducked, expecting a wash of hot fire. Milluri paused and then blew, placing her right wing over her maw. A blast of air shot through thin gaps in her leathery segments, and some of the thorned spikes on her wing tore away, flying like small bolts.

Cyran gasped. The thorns pelted the ground around the egg and the shell itself but did not pierce its outer scales. Those hitting the egg fell away or became lodged in gaps between scales.

"Like all others of my kind, my breath is not effective against dragon scales," Milluri said.

Cyran stared in wonder, not having expected the thorn dragon's breath to be what it was. The lumps where the thorns on Milluri's wing had dislodged vibrated and slowly nudged higher, regrowing.

"Then a forest dragon could hatch this egg." Cyran picked it up. "We could return to Nevergrace..." But there would be a lot of questions about the egg and why he had returned. During his most recent flight to Galvenstone, he had seen another forest dragon somewhere around here—at the beacon tower, which he would pass on his way back to Dashtok. Perhaps the dragon was stationed there or was patrolling the forest's boundaries.

"The watery breath of a forest dragon, or the inaudible call of a moon dragon, may be able to do it, if those types are truly this thing's forebears," Milluri said. "Or it may only be a moon who could accomplish the task, since the egg appears to have much more of those types of scales."

Cyran hid a shudder. Then it would take shadow dragon fire? "We shall fly." He hefted the egg and mounted his saddle. Milluri flapped her wings, and they rose into the dawn and sailed west.

They flew over the Scyne Road and approached the first beacon tower. Soldiers stood sentry at several tiers of the structure and watched them. In the distance, a dragon circled above two other towers.

Cyran veered Milluri toward the dragon until it wheeled in his direction, and then he glided his mount to a lower battlement on the nearest tower. The thorn dragon flapped to slow her flight and eased herself onto a dragon's perch. Within a few minutes, a forest dragon swooped down and landed beside them.

"Dragonknight?" the guard on the forest asked as he lifted his visor. "What brings you out to the beacons?"

Cyran nodded at the guard. "I am acting on the king's orders. I flew to Nevergrace to speak with my people before the war." He lifted the egg, displaying it. "And I happened upon this."

The guard shoved his visor higher and leaned closer. "We should get it to the hatcheries at once."

"That was my intention, but... I sent a message via storm dragon. The reply I received from Galvenstone asked me to try to hatch it now." Cyran shifted uncomfortably in his saddle. "I assume the king wants every single dragon we can find on our side."

The guard slowly nodded his understanding. "We will need far more than Galvenstone currently has to have any chance of defending ourselves against Murgare. I am unsure if a hatchling will provide much aid, but—"

"That is why I stopped when I saw you." Cyran pointed to the forest dragon scales on the egg, brushing more dirt from its surface so the green color became more obvious. "I was told that the breath of a forest dragon might hatch it."

The guard scooted aside, and the mage behind him peeked her head around the guard's lance arm as the dragon turned its neck to better expose her. Wizened old eyes sparkled beneath her hood. "We can try, but I have never seen an egg of that sort —black and speckled with green. But dragon eggs in general are not common. Not anymore."

Eggs are not common anymore? The Dragon Queen had mentioned something similar. Cyran's heart crumpled with further anxiety. "If I could return to Galvenstone bearing a new dragon, it would make a great gift for Igare."

The mage nodded and placed her palm on her dragon's neck. The creature's lips moved, but it did not say anything aloud. Its scaled eyes briefly settled closed as it adjusted its body and seemed to shake its head with a doubting attitude.

"If the king wishes it, we shall try," the mage answered.

Milluri extended her neck, and Cyran clambered down onto the walk. He placed the egg on the bare stones.

The forest dragon sucked in a mighty breath as Cyran darted aside. Its jaws parted, and a river deluged from its open throat, blasting over the walk. When the creature's breath fizzled out, water dripped from the egg and pooled around it. Cyran tentatively approached, watching for any movement as his boots sank into a stream that poured over the edge of the tier.

The egg wobbled and shifted. It rolled half a turn.

Cyran's breath caught in his chest as he stared, his heart rioting and sending blood whooshing through his ears. He feared what he might unleash on the world. Eidelmere had warned him, had encouraged him to destroy the last egg in the clutch when he had the chance, but like with several other things, Cyran did not heed the dragon's advice.

The egg settled and fell still. Cyran waited for a minute and then five and ten. Nothing more happened. He cursed, frustration seething inside him.

"My dragon is old and wise in some ways," the mage said. "She was not born in the wild but in the hatcheries long ago. She says it takes the breath of the mother to hatch an egg."

Damn, only the mother? Is that true? Shadowmar... Another memory jolted in Cyran's mind, something he had mentioned to the Dragon Queen that he probably shouldn't have. There might be a way he could hatch this creature.

"Not the mother specifically, but one of her kind," the mage continued.

"There is a moon dragon at the last tower before Galvenstone," the guard said. "He is stationed there during the day and patrols this area at night. We will wake him."

"I do not want to spend any more time on this." Cyran scooped up the egg.

The guard's pinching eyebrows betrayed his bewilderment. "As you suggested, we should give our great king a sign of hope in this dark time. It should not take much more than an additional few minutes."

Cyran silently cursed himself and the situation he placed

himself in. "We could try, but I do not want to take away from your watch."

"Nonsense." The guard pointed to the thin line of a tower in the distance. "It is not too far."

"My dragon says she has never seen an egg like this before, either." The mage leaned closer. "It is much bigger than a moon's egg and even bigger than the egg of a forest dragon. Hybrid eggs are never laid in civilization or the hatcheries, but even if it was laid in the wild, it should be of a size between the two who created it."

Cyran shrugged as he mounted Milluri.

"Where did you say you found this egg?" the mage asked.

"Outside of Nevergrace." Cyran urged Milluri to take flight, hoping to soar away and not meet with the moon dragon. His mount spread her wings and dropped from the battlements, the wind catching her and lifting them as she glided away. The forest dragon followed them. "Bloody hell."

Cyran landed outside the last beacon tower, one that sat on a hill between Nevergrace and Galvenstone. The forest dragon alighted beside them, and an archer on the beast's quarterdeck descended and rushed inside the tower.

"Come," the guard dismounted and waved Cyran on.

Cyran hefted the egg and followed the man through an entrance at the base of the tower. They continued to a stall where a glistening black dragon waited, its eyes small and sunken and nonfunctional.

Another mage stormed down the stairs as best he could on only one good leg, pulling his hood over white hair. "War could arrive at our doorstep any day, and you wake me and my dragon for a menial task? If you were not a dragonknight, I would have you flogged. You were nothing more than a squire of the outpost not even a year ago."

Cyran winced.

"It is for the king," the guard said.

The moon dragon's mage paused in front of Cyran. He reached out and ran a hand over the egg. He shivered but left his hand on its scaled surface. Cyran's heartrate ramped up. Could this mage sense what was truly in there?

"We are here to see if your dragon's breath can hatch the egg, or if whatever is inside of it died long ago." Cyran pulled away.

The mage squinted and glared at him before hobbling off. Cyran set the egg before the moon dragon, and its neck snaked out. Its nostrils twitched as it sniffed. Its mouth gaped open, and its tongue and inner throat vibrated. Cyran cringed and covered his ears, but no sound came out.

The dragon nuzzled the egg, turning it over. It opened its maw again and repeated the silent call. The egg did not wobble or shift.

"This egg will not hatch," the moon's mage said. "Either the creature inside is dead, or its mother was not a moon dragon."

"It was worth a try." Cyran shrugged, as if suddenly unconcerned. This dragon's breath was never going to hatch the egg. "I wished to give us all a moment of joy amidst the turmoil, but this egg is probably ancient, its occupant long deceased. Please allow me to keep it here until a time comes when things are safer. Then we can have a midwife from the hatcheries look at it."

"Why not take it to Igare now?" the forest's guard asked.

"And hand him another disappointment?" Cyran shook his head. "I will not do that right before the war."

"You're the dragonknight." The guard grunted in capitulation. "Do whatever you think is best."

Cyran faced the moon's mage. "You should not take your rest at this last beacon tower in any of the coming days, and you should not stray too close to it again. But, please, keep a particularly close eye on this one. Watch it from afar, preferably from a hiding spot in the trees. If Murgare comes to Nevergrace, this will be one of their primary targets."

The mage gave him a brief dip of the chin. "But if I am positioned too far away, I may not be able to spot an attacking dragon here."

"Have your creature use its breath on the kindling at the top of this tower every hour of every night hence," Cyran added. "To test and see if the wood has changed in any way. I am unsure what your dragon will notice, but you *must* alert Galvenstone immediately if the kindling changes at all in how it sounds to your dragon's ear."

One of the mage's eyebrows arched onto his wrinkled forehead. "What do you expect to happen?"

"Murgare will burn the wood here to stop any kind of signal from reaching Galvenstone."

"But I will be able to see a fire from leagues away. So will the watch in the king's city."

"Not if the wood burns with the black fire from a shadow dragon."

The mage's eyebrow fell back into its usual position. "But the soldiers up above us will still sound their horns."

"The soldiers will already be dead."

42

SIRRA BRACKENGLAVE

Shadowmar thumped onto the ground as snow dropped in thick clumps and gusts flung the flakes about. The Lake on Fire sprawled away into the southern horizon and a dark stretch of precipitation. Sirra dismounted along with Yenthor, Zaldica, and her other archers and companions.

The Murgare soldiers stationed between the town of Icetooth and the River of the Helm must have numbered at over one hundred thousand men, not including ten thousand knights. A couple thousand dragons also waited, and hundreds of ships still choked the harbor, although many of the largest ones sailed south while the others were being loaded. Oomaren had indeed given the orders for some to set sail.

Guard and dragons faced Sirra as she paced along, assessing everything. Kyelle and Sir Trothen and Vladden followed her. Men and women whispered as they passed, "It is the prior genturion of Northsheeren and the Dragon Queen herself."

"Then it is time for all the legions to fly with the ships."

"Not yet. Oomaren's orders were for us to await his signal."

"We will crush Belvenguard as easily as other dragons can crush the eggs of pygmies!" one man bellowed.

Others roared, spurred on by anger and the long wait most of them had probably seen at this shore.

Sirra's curiosity piqued as she waded through ranks of dragons and guard and soldiers, headed toward the center of the masses, a place she had seen when flying in. The area had been cleared for one massive dragon, the rest of Murgare's army creating rings around this focal point. As she walked on, more and more of the people around her appeared exotic—strange helms or sharpened teeth, painted faces or bodies or furs, and instead of standard bows and spears and swords, some bore clubs and spiked morning stars and flails. Many of the onyx guard had also arrived and formed small contingents around and within the masses, watching everything.

After striding through an encircling perimeter between a mist and a fire dragon and their teams, Sirra entered an expanse surrounding the largest cave dragon she had ever seen, although she had seen this same beast once before. The creature's twin pair of wings were stretched across the void, rather than tucked up against its body, to maintain its space. Near the beast's closed eyes and curled horns that the heavy snow settled upon, several men were involved in a heated discussion.

Sirra approached them, noting Kyelle hurrying to stay at her heels and Trothen following the young queen.

"We cannot wait here any longer," Westfahl, the king of the dwarves, said to Arch Genturion Ravenscroft, the man in violet and blue dragonsteel who had been placed in command of every Murgare legion and soldier here. Pygmy dragons flapped about the area, freighting dwarves between different cave dragons. "The cave dragons cannot sustain themselves on stone of lesser quality, that outside of our mountains. If this Oomaren does not show himself by nightfall, we return to Darynbroad."

Ravenscroft raised a placating hand, which infuriated the dwarf further, making the dwarf's cheeks redden. "Genturion

King Westfahl, I understand your concerns, and I beg you to wait for the signal."

"I have not even been informed of what this signal is."

"We shall all know when we see it, but—"

"The true queen of Murgare is brave enough to join her armies." Sirra interrupted their conversation, and both man and dwarf turned to regard her. She motioned as Kyelle stepped forward. "This is Kyelle, daughter of King Restebarge and Queen Elra, the new queen of Murgare."

Westfahl bowed his head. Ravenscroft genuflected.

"Please rise," Kyelle said. "I wished to come and see the state of the north's armies for myself and to speak with the genturions about the war." She faced Ravenscroft. "You are the acting arch genturion here?"

Ravenscroft stood. "Yes, my queen."

"What do you have to report?"

Ravenscroft stood straighter. "Oomaren, the king regent, ordered the amassing of all the banners, my queen. They have nearly all come, along with all of the north's willing dragons."

"All but the Smoke Breathers." Sirra removed her helm.

Ravenscroft's eyes closed briefly. "I am sorry, Dragon Queen. I suspect I know what it is you wish for, but the landing galleys have already sailed. The dragons will soon follow. No one can stop such massive wheels of war once they have begun turning. Well over a hundred thousand men are ready to face their ancient enemies and avenge their late king. So are the dragons."

"We will discuss how this happened later." Sirra frowned at the arch genturion, picturing all the legions of Murgare swooping south, the dragons taking turns landing and resting on the galleys built to help them make a crossing too long and arduous for most of their kind, a crossing they should probably never make.

Ravenscroft glanced at the onyx guard who had taken up

positions around the central circle. "The onyx guard arrived not long before you. We expect the signal at any moment."

Sirra eyed the guard members, who watched her with disdain.

"We will call the galleys back," Kyelle said, and Trothen stepped up beside her.

Ravenscroft's eyes widened. "Genturion Trothen." He bowed his head. "We heard you were removed from your station and detained."

"I never gave such an order," Kyelle said. "Nor did I release him from his position as the genturion master of Murgare."

The cords in Ravenscroft's neck jerked when he swallowed. "Please forgive my ignorance on the matter, my queen, but the ceremonies were performed. Oomaren is the king regent. He is overseeing... you, a queen who is still too young to rule."

"We will share words with this Oomaren." Westfahl huffed and motioned to Genturion Master Dahroon, the dwarven battlemage who stood just behind his king. Dahroon's red beard was prickly from the cold, and pale light flared in his hand as snow accumulated on his helm.

Sir Vladden strode forward and stared at the dwarven battlemage and his magical flames. A look of utter fear crossed the guard's expression, although he reached out with his one arm, apparently wanting to feel the dwarf's beard.

Dahroon glowered at Vladden. "Who is this walking corpse? And why is he trying to touch me?"

"Forgive Sir Vladden," Sirra said. "He is the half-souled and our current messenger."

Dahroon raised a thick eyebrow and retreated a step from Vladden's reach.

Sirra cleared her throat as she faced Westfahl and Ravenscroft again. "Oomaren should not be making such decisions for the queen when war between all of the kingdoms is at hand and the balance of all of Cimeren is at risk."

Ravenscroft bowed to Kyelle. "It was my understanding that during times of grave need is exactly when the regent should be making decisions for the kingdom and not someone... lacking in experience, no matter how wise they are. It was not my intent to belittle your authority or act against your wishes, but I have taken oaths—long before Oomaren's rise—to uphold a certain order of rule."

Kyelle did not blink or acquiesce. "I sympathize with your predicament, Arch Genturion, but from this moment, I will—"

"I will act as Kyelle's queen regent," Sirra said with no hint of jest. "Until Restebarge and Elra are avenged and Cimeren and Murgare have been appeased. I, the Dragon Queen, will act as the advisor to the queen. Let this be known." She turned to all those around them.

A cloud of dragons blotted out the muted northern sunlight.

"The sign!" someone shouted, and muttering and cries rang out over the lands.

The dragons flew together but not in strict legion formation. Most of them were of the ice or snow varieties, and they drifted and weaved about as if overflowing with vigor. Some creatures snapped out at others who shrieked or beat them back.

"It is the Smoke Breathers and their beasts," Sirra said.

"How can you tell?" Kyelle asked.

"Their dragons are more feral and powerful, as they live in the wild and hold sway over the clans." Sirra spoke with reverence. "The dragons of the valley would only have come if they truly believed this war was a matter they must face, for themselves and all of their kind."

"They are menacing." Kyelle's expression fell flat.

"The Smoke Breathers do not look like simple barbarians now, do they?"

"No, it is not the signal," someone in the vicinity added definitively. "This is not the coming of the king himself."

Most of the incoming dragons landed in the distance, but one headed straight for the center of the legions. It shrieked and wheeled about, circling above them before thumping down onto the ground and one of the cave dragon's extended wings. The cave dragon roared, and its eyes flicked open as it retracted its wing, spilling a small avalanche of snow.

"It did not take the clans long to respond after all," Sirra said as the Claw dismounted.

"The Dragon wished for her children to gather and join the cause, and so our people did as well." The leader of the Smoke Breathers said it as if it were the simplest of tasks to amass thousands of men and hundreds of feral dragons. He nodded into the distance. "The landing galleys have departed."

"They had..." Sirra paused as she looked southward. Many more ships had already disembarked, their sails filling with wind as they carved through the waters.

"They took your coming as the signal, although the Smoke Breathers cannot be what Oomaren had in mind." Ravenscroft shook his head. "The king regent would not have known the intentions of the clans of the brotherhood, but everyone has been primed to watch for a signal that was supposed to arrive anytime from this past day to the day after this. Oomaren is attempting to accomplish one last massive undertaking."

Sirra faced the genturion, a burning itch of curiosity and worry rising inside her.

"We saw something coming from the east." The Claw pointed. "It should be here soon. Before nightfall."

Sirra stared, and they did not have to wait long before a dark mass appeared on the horizon. Over the next hour, it drew closer, the cloud made up of many dragons packed tightly together and moving slowly. Something enormous was suspended beneath the cloud.

Sirra trembled, anxiety rising within her, a sensation she rarely experienced.

"In comes the king regent with his prize," Sir Vladden said before even turning in a stilted shuffle to gaze upon the spectacle.

When the individual dragons of the cloud became apparent, so did their cargo. The swarm of beasts from Northsheeren held ropes and a massive sling. Within the sling was another dragon that Sirra had only encountered once before—the whale dragon from the Ilmoor Sea.

The gargantuan beast roared as it flailed about in its makeshift harness, and the legion veered south and slowly lowered the creature earthward. They soared over the amassed legions, who had fallen into an eerie silence punctuated by cries of terror as the beast passed overhead.

The whale dragon was flown out over the lake and then settled onto its surface, the dot of a mage on its neck appearing like an ant on a hill. The sounds of steel sawing through taut rope carried over the water, and the lines snapped and broke away from the flying dragons. The beast sank into its new abode, sending out towering waves that rocked the landing galleys and hammered the shoreline.

"The sign has been delivered," Ravenscroft muttered. "Such a beast will surely destroy any traps awaiting our ships, sink Belvenguard's fleets, and batter the walls of Galvenstone."

"With such a force battering their walls, any mounted ballistae in the city will be disrupted," Westfahl added, his cheeks pale. "I never imagined that I'd see a beast larger than one of our cave dragons."

A dragon from the cloud that had been freighting the beast soared over the shoreline. A man with a golden crown on his head lifted a sword, and its steel sparkled in the fading sunlight. A conjuror's purple flames flared behind him. His ice dragon roared and spewed its breath over the area, sending sheets of frost tumbling from the sky amidst the snow. A few fire dragons swooped past behind the frost and breathed, their flames catching the plummeting ice and lighting it up in red.

When the sky sea rains blood.

Deafening cheers erupted all around the countryside and were accompanied by the thumping of wings and beating of weapons against shields. The tumult pounded the air and shook the earth as the mass of ships along the shoreline set sail.

Sirra glanced about, taking it all in, realizing the path of the future had been laid out. If she wished to continue to back Murgare—her kingdom and her people—she could no longer hope to avoid where this path led, a destination of destruction for both Cimeren and the *neblír*.

Tears trickled down Sir Vladden's cheeks.

The Claw caught Sirra's eye as he said, "Live with wonder."

She swallowed a dry lump in her throat. "Die before you've lost it all."

43

JASLIN ORENDAIN

Voices carried into the alcove. Jaslin's skin tingled. They were both here in the grove—in private—like Vysoria had said they would be.

Jaslin waited a few minutes, until the two men's conversation fell to a hush. Fallen leaves rustled in the wind and flew about, gathering in clumps. Early winter's chill had already settled around her. She took a deep breath and strode out around a bust of an old king of Belvenguard.

A man in white cloth was pressing himself against another man in a dark cloak, both beneath a tree clinging to a few golden leaves. Jaslin let the book she carried fall, and it hit a flagstone with a crack that seemed as loud as thunder. The two men lurched, one stumbling and hobbling, the other jerking away to place distance between them.

Jaslin stared wide-eyed as she placed a hand over her mouth in feigned shock. "I... What are you doing?"

Lisain tightened his robe around his waist as he glanced about the rows of trees. The dragonmage shuffled around and faced Jaslin.

"What are you doing out here?" the dragonmage asked. "Spying on us?"

Jaslin shook her head and pointed to her book. "I was reading where it was quiet. There is so much going on everywhere else inside and outside the keep."

"Will you be off, child?" Lisain asked.

She nodded. "Of course."

"Wait." The mage braced himself against the nearest wall. "You are one of the new nobles. You rode on my dragon."

Jaslin pretended to finally recognize him. "Oh, I did, indeed."

"This was no accident." The mage spat. "One of the others put you up to this. What do you want? To be caught when you leap from the wall again? Mayhap I'll let you fall this time and rid myself of you and the other young scoundrels who use my weaknesses against me."

Jaslin's hands trembled, and she knitted her fingers together and rested them against her thighs. "I-I know of a place where you two can do as you will and won't have to worry about anyone stumbling upon you."

"What do you want?" The mage shambled closer.

Jaslin retreated a step.

The king's boyish clergyman stepped up beside the mage, eyeing her. "None of the six good gods find fault with anything I have done, or else they would probably no longer speak to me. And I always seem to hear them better than anyone."

"Then it is only because you fear that the king will discard you if he finds out?" Jaslin asked, attempting to display a confident assertion.

The two men shared a glance.

"What do you want, little girl?" the mage asked again.

"I have an errand I must look into." Jaslin held her ground. "One that concerns Nevergrace."

"And?"

"I wish to travel south. Quickly."

"How far?"

Jaslin swallowed, her mouth suddenly as dry as old wheat. "The Southern Isles."

Both men stared at her for a moment with slack jaws. The mage bellowed. "You must be as mad as a marsh dragon. War is brewing and everyone is needed in Galvenstone, and you set up this little ploy to try to pressure me into taking you to the *Rorenlands*? It would take too long to travel there, even upon my swiftest of storm dragons." He shook his head. "It would be much easier just to kill you here and hide your body." His staff was suddenly in his hand, and he reached back as if to strike her.

Jaslin held out a hand to ward him off as more leaves swirled around them. "I do not judge love or you, but do you not wish to know where you can go so you don't have to meet secretively near the keep?"

Lisain pursed his lips. "There are already those who are suspicious. If we two are seen leaving the same chamber around the same time, rumormongers will become even more interested. Soldiers around Galvenstone will recognize me in any tavern or whorehouse. Do not think we are fools or have never considered such things. And if we try to conceal our identities in any establishment in the city, it only brings more attention from people who want to see if they can recognize the suspicious hooded men."

"What if I told you of a city beneath this city?" Jaslin asked. "One where merchants roam, and everyone remains hidden. You would blend in like any other there."

Lisain tapped his lips. "You cannot have access to the merchant tunnels."

"I know where there is access, and I have seen inns with chambers for rent down there."

The mage relaxed his coiled strike. "You will simply ask for bigger and bigger favors as time goes by."

"I will only ask this one thing, and I will also help you in another way so you won't have to find a quiet place to hide in Dashtok." Jaslin shot them a knowing smirk.

"Igare would probably never understand." Lisain shook his head. "And Riscott absolutely never will. The orator would have my head or have me exiled. At Dashtok, I stand and work for the good of Belvenguard and all of the realm. If I am sent elsewhere, my purpose will be lost, my abilities wasted."

Jaslin gave them a casual shrug. "In time, you will not have to worry about such things."

"And how could you possibility be so certain of that?" the mage asked.

"Because I am the lady of the Never's handmaid, her closest friend and only confidant here. And I once saved her life. She would do anything for me. When she is married to the king, she will gradually introduce the notion of you two when they reminisce and share stories in their bed. She will remind Igare of how valuable his clergyman, Lisain, is to the kingdom. She will tell him that some things, such as who we love, are of no consequence. And her opinions will fill the king's ear more often than Riscott can mutter his hate. Within weeks or months, Igare's indifference on the matter will only strengthen. Menoria will also remind him that he is the king, and his orator cannot punish any councilmember without his consent. Once this occurs, any future threats from young nobles will become obsolete."

The mage's scowl lifted and nearly twisted into a relieved grin. "Even if you can do all that you claim, your visit to the isles can wait until after the coming war. We will discuss it again then."

"It cannot." Jaslin reached out and touched his cloaked forearm. "No one knows when this war will begin, and its outcome" —she kept her suspicions about a traitor in the council to herself, in case the traitor was Lisain—"will be negatively affected if I do not find out what the Never needs to know. It will only be a brief stop. There is something there I must see, and that is all. But we must depart at once."

The mage faced the clergyman and asked, "What if the war begins when I am gone?"

Lisain's eyes moved about beneath his closed lids.

"Then you will remain safe from legions of Murgare dragons," Jaslin said.

"But Igare will have my head for leaving without his consent." The mage grimaced.

"You have the swiftest dragon, but it is of the small storm kind," Jaslin began. "Storms can never fly an armored guard into battle or carry archers who—"

"The Hunter and Merchant foresee safe but hasty travels to the south," Lisain said, his eyes still closed. "If you stay to the west. It is to the east that the Siren sees a brewing darkness marching upon our lands. The Siren also speaks of questions that need answering, and even though the north has likely set sail, they will not reach us for days." He strode forward and placed a hand on Jaslin's left breast.

Jaslin grunted in protest and tried to pull away, but Lisain grabbed her by her arm and held her still, closing his eyes. He muttered something under his breath, and the pain on her chest from the assassin's knife wound vanished. Lisain stepped back with his head bowed. Jaslin lifted her tunic at the neckline and peered downward. The puncture wound that had sunk through her skin was gone, completely healed.

"The Siren grants the ability to heal flesh." Lisain forced a smile and nodded at the mage. "It is only him and other mages and the mortally wounded who I cannot heal, which troubles me. That is probably what draws me to him." He patted the mage's shoulder. "His mystique."

How did the clergyman even know she had a wound? Surely if anyone sent an assassin after her, it was Keliam, not someone in the council. *Or perhaps Keliam worked for someone in the council.*

"The Dragon's pit of burning arseholes." The mage spat again. He was young and svelte, although crippled like most mages. "If we are to do this, I will still require coin and a secret from you in exchange, handmaid. I have little faith in goodwill. And your secret must be something dark, something you do not want anyone else to know."

Jaslin hesitated. She could not tell him of her true intentions and suspicions in regard to a traitor in the council, not yet. That could ruin her entire plan. Nor could she tell him about the coin she was forced to take from Menoria, or if he demanded more, he could realize that Jaslin didn't have enough to pay him. "My shard," she blurted before the silence had spanned too long of a duration. She swallowed and retrieved the crystal fragment from her pouch. "It holds some magic from the past age. From the elves of Cimerenden." She twirled it before the mage's eyes.

"And why would anyone, including myself, give a farthing's fuck about this secret?"

"Because it controls me." Jaslin's head drooped. "It asks me to do things I should not want to do. But it was a gift from my deceased brother, before the woods took him, and so I cherish and despise this shard. My other brother doesn't want me to have it because he suspects it is evil. If any conjuror discovers that it holds magic from the ancient elves, it will be taken from me—by force or stolen. Then my heart shall break a final time. I will also then lose any control I have over bone and earth magic."

The mage tapped his finger against his cheek as he scrutinized her. "And coin? How much do you have on you?"

"One gold crown."

"I will take that now, but ten more crowns will be due upon our return, because I am risking much with this venture."

A swirl of dread stirred in Jaslin's stomach as she recalled Cartaya saying that this man would be dangerous if he was not paid. She did not have a single crown to her name, but Menoria did. Menoria would probably not have ten crowns on her person —none of the lords or ladies of Nevergrace had much coin—but once she was queen, she could pay off Jaslin's debt. Aiding the kingdom and unmasking a traitor in Dashtok before such a person could assist Murgare by causing chaos within Galvenstone would be well worth it.

"Let me say this again so it is clear—you will pay me ten crowns once we return." The mage glared at her, and the clergyman patted his arm. "Or your life will be in jeopardy. The people I owe coin to do not accept excuses."

"There is no need to be so intimidating." Lisain smiled at his friend. "This young woman is a trustworthy handmaid of our future queen. She will pay you."

Jaslin swallowed. War would likely be upon them at or soon after their return. That should distract the mage for a while.

"Then we best hurry and return to Dashtok before the rains turn to blood," the mage said. "Even storm dragons cannot fly to the Rorenlands in a day."

Jaslin held out her hand and dropped the gold coin onto his palm, concealing her nerves and indicating the exit from the grove. "Shall we?"

∼

Clouds whipped past Jaslin's head, engulfing them in white fog as her heart raced erratically in her chest. The biting chill of the wind carried through her furs and stung her cheeks, but the heat radiating from the storm dragon directly beneath her was more than enough to keep her from growing too cold.

"Is it all you dreamed of?" the mage asked from his position behind her, she in the guard's saddle, the dragon's head just before her. The mage's tone was full of disdain.

"I am Jaslin," she said over her shoulder. "And you are?"

A moment of silence passed before he reluctantly said, "Tallius. And if you, Jaslin, do not fulfill all of your lofty promises, I will—"

"You will let me fall or kill me. I understand. It would not be a difficult thing for you to do. I am not powerful or treacherous, and I have no intention of deceiving you or not carrying out my end of the bargain. Igare will eventually accept you and Lisain, and you will no longer have anything to fear." *And my queen will hopefully pay you the coin you demanded.*

They soared along with only the roar of the wind and thumping of the dragon's wings filling the void in their discussion. Rain began to fall from the sky sea.

"I am not the only one in the Summerswept Keep with secrets," Tallius eventually said. "I have heard many things while giving rides to the young nobles."

Jaslin's ears prickled. "If you are trying to entice me into revealing something else about myself that I'd like to keep hidden, I am afraid I do not have much else to tell. Unfortunately, I am not very interesting. I am a simple young woman from the Never."

"But that is not true. Cartaya and Tiros have taken an interest in you. Everyone in the castle, besides maybe your lady, knows that."

"I am not trying to hide the matter from anyone, and I have nothing to lose if you expose it. My only secret is that I cannot wield magic without my shard. No one realizes that."

He grumbled something. "That is not even why I brought up

what I said. You are suspicious and untrusting. I was merely... gossiping."

Jaslin shrugged, as if she were uninterested. "I am sure everyone in the castle has some secret, whether big or small."

"Some much bigger than others. The orator's boy, Jaken, is likely to wed the princess—a marriage promoted by the orator through much advising and performing of favors. Many suitors from the great cities have come to the Summerswept Keep and have been denied by Igare. But Jaken has no physical interest in Nistene."

"Anyone who has spent more than a minute with those two and Vysoria can see that for themselves. He is in love with, or at least lusts after, the conjuror's daughter."

Tallius chuckled in a dark timbre. "But young Jaken would *gladly* marry the princess if Igare were dead or would pass soon after the wedding. Or so Jaken recently said directly to Princess Nistene on the back of this very dragon. He told her she was not pretty enough to be his wife, unless she were a queen. They also discussed it in a manner that made it plain this was not the first time the topic was brought up."

Jaslin's mind spun with scenarios. The king had no son. *Jaken would then become king of Belvenguard.*

"It makes me wonder if Igare or anyone else has heard of or suspects the young man's aspirations," Tallius said.

Jaslin rode along in deep thought, pondering what Jaken and Nistene would be willing to do for ambition and love, as well as what Igare and his councilmembers might do if they knew.

Clouds whipped past as the storm dragon barreled onward.

44

CYRAN ORENDAIN

Cyran eyed the inner stairs spiraling up inside the last beacon tower. They reached to the equivalent of probably thirty or more stories. He shook his head as the egg weighed heavily in his arms, and he hurried back outside.

Once he was on Milluri again and in his saddle, he watched the skies and area around them for Nithinix and his archers. They had not yet arrived, although they should have long before now. He waved farewell to the team on the forest dragon, and his thorn lifted from the ground. Milluri flew about the tower, circling it as they rose. When she reached its pinnacle—an open bowl of a level that was stuffed with kindling and logs—she drifted in closer. A combination of dread and exhaustion seeped from the five soldiers who stood around its perimeter.

"A true dragonknight of Belvenguard," one said to another. "Why has he come here?"

"Do not let me disrupt your watch, good men of the realm." Cyran raised a hand in greeting. "I am only here to check on the beacon and make sure it is fully prepared. War is now imminent, and the time of waiting will soon be over."

Milluri extended her neck to the logs as she flapped her

wings and hovered, and Cyran leaned over and lowered the egg into a gap in the beacon's fuel.

"Is that a dragon egg?" One of the soldiers gawked.

Cyran gave him a nonchalant grin, although his tone was earnest. "We cannot let *any* others know where I have left this. Not until we are safe and we know whose side everyone is on. Not a word to anyone, unless the king himself demands it of you."

Three of the soldiers nodded their understanding.

"But if we have to light the beacon, the egg will burn," another soldier said.

"It is a dragon egg." Cyran released the egg, and it rolled down into the pile. "It cannot be burned by fire."

"You fool," another soldier said to the one who had spoken, slapping him on the back of the helm as if he had completely lost his mind. "Fire harming a dragon egg, bah." He chuckled derisively.

The first soldier flushed, and his posture stiffened.

"Pray you never have to light this beacon," Cyran said. "But do not hesitate to do so if the time comes and dragons swarm in from Nevergrace, or if they skim over the Evenmeres here."

The insulted soldier's face then paled. "So many are already fleeing for the dells and valleys in the south. Even soldiers are doing so. They say Murgare's landing galleys are sailing across the Lake on Fire. They say we cannot survive the coming storm."

A weight tugged at Cyran, but he feigned optimism. "Nevergrace has never fallen into ruin, not even when the Dragon Queen took her from us, and we soon took her back. Galvenstone is even stronger. The north will come in a blaze of arrogance. That will be their undoing."

The soldier barely nodded.

"Stand proud, soldiers of Belvenguard." Cyran clenched a fist, and Milluri circled about. "Dark times fell on the kingdom long before we walked these lands, and our mothers and fathers prevailed. Do not forget that. We shall earn our own stories that we can then tell our children."

The soldiers stood a little more rigid and proud.

Cyran glanced eastward. There was still no sign of Nithinix and Vyk and Ineri. They should have met him at the beacons by now. A sensation of worry flooded his core. Had they accepted Murgare's offer and fled as well? With those promises and the odds stacked against them, everyone at Nevergrace might have. After all these centuries, the people of the outpost could give up and allow the enemy to soar past them unopposed.

Milluri circled the tower, catching the currents and tilting as Cyran squinted into the distance. The Evenmeres loomed like a silent threat running across the northern border. Curtains of winter rain hovered over the woods and raced south.

"It was Eidelmere who convinced us we should assist him and aid with your rescue," Milluri said in Cyran's mind. *"Now I regret that the dragon ever found us."*

Cyran's guilt and remorse swelled. *"Please, do not fear what is to come, and do not blame him. The darkness would still have eventually found you and your kindred. I will make you the same promise as I made him—that when this war is over, I will free you, and you may return to your home. I will never call you back to do anyone's bidding. Never."*

"Eidelmere said as much. He said you would free us after the shadows passed, although I doubted him. I fear we will be kept and used as war engines for the ambitions of man. We have already lost one dear friend, and I do not know if I will ever see Nithinix again."

Cyran's heart melted. *"I can only promise, as I have nothing more that will solidify my vow, but I mean it wholeheartedly."* Still no other thorn dragon appeared from the east. *"Why did you ever listen to that old... brave dragon, anyway?"*

"I knew him from when I was a hatchling. He was much older

than I, and he taught me about the ways of the dark woods and old growth angoias."

"Eidelmere taught you?"

"Indeed. But the forest changed since he was taken by man and housed at Nevergrace. The Evenmeres are an eerie place now, for both forest and thorn dragons. Our kind are dying out, and few are left in the wild. The creatures lurking in the woods hunt and ambush us whenever we slip and are not as cautious as we have to be."

"Shall we find you a new home away from all of it?"

A sense of nostalgia and longing flooded the other realm, but the dragon did not answer.

Cyran gritted his teeth. It had been much longer than the hour he had given his companions, and Igare wanted him back at Galvenstone to help defend the city and the castle. After everything he had already done, he still had to submit to duty and did not have time to return to the outpost again.

If war had suddenly descended upon Nevergrace, surely there would be smoke, and the farther beacons would have been lit. The choice of accepting Murgare's offer would lie with each of his comrades, as well as with each and every person at the outpost, but they probably did not know what was approaching from the south. If the legions from the Rorenlands came, would they spare those who accepted the north's offer? There would probably be few, if any, in this kingdom who would survive this war if the other four kingdoms came at Belvenguard from each side.

Cyran exhaled slowly, and his heart teetered on some invisible cliff as he wheeled Milluri around and headed west toward Dashtok.

∼

The walls of Galvenstone extended along the shores below, the lake shimmering to the north as rain drizzled over it all. Swarms of soldiers bustled about the battlements, stacking bolts near ballistae that were larger and more powerful than the ones most dragons could carry on their quarterdecks. Galleys and carracks and caravels and other types of ships Cyran did not know the names of choked the harbor. Catapults and enormous crossbows were being wheeled up behind the walls, and mounted versions were being built along the battlements. Knights on horseback gathered in masses.

A legion of stone dragons, with their two pairs of wings and mounted trebuchets, lined up inside the bailey, and soldiers hurried back and forth, loading their crates with projectiles. These beasts would be powerful, but they were slow and could not fly far without rest. They would not be able to stop the coming legions and the Dragon Queen's beast from reaching the city. Galvenstone's best course of action now might rely on how accurately they could gauge when Murgare would arrive. Then they could fly out and meet their enemies, bringing the combat over the lake instead of along the shores of the city.

Cyran swooped lower and, when there were no other guard waiting to land, settled onto a designated area in the bailey. The scene around him did not appear as it had when he'd left. Hardly any dragons swirled in the skies overhead, and none were taking flight. The cold of winter had also finally settled around the southern end of the lake, and the season's rains had begun.

"Hurry, damn it!" a dragonsquire shouted to another young man who stumbled as they wheeled a cart in which a silver dragon helm was suspended from ropes.

Two other squires pushed a cart carrying the ridged and overlapping caps of armor for a dragon's neck and rammed into the stalled cart. "No more fucking mistakes," a squire at the second cart said.

Cyran dismounted, a sense of urgency flooding him. He hurried past the carts and up the stairs to the battlements where dragons were stationed in tight intervals. As far around the city's walls as he could see, dragons were being armed and armored.

Soldiers and archers manned heavy ballistae placed between each stationed dragon and faced the lake. Other squires wheeled dragonbolts in by the cartload. Cyran paced along the walk, dodging several men who rushed about. Most did not say anything, but when they did, it was often a curse or shout ripe with anger.

A rose dragon Cyran passed by opened its mouth and coughed, a sound he had never heard one of the creatures make before. Thankfully, none of the other beasts around him appeared sick.

Not far away stood a svelte man in gold and red armor who spoke to a group of guard encircling him.

Paltere. Cyran picked up his pace, and two squires almost ran him over with a cart.

"Watch yourself!" One young man shook a fist at him.

The squires' cart held dragonbolts with sharpened and curling hooks rather than typical broadheads. The projectiles were fashioned like massive fishhooks, as if they were never meant to be dislodged from their target, but they would not plunge nearly as deep or create nearly as deadly a strike as a typical bolt. Coils of rope as tall as the squires accompanied each of these strange projectiles.

Cyran didn't ponder the bolts' style for long before rushing on and weaving his way through ranks of guard and archers. The mages were not about.

"Cyran." Sir Paltere waved him forward. "I am glad you returned. The time is upon us."

"What happened?"

"The storm dragons spotted the fleets of Murgare sailing south. The north has legions so thick they blot out the sun and cover the far end of the lake and all their ships in shadow."

Cyran's heart lurched up into his throat, his palms suddenly damp as he flexed his fingers. "How long do we have?"

"Their landing ships cannot sail fast, and it seems they are biding their time, hoping to arrive rested and ready for battle. But they must have launched their ships days or even a fortnight ago already. The storm dragons will keep us informed, but it should not be more than a day or two before they arrive at our shores. It could even happen much sooner, during the early hours before dawn tomorrow."

"The sky sea is going to release the largest squall of blood any have ever seen," an archer nearby said.

"Then the old tales about an elf riding a dragon and bringing about the end of the world are wrong," a guard beside him muttered. "The end is already here, and there are no elves."

45

PRAVON THE DRAGON THIEF

The smoldering ruins of Trasten lay far to the south as King Jabarra's legion continued their steady tromp northward, the drumming of sand dragon feet pounding around them.

Pravon tilted his chin toward his shoulder. "I would have guessed that this genturion, or Kridmore—whoever is actually in charge—would have brought us west to take Somerlian."

"It seems we head for the narrow gap between the Ilmoor Sea and Arrow Lake." Aneen's teeth crunched through the peel of a brown fruit of the Rorenlands, its spray misting the back of Pravon's neck.

"Then it will be to the foothills or the forest beyond before we sack Valan."

"Surely this army cannot pass through a forest."

Memories of their recent deeds shuffled through Pravon's thoughts as he ran his fingers through his long locks, which were gritty with sand. "We could just flatten the entire forest."

Aneen fell silent.

They had encountered less resistance in Lynden and Trasten than they had in Progtown before the townspeople and what legions remained in each city—those who had not been sent to

Galvenstone—fled northwesterly. After the events at Progtown, word of the coming army from the Rorenlands had probably reached other cities, and not as many people and dragons had remained behind hoping to defend their lands. Those who had stayed and then ended up fleeing after the sand dragons arrived would now be hoping that Galvenstone would provide a safe haven and protect them.

"Why Valan and not Somerlian?" Aneen asked. "Somerlian is the second-largest city in Belvenguard and has the second-mightiest legions. If I were Genturion Master Ristanus"—she said the name with a feigned arrogant air—"I would want to take out my strongest adversaries before they had a chance to further prepare for our coming, and before too many of our ranks died. This way, Somerlian will also have more time to learn about the tactics of this army and come up with better defenses."

Pravon shrugged. "I've given up on attempting to understand the decisions of the Dread King and our contact. Kridmore's actions were not clear even before we joined Ristanus."

They rode along, and hours and then days and nights wore on and faded away. The legion threaded the narrow gap and trudged through the hills beyond, taking only short respites at night to sleep.

One morning, an hour after dawn, before these areas far to the north of the Rorenlands warmed with sunlight and lost the bite of early winter's chill, they descended the last of the hills and overlooked the city of Valan, its valley, and the Scyne River to the east. Sprawling grasslands and fields of wheat extended to the north and west. Blue and gold flags fluttered from the walls of the city and from a castle in its center.

Ristanus waved on the legions, and a horn of the Rorenlands blared. Dragons bellowed.

No creatures or men of Valan answered. No dragons rose

into the air. No soldiers poured out or flooded the walls and manned the ballistae.

The sand dragons lumbered onward, but there was no need to blow their sandstorm breaths and conceal themselves.

"This could be a ruse." Pravon clenched his steed's scales tighter. He had long released the creature from the hold of the black poison, but this beast still did not seem overly concerned with the death of his mage, and the dragon had not resisted them. The beast was content with moving along as one of the herd. Whether sand dragons were less intelligent or felt less emotion than others of their species, Pravon could only guess. Perhaps they were simply more stoic. Their legion had probably lost close to half of their numbers during the destruction of the three cities, but neither the dragons nor the genturions seemed deterred.

"The Assassin be with us." Aneen shifted about, searching for items beneath her cloak. Her other hand clenched Pravon's shoulder. "I do not like the silence. Nor the lack of cover. I think you could be right."

Their legion marched closer and closer, and still nothing other than the snapping flags stirred within the walls. It was the silence that bothered Pravon the most. It chewed at his resolve and strummed his nerves. Any nearby crunch or taut creak of a crossbow winding tight caused him to lurch.

When they reached the outer walls, still no soldiers emerged to loose a barrage of dragonbolts. Pravon gripped his tainted spine in his fist, prepared to drive it into his mount and control the beast once again. They would then conceal themselves in haze and flee from this place.

Kridmore's and the genturions' beasts roared, reared like horses, and lifted massive legs to stomp and kick at the walls. Stones gave way and catapulted inward, the cracking caused by their release echoing across the valley. The legions plowed on through the gaps they created, ramming down more of the walls with each passing dragon.

Pravon's mount slipped into the city as other beasts trampled buildings and crushed houses. Stones toppled and hit the ground, sending up dust clouds. In what felt like less than an hour, the city had been decimated, and Pravon and Aneen passed through a gap in the far walls.

The majority of the legion flowed behind them.

Ristanus did not raise a fist in celebration or victory. He simply led them north across the fields and grasslands.

"What lies to the north of here?" Aneen asked once they had left the dusty wreckage of Valan behind. "I wasn't sure if we would make for Somerlian or Valan, but we have to head for Galvenstone now. The larger war should be looming there or could have already begun. The powers that be must intend for our legion to become part of it."

Pravon shook his head in disbelief. "If we maintain this heading and do not veer easterly for Bransheer or the Weltermores, or westerly toward Galvenstone, then there is only Nevergrace between us and the Evenmeres."

"But that castle is already in ruins, after the Dragon Queen's takeover. What could the Dread King or Kridmore possibly want with the outpost?"

"I do not know, but I believe we will soon see what Kridmore's and the Dread King's true intentions are."

46

JASLIN ORENDAIN

The storm dragon landed in a flurry of wings and rising dust, touching lightly on the ground. Jaslin shielded her face but still coughed as stifling heat radiated down on her. Sweat beaded on her forehead.

When the dust cleared, two men wearing robes that were attached to the tops of their pointed helms and fell loosely around their bodies approached.

"What do we tell them?" Jaslin whispered over her shoulder to Tallius.

"I have no notion." Tallius scowled. "You were the one who wanted to venture here, remember? I do not often travel to the Rorenlands, and never to these isles."

Jaslin's mouth had gone as dry as the sands around them. She did not know what she expected to discover here but, like in one of her stories, she envisioned landing, sneaking about an island, witnessing what she could, and finding supporting clues or information, not having to talk her way past foreign men. She did not move from her seat and held her head high as the locals neared. Behind them, masses of hunched men toiled under heavy sunlight, their backs browned as they dug picks into boulders and hefted away jagged stones. Others sweated as they plucked olives and dates from trees or tended to rows of grape vines.

"Are our ships behind on arriving at Belvenguard and hauling cargo?" One of the locals spoke with a thick accent and looked through a slit in his robes where the cloth had been pulled back along the sides of his helm, exposing only his pale eyes and the dark skin of his cheeks. He peered around Jaslin to Tallius and bowed his head. "I am Jarinede."

Jaslin glanced over her shoulder at the mage.

"You should do the talking," Tallius whispered. "They are used to only dealing with men, but I do not know why we are here."

"Your storm dragon is one of the king of Belvenguard's, no?" Jarinede's hand furtively moved to something at his waist as his expression narrowed with suspicion.

"I am Jaslin, and I have come on behalf of King Igare Dragonblade's newly betrothed—the Lady Menoria of Nevergrace." Jaslin straightened, attempting to appear bold.

"Ah, the king takes another wife," Jarinede said.

His comrade elbowed him and spoke in a foreign tongue, his tone terse.

Jarinede bowed his head. "Forgive me. I forget that men in the northern kingdoms, even kings, do not take multiple wives."

Jaslin waved away his concern.

"Then, his prior queen has passed?" Jarinede asked.

Jaslin nodded. "We are here to have a look at the isles and where we will be shipping…"

Jarinede's eyes shut briefly. "We treat our slaves here as well as any others in the kingdoms." He waved an arm, lifting his pale robe as he gestured at all those working the trees and vines and rock. "They work, but they have deserved such a life, no?

We feed them and provide shelter. They work no longer than the daylight hours." He studied Jaslin for a moment. "The new queen worries how the thieves and rapists and murderers of her kingdom are treated in the Rorenlands?"

Jaslin's jaw fell open before she recovered her composure. "She... no. She is not overly concerned with their welfare. As long as they are not being tortured. Or sustaining other unnecessary suffering. Nothing other than work and lack of freedoms."

Jarinede's posture relaxed, and he smiled and released a tense breath. "They do not have freedoms like those they experienced before their sentencing. And Belvenguard will still receive a share of the goods... what is the word"—he shook his head—"equal to the amount of workers provided."

Jaslin planted as honest a smile on her lips as she could muster. *These are indeed penal isles and colonies.* "I am simply here to look over the area and workers. Then I will be off as quickly as possible to report my observations to Lady Menoria."

"Come." Jarinede stuck a hand out of a side slit in his robes and waved her on as he pivoted about. "Here in the isles, we still cherish our alliance with your king and will show any royal of Belvenguard anything you wish to see."

Jaslin dismounted, taking one last look at Tallius, who remained comfortably in his saddle. He raised an eyebrow at her and smirked but made no move to follow. Jaslin passed by the other soldier or slaver, who eyed her warily.

"Our king's vineyards are primarily on the south isle, but we have some vines from here to the west." Jarinede motioned along the rolling hills of vines that looked more like small trees attached to stakes. "The boulders the slaves break up and cart off are used to build and fortify the walls around each island." He looked back at Tallius's dragon. "To keep thieves and corsairs away. The walls do nothing to stop dragons, but we seldom see such beasts here."

Jaslin nodded and studied the lands and workers, pretending to assess their labor.

"The olives and dates are on the drier side of the isle." Jarinede kept walking.

They passed by a group of young to middle-aged men, all of whom had scraggly hair but were clean shaven with sun-leathered skin. They wore cloth only around their groins and had no boots or sandals of any kind. Some of the men glanced up at Jaslin but quickly looked at Jarinede and returned to their work. Only one man continued staring at her, and Jaslin caught sight of something on his throat—the tattoo of a raven within a triangle. When their eyes met, drool strung from the man's lips, and Jaslin shuddered.

Jarinede stepped toward the slave, shouting something in a foreign tongue, his arms lifting his robes and making them look like wings. The man cringed and fell to the ground. Jarinede paused, glanced back at Jaslin, and forced a smile. "Pardon this man."

Jaslin gave the slaver a quick nod of assent, wondering what the prisoner might have tried to do to her if Jarinede were not here. She also considered what Jarinede might have done to the slave if she were not present. But such thoughts would not provide answers to the questions she sought. They were not why she had come to the isles. Her predominant question remained —what would a man of the south have to do with killing queens in the north?

"Show me where and how the tattoos are applied." Jaslin strolled along behind Jarinede, pretending to be at ease.

Jarinede paused and glanced back at her. "We do not mark slaves here. The Rorenlands brand our own murderers and other villains when we ship them to the isles. I can show you."

Jarinede pointed to a sandstone building atop the hill and led her onward. "We have only received a few men today, but you will be able to see that the brands were applied some time ago and are nearly healed."

"All the men sent here are already marked with the tattoo of a triangle and a raven inside of it?"

"Indeed. The villains from Belvenguard are marked the same before our king's ships deliver them from your kingdom to ours. It takes an experienced and practiced hand to create the tattoos, and so we have an artist aboard each vessel. The slaves receive their brandings as soon as the ship carrying them leaves port."

Thoughts churned in Jaslin's mind. "Are any slaves ever set free? Maybe released after a time of service?"

Jarinede chuckled and studied her before realizing her question was sincere. "No."

That would mean all the men in the kingdoms who bore such a tattoo should reside at these isles. The merchants who told her about the markings were right, unless... "Have any branded villains ever overtaken the ship bearing them here and sailed away before arriving? Never to be caught?"

Jarinede stopped outside a woven slip of a door and pulled it back. Inside, the building was dark and cool. "It has probably happened at some point in history, but never that I am aware of. It may be easier for men with marked throats to hide in our kingdom"—he gestured at his robes—"but not in Belvenguard. And an entire ship of villains returning to any kingdom would draw much attention."

Jaslin pondered that. There had been word of possibly three tattooed assassins being sighted in total, including the man who attacked Jaslin in the undercity, and that man's skin was too light for him to be a native of the Rorenlands. Even double or triple that number of assassins was not enough to man a large ship, and a vessel would not likely have departed on such a long voyage until it was fully stocked with human cargo. The coin received for three or so slaves would not be worth the effort of passage to the Rorenlands.

"Have the slaves also had their tongues removed prior to arriving here?" Jaslin asked.

Jarinede flinched and shook his head before stepping into the building. She followed the slaver through the doorway. Lamplight fluttered inside a long hallway. The temperature immediately dropped to a manageable heat. Jarinede turned a corner and led her into a chamber. A dozen men dressed like Jarinede, but who held whips with many lashes, encircled five naked men. One of the slavers addressed the arrivals. Each naked man had a tattoo on his throat, each marking only lightly scabbed and peeling. All were the same style—black, triangle, raven. The voyage by ship would have probably been a long one, allowing time for the tattoos to mostly heal.

Jaslin hovered near the doorway. "Were some of these slaves assassins?"

Jarinede's fingers appeared under his cloak as he rubbed his clean-shaven chin. "They are murderers and rapists and thieves who have stolen items of much value or from someone they should not have, someone important. None are trained assassins. We would not allow that here. While we are strong and can control these villains, there are more of them here than there are of us. No good." He shook his head.

"Is this where you remove their tongues?"

The slaver's eyes gaped. "We do not remove tongues. No. Please tell your lady we are not animals. The overseers here on the Southern Isles are not barbarians. The slaves are all allowed to keep their tongues. None talk back to us after their first day. Once they arrive, they learn the ways of their new life quickly."

These criminals arrive with their tongues intact and tattoos, and the slavers do not remove their tongues. "Has Belvenguard ever asked for you to return any of these men?"

"Never. Once they are here, they stay. They have been judged guilty of high crimes worthy of death, but the kind and just kings sometimes allow us to ship such men here instead."

"And you said the intricacy of the tattoos is hard to emulate?"

He nodded. "I am sure there are many others in the kingdoms who can make something similar, but not without looking at a marking while they do so."

Jarinede walked over to a pedestal that held an open tome. He ran a finger down a long column of what appeared to be names, although these possible names were foreign. In adjacent columns, there were names of Rorenlands's cities written in strange letters and dates, but the names were familiar. Jaslin had read them before in stories—Tablu, Jardoor, Kistengrove, Sarzuth. A final column listed strange words she did not understand.

Jarinede dragged his fingernail over the indiscernible column. "As I said—rapist, two murderers, and two thieves. Five of them this day."

A thought surfaced in Jaslin's mind. "Does Belvenguard also keep records of their villains that you ship here?"

Jarinede's expression contorted with incredulity. "Of course they would. Most of those who our ships bring have been judged in Galvenstone by the council or the lesser courts there. Not all of your judges are nyrens, or so I've heard, and those who aren't would want to keep records of who they convict and sentence."

The archives.

One of the arrivals screamed, and Jaslin lurched as the man charged a slaver, fists flying. The slavers' robes flared open, revealing something to the criminal that Jaslin could not see, and they fell upon the man, who shrieked and wailed. Two of the other arrivals assisted their comrade.

"You can find your way out?" Jarinede asked. "I will remain here and help with this situation."

Jaslin nodded, her stomach turning queasy as Jarinede flared his robes and marched toward the scene, seeming to rise taller. Jaslin looked at the tome. She flipped back through the crackling pages as the slavers and new arrivals screamed and cursed. She found several pages that included dates around the time when the Murgare queen and Queen Hyceth would have been murdered. A strange spelling of the word 'Belvenguard' was positioned next to some of the names of the arrivals. She waited for a frightened shriek to sound and ripped the pages from the book, rolled them up, and stuffed them into the waist of her leggings, concealing them with her tunic. Then she retreated from the chamber and the amplifying cries, rushing outside.

She bustled down the path toward the waiting storm dragon, her mind racing. Why and how would two criminals shipped to these isles end up in Belvenguard and assassinate the queen of the north and then Belvenguard's queen, knowing they would likely be caught and killed? Moreover, who would benefit from having queens murdered instead of the king? Also, conjurors needed to speak to use their magic, and the assassins did not have tongues. So those villains could not have performed any bone and earth magic to accomplish their tasks. The possibility that the tattooed assassins were somehow linked to Keliam seemed like the most plausible explanation. Why else would one have come after her? Another, more frightening, inkling poisoned her thoughts, but she dismissed the notion for the time being.

When Jaslin neared the toiling workers, the man who had eyed her earlier stared at her again. A sharp kick of dread landed in her stomach, and she hurried past them. None of the other slavers were about.

Footsteps sounded behind her. She started jogging, and the footfalls quickened. She glanced back. The man in question pursued her, hobbling along, drool swinging from his chin, reminding her of a lame but wild wolf running her down.

She shouted and ran, but the storm dragon was too far away. A strong hand grabbed her shoulder and shoved her forward, causing her to stumble and trip and flail. She crashed onto the ground face-first, skidding across gravel and dirt.

A heavy weight crashed on top of her, pressing her down. A soft punch landed on her back, and strong hands ripped at her tunic and leggings while she was pinned against the ground. Somewhere nearby, jeering sounded.

"I have to make it look real," her attacker whispered in her ear. "But, please—"

Jaslin gasped, trying to reach behind her, but she could not grab her assailant. Her eyes closed as she shouted, and anger and suffocating fear blazed inside her.

"Take me with you," the man said, his voice almost lost in Jaslin's terror. "Or kill me."

Jaslin's hand had already found a pouch at her waist, and before she even knew it, she was ramming the crystal shard into the flesh of her attacker, who was struggling with her leggings. Blood sprayed and flowed.

A scream blasted in her ears, and suddenly the weight was gone. Behind her, her assailant managed to mutter, "Others in the guild were taken by a dragon from Belvenguard."

Jaslin rolled over, lifting her shard. The fragment dripped with blood that ran over her fingers.

Her attacker was on his knees, holding two blood-soaked hands over a wound on his side. Amber flames bloomed beneath his palms and shot outward. His eyes turned a similar color and smoked.

He winced but mouthed the words, "Thank you," and exhaled. More fire erupted across his shoulders, and he collapsed in a ball of flames.

Three slavers rushed closer before standing frozen, their eyes gaping as they stared at Jaslin and her bloodied shard.

47

CYRAN ORENDAIN

The hours rolled by like days and the days like years. Cyran paced along the battlements under a misting rain while overlooking the lake. The progression of Murgare's legions had slowed for some unknown reason, although it could not be much longer now before the watchtowers on the lake blared their horns three times to announce the sighting of the north's dragons.

Milluri perched on the merlons nearby, her eyes closed in sleep, dragonsteel pauldrons, neck plates, and a helm strapped to her and dripping with precipitation. She had been edgy, but over the past few days, she had decided it would be best to rest before the coming storm. The pain in Cyran's heart from his broken bond with Eidelmere had not lessened, but he tried to ignore the sensation and focus on the present and his new dragon.

"No one can find her." Menoria hurried up to Cyran, two kingsknights trailing closely behind her. "I have not seen her in at least two days, and no one knows where she has gone."

Hopefully she is rightly scared and ran away to hide and read.

Cyran's palms grew damp. Even though that was what he hoped for, he doubted Jaslin had done such a thing, not after what happened during the takeover at their outpost. He would never see his sister in the same light again. But if he and Menoria could not find her, then perhaps the armies of Murgare would not be able to either. "If I see her, I will insist that she take refuge with you in the keep."

Menoria nodded, her face wan. She swallowed as she looked over the lake and then to the sky before rushing off.

Paltere paced by for about the twentieth time in the past hour, always whistling. Evenfall settled over the lands.

"How do you deal with the waiting?" Cyran asked the other dragonknight. "At Nevergrace, the attack came without warning, and I was always trying to catch up with what was occurring. Now I think I prefer it that way."

Paltere curtailed his whistling. "I find joy in what I can. In music mostly. You are a man of song, are you not? You are a man of the Never."

Cyran nodded. "But right now, I don't think my fingers will be able to play the strings the same way as usual."

Paltere clapped him on his pauldron, which glowed green in the fading light, green for the forest dragons of the Never.

"How many of our dragons are sick?" Cyran asked.

The middle-aged dragonknight furrowed his chin and rubbed at his scruff. "More than I'd like there to be and yet not too many. There is nothing that can be done about it now."

"Have we lost any of the beasts? And have the nyrens looked at the body to see what is causing the sickness?"

Paltere shook his head. "We have not lost any."

"That is something, then."

"Indeed, my young comrade. Just remember everything you have been taught about the lance and what you have learned of your new dragon. I am sorry about the loss of your other creature. I've heard it is nearly unbearable."

Cyran's head drooped, the empty sucking feeling in his heart increasing many magnitudes with its acknowledgment.

"Stay strong for now." Paltere squeezed his arm. "One day soon we will find time to mourn." He resumed his whistling right where he had stopped and strolled away.

Hours crept by and faded away. Torchlight burned brighter as night fell, the flames sizzling under the rain, and the light of the thousand moons made the sky sea glisten through the storm overhead. Over time, the rain turned to a mixture of ice and then drifting flakes of snow, something the people of Galvenstone said they did not see every winter. But the drifting snow did not last. Sheets of rain drifted in over the lake and bombarded Dashtok and the city.

The beating of wings sounded to the east, and a dark form plunged down toward the battlements. People screamed and shouted. A horn blasted. The beast swooped over the area, and people collapsed in fear.

Cyran ripped Eidelmere's Flame from its sheath as he crouched, glancing toward Milluri, wondering how many of their soldiers would actually be able to face the evil that would soon descend upon them. He paused. This was no shadow dragon passing by. Only one kind of dragon could be stealthy enough to arrive out of the night and from the east without warning—a moon dragon—and one moon dragon would hardly be able to destroy Galvenstone.

He stood straighter and waved to the flying beast and its riders, hurrying to the edge of the battlements. "Moon dragon! What news from the east?"

The dragon wheeled back around and slowly descended until it hovered just over Cyran's head. Other soldiers started to gather and approach. Sir Paltere pushed through them and joined Cyran.

"There you are, sir dragonknight." The mage on the beast's back peeked around a shielded guard and looked at Cyran, the mage's eyes wide with fright. "The beacon towers burn, and all the soldiers there are dead."

Cyran's skin prickled with an icy cold. This was the dragon and mage he had spoken with and given orders to at the beacon tower.

"If the beacons were lit, the watch would have seen them," Paltere said. "Galvenstone's bells would be ringing, our horns blasting." He raised a hand to shield the rain and gazed eastward into the night. No firelight carried across the distance.

"Not if the beacons were burning with black fire," Cyran said.

Paltere regarded Cyran, bemused for an instant. "As you mentioned to the Dragon Queen."

"We came to inform Galvenstone as soon as we noticed," the mage continued. "The beast that we assume carries the Dragon Queen slowed for her legion to join her, but they will soon be on their way here."

"*Shadowmar.*" Cyran swallowed, picturing the Dragon Queen's mount somewhere out there in the night with a legion of her own. He shouted, "Guard and archers and mages of Belvenguard, mount up. Murgare comes by way of the lake *and over the Evenmeres!*" *Other kingdoms could soon be attacking us as well.*

Paltere swung about and yelled to his guard, pointing at dragons and barking orders. Bells pealed in the night, rattling ears and snapping a tense silence. Horns blasted around the city and castle. Torchlight flared inside the keep.

"To arms!" Riscott rushed along the battlements, his robe

whipping behind him. "As we have laid out the plans. In the midst of chaos, do not forget your duty."

Suspicion arose in the back of Cyran's mind. What had the orator ordered everyone to do?

Behind the orator, Igare strode with determination, watching from under the roaring rain as the archers and guard mounted their steeds of scale and fire. The king nodded to those who passed by, the remainder of his council following him.

The thumping of massive wings mixed with the chorus of bells and horns, and hundreds of dragons rose from the castle and baileys and outlying areas.

"They are coming from Nevergrace as well?" Igare asked as he approached Cyran.

Cyran nodded solemnly, trying not to think of his people there and what might have happened to them.

"Take your positions!" Igare bellowed. "Murgare attempts to surround us. The majority of our forces will confront and attack the north's masses out over the lake, but we shall keep reserves around the walls here. A smaller legion will protect our city's eastern border."

Conjurors in mauve cloaks scrambled up quarterdecks or crawled into turrets, following archers. An array of other men and women in plain tunics did likewise, the minimally trained who held some power over bone and earth magic.

"Riscott has already matched all our conjurors who have been named as battlemages, and their trainees, to others of the guard," Paltere said to Cyran. "There are not nearly enough who wield bone and earth magic to go around. Not that you could use one of them with your empty quarterdeck."

Cyran glanced at the unmanned mounted crossbow on Milluri and then at her turret, which was also unoccupied. Vyk and Ineri must have either died facing a legion of Murgare, or they had accepted the north's coin and fled. He searched about the area for his assigned dragonsquires, who were to be his archers if Vyk and Ineri did not show.

Two young men, appearing more like boys, huddled together against a far wall, staring with wide eyes at the chaos raging around them.

"Mount up!" Paltere yelled at the squires, and the boys turned and fled.

"We have no time to wait for more squires or even soldiers who may be brave enough but aren't well trained with the bow while on dragonback." Cyran clambered onto Milluri's neck and into his saddle. He grunted as he shifted in his seat. "And so my dragon and I will have no use for a conjuror—we never had any magic-wielding people at Nevergrace—but I'll attempt anything I can to aid Belvenguard."

"You are to fly out over the lake with us," Paltere said. "Per the orator. To help stop or at least delay a siege of dragons that could decimate the city." He paused. "You are a dragonknight. Do not forget that. You have no mage—no middleman—who would otherwise have to determine your dragon's path. You and this thorn dragon will be far superior to any other guard and their beast. Just try to get in close and fight from there with a dancing and weaving lance." Paltere drew two swords, placing the back of one of his hands against his forehead and angling the blade downward. He placed the palm of his other hand against his belt and angled the weapon upward so both blades overlapped, which created a halo with sheens of red and gold. "Till the end of days we soar. Till the end of nights we reign. You honor me. My soul sees yours."

Cyran pressed the hilt of Eidelmere's Flame against his forehead, mimicking Sir Paltere as he repeated the words in a clear and bold tone, wishing he still had his silver elven sword. The green glow of the forest dragon surrounded him.

Paltere sheathed his blades, pivoted about, and strode away for his sun dragon.

Cyran imagined Milluri's armored form rising, picturing every move they would need to make to lift into the gushing sky and accompany Paltere as they led the forces gathered at Galvenstone against the coming of Murgare and the Dragon Queen.

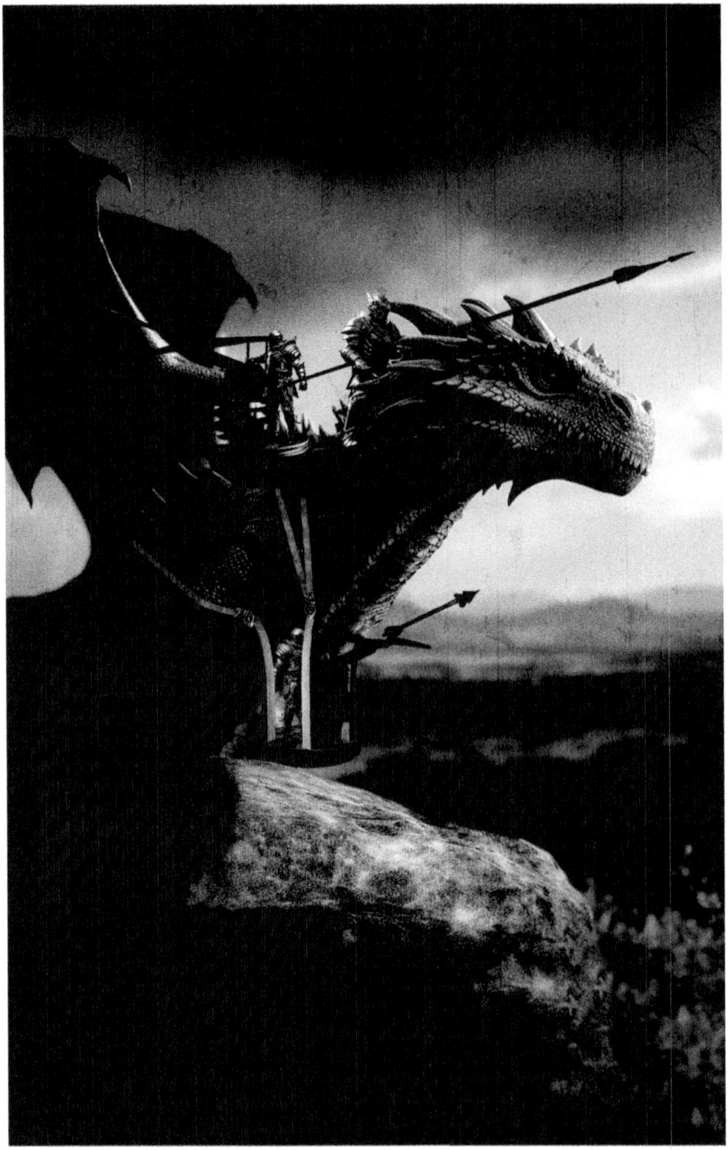

48

SIRRA BRACKENGLAVE

ONCE BEYOND THE LAST COPSE OF ANGOIAS, SHADOWMAR DIVED down toward the pine canopy below as snow fell in heavier and heavier clumps across the forest and the fields beyond. A few fire, ice, mist, blood, and bone dragons barreled along behind Sirra in multilayered tiers of death. None of Belvenguard would escape their fury. Thankfully, she had left Sir Trothen, Kyelle, Sir Vladden, and Quarren behind.

Less than half of Sirra's original legion had completed the arduous crossing after diverting from their main army and the lake far to the north, hopefully before the watchtowers of Belvenguard could have spotted them. As a further precaution, the mist dragons in the legion had also helped conceal them during the night.

Nevergrace loomed in the darkness ahead, its silhouetted twin towers and broken keep dotted with torchlight. The attack here would be swift and severe.

Sirra banked Shadowmar westward, her resilient mount ignoring any weariness. The others angled for the center of the outpost. As Shadowmar streaked closer, staying low to the canopy to hide her bulk from the lighted sky sea, a horn blasted multiple times within the Never's walls. Another horn answered as Sirra descended upon the castle.

"Portside bow!" Yenthor shouted behind her.

A forest dragon rose before her, cutting her off from her objective as it beat its leathery wings and shrieked. Shadowmar folded in her wings and hurtled along even faster as Sirra muttered a word. "*Dramlavola.*" Vigor flowed through her limbs as she braced her shoulder against her lance.

The thump of releasing crossbow ropes sounded from above and below the forest dragon, and two bolts screamed toward them.

"*Aylión.*" Sirra saw the future paths of the projectiles and whipped Shadowmar in a tight circle, rolling her upside down in an instant as one of the bolts buzzed by just beneath her skull. The other sailed harmlessly skyward.

After completing their barrel roll, Shadowmar roared and beat her wings, screaming onward. Sirra positioned her lance as they neared. The guard on the forest dragon realigned his weapon, apparently believing he would be able to strike Sirra.

At the last moment, just before colliding, Sirra veered Shadowmar upward and to portside, her lance already poised for the new trajectory. The guard bellowed and attempted to keep up with her movements as he shouted something to the mage behind him while repositioning his weapon.

Sirra's black lance clashed against her opponent's shield, and sparks flew like a bucket of molten metal that had been cast into the air. A crack answered. The guard's shield exploded, and he was catapulted into the air, a limp form sailing through the moonlit night. The dragons brushed past each other in a thumping of wings as Shadowmar roared. Sirra glanced westward at her target—the beacon towers—and then back to the unprotected mage on the forest dragon, considering if she should relieve the dragon of that man before leaving the outpost to the rest of her legion.

A rope in the turret below Shadowmar snapped, and the whistling of a bolt carried out for less than a second before ending abruptly with a thump and crunch. The projectile's fletching protruded between the eyes of the forest dragon. The enemy beast's wings slowly stopped flapping, and the dragon tilted before falling still and dropping like a stone.

Yenthor yelled his approval of Zaldica's shot, and Shadowmar raced onward. The first beacon tower between the outpost and Galvenstone loomed ahead, and soldiers stationed there shouted and pointed weapons. A spark flashed in the night but quickly died out in the snowy cold. Another followed. Yellow flame bloomed.

Shadowmar's jaws gaped as they came upon the tower, and her black breath spewed past her teeth, snuffing out and swallowing the initial burst of fire created by the soldiers. Black flames writhed, and the logs on the beacon tower crackled and blazed with shadow, resembling ghostly specters dancing on a pyre.

A Belvenguard soldier screamed and leapt from the top of the tower, plummeting many stories to the earth and landing with the cracking of bones. Sirra shook her head. Such were the atrocities of war. She had often seen similar and bizarre things over the past five centuries.

Sirra banked Shadowmar downward and to the south, skimming low over the ground, the tree line of the Evenmeres just to their right and shadowed by night. The next beacon tower might have heard the horns of the outpost or could have seen the initial spark created by the first, and they would soon light their signal.

She glanced back. The dragons of her legion dived and looped around the castle, lighting up battlements and ballistae with their fire, frost, amethyst fire, crystal shards, poisonous gas of the bone dragons, and acidic red discharge of the blood dragons, which would dissolve whatever it came in contact with.

Another forest dragon was hit with several bolts, and the creature spiraled downward at a slant, crashing and plowing a swath through the fields beyond the castle.

Shadowmar hurtled toward the next tower and unleashed her breath, lighting up its beacon with the color of night. They soared on without pausing.

Behind her at Nevergrace, no more forest dragons attacked her legion, and the north's dragons wheeled around and flew after her, leaving the walls concealed by mist breath. There was no reason to make sure all the people at the outpost were dead. Only their dragons would cause her legion any issues. Now it was time to descend upon Galvenstone unannounced and from the east.

Leagues across the darkness and to the south, rows of torchlight dotted the night. The torches filled an expanse of land as large as a flattened mountain. A legion of sand dragons from the Rorenlands was supposedly marching northward and might try to aid or destroy Galvenstone. The Rorenlands' motives and objectives regarding the other kingdoms were obscure. There probably wasn't anyone in Murgare who understood what that kingdom was planning, unless Oomaren was behind an allegiance with them. But it did not matter. The sand dragons would arrive too late to stop her attack or defend the outpost or the capital city of Belvenguard.

Shadowmar set the next few beacon towers ablaze as they whipped past them. The last tower on the hilltop neared and seemed the tallest and most ominous of all.

Behind Shadowmar, there were still no bright fires or anything else to signal that something was out of sorts in this part of the kingdom. In front of them, the marshlands blurred by, and the lake glistened with moonlight that was distorted by rain.

Shadowmar's jaws gaped as they came upon the last beacon tower. The screams of soldiers were silenced by black fire nearly as soon as they erupted. The kindling in the bowl atop the tower flared in darkness and crackled.

Sirra slowed her mount and hovered, waiting for her legion. In the distance, the walls of Galvenstone sat silently on the hilltop.

49

JASLIN ORENDAIN

THE STORM DRAGON BARRELED NORTHWARD EVEN FASTER THAN when they had flown to the penal isles. Tallius must have been worried about being gone for too long and about the impending war.

Clouds hurtled past, creating a haze around them. Flashing recollections of the assailant Jaslin had most recently set aflame replayed in her thoughts again. The man probably deserved what she had done to him and was likely a rapist in his prior life, but images of the criminal burning still unsettled her. And why had he wanted to escape on a Belvenguard dragon like others in some guild supposedly had? He was the second man she had killed with her shard and its magic, the first no less terrifying, although she did not have to witness the progression of her flames with that assassin's death. It seemed like when she was in mortal danger, she could command magic, as long as she had her shard, and her powers could be deadly. She would have to be mindful and careful when attacking in anger or out of fear, especially if her would-be assailant did not mean her harm.

As they flew, twilight fell over the sky sea, and night dragged on.

Rain let loose from the clouds and pummeled them. The tolling of bells carried up to the sky and were followed by horn blasts. Tallius muttered something. Their dragon dived. The clouds parted, and land opened up beneath them, Galvenstone and Dashtok centered directly below. Several watching storm dragons and riders nearby must have recognized them and allowed them to pass without obstructing their path or slowing them down.

Jaslin's stomach clenched and felt like a ball of lead sitting in her gut before it rolled up into her throat.

"The sky sea is already raining blood." Tallius leaned over and against his dragon's neck, and they plunged downward even faster.

The storm dragon did not ease from its descent until the castle and its torchlight rose up and nearly hit them. Then the dragon threw its wings out, bracing as wind snapped its leathery segments out like sails and flung the creature upward. They glided over the battlements as guard and archers mounted their beasts.

Igare exited the keep with his council. Soldiers holding lamps walked on either side of him, and Menoria trailed behind them, her kingsknights flanking her.

"There!" Jaslin pointed. "Take me to my lady."

The storm dragon dipped one wing and lifted the other, whipping about before slowing and settling onto a merlon outside the keep. Dragons leapt from the walls and swirled in the skies.

"Menoria!" Jaslin scampered down from her saddle as the king and his council paced away.

The lady turned, aghast. "Jaslin? Where have you been?"

Jaslin rushed over to Menoria and hugged her before quickly pulling away. "What has happened?"

"Dragons have been sighted over the lake. They are now

close enough to be seen by the watchtowers. There is also a rumor spreading that the beacon towers have been sabotaged."

Gooseflesh prickled across Jaslin's arms. "Then we still have some time before they arrive?"

Menoria nodded subtly as her fingers clenched Jaslin's wrist. "I've been needing your assistance more than ever these past days, and your ear, but I often cannot find you anywhere. Times have... not been easy." She stared at the stones of the walk. "Being betrothed to a king is difficult enough. Add in a time of impending war, and I—well, I've been beside myself. I have dearly missed you, my handmaid, my friend."

Jaslin gripped her lady's hand to reassure her as dragons roared and shrieked around them. "I am truly sorry, milady. There were certain things I was forced to deal with, as they affected Belvenguard and Nevergrace more deeply than I could ever have imagined."

Menoria's head snapped up, and the lady scrutinized her. "How so?"

"We should not discuss any details out here. I do not want to frighten anyone further, or start rumors that may be false."

Menoria paled and glanced around at the swarming soldiers on the battlements. Below, warhorses snorted and whinnied. Hoofs clopped on cobbles as contingents of knights rode out to the shoreline.

"There is still the matter of coin." Tallius cleared his throat loudly and hobbled up to stand with Jaslin and Menoria.

A sinking feeling pulled at Jaslin's stomach.

"Ten gold crowns," Tallius said as he faced Menoria and held out an open palm.

"Ten crowns?" Menoria glanced back and forth between him and Jaslin, perplexed. "Whatever for?" Her attention settled on Jaslin. "What have you done?"

Tallius scowled. "She owes me for passage on my storm dragon. It was a long venture."

"Even I do not have ten crowns I could drop at a moment's notice," Menoria said.

"We are at war." Jaslin indicated the chaos around them. "Surely your need for coin can wait until we determine *if* we will survive."

"Ten crowns could be the only thing that ensures my survival." Tallius folded his arms across his chest. "The people I owe coin to do not accept excuses. If I do not have it, I will name you as the one they should seek out."

Jaslin clenched her jaw. More dragons screamed past overhead.

"Enough of this talk." Menoria glared at the mage. "I will be queen of this kingdom, and I will pay you as soon as the war is over. With interest, if needed. But not now." She tugged at Jaslin's sleeve as she swallowed and then spoke more quietly. "Cyran is heading out to face the incoming legions, and he is in a weaker position than many others of the guard. The orator did not supply him with a conjuror, and the archers Riscott assigned to him at the last minute, when his did not show, fled. Not that those squires were even adequately trained in using the crossbow while flying."

Fear shot through Jaslin like pain from fire. She looked northward, picturing Tamar and his death. Cyran would soon follow their brother's path. *No archers?* She did not have any real experience with conjurors riding dragons—had never even seen such a thing, as Nevergrace did not have such people—but with the odds of this war stacked against Belvenguard, her people were trying everything they could to aid their legions. She whipped about, her mind flashing with thoughts and ideas as she grabbed Tallius by the robes and shook him. "Take me out there."

Tallius stumbled back a step, his expression of anger breaking before snapping into one of shock. "You must be mad."

Jaslin gripped his robes tighter, pulling him off-balance and onto his weak leg. "I must do this for my brother. He is all I have left."

"You cannot even pay for your flight to the Rorenlands. I will not put myself in the middle of battle for you. You can go if you wish, but you must find another dragon and mage to take you."

Jaslin tugged him farther away from Menoria and whispered in his face, "I will not accept no as an answer. I will earn or even steal whatever coin is needed from my lady once she is queen. I will even take it from the king if I must."

Tallius's eyes narrowed. "Be careful of what you say. People who steal from the crown either find themselves dead or on the Southern Isles."

"I have stolen a crown already, as you have probably now realized." Jaslin grabbed her shard, and her hand grew hot. Smoke rose from the mage's robe. "This *must* happen. You saw what I can do to a man, what I did in the Rorenlands. I wield the flames of bone and earth magic, and no one but you and I know it."

Tallius pulled back in surprise, stumbling and falling onto his backside. He held a hand up to keep her away as firelight and shadows gamboled across his face. "Stay away from me!"

"Jaslin!" Menoria stepped closer.

"I will not," Jaslin said to the mage. "But I will pay you for your service."

His eyes flashed with fear and then realization as some dark lust of his was tempted. "I could do it, but it would cost you much. Enough to pay off all of my... a small fortune."

Jaslin shrugged off his demand, unsure if either of them would survive this day or the next, although something in the back of her mind shouted a warning. "I will deliver a reasonable amount of coin for the deed." *Cyran.* She glanced back out over the walls.

"If you do not, I will inform everyone I am indebted to that they should come after you." Tallius reached out for aid, and Jaslin assisted him to his feet. "They could kill me first, but then they will surely kill you as well."

Jaslin nodded abruptly as if she were unconcerned.

"Then follow me back to my dragon." Tallius hobbled away.

"You cannot go." Menoria grasped Jaslin's collar, holding her still.

Jaslin grabbed her lady's fingers, breaking Menoria's grip and patting the back of her hand. "I am again truly sorry, milady, but the last living member of my family needs all the aid he can get. There is something I must do. Then I will return. We will live out this war together within the keep."

A tear slipped from Menoria's lower eyelid as her lip trembled.

50

CYRAN ORENDAIN

MOONLIGHT SHONE THROUGH THE SKY SEA AND RAGING RAINS, silvering the Lake on Fire as Cyran and Milluri soared onward. It would be to their advantage and Murgare's hindrance to meet the coming legions out over the lake rather than at their city's walls.

The crying of dragons chased at their heels, and a few silver dragons whipped past them. Thoughts of heading to Nevergrace tormented Cyran, but the vast bulk of Murgare's legions had to be coming over the lake. Only a small amount of them could have veered off, crossed the marshes, and headed toward Nevergrace and the beacon towers without being seen. He should maintain his heading and clash with the enemy over the lake where the Dragon Wars once raged and resulted in hundreds of thousands of deaths. The north must have planned to use the cover of night to get as close to the city as possible before the watchtowers spotted their incoming legions.

Many more shrieks and roars arose in the vast darkness, these coming from somewhere far ahead. Firelight blinked down below and to the north, arising from fleets of Murgare ships racing for Galvenstone. The vessels seemed to almost span the entire width of the lake, reaching from the eastern marshes to the western shores, but that could not be true. There would have to be thousands of them to do such a thing. More likely, many were rafts or skiffs carrying torches to strike fear into the hearts of their enemies. But there were probably thousands of dragons creating a cloud of shadow in the moonlight above the fleet.

Cyran swallowed and glanced back. The masses of his legions were still rising from the castle and keep, and the sky between him and the walls of Galvenstone were littered with dragons in haphazard formation.

"Halt here!" Cyran called to the faster flying dragon types soaring around and past him.

"We will not be able to put much more distance between the city and our legions," Paltere yelled from somewhere close by. "We shall meet these demons with our entire force rather than thin our ranks and sacrifice the might of our attack for distance from our kingdom."

The dragons racing away banked left or right and wheeled about. Those behind them fanned out and flanked Paltere, taking up a wedge formation. Many moon dragons, with their sightless dark eyes, took up the forefront.

"Your kingdom breathes behind you, dragon riders!" Paltere shouted as he stood up in his stirrups and raised his golden sword overhead, its radiance creating a halo around the blade and lighting up sheets of rain. "Your families, your women and men, your children. Your brothers and sisters. The lands that have raised you and that you have looked upon since you were children. That is your kingdom." He pointed his sword behind them. "Belvenguard. Therein waits your king, Igare Dragonblade. Those are the lands of your fathers and mothers. Lands of song and of celebration and heartache."

He paused and looked over the hundreds of dragons in

formation and those still swooping in to join their ranks. "We have never held her from the hands of our enemies with wishes and prayers, and we will not be able to call our lands our own if we do not stand against the storm now. The sky sea has begun to drop its blood. Night fades. Dawn will rise soon. And what you will see when the sun comes up may make the bravest of you tremble, the most valiant of you consider fleeing. But we are brothers and sisters now. Each and every one of us. From the oldest archer to the youngest mage."

A collective breath was sucked in all around them and slowly expelled as Cyran glanced at the masses of guard and archers and mages and their beasts. Everyone looked at each other.

"This moment has tapered our bloodlines down into one family," Paltere said. "Anything that has been said or done before is forgiven. All we have is now and the future we seek this day. This is nothing else. And when daylight shines across the lake and lights its waves up in orange, you will see your enemy, something each of us must stand against, or all of us will fall. You will not know fear. You will not tremble. As sure as my arm will wield my lance, you will strike with your bolts and magic and dragons. For we are one. Without any one of you, Belvenguard will cease to exist, and all we were shall be forgotten. The legions of the north will then pour over our lands and desecrate our cities and our homes. They will fire the trees and the grass and burn every village to the ground. The lands of Belvenguard shall become an extension of Murgare and of evil." He paused again. "But not if you stand and ride with me. Not if you defy the greatest of evil in the face of despair. For hope cannot be taken from you until your soul is lost. And today, when I look upon each of my brothers and sisters and the glorious dragons of Belvenguard—our saviors and our treasured mounts—my hope soars." He shouted and jabbed his sword into the sky.

Men and women roared and hollered.

"Till the end of days we soar." Paltere raised the back of his hand to his forehead, blade down in the salute of the old guard. "Till the end of nights we reign. Your *all* honor me. My soul sees yours!"

Deafening cries rang out and blasted across the lake, rolling northward like thunder, and the tumult was answered by the shriek and roar of Belvenguard's dragons. Silver and gold fire flashed as the beasts blew their breaths overhead. Lightning arced, and rivers of water streamed. Starlight flashed in bursts.

A line of ten ally stone dragons flew low over the water, the many archers on their quarterdecks swiveling in their frames, the soldiers manning the trebuchets, preparing. The gargantuan beasts flapped their two sets of wings and slowly and steadily, like ships at sea, passed the forming ranks above.

"With me!" Paltere spun his sun dragon about, and it flapped its massive wings and roared before flying north.

~

The wedge of the legions drove onward as Cyran steered Milluri, attempting to stay at the forefront as they soared over the water.

Rays of muted morning light rose and painted the eastern sky and plummeting rain in red. A red dawn. Blood rain.

"Cyran!" someone shouted, their voice distant.

Cyran slowed Milluri and veered right, away from the advancing legions. He glanced about. A blue flash wound around the margins of the wedge, darting in and out like a bee.

"Cyran!" The voice was female, possibly even his sister's.

Cyran wheeled Milluri around and flew toward the weaving storm dragon as his stomach sank lower and lower with each beat of her wings. *Jaslin?* "Jaslin!" He angled closer.

The storm dragon curled and whipped around before

streaking toward him. The creature's jaws gaped, and it thrust its wings out and braced against a rush of wind, slamming to a halt.

"Jaslin?" Cyran asked.

The rider on the guard's saddle brushed her auburn hair with faded ends from her face. It *was* her.

"Jaslin!" he said. "What are you doing out here? You *must* return to the castle. The entire army of Murgare is coming."

Jaslin raised a hand to pacify him. "I have to speak with you first."

Cyran swallowed his fear for her and his rising anger. "Quickly."

She nodded, but her lips slackened and she paled when she looked behind him. "It's true—you do not even carry any archers."

Cyran's eyes briefly shut. "They did not return from Nevergrace, and my squires ran off."

"Every other dragon out here probably has their guard and archers."

"But they are not dragonknights."

She shook her head. "Many also have conjurors to aid them. I... have discovered that I can wield some power when I hold the shard of the decanter."

"What kind of power?" Cyran's forehead tightened.

"Bone and earth magic."

Cyran's hand fell from the handle of his lance.

"I can help you," she said. "I could even try to be one of your archers."

His fear for her amplified. "No. Absolutely not. You have never even loosed a crossbow."

"I was afraid you may say that." She swung one leg over her saddle, and the storm dragon held its wings out, hovering on the air currents and drifting closer until the two dragons' wings touched. "I'm not leaving until you let me try one thing. Only then will I go."

Cyran gritted his teeth and cursed under his breath. "What is it that you want to do? I will not allow you to ride on my quarterdeck and practice with a crossbow for the first time while in the midst of war."

She climbed out of her saddle, scaled down her mount's neck, and crawled out onto its still wing. A rope was tied around her waist. She glanced back at the mage guiding the storm dragon and shot him a look, as if enforcing some prior agreement. Cyran scrutinized the man as well, etching the mage's face into his mind.

"Cartaya said that bone and earth magic is solely limited by the imagination, and I can only harness it with the shard," Jaslin said.

Cyran rose from his saddle and stood as he walked along Milluri's neck, feeling each movement his mount would make, seeing each of her scales in the other realm, knowing when and where to move and doing so with ease. He stepped onto the quarterdeck as Jaslin scrambled onto it and tugged on the rope attached to her harness, pulling out more slack. She smiled at Cyran as she rose in a hunched posture, one hand on the planks, as if afraid she would topple off at any moment. She shuffled for his stack of bolts.

"Even if you can put some additional power into one of my bolts, it probably won't last until I can loose it, *if* I can even loose it," he said. "I am alone, remember?"

"Can you not fly your dragon from the quarterdeck? At least until you're in close enough range for a tilt?"

Cyran's thoughts wavered. He recalled Eidelmere and their flight through the Evenmeres.

She placed her hand on one bolt. "If you could have a bolt carry any single ability or enchantment, what would you like it to be? I've heard others mention a bolt that will not be affected by wind and that can possibly even seek its target."

Cyran pondered that for a moment, recalling his difficulty with hitting his targets. "I would like to unseat the Dragon Queen and kill her in the process."

Jaslin glanced at his lance, and her eyes narrowed. "I'm not sure if such a thing would work. You probably won't encounter her first, and then my power would be used up and wasted on another."

Cyran looked at the legions steadily flying past them. "In that case, I wouldn't want to waste any magic by having it help me hit my enemy. One regular bolt would never bring down the shadow dragon. I would want something imbued with damaging effects so that if I have a chance to shoot down Shadowmar and can manage to hit her anywhere, she will fall from the sky. To have any hope of winning this war, the Dragon Queen's beast must be killed. And the sooner the better."

Jaslin's eyes closed, and her hand went to her waist. She pulled out the crystal shard, and a sense of foreboding filled Cyran. She muttered to herself as she squeezed the shaft of the bolt she had chosen. "What would kill a shadow dragon?"

Cyran paused as ideas somersaulted in his mind. "I don't know. She doesn't seem to have a weakness. Unless she can also be affected by her own venom..." Memories of Eidelmere being ensnared by those black veins that throbbed and reached for his neck spewed through Cyran's mind and hammered at his heart and its eternal wound. Eidelmere's soul was gone. It was only right that Shadowmar should lose hers as well.

Jaslin nodded. "I heard the same notion from a nyren." She fished out another item—a vial filled with black liquid that bubbled. She reached for the bolt's broadhead and tipped the vial, dribbling its contents over the striking surfaces. Amber light flared beneath her hand on the shaft and radiated outward.

Cyran gasped and stumbled back.

His sister placed the shard against the broadhead, and the fragment seemed to melt into place. Amber light glowed and then darkened as it enveloped the liquid and created a black halo of shadow that masked the bolt's tip.

Cyran's heart rattled in its bony cage. What was she doing?

Beads of sweat poured from her forehead before she retracted her hands from the bolt and fell back. Her eyes gaped as she stared. "There. I've done whatever I could, and I pray I have created something powerful enough. Hopefully this will be able to affect a shadow dragon. My power is gone now, along with the shard that came from Tamar's last gift to me. You have one chance to use it on whatever enemy you must."

Emotions lanced through Cyran's chest like lightning. "Jaslin... I..."

"I'll return to the castle and help care for Menoria as best I can, Brother." She stood on shaky legs and stared at him for a moment before rushing up and wrapping him in an embrace. "Promise me that I will see you again when this is over."

Cyran could barely nod in response, and she crawled back onto the storm dragon's wing and returned to her saddle. The mage's dark expression did not shift as the creature whipped around and streaked south, back to Dashtok.

The broadhead of the bolt his sister had held was still sheathed in darkness.

51

JASLIN ORENDAIN

Dawn's light rose in the east as the storm dragon Jaslin rode hurtled through curtains of rain and past the harbor and the ships that had set sail to meet the fleets of Murgare. Other vessels remained behind, in reserve to guard the city.

She watched the wind billow sails of red and gold and puff them up with a pride and boldness. Galvenstone would stand proud against the north, but did they have a chance of surviving?

They tore along, easily passing a galley far below, and a strange thought struck Jaslin. What could catch a sailing ship other than a dragon? Perhaps a faster ship, but it would have to have set sail around the same time. That would mean a dragon could have taken any prisoners who had been tattooed from a ship bound for the Southern Isles and brought them back to Galvenstone. And what kind of dragon would most likely be sent on such an errand? The fastest of their kind.

The storm dragon landed on the battlements, and Tallius dismounted. Jaslin followed him.

"Do you still demand your payment now?" she asked the mage.

Tallius folded his hands as if he were a kind soul considering her proposition before he formed a solemn expression and nodded.

"Then follow me." Jaslin paced away and entered the keep.

The mage shuffled along, trying to keep up. Jaslin strode down hallways and descended stairways until Tallius fell behind and she arrived at the throne room. The double doors were open, and kingsknights in gilded armor stood beside them.

Jaslin tentatively approached, and the kingsknights made no move to stop her, so she continued through the entrance. Inside the chamber, Igare paced around the throne that was adorned in red and gold dragon skin with wings extending out to each side. He rubbed at his cheek, his hair dangling over his face. His four councilmembers surrounded him, speaking in hushed voices. Jaken, Vysoria, and Princess Nistene sat in a corner, holding their own private conversation.

"Jaslin!" Menoria hurried from the dais, her skirts swishing along the runner as tears dribbled down her cheeks.

"I have returned safely, milady." Jaslin hugged her. "When I left my brother, the battles over the lake had not yet started."

Igare stared at Jaslin. "Handmaid?" Shock pulled his eyes wide. Riscott also looked surprised to see her.

"I am sorry that I was away for a bit." She bowed.

"You should take your lady to my chambers and wait out the war there," Igare said to Jaslin, his face pale, his hair disheveled. "My council and I will likely be needed for many hours to come, and I do not intend to rest until Galvenstone is victorious."

"Milord." Jaslin quickly bowed again. She grasped Menoria by the arm and turned to guide her out of the chamber.

"The safest place will be in the king's chambers," Menoria whispered and steered Jaslin in a different direction. "They are this way."

Jaslin paused, but Menoria led her toward the winged throne with a dragon skull above it and then to a side doorway.

"The king's chambers will be the last room in all of Dashtok and the Summerswept Keep to be breached," Menoria said.

They passed Riscott, Tiros, Cartaya, and Lisain, who whispered amongst themselves.

"If they punch through our legions and reach the city, we should take the king to Avleen and the Sivwood," Tiros said.

"Nonsense." Riscott shook his head. "If the worst happens here, then Somerlian would be our safest harbor. The Somerlians still have legions, and the Rorenlands's sand dragons have not yet sacked their city."

"I say that no matter what happens, we remain in the keep and face our enemies." Cartaya roamed about, white fire flaring in her palm.

Why had one of the most powerful conjurors in the kingdom not been sent out with one of the dragons?

Lisain bowed his head. "The Great Smith and the Siren look upon today as a day when all of Cimeren will shift. Any hints of the outcome cannot be foreseen. Not even by them."

Jaslin slowed her pace so she could keep listening, but Menoria tugged her through the doorway. Kingsknights as quiet and still as statues stood inside the hall beyond, and Menoria's two kingsknights took positions in alcoves, joining the others who watched over the king's chambers. Menoria ushered Jaslin past one doorway, making toward another at the end of the hall.

"What's in there?" Jaslin paused, pointing at the second doorway, which was even more elaborately decorated than the king's.

"Those are the queen's chambers." Menoria tried to pull her along, but Jaslin resisted. "That is where I'll reside after Igare and I are wed."

A chill crept up Jaslin's spine and ran across the nape of her neck. She had to see where Queen Hyceth's murder had occurred. "Is that where the former queen was assassinated?"

Menoria swallowed. "I believe that is what Igare said during that awkward first dinner when Riscott's mother asked everyone your prying question."

Jaslin ignored the memory and stepped closer to the door. "What was she doing at the time? And also just prior to her death?"

Menoria's pale expression of bemusement suggested she had no idea. "I did not ask Igare or anyone else that question. Maybe you should have, or you should have had Fileena do it."

Jaslin tried the handle, and the door swung inward. Faint torchlight flickered across the stones near the entryway, but towering windows extended up the far wall, and muted sunlight leaned into the room. Jaslin slipped inside.

"Igare asked us to wait in his chambers," Menoria said.

Jaslin studied the room—a bed, chairs, tables, lounging furniture, chests, tapestries, a hearth, and many windows. Jaslin roamed about the chamber and glanced behind the tapestries, but they only concealed unfaded stones. There were no passageways or other means of entering or exiting.

"We should go," Menoria chided her.

Jaslin searched about the hearth, which was large enough to step inside. The stone walls on each of the three sides of its interior were solid. The flue was choked with black soot. She examined the towering windows, most of which were stained glass and did not open. Only a couple smaller ones had latches. She popped one of these latches open and pushed the window outward.

Hobbling footsteps echoed out in the hallway. Tallius was still following her.

"What are you doing? Menoria asked.

"I owe that dragonmage a lot of coin." Jaslin searched the

sills of the windows that could open for evidence of tampering. She had seen such a thing in the lord's chambers at Nevergrace, after the new lord and previous lady were murdered. There had been fresh scratches in the rock around the window, as if someone had slipped a tool inside and released the latch. There was nothing here to indicate any kind of furtive entry. Nothing was forced, either. The windows overlooked the lake, and the walls of this chamber were some of those composing the outer keep. These walls plunged straight downward for many stories and then became sheer cliffs that descended to the lake.

How could an assassin have snuck into this chamber? Whoever had killed the lord and lady at Nevergrace had probably scaled the keep, but they had only climbed five stories and opened an aged and loose window. Even if these tattooed assassins could wield magic, unless they had spent an entire day or more climbing cliffs and walls without being seen, they would have had to slip past many kingsknights in Dashtok to get in here.

Jaslin checked the remainder of the windows as more shuffling footsteps echoed in the hall outside. She recalled taking the gold crown from Menoria, and her stomach cramped. "I owe the mage more coin than I will ever own."

"Are you searching for coin in here?" Menoria asked. "Do not fret over it. Once I am queen, I will be able to get you out of whatever predicament you've found yourself in, as long as you promise to never do it again."

The footsteps stopped outside the queen's chamber. Tallius glared at them from the entryway.

52

CYRAN ORENDAIN

A dawn as red as blood dripping across the horizon lingered.

The moon dragons blinked over sightless eyes and circled away from the front lines and to the rear. In the early light, the armor on the legions behind them glittered across the skies. Sunlight slowly crawled from east to west but was initially shaded by the forest before it rose and fell across the marshlands and then the surface of the rain-splattered lake. The waters lit up, contrasting with the murk of the marshes.

The easternmost of Murgare's fleets appeared under the light. Galleys and carracks sailed along, as well as larger ships where dragons rested in the center of their bulk. Some of the largest vessels could have been bigger than the entirety of Castle Dashtok. The sunlight angled outward, revealing row after row of ships that indeed stretched across the entire lake, more vessels than it seemed there were people in Galvenstone.

Cyran's blood turned to an icy froth as he waited out over the lake with the legions of Galvenstone under a drenching rain.

When the sunlight reached higher, the clouds of enemy dragons swarming in the skies emerged. Thousands of them whirled and circled about in a pre-battle dance of shrieks and acidic and fiery and icy breaths meant to strike terror into the hearts of the bravest men.

"Hold your positions!" Paltere lifted his sword high and slowed their more recent advance until his beast hovered in place.

The Belvenguard legions behind him formed a pyramid on its side, the wedge in front and the ranks sprawling up and downward and to either side in a precise battle formation honed by discipline, its walls primarily composed of gleaming gold and red and silver dragons.

"We shall remain here until they venture closer," Paltere said. "At that time, I will decide if we are to hold our defenses and shoot them down or charge."

Below, the fleets of Belvenguard eased past them, their sails only half unfurled. Their fleet numbered at less than a quarter of what Murgare had brought with them.

The throng of Murgare's dragons shrieked, and they swirled and dived and climbed and breathed with orchestrated choreography as they advanced. Some men and women of Belvenguard gasped or cried out and covered their ears, their faces pale.

Paltere sat resolute, a look of indignation playing across his features. The minutes the north took to approach seemed like hours and then days. Finally, Paltere again raised his sword above his head and swung it downward. "Charge!"

Belvenguard dragons roared in reply and beat their wings faster, spewing rivers of fire into the skies. The wall of their legions tore northward as Murgare barreled toward them.

Cyran angled himself low against Milluri's neck as they sailed, some of the faster dragons in the staggered forward ranks passing his thorn. He glanced back to Milluri's quarterdeck and the unmanned crossbow there. He longed for Vyk's and Ineri's company in this last battle. He would have to get close to an adversary to inflict any damage with his lance, and the more powerful and commanding the target, the more he would want to seek them out, which could be deadly for him and his mount. The Dragon Queen was who he wanted to confront more than any other, but unfortunately, she was probably moving against Galvenstone via Nevergrace.

He cursed and discarded his line of thinking, focusing on a bone dragon in the forefront of Murgare's hordes. The archers on the horrific beast's quarterdeck and in its turret sighted him. Ballistae arms thumped, and bolts screamed toward Milluri. The answer of more projectiles loosing from hundreds of dragons on both sides followed. Cyran imagined Milluri tucking in her wings and diving, and she did so, narrowly avoiding the bolts as they tore through the sky above.

"If you allowed me to fly of my own volition, I could react quicker," Milluri said in his mind.

A cloud of projectiles arced between the racing legions, those from Belvenguard lighting up the sky with an assortment of conjuror's flames and flaring ice or other colored magics. Thuds sounded as the bolts punched through leathery wings and impaled scale and bone and flesh on both sides. Other projectiles buried into quarterdecks with sharp cracks.

Dragons dropped from the skies in droves, spiraling downward on limp or cockeyed wings, smacking into the water far below and spewing geysers from the lake. Holes emerged in Belvenguard's formation but, for now, were quickly filled.

Cyran banked Milluri in a tight arc and came at the bone dragon as he poised his lance for a strike and leaned against his guard's shield. Both weapon and shield flared with the green light of the forest dragon. The guard on the bone dragon shifted, shoving his lance around to meet Cyran's charge, his armor creaking as he braced against his shield.

Milluri angled her wings slightly in response to Cyran's

thoughts, and she quickly rose on an air current and then plummeted. Cyran already had his lanced positioned for the angle he foresaw while the enemy guard panicked and attempted to adjust. The tip of Cyran's lance clashed with the upper portion of the guard's shield, skipped off, and rammed the assailant in the helm.

Dragonsteel folded inward and released a metallic crunch that blasted Cyran's ears. Leather snapped, and the guard launched from his seat and flew away. Behind the guard's saddle, a mage looked up with gaping eyes.

The bone and thorn smashed into each other with a mad flailing of wings and screeches, Milluri coming down on their much larger opponent. Teeth and talons flashed and buried into scales. Blood flowed. Cyran ripped Eidelmere's Flame from its sheath and, in a swift strike, severed the mage's head from his body. Cyran's blade easily cleaved through its target and continued on, hewing the bony scales and flesh of the beast beneath.

The mage's head dropped like a stone, his body still seated in his saddle while the bone dragon roared, shook its neck, and flew off, retreating into the north and taking its archers with it.

"I can make more accurate strikes when I steer," Cyran muttered.

The next dragon was already in Cyran's face, the guard's lance aiming for him, and he sent Milluri into a twirling dive, narrowly avoiding the blow. More bolts buzzed past as Cyran righted himself.

Paltere, on his mighty sun dragon, unseated a mage on a blood dragon, hurling the man into a crystal dragon. The mage's bones crunched on impact. The dragonknight's archers loosed, impaling an ice dragon with three of their magically flaming bolts. A mist dragon exploded from an obscuring fog, shrieking and descending upon a Belvenguard rose dragon, tearing at the rose with teeth and claws as their archers attempted to reload.

The mist snatched up an archer on the rose in its jaws, tearing the man from the quarterdeck and flinging him away as the rose breathed a puff of blinding light.

Leather snapped as the mist tore at the quarterdeck and snaked its long neck beneath the rose to bite the archer in the lower turret in half. The quarterdeck slipped sideways and tilted on the rose's back. The guard and mage shouted as their quarterdeck sat poised for a moment on their dragon and then tilted and plummeted, flipped end over end.

Cyran wheeled Milluri about and drove at the mist, his lance ready. He skewered the beast in the side of its neck, and it flung its head back, blood dripping from its teeth as it expelled its foggy breath overhead. The mist dragon wrenched away from Cyran's lance just before a barrage of flaming bolts slammed into its chest. The beast went still and fell from the sky.

A mass from Belvenguard's legions dived down toward the lake's surface and Murgare's advancing fleets, their archers lighting bolts with typical fire while conjurors placed glowing clouds of blue or violet or white over other broadheads. A stone dragon's trebuchets loosed, hurling boulders at the north's ships. The heavy projectiles crashed through hulls and sent two halves of a galley spinning away before they started sinking. Flaming bolts buried into more ships, lighting them ablaze.

Belvenguard's fleets advanced, archers on those vessels also loosing droves of fiery bolts at their adversaries on the water. Carracks rammed into galleys, and planks and beams crunched and flew out over the lake along with a handful of sailors.

Bubbles erupted, and Belvenguard lake dragons—looking like nothing more than small stones on the water—surfaced with their concealed mages and guard, who had disguised their protruding heads as birds. The beasts' multiple long necks writhed below many snapping heads. They bit into Murgare's ships and flung away masts and men, capsizing and sinking many of the north's vessels. Hundreds of Belvenguard soldiers on ships cheered, and for a moment, it appeared that Cyran's people would hold their own on the water.

Cyran steeled himself, preparing to help defend against a similar wave of Murgare's dragons that would retaliate and aim for Belvenguard's fleets, but none of Murgare's legions dived toward the water. They maintained their chaotic attacks in the skies. Cyran had Milluri climb back up into the thick of battle while wondering what trap Murgare had waiting below. They had to have something else planned if they did not need at least some of their legions to destroy the fleets.

A deep roar sounded, and Cyran slowed Milluri's flight. Below, a titanic wave emerged in the gap between most of the northern and southern fleets as Belvenguard lake dragons persisted in decimating Murgare vessels. The wave rushed south, battering into Igare's ships. The massive form of a beast surfaced, its back blue and humped and scaled. It rammed into the first row of Belvenguard's fleet, tossing vessels aside like sticks and capsizing most. Then it continued its advance, plowing through more ships and not even flinching when bolts struck its humps. The fleets of Murgare rallied behind the beast as enemy soldiers bellowed and fully raised their sails, the wind pushing them toward Galvenstone.

"Their fleets are advancing on the capital!" Cyran pointed downward, but no one seemed to hear him amidst the din.

Milluri dived.

53

JASLIN ORENDAIN

"You will not lose me until you have settled your debt, handmaid." Tallius slowly shuffled into the chamber toward Jaslin and Menoria.

"I did not intend to lose you." Jaslin smoothed her tunic, feigning boldness. "You simply fell behind. I cannot pay you until we return to my lady's chambers. I keep my coin there, but I will retrieve it and return at once so you don't have to hobble the length of this castle."

Menoria scrutinized her, suspicion narrowing her eyes.

Jaslin cast her a quick wink and whispered, "I must keep him here and draw another to somewhere private."

Menoria swallowed, and her hands trembled. She faced the mage and spoke loudly. "I will accompany my handmaid and make sure she returns immediately after fetching her coin and that she pays you what you are owed."

Jaslin forced a smile and strode past Menoria, exiting the chamber and a quietly cursing Tallius. They passed the kingsknights—who made no move to follow Menoria now and remained waiting outside the king's chambers. The kingsknights must not have seen Tallius or anyone in these chambers as a threat. Jaslin reentered the throne room.

After the king and the council's conversation paused and Igare paced away, Jaslin folded her hands and asked, "Your Grace?"

Igare glanced up, an eyebrow raised.

"I apologize, but the lady is distressed," Jaslin said. "I have found that a good story settles her more than anything. If you'll allow it, I'd like to read to her until she either falls asleep or this war is over."

Igare nodded. "A wise decision."

Jaslin bowed her head, stepped closer to the councilmembers, and asked them, "Do the archives of Dashtok hold any stories or only records?"

Lisain scratched his scalp. "There is only one set of chambers for scrolls and books. Most things stored in there are records, but I think there are some stories."

Jaslin studied the three young nobles across the way. Were the queens of Murgare and Belvenguard killed because of one or more of them? An assassin, even a master assassin—and according to the slaver at the Southern Isles, those men were no such thing—would be hard-pressed to sneak their way into well-guarded chambers in the most secure castle in the kingdom. And the assassins would have had to do it not only once but twice, probably without scaling the cliffs and castle walls and coming in through one of the queen's windows. At least one had also supposedly used magic to aid them, but without a tongue, they could not speak and thus could not use bone and earth magic.

The councilmembers were studying Jaslin closely now, and she asked, "Are there any old legends of valor and courage you would recommend we read to give us hope?"

Cartaya's forehead wrinkled. "Old histories are kept in the

minds of the nyrens or at the citadel in the south, so do not waste time searching for true tales of valor. Stay in the east wing if you want to find a fable. The western section is all records."

"Records?" Jaslin hoped she said the word with just the right amount of interest—not too much, which could make it seem like she wanted them to know she was interested in such documents, but not too little that the suspicions of these four were not raised. She quickly bowed again and hurried away toward the exit, as if her life depended on finding the archives. Menoria caught up with her and took her arm.

"What are you attempting to do?" Menoria asked. "You are acting very strange."

"I want to tell you my suspicions," Jaslin said, "but if I am wrong, I fear the consequences. I must be certain first, or you will never believe me."

Menoria released a quiet gasp. "Does this all have to do with a potential traitor in the king's council? What your brother talked about with his squire friends?"

Jaslin bit her lip and slowly nodded. "Igare gave us permission—so the soldiers and knights won't stop us—but we must see if one or more of those four tries to intervene." She glanced over her shoulder. All four of the councilmembers were watching them depart, and Lisain whispered something to Cartaya. Tiros's hand trembled as he stroked his beard. Riscott sneered.

"Let us hurry and find stories that will last us through all the bitter days of this war," Menoria said loudly and tugged Jaslin along, leading her out of the throne room, through hallways, and down staircases until they arrived at the archives.

The chamber's twin doors looked as old as the keep itself. Their wood was cracked and splitting. Menoria heaved, and one door groaned and creaked as it grated inward. The lady stepped inside and headed east before Jaslin pulled away.

"If you are truly interested, find all the stories you can," Jaslin said, "but I will be searching the records and could use your help."

Menoria glanced back at the doorway and then to the other wing before nodding. Jaslin rushed off, and the lady waited for only a moment before following her. They paced between stacks of parchments and books.

"What are we looking for?" Menoria asked.

"Recent records showing any rapists, murderers, and thieves sent from Belvenguard to the Rorenlands." The assassin who had attacked Jaslin was not dark-skinned enough to be from the Rorenlands.

The walls around them boomed, and Menoria cried out and glanced nervously about. "What was that?"

"The dragons of Murgare are here." Jaslin swallowed her fear and searched the rows of tomes before someone's footsteps echoed in the hall and then paused before entering the archives. Jaslin's skin tingled with apprehension. The traitor might have come to stop her, or Tallius could have trailed them, seeking more than coin.

"This is the section for court convictions." Menoria pointed a shaky finger at an entire row of shelves that extended into the darkness.

Jaslin pried a lamp from its wall mount and scanned the tomes, which appeared to be sorted by timeframes. She ran down the aisle, holding her lamp aloft and shining its light over the works until she came upon books with recent dates pressed into their spines. She pulled down several and laid them out on the floor as Menoria joined her. Together, they thumbed through pages and flung books aside that did not contain what they were searching for.

"Here!" Menoria slid a book in front of Jaslin and pointed at the names of convicted villains.

Jaslin leaned closer, searching for dates and what each villain's crime was. She turned back a page. There, she found a list of names and the words 'Southern Isles' beside them. The dates were within the last few months. She lifted her tunic and pulled the crumpled pages of the isle's records from her waist, unrolling them and flattening them out as the stones around them banged again. She scanned the names. Nineteen men from Belvenguard had arrived at the Southern Isles within the past month. She found their same names in the tome on the floor. Then she paused with fear as a jolt of realization shot through her. Twenty-one men had been sent from Belvenguard. Only nineteen had arrived at the isles. The missing two had the same listing for their conviction—thief guild member and footman.

A thunderous clap rattled the walls, and the approaching footsteps stopped at the aisle they were in. A silhouette stood watching them. "There are no stories in this section." Riscott's voice carried as he advanced and repeatedly banged a fist against the shelving.

Jaslin's heart leapt into her throat, and her pulse pounded in her ears as she frantically turned more pages. "I need to confirm something before he stops us."

Riscott's slapping footsteps neared as Jaslin flipped back to the dates preceding Queen Hyceth's death. Her hand trembled when she found the timeframe and what she sought. Two additional men had not arrived in the isles, even though they had been sent with a previous shipment of prisoners. The words 'thief guild member and footman' were also written next to their names.

At least four thieves who were part of a guild had disappeared from the Rorenlands's cargo. Then they reappeared as assassins in Belvenguard. One attacked her, and two of them killed queens.

54

SIRRA BRACKENGLAVE

Shadowmar streaked for the walls of Galvenstone under a downpour. The outer gates were closed and sealed as dawn rose behind Sirra. Horns blasted, and dragons swarmed over the city, many of them hovering beyond the eastern walls.

The beacons had not been lit, and yet someone still knew that Sirra and her legion were coming by way of Nevergrace. She gritted her teeth and adjusted her helm with an open palm. So many more would have to die this way, but Igare Dragonblade was there in the Summerswept Keep. He was the reason for the entire war.

Sirra slowed Shadowmar's flight, allowing the others who had completed the journey with her to catch up.

"Galvenstone knows we're coming from the east," Yenthor said to the guard on a mist dragon as the beast reached them and slowed its pace.

"Then my mount's breath will not aid us much," the mage behind the guard replied.

Two feral ice dragons with Smoke Breather guard and archers stalled and flapped alongside them.

"Live with wonder." Sirra drew her sword, and black flames crackled as they ran up its length.

"Die before you've lost it all," Zaldica and Yenthor muttered in unison along with the others.

"Strike at the heart of the Dread King." Sirra pointed with her sword, and Shadowmar reared back and flapped harder, propelling them onward. The others trailed her.

Rivers of gold and silver fire blasted under the pale light of dawn as the dragons patrolling around Galvenstone bellowed and descended toward Sirra and her small legion. Yenthor's crossbow's arms thumped and vibrated, the loaded bolt screaming away and puncturing a silver dragon's chest. The enemy beast roared, spewing more fire, and it plummeted, crashing onto the walls of Galvenstone.

Shadowmar soared higher to meet the incoming dragons. Ballistae on the city's walls swiveled about and loosed projectiles the size of lances. Sirra weaved her mount around the bolts as they sailed closer to the capital.

A golden sun dragon dived at Sirra, and she angled her lance upward as the beast flexed its neck, which exposed its guard and his poised weapon. Sirra bobbed Shadowmar to the side, and the guard's lance skipped off her shield, the impact barely carrying through to her armor. Her weapon flashed black and clashed with the guard's shield, ramming it in the center and collapsing dragon-steel in upon itself. The blow threw the guard back in his saddle, bending him over backward at the waist, snapping his spine.

Shadowmar flapped and rose, lunging upward, and Sirra skewered the newly exposed mage. The sun dragon roared and shook, flinging away the bodies of the guard and mage while tearing at the harnesses of the quarterdeck and turret and flying away.

Sirra turned to the next assailant—a rose dragon that

blasted a gush of blinding light. Sirra's eyes clamped shut, but she knew the rose would not be affected and would fly through the light and use their moment of weakness to attack. Zaldica shouted in fear and frustration as her bolt flew into the starlight.

Sirra summoned the power of the dragon realm. "*Aylión.*" In her mind, she instantly saw where the rose dragon would dart through the light. She angled her lance to meet its charge, her eyes still closed.

The rose dragon shot forward, its jaws gaping, its teeth bared as the light dimmed. Sirra's lance skewered it, ramming through its mouth and erupting from the back of its head. The dragon's archers blinked, trying to dispel the blinding light as Shadowmar grabbed the dead dragon in her talons and ripped the dragon's neck from its body before allowing both to fall to the earth.

They soared higher and closer to the outer walls, weaving past incoming dragons as bolts flew and lances clashed.

Below, people ran frantically about in the streets of the multitiered city, screaming and pointing. Shadowmar's jaws gaped, and black fire erupted from her throat, blasting at the walls and ballistae as more bolts tore through the air.

The projectiles that raced toward them were partially consumed by her fire, and the wooden frames of the ballistae were demolished instantly. The metal arms of the weapons scorched and sagged, and their steel braces collapsed. Ice breath from the Smoke Breathers' mounts followed, dashing against the walls and freezing soldiers and crossbows in place. Fire and mist and bursts of crystal shards answered, each beast trading places with the next while swooping down past the other in the trained battle formation of the *kiölen*.

Catapults hurled boulders at them and took out an amethyst dragon by crushing its wing. One of Galvenstone's massive bolts buried into a fire dragon's shoulder. The dragon veered and spun about, releasing a flurry of angry flames before spiraling downward.

Sirra drove Shadowmar around the circle of walls, her mount gushing her light-absorbing fire. In the distance, the fleets of Murgare were racing closer, the massive whale dragon at their head smashing through the defending vessels.

The legions of Belvenguard that swarmed out over the lake turned about and winged their way back toward their city and Murgare's whale dragon and ships, Murgare's endless legions pursuing them. One dragon with only a single rider raced out in front of all the others, heading for the whale dragon, and Sirra's heart twisted with bitter anger.

The young dragonknight of Belvenguard.

She veered northward, the Smoke Breathers following her, their vicious dragons tearing into their enemies.

"Focus on the city." Sirra motioned for the rest of her legion to direct its attacks at Dashtok and the Summerswept Keep. "I will return shortly."

She continued north, planning to stop the dragonknight from interfering with the whale dragon and to also trap Belvenguard's legions between her and the rest of Murgare's ranks. Then the whale dragon could batter the foundations of the city, and all of Galvenstone would crumble.

55

CYRAN ORENDAIN

Murgare's enormous beast left a trail through the water, its wake parting behind it like twin tidal waves. Ships in the creature's path listed and sank, the monster smashing into their hulls from below. The Belvenguard vessels farther away were battered by its wake, which capsized many.

How can anyone hope to stop this thing? Cyran used his link with Milluri in the other realm and drove her faster.

A massive black beast dropped from the sky ahead, coming from Galvenstone. Cyran's heart fell into his guts as soon as he recognized the one-eyed monster of a dragon—Shadowmar. Her having come from Galvenstone did not bode well.

Shadowmar swooped down toward him, the beast's talons extended as if she meant to scoop him up like an eagle did with a rodent. Cyran rolled Milluri to the side, avoiding the claws, and Shadowmar hovered above, tilting her head downward until the Dragon Queen glared at Cyran through her spiked helm. Sirra's archers in the turret and those on the quarterdeck kept their bolts trained in his direction. He was at a serious disadvantage.

"I have watched you go down on two dragons already." The

Dragon Queen's voice was calm and collected as it projected across the distance, and her mount drifted closer through the pounding rain. "Do not make it a third time, or I fear it will be your last."

Cyran kept his eye on the beast's talons and jaws, which dripped with blood and precipitation, as he had Milluri climb to the side and to an altitude even with Shadowmar, his fury and hate blazing in his chest. "I was the one who knocked you out of the sky and left you for dead the last time we met in battle, remember? I'm sure that hasn't happened too many other times in the past centuries."

If Sirra scowled or grimaced, Cyran could not tell.

"You can still turn your fleets and legions around." Cyran sat taller in his saddle. "All of Cimeren does not have to burn. There is still time, although not much."

"It is not in my power to do so. The people of the north seek revenge for their murdered king, as well as for many other atrocities."

"It is Murgare's atrocities that must be atoned for and remedied."

The Dragon Queen slowly shook her head. In an instantaneous burst of speed, the shadow dragon lunged forward. Sirra's lance swiveled and rammed into Milluri as Cyran barely managed to spin his mount to the side and raise his own weapon. The length of the queen's lance struck the thorn dragon's head and neck, knocking her aside and twisting her around. Cyran cursed as he whipped his lance back at his attacker, and its length hit the side of Shadowmar's neck but did not seem to deal much damage.

Shadowmar's wings stretched out, the curling claws at the tips of her extremities latching on to one of Milluri's wings and tearing gashes through her leathery segments. Then Shadowmar tilted backward and, with the motion of a disc thrower, heaved Milluri in a tight circle. Cyran's heart shot into his throat, and the shadow dragon launched Milluri away.

They plummeted like a stone bound to a single feather, dropping quickly around one wing that tried to flap. The waving surface of the lake rose up in seconds, splaying out around them. Cyran struggled to remain in his seat as he reached into the other realm. Milluri's fear and pain hit him like a punch to the gut. He stroked the fiber of her true name, her soul, passing soothing thoughts and feelings into her. *"Even if we die today, we will not be lost. We still have the* neblír."

Milluri's fear ebbed a little, only lashing out in broken waves. Anger and determination smoldered and bloomed, countering her other emotions. Her shredded wing beat at the sky as the lake's surface neared. The tatters of two segments whipped in the wind, but the remaining segments billowed, and the force of their halting descent nearly threw Cyran over her head. They leveled out in a bracing arc, and Milluri glided over the lake and shrieked.

Cyran swallowed and regripped his lance's hilt. His mount's wing was damaged, but she could still fly. If all of Cimeren was to burn when this war was over, they could not leave to lick their wounds.

High above, the Dragon Queen flew headlong into the fray, directly into the midst of Belvenguard's legions. She unseated a guard as her archers dropped an approaching silver dragon with four bolts. Then she quickly realigned her lance as her steed wheeled around, and her weapon struck the mage on the dragon she was targeting, catapulting the mage from her position against her dragon's scales. Her archers shot three more bolts into an amber dragon, who spewed amber sludge into the air before plunging downward.

Above them, clouds of mist roamed, and fire and ice and mist and crystal and bone and blood dragons swooped down upon the legions of Belvenguard, clawing and biting, their riders loosing bolts or puncturing flesh with lances. A cave dragon more massive than any beast in the sky emerged and trailed Shadowmar, a legion of dwarves on the beast's back loosing volleys of bolts as well as boulders from twin trebuchets. Both types of projectiles hammered into Belvenguard's legions and killed far too many.

A dozen dragons from Galvenstone tried to face the Dragon Queen, but her beast and archers and her lance dropped them or unseated their mage and guard or buried bolts into scaly hides one after another. Sun and rose and cloud dragons behind the fallen twelve veered around her, trying to flee the carnage and return to protect the city.

"We must *stop her this time, or Belvenguard will fall,*" Cyran said only through the other realm.

"*I cannot contend with that beast, and you cannot contend with her.*"

Cyran clenched his jaw as they swooped upward and soared as fast as they could. He glanced at the ships of the north streaking toward the city, the massive creature beneath the waves at their forefront. "*I do not see how anything other than a hundred ballistae projectiles could stop that monster in the lake. We have to trust that the defenses on the walls of the city will bring it down.*"

As he watched, the multiple heads of legions of lake dragons rose in the southern bay, their necks writhing about as their jaws tore into Murgare ships and flung wreckage about. The beasts avoided Murgare's massive dragon at the forefront but swung in and attacked the ships behind it. The remaining mass of the south's fleets bobbed near the shoreline of the city. Their sails spiked with wind as they attempted to gather speed and move out of the path of the beast beneath the surface.

Catapult ballistae from Murgare's fleets launched flaming

rounds and boulders in towering arcs that seemed to travel a league before a few smashed into the walls of Galvenstone, spraying fragments and rubble into the air. Ballistae on the walls returned projectiles but had to be careful to avoid their own ships while concentrating on the beast racing toward them.

Cyran cursed as Milluri soared along at a slower rate than before her wing was torn.

Fire and ice dragons plunged downward and unleashed their breaths upon Belvenguard ships, roasting wood and soldiers or locking them in ice. Boulders from catapults on both the northern and southern ships launched at each other, and those from Galvenstone also targeted the approaching beast in the water.

The Dragon Queen suddenly dived from above and joined her attacking legions. Shadowmar spewed black fire across a mass of fleeing Belvenguard ships, making them burn like phantoms. The shadow dragon's talons gripped one of the heads of a lake dragon and ripped it from its neck. Sirra's lance impaled another head. Her archers battered a different lake dragon with bolts.

Fuck. "We *have to* knock her out of the sky!"

"We cannot."

"I did so before."

"How?"

"Because I..." His thoughts turned and revealed themselves before sinking in his mind. "Because she never expected me to be immune to her magic from the other realm. She had probably not encountered that before, and it took her by surprise."

"Then it will not work again. You've seen how fast that beast of hers moves. I cannot match it, even if you could match her skill with the lance. Unless you wield some great power of your own, we cannot accomplish such a task." Milluri fell silent for a moment as they skimmed above the lake, streaking as fast as they could toward the moving battle. "And even if you held such power, the Dragon Queen would probably be immune to yours."

Rage brewed and erupted in Cyran's chest. "The Assassin's head on a pike! I could not grasp any of what she was trying to teach me, anyway. Eidelmere, where..." He stopped cold, his hand on his sword's hilt, on Eidelmere's Flame. *Eidelmere.* Memories stormed through his mind. He glanced back at his empty quarterdeck, his gaze drawn to the stack of bolts there. "This is what Eidelmere wanted." One bolt's broadhead was covered in black shadow. *Jaslin.*

Cyran stood in his saddle and turned around, feeling the other realm all around him, every beat of Milluri's wings and shift of her scale. He knew where and how she would move at least as well as he knew the movements of his own body, and he could imagine and control everything she did. He stared at the carnage before them and directed his mount toward Shadowmar, who danced like a dragon fae among so many other much smaller creatures.

Cyran stepped along Milluri's neck, bracing against the wind, his tunic whipping around him. And he marched along her spines for the quarterdeck.

56

JASLIN ORENDAIN

"What are you two doing?" Riscott strode closer to Jaslin and Menoria, his sneer speckled with shadows and firelight.

A deafening boom made Jaslin's ears ring and her skull throb. A row of books toppled from a shelf nearby, and they crashed onto and splayed out across the floor. Dragons roared and shrieked just beyond the stone walls of the archives. The crackle of fiery breaths followed.

"We should return to the king's chambers at once," Menoria said, but Jaslin shook her head.

Riscott did not stop his advance. "I fear you seek something that the council may want to know you are interested in." He raised a long dagger over his shoulder as if preparing to strike.

Menoria screamed and scooted away. Jaslin lunged at the orator. She hit him in the chest and sent him sprawling backward as she sailed with him. Riscott's back thudded against the floor, his wind blasting from his lungs as he groaned. His dagger skidded off into the shadows as Jaslin landed on top of him.

Jaslin grabbed him by the neck and squeezed, choking him.

"Get off me!" he tried to yell through a constricted throat while grasping at her clenching hands.

"You are the king's orator." Jaslin squeezed harder. "You know all of Igare's and Galvenstone's swiftest messengers. In the past, you have asked one or more of them, maybe even Tallius, to fly from the castle and track down the Rorenlands's slave ship, haven't you?"

Riscott's eyes bulged as he regarded her and altered his defense, releasing one of her fingers that he had loosened from his neck before attempting to jab his fingertips into her face and eyes. "You don't know anything."

Jaslin leaned away from his flailing attempts and turned her head to the side.

"What are you doing?" Menoria grabbed Jaslin by the shoulder and shook her. "You're hurting him."

"He knows who the traitor is." Jaslin's fingers cinched down tighter on the orator's flesh, causing his eyes to protrude from their sockets.

"I don't—don't know of any traitor." Riscott snarled. "Besides Garmeen of Nevergrace."

"That may be true, if there is no traitor," Jaslin said, "but it would mean that something else even darker is happening. *Someone* ordered a messenger to bring back a few of those who were convicted and were being shipped to the Southern Isles, those able-bodied and skilled prisoners who could at least pull off the appearance of being assassins, even if they did not truly possess such murderous expertise. Prisoners who were once footmen in a thieves' guild."

A deep purple hue flushed across the orator's cheeks. "You cannot make me talk. Only the king himself can do that." His fingers caught a lock of her dangling hair, and he snatched it up, yanking as hard as he could.

Jaslin winced as her scalp lit up with pain, and her grip loosened. "Tell me, damn it!" She muttered something under her breath.

Menoria tugged on her shoulder again. "Jaslin, stop this! I command you."

Riscott jerked on her lock of hair again, and Jaslin cried out, losing her grip on his flesh. Riscott smirked and used her hair for leverage, pulling her head off to one side while attempting to scoot away from her and sit up.

Amber light flared beneath Jaslin's fingers and wreathed the orator's neck. Jaslin and Riscott both gasped. She pulled her hands back in surprise before quickly recovering and grabbing him by the throat again. The orator shrieked and writhed beneath her. She expected Riscott to burn like the assassin, but it seemed that she now had more control over her magic.

"Jaslin!" Menoria stumbled away.

I do not need the shard to control bone and earth magic... but I must still utter an appropriate word.

"You lied!" Riscott wailed. "Tallius told us you could not command magic without your shard."

Jaslin clenched her fingers, and her magical fire flared, growing taller and hotter, although not yet hot enough to sear his flesh. "Someone ordered a swift storm dragon to overtake the slaver ships from the Rorenlands—those vessels that picked up convicted men from Belvenguard—didn't they? It is the only feasible way that people bearing those tattoos would have never arrived in the Southern Isles *and* could have reappeared here in Galvenstone."

"Yes!" Riscott screamed. "A dragon brought a couple men back each time."

"Who ordered this errand?"

"Me."

Jaslin's flames settled as she leaned back on the orator's chest, thinking. Riscott seemed the most likely one of the councilmembers to be loathsome, but he didn't fit this mold. "It would never have been your idea to have Queen Hyceth killed.

That would only further obstruct Jaken's—your son's—rise to the throne. Having the queen killed ensured that Igare would remarry and could then have a son of his own."

Riscott bounced his hips and kicked, but Jaslin latched on tighter, her magical flames ensnaring him and reddening his skin.

"No matter how much I want to believe it, *you* are not the evil plaguing Belvenguard after all," Jaslin said. "Tallius told me that he overheard Jaken and Princess Nistene discussing something that they had probably discussed before. He said Jaken claimed that he would only wed the princess if the king were dead and he could then rise to the throne of Belvenguard."

"What are you trying to say?" Menoria cringed, and the walls rattled around them. "That Jaken wants to kill the king?"

"No. That the assassin didn't even attempt to kill the king." Jaslin kept her grip tight on Riscott, and her flames did not weaken. "Only the queen. Two queens, actually. Then, while trying to find answers, like the guard of old, I kept asking myself who in the council would benefit from this and why."

"Not Riscott?" Menoria asked.

Jaslin shook her head. "Clearly not. But I could not understand how it would help Lisain or Tiros either."

"Then Cartaya?" Menoria stepped closer and covered her open mouth.

Jaslin shrugged. "If she wanted to marry Igare, then it is possible that she had the queen murdered, but even though she appears young, I have a feeling she is not. I think most people realize this. Igare would not wish to marry an older woman whose womb is likely barren. Cartaya would not expect him to even consider her, and Vysoria—her daughter—is also younger than you and not a lady of any land. Both Cartaya and Vysoria would be unable to give Igare a noble son. Not like you could." She stared straight into Menoria's eyes.

Menoria flinched and retreated a step. "I had not... I could not have even fathomed such a thing—to kill my queen."

"I am not accusing you of anything other than being of the age and title to bear royal children."

Menoria's hand fell limp with relief and settled against her side as Riscott continued to gasp but remained still, fearfully watching the amber fire around his neck and Jaslin's hands.

"Then the princess has the motive," Menoria said. "So she could have Jaken."

"Do you think Nistene has any real power to order such things as assassinations?"

Menoria pursed her lips. "No. And Vysoria? She would not have much to gain if she would not become the king's wife. Who else is there with enough power to command such a thing? This all seems farfetched, like something in one of your stories."

"Not if it is so ingrained in a portion of the culture and kingdom that it is no longer considered abhorrent or intolerable by the council, who must have known." Jaslin's eyes closed briefly. "The king and his council have their informants. At some point, they would have learned of the same thing that Tallius heard Nistene and Jaken discussing."

"Then one of them would want to make sure the king had a male heir?" Menoria slumped to her knees. "So they had the former queen murdered?"

Jaslin slowly nodded as pieces of the events became solidified in her mind, but she could not voice her thoughts now. They were too gruesome. Menoria had to arrive at the same conclusion and say the words. "And the assassins had their tongues cut out so they could not speak to anyone who apprehended them. They would take all the blame without any opportunity to defend themselves. The problem was that they could not utter a word and thus could not perform bone and earth magic. The idea of them using magic to sneak into the castle, and the claim of finding one of them magically hovering and hiding in the rafters, was a mistake. A lie. My brother also realized this."

"Are you saying that Tallius is behind all of it?" Menoria crawled closer still.

Jaslin shook her head. "And Riscott, Lisain, Tiros, and Cartaya would have nothing to gain." Her grip on Riscott's neck tightened further still, and she clenched at the cords in his throat as her warm fire ran across his face. She glared down at the orator. "It was *him,* wasn't it?"

Riscott kicked in an attempt to unseat her. "We are all going to die today in this war."

"Tell me who gave the order for a storm dragon to retrieve the would-be assassins!" Jaslin snapped.

"Igare." Riscott clamped his eyes shut. "It was the king himself."

Menoria gasped and swooned as her jaw worked, but no words escaped her lips.

The light of Jaslin's fire flared to a blinding luminescence. "Igare did not want Jaken to wed his daughter or have reason to try to kill his king. After Igare learned of Jaken's ambitions and true desires, he probably despised the young man. So Igare had his own queen assassinated so he could one day soon take Menoria into his marriage bed in hopes that she would give him the son he never had."

Riscott's eyes ran wild with blind terror as his tongue fumbled to speak. "I-it is true. All of it."

Jaslin leaned over to stare directly into the orator's eyes. "Then there is no supposed traitor in the council after all. Igare's councilmembers, and probably a few of the kingsknights and at least one dragonmage, knew of all this and are still undyingly loyal to *him*. The murderer of the queen was only a secret kept from the masses. The people needed to hear a lie."

Riscott swallowed and nodded.

Jaslin's mind ran wild. "And why did those thieves return to Galvenstone?"

"They were made promises—that their destitute families would be well cared for in their absence, if they obliged the king's wishes. Several were given a choice to either go on to the Southern Isles or return to Belvenguard, take up a cause, and be put out of their misery. The men we took willingly allowed the kingsknights to cut out their tongues."

Jaslin's hands trembled on the orator's throat as she slowly released him. "Then these thieves knew, or at least expected, what kind of accusations they would face, and that they would die."

Jaslin's mind spun. That would mean that the assassin who came for her was not sent by Keliam after all, but rather by Igare or his council, even before she had traveled to the Southern Isles seeking answers. That was why the king and Riscott had been so surprised to see her return, not because she had been away for a while. She had not noticed the other councilmembers looking as shocked. Cartaya and Tiros had seen her after the assassin attacked her, although the assassin could have been trailing her for days, and no one might have known when or where she was supposed to be killed. The king and his council probably wanted to get rid of her after she discovered the shadow dragon poison being smuggled into the city, poison the watch at the wharf had taken no interest in. She had had to force two kingsknights to witness the illicit poison in front of many people in order for someone to take action. The king and his council, not some thieves' guild, must have been behind all of that and also what Keliam was doing.

The ceiling bucked overhead, as if a massive dragon had taken roost there.

Jaslin shuddered with realization and sheer horror. "And why did they kill the first queen?" she shouted over the tumult.

Riscott swallowed a dry lump. "For the same reason that one of our king's real assassins assisted in the murder of the Dread King Restebarge back when Igare believed he had the full support of all his cities' legions, as well as the legions from all the cities in the Weltermores and the Rorenlands—to start a war with our sworn enemy. So we could kill them all."

"Then we fight on the side of the true dread king..."

57

CYRAN ORENDAIN

Cyran wrapped his fingers around the tiller of the mounted crossbow and slid a harness up his legs before belting it around his waist. Milluri soared along with her tattered wing. After latching the harness to the crossbow's frame, Cyran swiveled about, getting a feeling for the ballista and its mechanism's movement within the quarterdeck.

His mind roamed into the other realm, and he felt himself and Milluri there as if they were one being. The other realm again melded with his, and glowing threads of fibers weaved about wherever there were dragons, and these threads glistened under the deluge from the sky sea. Whatever he thought, Milluri would do—dive, climb, swoop sideways or at an angle.

"I could fly more freely and easily if you did not control my every movement," the dragon said in his mind.

Ahead, the fray of battling dragons, their deafening cries, bolts launching from quarterdecks and turrets, and occasional blasts of breath battered the sky over the lake just north of Galvenstone. The Dragon Queen unseated another guard and mage on a topaz and then a massive sun dragon, and Shadowmar ripped off half of the sun dragon's wing with her teeth.

Cyran suppressed a shudder of horror at the sight and grabbed the bolt Jaslin had melted her shard into. Swirling black mist encased its broadhead. Shadowmar had to be stopped, or Belvenguard would surely fall. He took over Milluri's flight and veered her upward, toward the fray and the shadow dragon, and her fear and determination laced the *neblír*.

"We must do this," Cyran said to his mount. "Afterward, I will set you free and never call you back."

A sense of hope sparked and twined with Milluri's fright.

Two ice dragons buzzed past, and Cyran ducked and weaved his mount as he tried to keep his bolt aimed in Shadowmar's general direction. Several ropes hit the deck around him, and he glanced up in surprise. Multiple soldiers were rappelling down from a Murgare moon and a blood dragon, the men descending so quickly they were nearly upon him.

Cyran ripped Eidelmere's Flame from its sheath as one soldier in thick furs, without any plates of armor, dropped onto the deck and swung a bearded axe. Cyran parried the blow with his sturdier dragonsteel blade, his attacker's weapon locking up with his. Both axe and sword pressed against each other as Cyran's eyes met his adversary's through his own visor and the horned and tufted helm of his opponent, the man's steaming breath pouring through his beard.

The green glow of Eidelmere's Flame blazed brighter.

Cyran pushed against the weapons, but he could not overpower the man and more of them were coming. He yanked his blade back, allowing the axe's momentum to carry the weapon at an angle past him. Then he swung again, cleaving into the chest of the man and releasing a spray of blood. The attacker fell as Cyran spun around just in time to see another axe swiping for his head. He leaned far back at the waist, and the weapon passed just over his nose with a sharp whistle. After righting himself, Cyran raised his rear-positioned leg and lunged forward, kicking the adversary in the chest and launching him over the edge of the deck as the man emitted a bellow of surprise.

Four other enemies had clipped roped harnesses to the holds on Milluri's deck and surrounded Cyran, all advancing and preparing to attack simultaneously.

Shit.

Instinctively, Cyran unlatched himself from the crossbow and widened his stance, crouching as he sensed his mount's impending movements. Milluri shook herself. Cyran leaned side to side just as she did so, keeping his balance, but his assailants all toppled over and smacked into the deck, hitting the ends of their tethers, which kept them from sliding off. Cyran leapt aft, slicing through one of the enemies' rope lines and then hacking through another. As the attackers regained their balance and stood, Cyran hewed through the last two ropes.

The adversaries charged Cyran with raised axes as he went down to a knee and remained calm and limber, bowing his head. Milluri shook much more vigorously this time, and all four assailants sailed away into the sky, screaming.

Cyran retained his balance in the center of the quarterdeck before darting back to the crossbow and clipping himself in.

In the distance, the Dragon Queen banked her beast, wheeled about, and soared away far too fast, but Cyran pursued her through a barrage of bolts from both sides, dipping just below them. Shadowmar burst out of the fray and then swung around to the east and circled. Cyran drove Milluri onward and out of the chaos of battle before the beating of massive wings sounded behind him.

A cave dragon larger than any other flying beast chased him as it flapped four colossal wings. A dozen dwarven archers and two trebuchets on its quarterdeck were prepared to loose, even more archers in its turret below. A couple of brown and white speckled dragons flew behind the beast, bearing only a dwarf or two each. All of them pursued Cyran and Milluri, likely having noticed they were after the Dragon Queen. A conjuror on the cave's quarterdeck hurried about, pulling around a long rope that was attached to his waist as he cursed and shouted, pointing at and touching bolts, lighting most with blue flame and one with what looked like lightning. Another dwarf shouted something at the conjuror, and the guard at the front of the beast bellowed and gestured.

Three archers loosed, and their bolts screamed toward Cyran. One sailed overhead, but Cyran had to use the other realm to whip Milluri aside and dodge the other two—one of them passing directly through a gap in her torn wing.

The dwarf archer with the lightning bolt swiveled about and took careful aim as those manning the trebuchets yelled and prepared to loose.

A sinking feeling pulled at Cyran's guts. Some bolts could be bestowed with magic to seek out targets and not be affected by wind and other factors. Maybe the lightning bolt was one of those. The dwarf archer paused and sighted him.

A rush of wind sounded, and a thorn dragon burst up from below. A bolt with a hooked tip flew from the thorn and punched through one of the cave dragon's wings, burying into its exposed flesh just behind a steel pauldron. Another projectile struck the beast perfectly in one of its nostrils, ramming upward before disappearing. The creature barely made a grunt of protest, but it tossed its curled-horned head, blowing steam from its nose, although it was unable to expel the bolt. It would probably take more than a dozen bolts in vulnerable and vital locations to bring such a monster down.

A forest dragon soared upward across from the thorn, and the archer on the quarterdeck loosed another bolt. The projectile struck their adversary on its flank just behind and above its turret. The two pygmy dragons screeched in fear and dived away.

Many of the dwarven archers spun toward their new assailants, but the thorn and forest dragons had already risen above them, pulling cables that were attached to the bolts anchored in the cave dragon's side and flank. The cables wrapped over the top of the dragon and tangled up one of its wings while the thorn and forest arced and crossed overhead, the dwarves trying to track them as they twisted and turned in close proximity. Several bolts flew, but all were well behind their targets.

The cables wrapped around the cave's other wings, binding them, and the Belvenguard dragons weaved circles filled with erratic movements so they would not be predictable and easy targets. After two more passes, the enormous wings of the dwarves' beast had been wrapped in loose coils of rope, and the thorn and forest dragons flew directly away, drawing the cables tight and cinching them down. The cave's wings buckled at its joints and folded inward. Its strength resisted some of the tension, but it was not enough for the beast to keep flying.

Dwarves bellowed in anger and fear as their mount's wings struggled and thrashed, most of the beast's movement coming from near its shoulder and not the outer portions of its limbs. The dragon tilted starboard and dropped from the sky.

Cyran shouted with elation and relief.

The other thorn dragon released its cable and whizzed past Milluri. The archer on the quarterdeck pumped a fist in the air, the exposed portion of his face beneath his helm nearly as red as blood, and saliva spurted from his lips as he bellowed.

Vyk! The hooked bolt with the attached rope had been his shot.

The archer in the turret—Ineri—yelled, "We had a little delay, dragonknight, after the messages from Murgare, but we came to our senses." The other distracting bolt that flew into the cave dragon's nose had been hers.

"We apologize for our late arrival," the guard at the forefront said, his voice familiar, the mage behind him fully protected by his bulk. Fine blond hair streamed from beneath his helm.

Cyran did a double take but couldn't see past his gray and green armor. "Dage?"

"They will make anyone a guard these days." Dage tilted his lance in acknowledgment.

Vyk bellowed another incoherent cry as veins throbbed along his arms and in his neck.

"Better late than never." Cyran glanced back at Shadowmar, who was reentering the fray not too far to the east.

The forest dragon rose up to meet them. "Nevergrace will also make anyone a dragonarcher now." Brelle was harnessed onto the quarterdeck, having been the other archer to help take down the cave dragon.

Cyran nearly lost his hold on his crossbow.

"Don't look so surprised," Brelle said. "After all, you're the one who became a dragonknight. And one of our new guard and his archers fled the outpost after we received those convincing messages from Murgare." She motioned to their guard, the smallest guard Cyran had ever seen. Their mage was not well protected. "Laren and I were all that was left."

"Laren?" Cyran studied the small man behind the helm of gray and forest green, imagining his boyish smile.

"We thought we'd try whatever we could to help," Laren said.

"And you weren't hard to spot," Ineri added. "You're the only archer out here who doesn't have a mage and guard on his mount." She reloaded another bolt, nodding toward the Dragon Queen. "And you're the only other on a thorn dragon."

Cyran nodded in gratitude before turning to study Shadowmar's path while Milluri shared a silent greeting with Nithinix.

"I assume you have some plan devised." Laren motioned to the enhanced bolt in Cyran's crossbow.

Cyran shrugged. "I'm making it up as I go."

"Take her down!" Vyk screamed, and a cloud of spit erupted from his lips. "We have your back. Now!"

Cyran whirled Milluri around after the shadow dragon and its flailing barbed tail. *It hasn't used its tail on other dragons here.* At least Cyran had not seen it do so during this battle, only with Eidelmere.

Milluri weaved about, trying to keep up with the agile shadow dragon as the beast dropped droves of Belvenguard mounts in her wake. They gained on their target, and Cyran swiveled around, steering Milluri while taking aim.

A memory hit him like a deluge of watery breath.

Eidelmere. He recalled the training and wisdom Eidelmere had tried to instill in him when crossing the Evenmeres—to trust. Trust a dragon fully. Let his mount fly on its own. Grant it free will. It knew what it was doing. *Let go.*

Cyran's eyes settled closed as he hesitantly allowed his control of his mount to slip away. Tears rose up like a tide in his eyes.

I trust you, Eidelmere. I was wrong in how I blindly accepted duty and a method I thought was most advantageous, one that would not be to the liking of any dragon. I see that now, and I wish with all my heart that I could go back and tell you this. "If you will, please guide us now."

Milluri braced with her wings, spreading them wide as she jerked and slowed, throwing Cyran forward, and for an instant he wondered if he had made a poor decision. Then the thorn dragon whipped upward in a burst of movement, flapping and thrashing around a bone dragon that spewed a rush of green acid fog.

"*Milluri, we have to work together to accomplish the impossible here,*" Cyran said into the other realm.

"*You aim. I'll maneuver,*" Milluri answered, shocking Cyran for a moment as her voice sounded like Eidelmere's in his head.

"*Find the best path amidst the chaos.*"

Milluri dipped and turned. Cyran kept his bolt trained on Shadowmar's swerving figure as best he could. He knew every movement Milluri would make—when and where and for how long—only he no longer controlled her decisions. This was the way it should be with knight and dragon, the way it was always meant to be. Somewhere, the two realms overlapped and became one. He forced a deep breath and let the sensation and trepidation of lack of control drift away into the din of battle.

"*I trust you, Eidelmere,*" Cyran said into the *neblír*. "*Your sacrifice, one you will never benefit from, will hopefully save some of your kin.*"

Milluri glanced back at him with a narrowed look of confusion before flying faster. They climbed over a blood dragon as the beast of Murgare battled with a rose, and after passing by, they dipped lower.

Just ahead, the Dragon Queen's steed flapped her shadowy wings, aligning for a tilt with Sir Paltere's mighty sun dragon. Paltere shouted something at the Dragon Queen, her quieter reply indiscernible. Her archers loosed volleys of bolts at the dragons around them. Cyran realized that when he was on the back of a dragon, his aim was not the best. He needed to get in close, as he had only one magically charged bolt. Milluri veered toward Shadowmar.

One archer in the beast's lower turret pointed at Cyran, and another beside the first loosed. The bolt streaked at Cyran faster than he could think, its tip coming directly for Milluri's skull.

The thorn dropped beneath him, barely avoiding the bolt that sailed past her head and barreled straight at Cyran.

Cyran's knees gave out, and he collapsed onto the quarterdeck as the bolt slammed into his crossbow, bursting it into splinters and chunks of metal. He was flung back with immense force, and the strap on his harness snapped. He rolled out to the edge of the deck as the offending bolt deflected and whistled away.

Milluri tilted to one side, working against Cyran's momentum and keeping him on top of her quarterdeck. He clambered to his hands and knees as his mount dived away from Shadowmar, throwing him off-balance. The remnants of his crossbow flew away, and the flaming black bolt rolled off the deck and onto Milluri's tattered wing.

Cyran sprinted and lunged for the projectile, leaping from the deck and out onto her limb. The bolt hung on to the bony segments of her wing but rolled and tipped into one of the gaps that had been created by Shadowmar's talons. Cyran leapt again, as far as he could, and grasped the shaft of the bolt as he fell through the opening in her wing. Milluri rolled upside down around him, and the lower turret nearly slammed into his face.

He flinched. His shoulder hit the turret's poled frame, but he grabbed onto it, also squeezing the bolt with his other hand and straining to heft its bulk. He scrambled inside the turret, dropped the bolt onto the empty crossbow there, and cranked its windlass.

"That thorn is wounded and carries no rider," a Murgare archer on the far side of Milluri bellowed.

"The young dragonknight commands that creature," the Dragon Queen said. "Do not assume—"

Milluri angled herself directly upward, climbing as Cyran swiveled in the turret, which had been the first position he had ever known on a dragon. He ignored the swarming memories and tension, feeling Milluri's body and soul—where she meant to move, the instant she decided something else, every fiber of her being in the other realm.

The dragons and sky and rain and lake around them all became luminescent fibers, shimmering and throbbing in webs of light. Cyran felt the *neblír* around him and fully entered the realm.

Milluri ascended straight upward, and her body tilted just past vertical. Her head fell backward while she rose. Her underside rose up and revealed itself as she matched altitude with Shadowmar, and the moment Cyran was exposed and he saw the black scales of the beast above, he swiveled and loosed, aiming for where his target *would* be when the bolt crossed the gap.

The crossbow thumped, its arms banging and thrumming as its projectile screamed away.

Shadowmar's last red eye flashed in the light and the threads before the bolt drove deep into it. The Dragon Queen cried out as her mount tossed its head back.

Milluri twisted in an evasive spin as bolts launched at them before the shadow dragon of legend jerked and opened her jaws, roaring so loudly that Cyran's ears rang. Then the beast fell completely silent. Black fire brewed in her throat, threatening to be spewed forth.

She is still not dead.

But, for a moment, she was stunned by Jaslin's bolt.

Milluri fell all the way backward, flying upside down as Cyran scrambled from the turret and scaled her neck before she rolled to right herself and soar at the blind Shadowmar from below. As Milluri completed her barrel roll, Cyran climbed the side of her neck, using her scales as hand- and footholds. He threw himself into his saddle and grabbed the handle of his lance as Milluri darted upward, and the archers in Shadowmar's lower turret hollered.

Cyran angled his lance just as he and Milluri collided with the partially immobilized beast, and he drove his weapon's entire shaft through the bottom of Shadowmar's jaw, crunching through mandible and then skull and brain before piercing through the top of her head.

Cyran released the lance as Milluri rammed into Shadowmar's lower jaw. The lance's mount snapped, and Milluri thrashed her injured wing, attempting to shove herself away as the shadow dragon jerked and then fell still, her wings pausing in mid flap.

The beast dropped from the sky like a boulder, and Milluri twisted out from under her descending form.

As Shadowmar fell from the heavens, a stinging sensation struck Cyran, a reminder from his prior encounter with the Dragon Queen. He rose from his saddle and scrambled along Milluri's neck, glancing back as often as he could before once again dropping down into the turret. He grabbed a hooked projectile with a cable attached to its end and placed it in the crossbow.

A storm dragon shot past like a bolt of lightning, heading straight for Shadowmar, whose massive, flared wings now caused her body to fall more slowly. The storm streaked past, and the Dragon Queen caught its foot, which lifted her from her saddle and carried her away.

But Cyran had already loosed his bolt. The crossbow's arms rang, and the projectile screamed along. It impaled the storm dragon's neck, and the cable zipped across the turret's floor as its coils unwound. The storm dragon hurtled away until the rope's slack ran out, and the beast hit the end of the line. It whipped around with a crack, jerking Milluri sideways. The storm dragon thrashed and fluttered weakly on the end of the line but could not gather enough strength to put up a challenging fight.

Shadowmar's plummeting form—with the lance of a forest dragon protruding through her skull—collided with the Lake on Fire and a dozen Murgare ships. A gush of black breath was expelled from her jaws, and this fire and an enormous geyser of water were hurled outward, burning and capsizing many more.

Lake dragons swept in, spewing breaths that boiled the water around them as they lifted their three or six heads and snapped at the carcass of the shadow dragon, devouring her scales and flesh.

58

CYRAN ORENDAIN

The legions of Murgare fell still and watched as Shadowmar was devoured. Fear and shock rippled through their guard and archers and dragons. Their attacks faltered. Their ranks broke apart.

The earth rumbled below Cyran, vibrating the entire lake and its waters. The enormous beast in the deeps pulled back from having rammed the cliffs below Galvenstone and Castle Dashtok. Walls crumbled, and stones plummeted into the lake. One of the castle's spires wobbled, tilted, and then collapsed, spilling over the cliffs and crushing Belvenguard soldiers and knights below.

"We have to stop that beast!" Brelle pointed and flew into a fit of cursing.

"How?" Laren asked.

Murgare ships that had been trailing the monster ran ashore, and planks dropped. Masses of soldiers and mounted knights erupted from the vessels and charged into the ranks of Galvenstone's mounted and standing army there. Steel clashed in jolting rhythms. Screams punctuated the din. A score of the north's larger dragons worked in teams, carrying colossal crates.

These beasts landed around the shores, and the walls of the crates fell open, releasing more enemy soldiers. The dragons blew fiery or icy breaths and seared or froze masses of the south's army around them, the sounds of crackling fire and freezing steel jostling in volume.

"We have to do something!" Brelle gesticulated frantically.

"We have the greatest archer in all the kingdoms." Vyk gestured at Ineri.

Ineri coughed. "I cannot hope to do anything to that beast, even with all my bolts."

"But there has to be a mage somewhere on it." Vyk squinted, and their thorn dragon dived.

Cyran tried to keep up with them as Milluri dragged the limp storm dragon and its Dragon Queen rider behind them, but they fell behind. Laren and Brelle's forest dragon raced past them.

The beast in the lake slowly circled, its one massive hump still above the surface.

"The mage must be there," Cyran yelled to his comrades as he pointed at its hump. "Hidden in its scales." One ship followed the beast closer than any of the others, and the outline of a red fin stood out on its black mainsail. "Unless the mage is on a ship nearby, guiding it, but that part of the creature has been above water most of the time."

Ineri wound her windlass as Nithinix dived. A Murgare legion nearby roared and chased them, led by the largest ice dragon in the north's army. A man of importance stood at the forefront of the beast's quarterdeck, his arms crossed.

Murgare's new king? Cyran grabbed another bolt and cranked his windlass, although his friends and new target increased their distance from him. He glanced down at the storm dragon dangling at the end of his cable and hooked bolt. He could not cut the beast loose even if it was dead. Its cargo was too precious.

"I see something." Laren's voice carried back to Cyran as the former squire leaned forward, and the mage behind him attempted to peek around his lance. "There!"

Laren's forest dragon dropped and then angled upward, skimming over the waters, the massive enemy beast still too far ahead for Cyran to pick out anything on its back. Vyk and Ineri's thorn dragon overtook the forest.

The creature below spun about and began swimming faster, building momentum, once again charging toward the shores and cliffs as battles raged on the shores.

Ineri's crossbow rope snapped, loosing a bolt that sparkled in the sun as it screamed along. The archer sat poised, watching her projectile without blinking. It flew for what seemed like half a league before spearing an area on the hump of the beast.

For a moment, nothing happened.

Cyran glanced at the dragons pursuing his comrades. The ice dragon that might have been bearing the north's king gained on Laren's forest dragon. Milluri beat her wings faster, sensing Cyran's agitation.

The plowing form of the beast in the lake slowed. It did not collide with the cliffs or smash the walls below Galvenstone. No quakes sounded. The beast simply swung about and submerged into the lake, its wake carrying northward before slowly fading.

More of Murgare's legions paused their attacks, some shouting in fear. Others turned to flee, pulling more with them.

"Ineri!" Vyk cried out. "A one in a million shot. The greatest archer Cimeren has ever known. Murgare's bane!" He screamed with unrelenting rage.

A clash of metal rang out.

The lance on the ice dragon rammed into Laren's shield as Laren's mage attempted to spin about and face their adversary. Bone and dragonsteel crunched and cracked. Laren was launched from his seat, his limp and broken body flying into the distance and plunging into the water.

"No!" Cyran swiveled in his frame, aiming.

A sun dragon swooped down, and Sir Paltere's lance struck the ice dragon's guard on the helm, instantaneously decapitating the man. The guard's body slumped in its saddle, and the king on the quarterdeck bellowed and pointed.

Bolts flew between the sun and ice dragons as Milluri raced closer, but Cyran would not loose and risk hitting Paltere.

Paltere's sun dragon took two bolts in the chest as the dragonknight's mount twisted around, and Paltere stabbed the mage on the ice, flinging the man from his seat. The sun dragon latched onto the ice's neck with its talons and buried them deep. Three rose dragons and two silvers flew in to aid Paltere, loosing bolts into the Murgare beast, and together, they sank talons into its quarterdeck, shredding the mounted crossbows there. Blood streamed from Paltere's mount in rivers, but the ice dragon had taken many more bolts. Its head drooped, and its eyes closed.

Cries of alarm and disbelief rang through the remainder of the Murgare legions as they stopped their advance. Many whipped about and flew away. Their fleets that still roamed behind where the beast had been realigned their sails and circled about on the water. Their soldiers on the shores retreated to the edge of the lake.

The wounded sun dragon and the roses and silvers hauled the ice dragon toward Galvenstone, the Murgare king screaming from its back.

Cyran stared at the area where Laren's armored body had sunk into the Lake on Fire.

59

PRAVON THE DRAGON THIEF

THE SWARMING MASSES OF DRAGONS IN THE RAIN FAR OUT OVER the lake resembled whirling dark clouds, although their screeches and roars and the clashes of battle rolled over the water, making it clear they were not simple clouds. A dragon larger than any of the others in the sky fell into the lake.

"That had to be a dwarven cave dragon." Aneen pointed into the distance.

"When do you think we will march to Galvenstone?" Pravon asked Aneen as they sat on their sand dragon. They had ended up traveling northwest but not to the king's city. A beacon tower loomed beside them, and the marshlands sprawled away from them all the way to the lake. The Evenmeres stretched to the north and behind them.

"Maybe Kridmore doesn't want to take the chance of getting us all killed." Aneen swung a foot over their mount's neck so that both of her legs dangled over the same side.

Pravon scoffed. "That would be a first. And if we do not offer aid, surely the Dread King will hold our blood contracts against us. The Assassin will not be pleased."

"We killed plenty of the north's dragonmages early on,

before tensions escalated with the Dragon Queen's overtaking of the outpost. Kridmore even burned that one circular village just to murder a couple mages. I'd say we did our part in keeping Murgare's legions smaller. We also accomplished everything we were supposed to at Nevergrace, including assassinating the lord and lady there to ensure war. We caused chaos in the south while punishing those cities that did not respond to the Dread King's call for their banners. That drove a lot more legions and people to Galvenstone, as the king wanted, and those people will not soon forget the price of their disloyalty. Igare should be pleased enough."

Pravon glanced over his shoulder with a raised eyebrow. "Igare the Dread King? Pleased with us for not aiding his legions once the war began?"

Aneen's forehead furrowed with worry. "I hope The Guild of Fire and Shadow can help us disappear as soon as we determine which side is the victor."

They watched the war rage until one small spot in the sky streaked toward them. A storm dragon appeared and quickly soared closer. The dragon touched down and cried out as the man in front of a hooded mage dismounted. This man was also hooded, only his pointed chin with a dimple and his crooked yellow teeth visible as he marched toward them.

"The king wonders when you plan to arrive and aid his city," their contact said as he approached Kridmore, indignant, his jaw set rigid. He wiped at the corners of his lips with two fingers. "The war has long begun. You were ordered to march the Rorenlands's legion to Galvenstone after destroying Somerlian, which you also neglected to do in favor of destroying Valan."

"Somerlian did not fit our course," Kridmore said offhandedly as he jerked his gilded dagger from the base of his mount's skull. He dismounted and slowly approaching their contact.

"*Your* course?" Spittle flew from their contact's lips. "Since when do *you* decide your course and the terms of your blood contract? My king will not be pleased once he learns what you have—"

Kridmore rammed his dagger into their contact's midsection, and the man doubled over with a sharp grunt. Violet light flared in Kridmore's palm and extended outward, forming a blade. The assassin swiped with his ethereal weapon, decapitating the man in a flash. Their contact's head hit the ground and rolled out from under its hood, staring blankly into the heavens, its eyes shriveling and turning black.

Fuck. Shock locked Pravon in place on his saddle. He did not recognize this messenger, but he knew the king behind the man. After a moment, the messenger's face wavered and changed—some work of magic. His pointed chin retracted and rounded, and a gray goatee revealed itself. His yellow teeth turned white and straightened. *Riscott, the Dread King's vile orator.*

Pravon's heart slowed to a crawling waver in his chest.

Their contact's storm dragon shrieked and flapped its wings, lifting away as Kridmore pointed at it with his dagger and uttered a word. The dark gem on the dagger's hilt glittered, and a ripple of energy shook the air. The dragon stretched and flexed its neck as if suddenly turning feral. It shook, and its mage shouted in surprise and was thrown from her seat. The mage landed with a thud.

Kridmore hurled his violet blade at the dragon as the beast wheeled about, preparing to soar away. The magical weapon pierced through the side of its chest, and the creature's flapping slowed. Its eyes blackened, and it tilted and dropped, crashing onto the earth.

Kridmore approached and loomed over the mage, who scooted away as fast as she could. Her hood fell back, revealing a young and defined face—a woman Pravon recognized as one of

Igare's swiftest and most loyal messengers, although he did not know her name.

"You... you severed my bond with Iostixis." The mage gripped her chest, as if in immense pain. Her eyes widened as she eyed the gem on the hilt of Kridmore's dagger. "The Sky Sea Pearl? It has been found? After all these years?"

"It was lost in the Elechon after the Dragon Wars." Kridmore flipped the dagger around and held up its dark gem. Clouds of swirling jade and teal mist floated beneath its surface. A darting red light followed the clouds. "Along with all of Cimerenden and the elves. But its time has come."

Kridmore drove his blade into the mage's chest, and she screamed and then slumped over.

"You were saying there *might* be a problem with our contracts?" Aneen said to Pravon, her tone riddled with surprise and sarcasm. Her words jolted Pravon's mind and made it function normally again.

In the far distance, a colossal dragon as black as night spiraled down from the carnage in the sky. The clouds of dragons parted, and swarms of them fled northward.

"The Dragon Queen has been defeated?" Pravon's disbelief surged.

They stared at the chaos of racing legions and sailing ships that still flung projectiles at Galvenstone. Boulders and volleys of bolts launched from the walls of the city at its attackers.

The earth shook beneath their dragon's feet, and portions of Galvenstone's walls toppled.

"The great beast from the sea," Aneen whispered.

Pravon glanced at the dead messenger, mage, and storm dragon. Their blood contract had been violated in as detrimental a way as possible. The Assassin and Thief would not look kindly upon them now. "Is it now time to disappear? For good?"

"Not yet." Aneen shook her head while watching the battle.

Another major event must have occurred, as many more of Murgare's legions retreated. The lake waved so massively that, for a minute, Pravon feared it might roll outward beyond the marshes and even engulf them.

"The beast from the sea has also been defeated," Pravon said. "I did not think that would be possible."

Silence reigned over their ranks, their numbers close to half of what they had been when they departed the Rorenlands to decimate the disloyal cities of Belvenguard.

When the clouds of dragons over the lake further broke their ranks, Genturion Master Ristanus and his two lesser genturions —Cavius and Nortimus—dismounted from their scaly steeds and stood as rigid as castle walls.

"King Jabarra should be pleased with many of the events and how the second Dragon Wars have unfolded," Ristanus said to Kridmore. "Even if Belvenguard is not yet fully destroyed."

The assassin sheathed his dagger and approached the genturions with arms spread in cheer. "My comrades, we have won. We are victorious. I wish to congratulate you on your achievements."

Ristanus gave him a subtle dip of his chin as Kridmore reached out to take the genturion's hand. Ristanus extended his arm, ready to clasp—

Kridmore drove a violet lance that was only taking shape into Ristanus's abdomen. It erupted from the genturion master's back with a crackle of light and steam.

Pravon lurched and instinctively yanked a dragon spine from his belt, burying it into the flesh of his mount. Aneen leapt off their dragon.

The two other genturions gasped and ripped blades from sheaths.

Kridmore flung Ristanus's body away and swung his weapon

through Cavius's defense. The violet blade impaled the genturion's chest. Nortimus swung his sword, but Kridmore easily ducked the blow and came up, ramming his magical blade into the genturion's neck. Nortimus's eyes blackened and shriveled in their sockets, and both genturions' bodies collapsed to their knees and then dropped face-first into the dirt.

The soldiers and knights and archers and giants in the legion shifted, weapons were drawn and hefted, and crossbows spun in their frames.

Pravon's heart bucked in his chest as he quickly wrapped his arms around his mount's neck, squeezed, and whispered, "Be free of your bond, my friend." He dropped from his seat. "Kridmore! What have you done?" He slowly backed away. "Everything we have worked for…"

The legions around them advanced on and encircled Kridmore.

"It is time for the ancient forest to come alive." Kridmore ripped off his dark cloak, exposing his face and long hair. Violet flames flared across his back.

Pravon gasped as he retreated farther away. Something huge shifted in the Evenmeres, and he continued backing away toward the southern fields. Aneen slowly followed him.

The advancing army paused in shock.

"My master—Beninthel, the ancient king of the elves—will have his revenge," Kridmore said. "For the Dragon Wars and what man and dragon did to him and his queen and all of our people. The curse he laid on himself and the elves who died around him will now come to fruition. And we will not rest until Cimeren is free of your filthy kind."

Kridmore is one of the Harrowed, a creature beyond life. One who has already died. Pravon trembled with fear as he crouched in the grasses.

Waves of earth rumbled and wound out of the woods,

carrying trees on top of them as they swiftly weaved toward the sand dragons and giants, who roared and shifted. Some of the Rorenlands's legion tried to wheel about and flee, but they were packed together too tightly, and their yolks and harnesses kept them that way as they bellowed with surprise and fear.

Floating lights darted from the woods, singing melodies that were hauntingly familiar. The grasses near the forest's boundary waved as other monsters with gray skin emerged from the woods and vanished into the foliage.

The rising mounds of earth knocked into the sand dragons and giants, throwing some of the beasts over like small trees. Then the earth opened beneath them—massive holes of darkness surrounded by rows of curled teeth.

Pravon stifled a gasp as sand dragon after sand dragon and giant after giant fell into each opening void and was swallowed by the abyss below. One creature beneath the ground fed and then rose, its tubular dark brown body cresting the earth before diving again and carrying a line of standing pines and oaks along with the dirt on its back.

"Earth dragons?" Aneen could barely speak as she flattened herself out in the grass beside Pravon. "I thought they were only legend."

As the legion of sand dragons was consumed by the earth, a score of figures cloaked in black stepped from the Evenmeres. Violet flames writhed across their backs and shoulders. A few of them moved differently from the majority—dead humans among mostly deceased elves. At least one young man from Nevergrace had been taken by the forest.

The tallest of the Harrowed spoke to Kridmore and the others of his kind, his voice blasting in haunting echoes over the plains. "The world of humans has been weakened beyond reckoning. The southern cities of this kingdom are in ruins, but their strength and numbers have been consolidated in a fortified and victorious Galvenstone. Here, the Weltermores and the remainder of the Rorenlands's armies could surround us. The north is in retreat, and their ranks will be disbanded, their numbers thin. We shall start with the defeated Murgare and raze every town and city and village to the ground. We will sweep south to north and east to west, and when the north is nothing more than fire and bones, then we will move on to Belvenguard. We will scrub Cimeren clean of every last human and dragon, like their kind did to ours."

Kridmore and the other Harrowed bowed their heads, and Kridmore ran to the last remaining sand dragon and leapt onto its back. He rammed his golden dagger into the base of its skull. The Sky Sea Pearl blinked with red light and then dimmed.

The undead assassin turned his new mount and followed the other Harrowed and their legions of monsters back into the Evenmeres.

60

JASLIN ORENDAIN

Jaslin tentatively escorted Menoria back to the throne room, following Riscott at a safe distance.

"We should flee this castle," Jaslin whispered.

"And go where?" Menoria asked. "Back to Nevergrace? There's a war raging around us the likes of which no one has seen before. We'd be killed as soon as we stepped outside. And I do not believe everything the orator just divulged while he was terrified."

Jaslin's stomach clenched. For now, she would have to pretend they knew nothing of Igare's abhorrent deeds and continue to treat him with kindness and respect... and not reveal their fear. Riscott paced along as fast as he could and rubbed at his neck, his skin red, and he wheeled on Jaslin and Menoria again just before entering the throne room.

"You will not speak a word of what transpired between us to anyone," Riscott reminded them for a third time, probably terrified of what Igare would do if the king knew what his orator had revealed to the king's betrothed and her handmaid. "*I* will personally deal with both of you once the war is over." His eyes were bloodshot, and his hands shook with fear and rage.

Jaslin held out her hand to remind the orator of what she could do to him if he tried anything.

"Just think of yourselves now as part of the inner circle of the royal family." Riscott's eyes gaped as he stared at Jaslin's hands and rubbed his neck. "You know what we know, and we protect Igare and the crown at all costs."

"We would not do anything to harm Igare or the throne," Menoria said in a somber voice.

"Where have you been?" Tiros rushed up behind Riscott, the nyren's cheeks red above his gray beard. "Your elite messenger is waiting. Igare needs you to"—he glanced at Menoria—"visit our contracted thieves out near the marshlands. To find out what is delaying the Rorenlands's legions. We need them here. Now!"

Riscott cursed and strode away with the nyren. Igare stood in the distance with the remainder of his council. The king of Belvenguard appeared as gentle and concerned as ever, and Jaslin had a hard time picturing him with a face of pure evil.

But evil is created by actions, not by someone's outward appearance or demeanor. This man, the true Dread King of Cimeren, had set up a situation that would lead to the deaths of tens of thousands. He only wore a mask of kindness. He was also the one responsible for the destruction and death that had occurred at Nevergrace. Jaslin shuddered.

Cartaya stood before Riscott and muttered an incantation. White flames sprouted from her palms as she waved them over Riscott's face. The orator's cheeks elongated, and his goatee vanished, revealing a dimple on his chin. His lips parted, his teeth turning yellow and crooked, and he wiped at his mouth. Riscott took a dark cloak from Tiros and donned it, pulling the hood down over his eyes. Then the orator rushed out a doorway that was off to the side of the chamber.

Jaslin exhaled a stale breath, but the clacking sound of a

mage with a staff shattered her moment of relief. Tallius hobbled toward her and Menoria.

"We could not reach our chambers," Jaslin said once the mage neared. "There was too much commotion with the shaking and booming walls. The future queen was frightened, and so we were forced to return here and wait until this is all over."

The mage shook a parchment at Jaslin. "The Guild of Fire and Shadow will know that my debt has been passed on to you no matter what happens to me, but I must leave at once. Igare has ordered me to take up another errand."

Jaslin swallowed her fear as best she could, and the mage departed, exiting the chamber through a different doorway than the one Riscott had used. Tallius also knew that Jaslin had traveled to the Southern Isles, and he could inform Igare or the other councilmembers of this at any time.

The walls boomed around them, and Menoria trembled. "I cannot believe much, if anything, of what that orator told us, but I no longer feel safe anywhere." She pressed her back into a corner and huddled there.

"We can stay here if you'd like." Jaslin wrapped an arm around Menoria to console her. "For now." The safest area would probably be in the vicinity of the king, although Jaslin feared that Igare would likely try again to have her killed once the war was over, if they survived.

Minutes and then hours crawled by as the walls rattled and dragons screamed and blew breaths that battered the stones around them. But no beasts must have made it past the city's defenses and survived long enough to mount a continuous attack on the keep.

A man in a messenger's tunic rushed into the chamber and bowed. "Milord, the Dragon Queen has fallen."

Jaken and Vysoria bellowed with elation, and a resounding

cheer went up and echoed around the chamber as Vysoria and Jaken hugged. Nistene tried to force herself upon them. The kingsknights remained rigid and silent.

Not too long after the first announcement, another followed. "Milord," another messenger said, "the whale dragon has been relieved of its mage, and the beast has fled into the deeps."

A collective sigh surfaced and buzzed around the rafters.

"Then the end is nigh," Tiros said, "and because those from all the dissident cities of Belvenguard have recently joined our legions and helped turn the tide, we do not even require the aid of King Jabarra's sand dragons."

"The Paladin and the Shield Maiden have seen the course of battle shift." Lisain was not as elated as the others, his tone bordering on melancholy.

Cartaya paced around the dais, but the flames on her palm fizzled out.

Why aren't the king's conjuror and her daughter out riding dragons and aiding our archers?

"It is time to take flight, milord." Tiros motioned at the side exit of the throne room.

Igare nodded, his expression conflicted with sadness and relief, his tone gentle. "We will show our support for our legions and celebrate with them, the true men and women of Belvenguard. Those loyal to their king. We barely survived this ordeal, and we did so only because we were forced to develop and implement new ideas such as dragon armor and novel bolts and strategically using more conjurors to aid the legions. The disloyalty of the free cities had become too prevalent, this in tandem with their mounting arrogance, but it will not happen again. Not until more centuries have passed and events have been forgotten. We would have outnumbered the north, if our people had all joined us, along with the Weltermores's and the Rorenlands's armies. The people of Belvenguard will be forgiven if they have realized their mistakes and have come to Galvenstone, but for a time, we will shun them as much as we would any outsider." Igare shook his head with disappointment as he motioned for his council to precede him as they marched out of the chamber. A wisp of black smoke slipped past his lips, and Jaslin's fears erupted anew. "After we celebrate this great victory, we will make preparations for my wedding."

Wedding? Jaslin's stomach then lurched, but she and Menoria slowly followed the king and his council through the side entrance and out of the keep. They emerged on the walls where a sun dragon more gilded and glowing and massive than any other of its kind waited. Its scales were free of blood and dirt, its saddles, quarterdeck, and turret manned but unmarred.

The archers and guard on the beast cheered when Igare approached, and the mage rose in his stirrups. Igare climbed onto a saddle behind the mage and settled into his seat. Cartaya ascended the rope ladder leading up to the quarterdeck and joined the archers as their conjuror.

"Brave warriors of Galvenstone, it is time to take flight," Igare said, and the men roared with approval. "We are victorious against the heinous north!" He raised a clenched fist, a look of despair and then determination seeping through his visage. His breath steamed.

The sun dragon lifted from the walls and swooped out around the city in enlarging circles. Legions beyond the walls erupted with cheers as their king flew past them, and Igare's archers loosed bolts that may or may not have been aimed at Murgare targets.

Lisain and Tiros remained behind, watching the spectacle with Jaslin and Menoria. Portions of the capital city were burning, and many structures smoldered. Out over the lake, the wreckage of ships appeared like islands, some still supporting masts.

Shouts and hollers of victory rang across the lake and rolled over the city. A burst of fire blasted from just above the king's dragon's back, not from the beast itself but from one of its riders. The breath flared and crackled and arced across the sky, directed at a Murgare dragon, who shielded itself and its riders. Although Jaslin knew little about the laws of the other realm, she knew dragons did not breathe at each other.

A storm dragon appeared out of nowhere and landed on the battlements nearby. The unarmored guard riding the beast addressed the remaining councilmembers. "The Murgare king has been taken by Sir Paltere."

A conflicting rush of emotion stormed inside Jaslin as she looked to Menoria and then into the city. Belvenguard was victorious, but the idea and image of her kingdom had taken up a shadowy residence in her mind.

Portions of the tiered walls around them were missing, and the bodies of numerous types of dragons littered the bailey below, along with mounds of rubble. Twisted corpses of men and limp arms and legs protruded from the debris.

Humans and dragons have once again accompanied each other in death.

61

CYRAN ORENDAIN

Milluri towed the dead storm dragon at the end of her cable to a cluster of rocks protruding from the lake as Belvenguard's legions soared overhead, celebrating their victory or heading back to Galvenstone. The thorn dragon lowered the body of her quarry—with the probably injured Dragon Queen still seated on it—and set it on the rocks before flapping and slowly landing.

Cyran gripped the hilt of Eidelmere's Flame and unsheathed the blade, holding it aloft as his wrath surfaced and, because of Laren's death, mounted and then blazed at full force. The weapon's shimmer bathed him and his armor in green as he watched the Dragon Queen warily and alighted. This woman could also be highly skilled in hand-to-hand combat, but there had been none at Nevergrace who could match Cyran's ability with the blade or crossbow when he was on the ground. He should be able to hold his own, hopefully, and even more so because her magic should not work against him. If not, the legions of Belvenguard would be able to kill her now that she was without her shadow dragon.

"You are now *my* prisoner, Dragon Queen." Cyran cautiously

stepped across the jagged rock, not knowing what to expect—her rage, shouting, cursing, a nonverbal confrontation, or a clash of blades—but he certainly did not anticipate what he found.

The Dragon Queen sat hunched forward in a slumped posture on the rock, her helm removed, her long brown hair dangling over her face as she stared at her boots or the stone between them.

Cyran watched her as he picked his way closer, taking note of the unevenness of the footing and recognizing the areas where he would be most likely to stumble. She did not make a move to stand or draw her blade, and his eyes locked onto her weapon's hilt as he imagined its crackling black fire springing to life.

"I have lost part of my soul." Her words caused the wound in Cyran's heart to burn. "My companion who has been there almost as long as I have been alive."

Cyran absently touched his aching chest. "Even you feel the pain of the *sïosaires*?"

She nodded, her hair waving, although it still concealed her face. "I have felt its pain only once before—when I was a young girl. That was a clean stab to the heart. This... this is a cutting edge against every surface of my beating organ."

"What did you do to Nevergrace this time?" Cyran gritted his teeth, focusing on his rage in an attempt to ignore their shared pain.

"What war requires." Her voice was only a whisper.

Cyran's heart sank, but he clung to his fury, gripping his sword tighter.

"I took out one of the dragons that rose against us," she said. "My legion felled another. We destroyed the ballistae and towers before they attacked us, but we did not fire the entire outpost or kill any more of its people than the situation required. Your home is still intact. At least what was left of it after our previous battle."

A wave of relief hit Cyran like a hammer to his sternum.

"Your friends attempted to warn you," she muttered. "I hope that you still do not understand it all, but I fear you do and that you do not care. Like so many others."

Confusion twisted Cyran's thoughts. "My friends?" Images of Laren launching from the back of a dragon replayed in his mind, twisting and stoking his anger.

"They had messages delivered to you and some of the others who might enter the guard."

Cyran froze. He recalled the parchments sealed with red wax. "*You* were behind those letters? Messages delivered in Belvenguard?"

"I was not. It was your friends who knew the truth and who wanted you to discover such things as well and then join them without ousting them as traitors. I only heard of their actions secondhand."

"Are you referring to Garmeen?" Cyran pictured the lean redheaded leader of the squires of Nevergrace who had been labeled as a traitor by Igare and his council before the recent events began. Cyran still meant to track down his previous friend and bring him to justice.

"Garmeen was only one of them."

"Who else do you allege to be a traitor?"

"Sir Kayom and Sir Ymar were two of the others."

Cyran lunged forward and angled the tip of his blade at her hair, where her throat would be hidden. "Do not make such accusations! Sirs Kayom and Ymar were loyal and brave guard." His breath spewed from his lips in hot bursts. "And you killed them both."

"They were loyal, in a sense."

"But you claim they were traitors."

"Only to the Dread King. They wished to remain faithful to Nevergrace and form their own kingdom there. Once you realized the truth on your own—they would have been risking their own lives as well as the lives of their families by telling someone outside their circle—they hoped to invite you into their confidence. I was not their friend, as they believed I was crafted by evil, but I respected them for how far they had come."

Disbelief surged inside Cyran. "What truth are you referring to?"

"The truth regarding the Dread King."

"The Dread King? Restebarge?"

Sirra scoffed.

"This Oomaren?" he asked.

She shook her head.

"Igare?"

She slowly nodded.

"Sir Kayom and Ymar would have never betrayed Belvenguard." Cyran took a deep breath but did not lower his blade.

"You probably believed the same of Garmeen, before the council convinced you otherwise."

Cyran was taken aback, but he quickly recovered and, with an ethereal hand, grasped onto the fury dissipating inside him. He would not let that emotion slip away. This master of treachery could not manipulate him if he did not allow the emotions she was attempting to tease out of him to surface.

"Menoria and Dage and Sir Kayom also received letters," Cyran finally said, recalling each instance.

"The former lady of the Never certainly did. Hers was a message of warning, which was similar to the one your hulking squire friend received. In the beginning, it seemed most likely that Dage would be the first to be called up into the guard at Galvenstone. Things would have played out differently if those sending the warnings realized sooner that you would in fact be the first to be tempted and deceived."

Cyran's thoughts tumbled around in his head.

"Sir Kayom never actually received a letter," Sirra said. "He was the one writing them, or occasionally Garmeen. Kayom may have tried to convince you that he also received a letter, so you would become more curious and seek answers. Igare and his council could have suspected this, and so they tried to keep Kayom and his squires apart when the former genturion of the Never was summoned to Galvenstone. When you arrived at Dashtok, you were told that Kayom had not yet come to the castle. Isn't that right?"

Cyran's jaw slackened. How could this woman know such things?

She continued, "It was either Igare trying to deceive you, or Kayom had the soldiers lie to you, so again, you would begin to suspect that something darker was occurring behind the friendly façade of the capital. The answer of who was behind this small affair is of no consequence."

Cyran snarled and latched on to his anger again. "Still, *you* killed them! I know that for a fact. And how can you even hope that I will believe this ruse of yours—that you know so much and some hidden truth about these matters?"

"I did not kill any of my hostages at Nevergrace, remember? I threatened to do so in hopes that Igare would release my queen, but I did not. However, I learned many things during my occupation of the outpost. The old nyren, Ezul, was quite helpful and knowledgeable."

"Ezul told you all that?"

She nodded. "He was a close friend of Kayom and Ymar, and I swayed Garmeen some time prior."

None of this could be true. This vile woman had attacked his outpost—his home—and had killed many. *Tamar...* No. Cyran shook his head. Tamar and Rilar had been ambushed by the monsters in the forest, before Rilar awoke and was taken by them.

"Your king wants you to be angry, not only at those from other kingdoms, but also at the people of Belvenguard if they do not obey his every whim," she said. "Above all else, he desires loyalty and devotion to himself."

For an instant, Cyran tried to picture Igare as evil, but he could not do so. Riscott, surely. Cartaya or Tiros, or possibly even Lisain, could also be treacherous, but not the kindly king of Belvenguard. This woman was lying to him, but why? To save herself? There would be easier paths to follow in order to do so.

"And what else is a king supposed to demand loyalty to?" Cyran asked, the tip of his blade still within a handsbreadth of her hair. "To the throne? Duty is linked to the king."

"The throne?" Sirra shook her head. "That is a touch better than to oneself, but hardly something to fawn over. Such a thing is what Oomaren desires—to have the people blindly follow whoever is crowned." She paused for a breath. "I fear that you have had and will continue to have many more problems arising from the notion of duty."

Her last words struck him in the heart like a bolt. Jaslin often said similar things. He shook off his doubts. "You must despise all kings. Faithfulness to the kingdom is the only other option you could list but, at best, would be another small step above devotion to the throne or crown. It is semantics."

Sirra studied her foot as she dragged the toe of her boot across the rock. "Could we ever hope to find a king who demands loyalty to the kingdom's people? That does not have to be so farfetched. A king is not required to want his people to be angry at outsiders or others within his realm if they question him, or even at those who cause harm. Such a king could ensure punishment only to those deserving but without emotion and through judgment formed by reason, evidence, and truth."

Cyran paused. Why was he even having this conversation with the Dragon Queen? This was the person who had locked him in a cell overlooking a cliff and repeatedly attempted to turn him against his kingdom so she could use his power against her enemies.

"Those were the kind of rulers that King Restebarge and Queen Elra were," she said. "And it was one of the reasons Igare despised them so."

Restebarge, the Dread King?

"There is a similar underlying reason why the dragons of Belvenguard are not laying eggs," she said. "It is also why most of the eggs that are laid are not hatching."

A ripple of fear ran up Cyran's arm. Those rumors terrified him.

"Dragons do not wish to be controlled and forced to do things against their will," she added.

Cyran pictured the dens at Nevergrace and how the squires had to keep the forest dragons behind gates or the creatures would flee back into the Evenmeres. "Murgare is no better in that regard. So do not try to take that angle. You control dragons and make them fight your battles as well. The same as with warhorses."

"The dragons of the north fight with us only when they want to, when they believe in the cause. The same goes for our mages. We do not force any dragons or mages to enter the legions like Igare and Belvenguard do. We do not own all the dragons of our lands, and those who fight with us are much stronger because of it. They also lay fertile eggs. Dragons become sterile when held in captivity for centuries."

"Belvenguard just destroyed your supposedly more powerful and free legions."

"Your vengeful actions may incite evil even in those who are good, and it could come back to bite you and others you love." The Dragon Queen fell silent for a minute, and Cyran was not sure how to respond to that accusation. "Murgare would have waited another century for Belvenguard and its dragons to further weaken before attempting to remove the line of dread kings, but Igare brought war upon Cimeren by killing Restebarge and Elra. Though I admit, Oomaren escalated the events as well. Igare is a tyrant who has anyone who stands against him killed by his weapon of the guard, and he terrorizes the people of other kingdoms."

"Stop wasting your breath. I believe none of this."

"Igare is too much like his great ancestor, the King of War and Wrath, who initiated the Dragon Wars with the objective of wiping out the elves of Cimerenden. Because he despised the elves for their power and did not want to ever have to answer to them or join them in council. Too much war and wrath also flows in Igare's veins. He carries the blood of the old dragons. Some say they can see it in his breath, the same as with his forefather."

"I am only here to take your weapons, wrap you in bonds, and deliver you as a prisoner to Galvenstone. You will be judged by the king of Belvenguard and his council. Now stand and offer me your hands for binding. Like you did to me and my comrades."

"And now a sixth kingdom arises. One of monsters and the dead who still linger only because of their need for vengeance."

A prickle ran up Cyran's sword arm. "Those in the Evenmeres?"

She nodded. "The creatures lurking in those woods are led by the Harrowed, victims of the Dragon Wars."

He recalled Rilar being turned into one of the cloaked

figures with violet flames raging across their backs. "The Harrowed were once people who fought in the Dragon Wars?"

"No. Not people. Elves. And the Harrowed King was once Beninthel, the king of Cimerenden. His ire festered for years but then erupted when men and dragons turned on his kind and his city and his queen. When these mounted dragons chased the last of his entourage into the Lake of Glass and burned them alive—creating the Lake on Fire—the elf king's rancor spewed into the mortal world. However, he did not kill his immediate attackers with bone and earth magic. He cursed himself and his own who were around him so they could arise again and seek vengeance. And he has recently reclaimed the lost Sky Sea Pearl of the elves, an enchanted item that can sever the bond between man and dragon. It splits our realm from the *neblír*."

Cyran's mouth worked a few times, but he could not find any words he thought would be wise to utter. Too many questions floated around inside his head.

Sirra said, "Legend claims that the curse of the Harrowed King was so sacrificial it gave him near limitless power of the bone and earth. It is said that he cannot be killed but by the hand of one of his own."

"By one of the Harrowed? Cimeren can never hope for such a thing." *Not even with Rilar as one of them.* Rilar had been a simple and gentle woodsman of the outpost and had no hint of his former self remaining after he was turned.

"Or perhaps by the hand of an elf."

But there were supposedly no elves left, although Cyran had encountered a few in the Evenmeres, who were soon killed. Maybe those were the last in Cimeren.

"And why in the Assassin's bloody hell do you think you can convince me that you know all of this? Including details concerning Igare's forebear?"

"Because I was there." She turned her head and finally

looked Cyran in the eye, her beauty and apparent youth striking him like a blade. "Nearly five hundred years ago when the Dragon Wars began."

Cyran's hand now trembled with rage and fear. He had heard such rumors about the Dragon Queen, although he had not believed them.

"How do you think I've lived for so long?" she asked, still studying him.

Cyran's muddled mind turned. He had not considered this beyond the obvious. "Because of your control of magic in the other realm—your ability to manipulate the *neblír*."

"I do not hold so much more skill than Sir Paltere, although he has never learned to harness it." She smirked. "Does he look as if he will live for centuries? Will you?"

Cyran leaned back. "What does it matter?"

She shrugged, her smirk planted on one corner of her lips.

An idea sprang into Cyran's mind and then solidified. But it was nonsense—something probably related to Jaslin's stories. "There is an old legend that says when an elf finally rides a dragon, the entire world will end."

The Dragon Queen did not give any indication of agreeing or disagreeing with his line of thinking.

He used the tip of his sword to poke through her hair and part it. He swept her locks back past her ear as he held his breath, unsure of what to expect. The top of her ear did not taper to a point, but a clean scar ran across the area.

She slowly turned her head, and Cyran used his blade to inspect her other ear. It appeared similar.

"You wear your hair long and unbound because you are... an elf," he said slowly, incredulity weighing against him.

"Probably the last of my kind." She pulled a blade from her waist, and Cyran stumbled back, regripping his weapon, which he had nearly let fall during his shock.

She held out a sheathed blade with a silver hilt. He recognized it immediately. It had been his blade, the one he had taken from a dead elf in the Evenmeres and that she took from him.

Sirra passed him the sheathed weapon. "My mother foresaw the error of Cimerenden's ways and what was to come. She took me from the elven city, disguised me as human"—she pointed at her ears—"and brought me north for the Smoke Breathers to raise me."

Cyran could barely understand anything she was saying as he struggled to keep his anger from plummeting into some deep pit inside him.

"My first dragon was white as snow," she said. "So was my armor. After I discovered my power, every man wanted to challenge me and prove his worth. Many had to die. Once I found Shadowmar and took up the black, the number of people hunting me diminished rapidly. The appearance I took on and brought to Murgare struck fear into the hearts of all. Simple intimidation has stopped many needless battles before they even began. It has also saved countless lives."

Cyran's blade drooped, and its tip clanged against rock, its green light dimming. "Your beast killed mine. With its venom, a substance that destroyed Eidelmere's soul so he was lost from the other realm as well. I *cannot* forgive that. Eidelmere was... he was more than my closest friend. He was part of me."

"The same as Shadowmar was with me." Sirra's head hung again, and she swallowed. "There is an antidote for the venom and poison of a shadow dragon."

"Whatever it is, it will not help Eidelmere now."

"But it may have already."

Cyran's heart twisted with pain. "Do not use my grief in an attempt to deceive me."

"I experience the same grief you do. The pain in our souls is matched, and I do not speak of it in hopes of deceiving you, only to enlighten you about aspects of the other realm that you do not understand." She paused. "There is only one antidote, but it is no tangible substance. I've recently learned that a new class of people called dragon thieves use the same method to stop their poisoned quarry from dying, and a natural ability to release and utilize this antidote is the primary reason why so few people actually succeed at being such thieves."

Cyran's anguish bloomed in his chest. "You telling me this now only torments me more."

"All it takes is love for such a creature, true love for a being and a species other than your own."

"Love for a dragon?"

She nodded. "But finding and feeling such a thing is not so simple. Few people truly love dragons. Even those of the guard and their archers respect and fear the creatures, but they do not love them." She sighed. "And to deliver the antidote, you must be there, like you were with your forest dragon. You have to release them from their pain and the poisoning of their soul. Eidelmerendren did not lose his soul that day. Even with everything that was occurring, you returned and held his wing. You were there. *You* saved him. Shadowmar was quick to anger, but she rarely used her barb, and she only sought to test you—to determine if you were of the same cloth as Igare or if you treated her kind differently. Your dragon did not die from her venom. He died of his injuries, a natural death. His soul lingers in the *neblír*."

Cyran's knees gave out, and he collapsed onto his backside, dropping his sword beside him with a clatter. His rage spilled out of his body and pooled on the stone around him. If this woman—potentially an elven woman—was manipulating him, she was a master, and he would likely fall victim to her impending attack. But she did not make any move toward him.

Milluri shrieked as other dragons circled overhead, their guard and archers emitting cheers.

"Be free," Cyran muttered.

No one said a word for a full minute.

I trust you, Eidelmere, and I will uphold my promise to you and your kind as best I can. "Be free, Milluriumillen. I release you from any bond with me and any other man. And I will release Nithinix at the first opportunity. *Mörenth toi boménth bi droth su llith.* Till the end of days we soar. *Mörenth toi boménth bi nomth su praëm.* Till the end of nights we reign. *Röith moirten íli. Ílith ëmdrien tiu gládthe.* You honor me. My soul sees yours."

The thorn dragon studied him and blinked. *"I seldom doubted you, Cyranorendain. Eidelmerendren insisted you were different and could be trusted. But know this—once a dragon's loyalty is earned, it does not fade or die. There could come a time when one of us may need the other again. But if not, then may it be in the other realm when I see you and Eidelmerendren again..."* She nodded, screeched, and flapped her wings, rising from the rock island and streaking eastward toward the Evenmeres.

A massive sun dragon descended toward them, and its wings beat faster as it prepared to land. The creature was too enormous to even be Sir Paltere's sun dragon. Someone of greater importance had come.

"The words you just shared with her were first learned by the Smoke Breathers and later taken up by the old guard before the guard became the weapon of kings," Sirra said.

Cyran sat still as the sun dragon alighted behind him. A gush of fiery breath lit up the sky, but the flames did not come from the jaws of the beast, rather from someone riding it.

"Live with wonder," the Dragon Queen said, making no move to flee or draw her blade.

Cyran's numb body would not respond to his commands.

"The appropriate response of the Smoke Breathers, dragonknight, is—die before you've lost it all."

∼

Thank You! And for the good of the realm, Please Read!

Through Fire and Shadow and *The Forged and The Fallen* series have been brewing in my thoughts and dreams for decades. It is the epic fantasy I've always wanted to create but which took life and blood and tears and lack of sleep to turn into reality. For years, I couldn't tempt myself to tread the same waters as such legendary fantasy writers, not without some spin or idea to add to the traditional fantasies I love most.

Now, with all that I am, I want to thank you, reader, for taking a chance on an unknown. For taking the time and risking your imagination on *Through Fire and Shadow*. Without readers, books and most stories would be lost, and without your support, I could not continue to write and dream.

Please, if you enjoyed *Through Fire and Shadow,* consider rating or quickly reviewing it on **AMAZON**. Every single review —for EVERY single book in the series—is important and aids me in practicing my art and standing out among millions of other books by encouraging other readers to take a chance while also showing Amazon the book is worth promoting. A review is the single most powerful thing a reader can do for an author—if not for Cimeren, Cyran and his friends, and the unfolding story. Reviews make all the difference in the digital book world where each year hundreds of thousands of authors spar for your attention and a place in your heart.

Creating this world and its characters and connecting with readers through story is an incredible feeling and the reason why I write. As weird as it may sound—I want to get out of bed each day to dream, and I would be honored if you could help guide me along the path of honing my craft and making this dream come true.

My vow and oath to you, reader, is that I will always treat my skills like a blade and continue to sharpen them, and I will not stop looking for stories to bring into our world.

Röith moirten íli. Ílith Ëmdrien tiu gládthe. You honor me. My soul sees yours. And even more importantly: Live with wonder. Die before you've lost it all.

A fan of all those who still dare to read and tread the worlds of imagination,
 Ryan
 R.M. Schultz

Review Here: **_Through Fire and Shadow_**

RECEIVE A FREE THE FORGED AND THE FALLEN PREQUEL!

Receive a free *The Forged and The Fallen* prequel novella by joining the Sky Sea Council!

Forged in blood. Fallen in death

The shining city of Cimerenden has reigned over the continent for thousands of years. But one man envisions a future where the dragon is tamed and used for war.

In the Valley of the Smoke Breathers, a spark ignites. The Dragon Wars arise, and Cimerenden is poised to fall.

Dragons swarm the skies.

The Dragon Queen rides.

The shining city burns.

The Taming and The Betrayal is a prequel novella set hundreds of years before the events in *Through Blood and Dragons*—book one in *The Forged and The Fallen* series.

<u>Grab your FREE novella here!</u>

<u>www.rmschultzauthor.com</u>

(Or type the info above into your phone or browser as the Kindle sometimes has its quirks. Or scan the QR code below.)

Receive a free The Forged and The Fallen prequel!

BOOK 3 COMING IN 2024!

The third book in The Forged and The Fallen series - Through Bone and Ice - will be published in 2024

Live with wonder. Die before you've lost it all.

GLOSSARY

Cimeren (SIM-er-en): The largest continent consisting of the five major kingdoms.

The Elder Tongue

Aylión (AY-lee-ahn): Word from the other realm to see a second into the future.
Deserité (DES-er-I-tay): Word from the other realm to know if someone speaks a truth or a lie.
Dramlavola (DRAM-lah-VOH-lah): Word from the other realm to amplify physical and mental capabilities.
Ëagothor (Eh-ay-GOTH-or): Word from the other realm to sense dragonmages.
Luënor (lu-EH-nor): An ethereal weapon summoned from the soul.
Mëris (MEH-ris): A dragonmage—one of those who can walk in the dragon realm and form a bond with a dragon.
Neblír (neb-LEER): The dragon realm.
Omercón (oh-mer-CONE): A hand-to-hand combat maneuver opposite of a parry—to meet the force of a blow—the *omercón* is to follow the force.
Opthlléitl (ahpth-LAY-EE-tel): Word from the other realm to speak in the voice of a dragon.
Sïosaires (sy-O-sair-es): The title bestowed upon a dragon or human who has shared a bond with the other species but the other has died, severing that bond.

Names

Aneen (a-NEEN): Female dragon thief in Pravon's party.
Brelle (brel): Female dragonsquire companion of Cyran's.
Cartaya (car-TY-yah): A conjuror who wields bone and earth magic. A member of King Igare's council.
Cyran Orendain (KY-ran Or-en-dayn): Young male point-of-view character from Nevergrace.
Dage (dayj): Hulking dragonsquire companion of Cyran's.
Dahroon (DAH-roon): Genturion Master and dragon battlemage of the dwarves of Darynbroad.

Eidelmere (EE-del-meer): Sir Kayom's forest dragon.
Emellefer (em-EL-lah-fer): Young serving lady of Nevergrace.
Farsten (FAHR-sten): A kingsknight appointed to protect Menoria.
Fileena (FI-leen-a): Mother of Igare's orator, Riscott.
Garmeen (gar-MEEN): Eldest of and the leader of the dragonsquires of Nevergrace. A known traitor to Belvenguard.
Geniar (Gen-E-air): A kingsknight appointed to protect Menoria.
Igare (I-gair): King of Belvenguard. Resides primarily in the Summerswept Keep of Castle Dashtok in the capital city of Galvenstone.
Ineri (in-AIR-ee): Female dragonarcher of Belvenguard. Sickly. Cyran's companion.
Jabarra (Jah-BARRAH): The new king of the Rorenlands. He resides at the Yellow Castle.
Jaken (JACK-en): The son of Igare's orator, Riscott.
Jaslin Orendain (JAS-lin Or-en-dayn): Cyran's younger sister.
Kayom (KAY-ohm): Genturion of the dragonguard at Nevergrace.
Keliam (KEL-ee-ahm): A merchant who sells suspicious goods down at the wharf in Galvenstone.
Kridmore (KRID-more): Dragon thief companion of Pravon's.
Kyelle (KI-el): The Murgare princess. Daughter of the late King Restebarge of Murgare.
Laren (LAH-ren): Young male dragonsquire companion of Cyran's.
Lisain (lis-AYN): A clergyman of the nine gods. A member of King Igare's council.
Luminsteir (LU-men-steer): The Murgare king's conjuror.
Menoria (men-OR-ee-ah): The young lady of Nevergrace.
Milluri (MILL-oor-ree): Thorn dragon who aids Cyran.
Nistene (nih-STEEN): Daughter of King Igare, the princess of Belvenguard.
Nithinix (Nith-IN-ix): Thorn dragon who aids Cyran's companions.
Paltere (pal-TEER): One of the very few dragonknights of Belvenguard.
Pravon (PRAY-vohn): Dragon thief point-of-view character.
Quarren (QUAR-ren): Dragonmage for Vladden.
Ravenscroft (RAVENS-crahft): Genturion master of the gathering legions of Murgare along the north shore of the Lake on Fire.
Riscott (RIS-cott): King Igare's orator. A member of the king's council.
Ristanus (Ris-STAN-us): Genturion master of King Jabarra's legion of sand dragons.
Restebarge (REST-ah-barj): The Murgare king.
Shadowmar (SHA-doh-mar): Sirra's shadow dragon.
Sirra Brackenglave (SEER-ah BRACK-en-glave): Female dragonknight from Murgare. The Dragon Queen.

Tallius (TAL-ee-us): A dragonmage who rides a storm dragon and is a messenger of King Igare.
Tamar (tah-MAR): Cyran's brother.
Tiros (TY-rohs): King Igare's nyren. A member of the king's council.
Trothen (TROTH-en): The prior genturion master of Murgare under King Restebarge.
Turin Bolenmane (TUHR-in BOH-len-mayn): A dragonarcher of Belvenguard who was lost during their kingdom's attempt to capture the Murgare King, Restebarge. This occurred in the prologue of *Through Blood and Dragons*. Turin rode the rose dragon Renorrax.
Vladden (VLAD-den): Dragonguard of Murgare.
Vyk (vike): Male dragonarcher from Belvenguard. Cyran's companion.
Vysoria (VI-sohr-ee-uh): Daughter of the Cartaya, Igare's conjuror and councilmember.
Weerin (WEHR-in): King of the Weltermores. Also known as the Burro King.
Westfahl (WEST-fall): Genturion king of the dwarves of Darynbroad.
Yenthor (YEN-thor): Male dragonarcher from Murgare.
Ymar (YA-mar): The master-at-arms and dragonsquire trainer at Nevergrace.
Zaldica (ZAL-dih-kah): Female dragonarcher from Murgare.

World of Cimeren

Belvenguard (BEL-ven-gard): The largest of the southern kingdoms. King Igare rules over Belvenguard.
Darynbroad (DAHR-in-broad): The small northern kingdom of the dwarves.
Dashtok (DASH-tock): King Igare's castle in the city of Galvenstone.
Eastern Reach: The eastern most lands of southern Murgare.
Evenmeres (EE-ven-meers): A massive forest the size of a kingdom that, along with the Lake on Fire, divides Cimeren into northern and southern halves.
Galvenstone (GAL-ven-stone): The capital city of Belvenguard wherein lies Castle Dashtok and the Summerswept Keep.
Lake on Fire: A lake the size of a kingdom that, along with the Evemeres, divides Cimeren into northern and southern halves. The lake was termed the Lake of Glass in the past age.
Marshlands: A borderlands between the Lake on Fire and the Evenmeres.
Murgare (MOOR-gair): A sprawling kingdom that makes up almost all of northern Cimeren.
Nevergrace (NEH-ver-grace): Also known as 'the Never.' A castle and outpost that lies along the northeastern margins of Belvenguard and against the Evenmeres's border. Cyran's home.

Northsheeren (north-SHEER-en): The primary castle of Murgare and where Murgare's king typically resides.
Rorenlands (ROAR-en-lands): A kingdom in the far south of Cimeren.
Summerswept Keep: The keep associated with Castle Dashtok in the city of Galvenstone. Where King Igare typically resides.
Valley of the Smoke Breathers: An icy wasteland in the far north where the brotherhood of the Smoke Breathers began and where they tamed the first dragon.
Weltermores (WELT-er-mores): A small kingdom in southern Cimeren that lies to the east of Belvenguard.

Terms

Battlemage: A conjuror who has the ability to place magic on dragonbolts and enhance a projectile's abilities.
Dragonarcher: A crossbowman or woman who mans a mounted crossbow on a dragon's quarterdeck or in its turret.
Dragonguard: The armed and armored warrior who is seated just behind a dragon's head and wields a dragonlance and shield. Their primary purpose is to offer commands to the crew on the dragon and to defend their dragonmage.
Dragonmage: One of the *mëris* who rides behind a dragonguard. Their soul is twined with their dragon's, and they guide and navigate the dragon.
Dragonknight: One of the rare few of the *mëris* who is not crippled by the dragon realm and can act as both dragonmage and dragonguard.
Dragonsquire: A squire to a member of the dragonguard.
Dragonsteel: Steel forged with the scales of any type of dragon. Such steel has an array of colors and properties based on the types of scales used.
Genturion: The commander of the dragonguard at each city and outpost.
Harrowed and the Harrowed King: Figures in black cloaks with violet fire flaming across their backs and shoulders. They are said to have returned from the dead to haunt the Evenmeres.
Nyren (NY-ren): A faction of scholars and healers trained to recall everything they have read or learned.
Quarterdeck: A wooden platform strapped to a dragon's back by cinches and harnesses. The quarterdeck can carry one or more mounted and heavy crossbows for use by a dragonarcher.
Onyx Guard: The Murgare king's specially and expertly trained soldiers.
Turret: A platform hanging below a dragon's belly and legs that houses a mounted and heavy crossbow for use by a dragonarcher.

ACKNOWLEDGMENTS

I wish to thank the following people for all their help and sacrifices in turning this story into a book.

To Matt Schultz for reading and editing the first sorry version of every book I write and making the story shine.

To Jason Weersma for cheering me on from the beginning.

To Laura Josephsen for the most detailed questions and concerns I'd ever consider.

To each and every reader in the Sky Sea Council and the Small Council. Without your support and insight and reviews, I couldn't have come this far.

ABOUT THE AUTHOR

After reading Tolkien, R.M. Schultz wrote his first 100,000-word fantasy novel as a freshman in high school. When he's not saving animals, he has continued writing across genres for over two decades but always includes fantasy elements. R.M. Schultz founded and heads the North Seattle Science Fiction and Fantasy Writers' Group and has published over a dozen novels.

R.M.'s books have won multiple awards, including bronze and gold medals for fantasy. His latest series is being adapted into a video game! The game is slated to be released in the fall to winter of 2024. He has written and performed several songs—calling them dragon shanties—for the world that will be included with the music played for the game.

Someday, he hopes to be knighted by George R.R. Martin.

www.rmschultzauthor.com

Copyright © 2024 by R.M. Schultz

All rights reserved.

No part of this book may be reproduced in any form or by any electronic or mechanical means, including information storage and retrieval systems, without written permission from the author, except for the use of brief quotations in a book review.

The characters and events portrayed in this book are fictitious. Any similarity to real persons, living or dead, is coincidental and not intended by the author.

ISBN-13: 9798884014183

Published by Sky Sea and Sword Publishing

www.rmschultzauthor.com